Eleanor Dark was born in 1901 and was educated at private schools in Sydney. Her father was the poet Dowell O'Reilly, and in her work is found the same elegance and delicacy that characterises his poems and short stories.

Eleanor Dark began writing in her childhood, contributing verse, short stories and literary articles to various Australian magazines. Her first novel, *Slow Dawning*, was published in 1932. Since then she has published nine novels: *Prelude to Christopher* (1934), *Return to Coolami* (1936) — both of these novels winning the Gold Medal awarded by the Australian Literature Society for the best Australian novel of that year — *Sun Across the Sky* (1937), *Waterway* (1938), *The Little Company* (1945), *Lantana Lane* (1959), and the trilogy of historical novels *The Timeless Land* (1941), *Storm of Time* (1948) and *No Barrier* (1953).

In 1978 Eleanor Dark was awarded the inaugural Alice Award, the bi-annual presentation of the Australian Society of Women Writers to an author who has "made a significant contribution to literature in Australia".

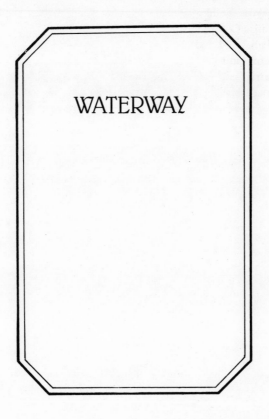

WATERWAY

By the same author

Slow Dawning
Prelude to Christopher
Return to Coolami
Sun Across the Sky
The Little Company
The Timeless Land
Storm of Time
No Barrier
Lantana Lane

WATERWAY

ELEANOR DARK

SIRIUS QUALITY PAPERBACK EDITION
PUBLISHED BY ANGUS & ROBERTSON

to M. O'R.

Angus & Robertson Publishers
London • Sydney • Melbourne • Singapore • Mánila

This book is copyright. Apart from any fair dealing for
the purposes of private study, research, criticism or
review, as permitted under the Copyright Act, no part
may be reproduced by any process without written
permission. Inquiries should be addressed to
the publishers.

First published by William Collins, London 1938
First Australian edition by F. H. Johnston, Sydney 1946
This Sirius Quality Paperback edition by
Angus & Robertson, 1979

National Library of Australia card number and
ISBN 0 207 13838 9

Printed in Hong Kong

CONTENTS

			Page
PART I	THE SUNRISE	- - - - -	9
PART II	THE COVE	- - - - -	83
PART III	THE CITY	- - - - -	173
PART IV	THE FERRY	- - - - -	273
PART V	THE SUNSET	- - - - -	331

AUTHOR'S NOTE

For the purposes of my story, I have revived the regular ferry service (which was discontinued some years ago) from Circular Quay to Watson's Bay and intermediate wharves. Although some of the events described in Part IV are based on real happenings in November, 1927, all the characters in the book are imaginary.

E.D.

MAIN CHARACTERS IN THE BOOK

Professor Channon	
Lesley Channon	*his younger daughter*
Winifred Sellman	*his elder daughter*
Arthur Sellman	*her husband*
Brenda Sellman	*their blind daughter, 6*
Lorna Sellman	*Arthur's sister*
Lady Hegarty	
Sim Hegarty	*her younger son*
Ian Harnet	
Denis Harnet	
Jonathan Harnet	*Ian's sons, aged 8 and 7*
Roger Blair	
Oliver Denning	
Lois Denning	*his wife*
Chloe Marshall	*his step-daughter*
Jack Saunders	

PART I
THE SUNRISE

"*The coast as he drew near Port Jackson wore a most unpromising appearance, and the natives everywhere greeted the little fleet with shouts of defiance and prohibition, the words 'Warra warra'—Go away, go away—resounding wherever they appeared. The Governor's utmost expectation, as he drew near the harbour, being to find what Captain Cook, as he passed it by, thought might be found, shelter for a boat; he was most agreeably surprised at discovering, on his entrance, a harbour capable of affording security for a much larger fleet than would probably ever seek shelter or security within its limits.*

"*In one of the coves of this noble and capacious harbour he determined to fix the future seat of his Government. . . .*"

From "An Account of the English Colony in New South Wales," by David Collins, sometime Judge-Advocate and Secretary of the Colony, 1798.

DRIVING at dawn along the high road past the lighthouse, Oliver Denning looked down over roof-tops at the harbour. It was barely light yet; the water was a pale, flat glow, something which was different from the fading darkness of surrounding land—no more. He would have liked, now that he was wide awake, and the memory of his bed less poignant, to loiter, but the call, if cryptic and incoherent, had been urgent. His profession, he thought, which dragged him rudely into hours which he might otherwise never see, gave him but little chance to study them. A movement far down over the surface of the water caught his attention—above the pale glow of a moving patch, paler still. He thought:

"The gulls fly inland thirteen miles—but there's still salt water under them, and the smell of the ocean. . . ."

It was so queerly silent. Humanity was asleep all along those dark, mysterious shores, and not till it wakened would the ugly noises of its myriad activities wake too. It was as quiet now, Oliver thought, as it must have been on the dawn of that day a hundred and fifty years ago which had marked the end of its primeval solitude. Now, with the aid of dim light, narrowed eyes, and a little imagination, you could annihilate the city, the growth whose parent cells had fastened upon the land that day. You could become a different kind of man, tall and deep-chested, black-skinned and bearded, standing upon some rocky peak with the dawn wind on your naked body, your shield and spear and throwing-stick in your hands.

It was this same place that you saw, this pale, flat water between dark headlands; but the headlands were not Blue's Point and Potts Point, Longnose Point and Slaughter-house Point. They were Warringarea and Yarranabbe, Yeroulbine and Tarrah. Far along that

11

slowly brightening waterway you could see a little island, dark in the middle of its silver path—not Pinchgut, where miserable convicts suffered or hung in chains, not a foolish little fortress, staidly renamed Fort Denison, but a lovely soaring column of weather-worn rock, holy place of your people—Mattewaya. . . .

The light was stronger now. You could see the red roofs and the spires of churches and the grey skyline of the city. You could see the dome of the Zoo on the opposite hillcrest, and the great, ghostly arc of the bridge. Your moment of wilful mysticism, your plunge back into a savage body and an inviolate land were over, and you were Oliver Denning, doctor of medicine, on your way to a job. You were one of the red roofs, and all about you, on this shore and on the opposite shore, from Balgowlah to Parramatta, were your neighbours, the other red roofs. . . .

Oliver laughed at himself. He was very well pleased that it should be so. His faith in mankind was strong enough to survive the periodical blasting revelation which came to him of the stupidity and littleness of individual men. In such moments, he thought, your soul seeks an escape—backward, forward, anywhere out of an unendurable present. In more wholesome mood you come back—gladly. You might regret a lovely solitude invaded, a land whose essence is the majesty of its ages, polluted by the crimes and cruelties of one petty generation of an upstart humanity. You might sigh for lovely places violated and lovely names forgotten; you might grieve for a brave and ancient race fading slowly to extinction, its language scantily recorded, its virtues unremembered, its miseries ignored.

But you must return with joy to your own life or it becomes a worthless thing. You must weigh its beauties and its uglinesses with detachment, and God help you if its beauties seem the less! What you see now, spreading itself over the foreshores, reaching back far out of sight, and still back into the very heart of the land, is something in whose ultimate good you must believe or perish. The red roofs and the quiet grey city become intimate and precious—part of a story of which you yourself are another part, and whose ending neither you nor they will see.

His mind retreated from that bleak momentary contemplation of the future, fastening itself more firmly into the little present which was his physical home. It did not seem so little, either, he reflected, when you were safely and normally ensconced in it. A lifetime! Your mind leapt backward towards babyhood and then began to move forward again, lingering, turning, considering, weighed down by a veritable mass of rich and varied experience. You were a little boy, and a bigger boy, and a young man, and a man not so young, and every stage had seemed long and full of significant events! Less confidently you went forward from the present—how far? Another thirty years at least, barring accidents. Yes, it seemed a very fair slice of time, this barely recordable blink in humanity's existence! And, crossing your own life, it held many other lives, touching, running parallel for a little while, closely woven, breaking away, so that you could never, at whatever point you chose, study a life solely your own, but always a life thrumming and alive with contacts, reacting to them in harmony or discord like the strings of a violin.

Discord. That word, he thought with a faint sigh, took him by the scruff of the neck and dumped him unceremoniously back in his consulting-room chair. Discord of the body, discord of the mind; to minister to these he existed. Somehow, from stores of more or less easily acquired knowledge, and from depths of most laboriously acquired wisdom, it was his job to restore harmony. He thought, inevitably, of Harnet, his next-door neighbour, who only a few weeks ago had sat in the patient's chair, the light marking deep lines and shadows on his bewildered face as he struggled with queer emotional side-currents of his love for Arthur Sellman's wife, Winifred. What, Oliver asked himself with dejection and humility, had he been able to accomplish there? There had been, possibly, for his patient, the temporary alle-

viation of having spoken aloud submerged and tormenting thoughts; the easing for an hour or two, a day or
two, even, of nervous tension; a little good which life
and circumstance would soon undo again!

And Winifred herself. How long could she go on
living there in the huge, ornate house next door to
Harnet's, living hardly and enduringly, her life and all
its joy laid at the feet of her little blind daughter? His
thoughts turned instinctively from a problem whose
apparent hopelessness was out of tune with his mood, and
following the smooth road of association paused gratefully upon the mental image of Winifred's father, old
Professor Channon. But even here the knowledge of
two X-ray plates which lay at this moment in the drawer
of his desk swam up into his consciousness like some
shadowy submarine monster seen dimly for a moment
and then lost again, as his mind separated that dark fragment of medical knowledge from the pleasanter conception of ordinary friendship. He found himself regretting
that his own university career had not led him to Professor Channon's lectures; stimulating, they must have
been, the astringent flavour of their irony softened and
mellowed here and there by a genial humour and a
native wit. More and more stimulating, in fact, until
they had reached, a few years ago, a pitch of unortho-
doxy at which the Senate felt it could no longer blink!
Well, perhaps it had not mattered. The years of enforced
leisure had borne fruit. For every score of students who
would have absorbed his views in the lecture-rooms, a
hundred people had read them, puzzled, irritated, amused,
but never bored, in that brilliant and provocative series
of essays upon a variety of human institutions, which,
impishly, he had called *The Sapience of Homo Sapiens*.
It was no wonder, Oliver thought, that in both his daughters there should flash a restless, keen-edged intellect,
setting Winifred, the elder, at loggerheads with her empty
life, spinning problems for Lesley which would never have
existed for a girl of lesser intelligence. "Poor Lesley!" he
thought, and, instantaneously, "Lucky Lesley!" For were

you to pity or to envy a young creature so intrepidly advancing upon life? Her vigour of brain and body, her beauty which was boyish and virginal, the half-contemptuous efficiency of her free-lance journalism, the determination and thoroughness of all her undertakings, were admirable, and yet in a way poignant, and he found himself wondering with some anxiety whether she really loved Sim Hegarty, and if so what she would do about it. For her determination and thoroughness extended to her convictions, and her convictions had the brilliance, the clarity of definition which only the convictions of youth can have. It was impossible, knowing her, to doubt the sincerity with which she condemned a system in which, by the simple process of marrying Sim Hegarty, she had, in a material sense, everything to gain. That was a knotty problem for a young girl to unravel, but Oliver smiled to himself, thinking that perhaps it was as well that life did so often demand its most intimidating decisions from the very young. Only the very young, after all, had the gay courage, the still unshattered nerve to make such decisions lightly and with confidence. And Lesley would make her choice somehow—her choice between Sim Hegarty, lovable, eligible, secure, spoiled darling of the world she mistrusted and despised, and Roger Blair, stormy petrel of the city's intellectual life; impulsive, dynamic Roger Blair, despiser of security, dropper of bombshells, leader of forlorn hopes! . . .

The smile begun for Lesley deepened and then faded with the thought of Roger, and Oliver glanced down the hill in the direction of the Bay, where the houses were older and more dilapidated, and where, in a furnished room, Roger lived alone and burned the midnight oil in the cause of culture. The smile was for an endearing and volcanic energy, an adventurous originality of thought, a personality which combined, rather amusingly, boyish and irresponsible enthusiasms with intellectual conceptions at once audacious and profound. But its fading left a sadness, a depression. Not all that energy and ardour would save *The Free Voice* for more

15

than two more issues. And feeling a restlessness in his mind, a familiar rebellion against coherent thought, Oliver released his brain and followed it along straying pathways of association. *The Free Voice*. There had been, once, a voice that cried in the wilderness: "Prepare ye the way of the Lord." "The Lord God." "God is the Spirit." Art, music, literature, the things of the spirit. . . . Yes, how neatly and inevitably, by the dependable path of words that pointed the way to interlocking thoughts, you came back to Roger's *Free Voice* so soon to be silenced, crying in the wilderness: "Prepare ye the way of the Spirit!"

No chain of association, but a mental leap, took him from here to Lois. It was a leap which his mind, by now, was accustomed to making, and which it made often and gratefully—a leap from turmoil into peace. That thought, even as he framed it, caused a little grimace of amusement to stir the contemplative stillness of his face, for peace was a funny word to apply to his odd, haphazard life with her. And yet it fitted as it could never have fitted the perfectly ordered routine of existence with his first wife, Helen. Lois sometimes forgot messages, which Helen had never done. She often forgot darning and buttons, and she almost habitually forgot meals. Quite frequently, he acknowledged somewhat wryly, she even forgot him. She would look at him absently as if she didn't know him, or perhaps didn't see him, and if he spoke to her at such times it was quite certain that she wouldn't answer sensibly, and quite likely that she wouldn't answer at all.

Chloe, used to her peculiar mother, had filled many gaps with an indulgent efficiency which both amused and impressed her step-father. Now, with the advent, three months ago, of the excellent if voluble Mrs. Trugg, Chloe was released, meals appeared, the telephone was answered, the house was swept and dusted and . . .

And Lois was in it. That, he realised, meant peace. The knowledge of her nearness. Beyond her his thoughts would not go. There, as at the top of a hill commanding

16

a beautiful view, he had to pause a moment, savouring happiness and wonder. He looked down at the harbour again, a last glance before shops and houses and a turn in the road would hide it from him, and, with the impression in his mind of that small group of interwoven lives, the packed red roofs seemed at once lovely and horrible like the Medusa's head—a matted tangle of innumerable interwoven lives. . . .

As he turned into a side street, he saw far below him, over the water, a last flash of wings.

* * * * *

The smoke from Winifred's cigarette made a blue haze round her head. She had smoked three, one after the other, standing there at the window, while the daylight wakened slowly and her figure changed from a dim white shape into a clear silhouette, dark against a silvery background. It was a queer thing, her husband thought resentfully, watching her from his bed, that she should seem so important, and that the thought of giving her the freedom she so badly wanted should make him recoil as if it were a kind of suicide.

He had no very clear remembrance of the scene last night. He had been, he supposed, a bit fuddled after George Hegarty's farewell-to-bachelorhood dinner. But he did remember that when he had come in to bed she had been just preparing to go off as usual and sleep in Brenda's room. And that he'd been angry.

Well, so he had a right to be. It wasn't as if she made any secret about her feeling for the fellow next door, and when your wife is in love with a fellow next door and makes (or rather, confound her, doesn't bother to make) excuses for sleeping in another room, and a room opening on to a verandah at that, surely to God a husband has the right to object? And other rights too.

He moved, and instantly a pain shot darkly and malevolently behind his eyes. It had been a good party —George knew how to give a party even if he were too darned ponderous to enjoy it when it was there. And

17

what with the party and the wine, and the talk and all the chaffing. . . . You come home and find your wife just going off, as cool as you please, to sleep in another room. Looking you over in that blasted superior way of hers. Saying not more than three words at a time in that voice which is supposed to make you curl up. And does—sometimes. But not last night. Not any more. You can let a woman go just so far and no farther; then you've got to assert yourself. . . .

What were men *made* stronger than women for if not for a bit of cave-man stuff once in a while? And if she tried any tragedy tactics this morning he would just point out again that if she wanted not to be parted from Brenda she'd darned well have to behave reasonably.

Reasonably. But that was just the way she never did behave. For better, for worse, for richer, for poorer. Poorer, of course, didn't apply to them, but it was the spirit of the thing. He'd given her everything. And what had she done for him in return? His forehead creased with another flash of pain behind the eyes, and he found himself thinking of the first years of their marriage—of her incessant badgering, her incomprehensible restlessness.

Always wanting him to *do* something. Finance some damfool, harebrained scheme. . . .

"I don't *want* any new investments, I tell you. All my money's safely disposed of. You needn't worry. I'm no wild-cat speculator."

"Arthur, I'm not *worrying*. Not that way. I just want to help this thing along. You aren't *doing* anything with your money."

Not doing anything! Women! Not many men had sounder investments. Conservative, but absolutely safe. All bringing in their steady six per cent. Not doing anything! But he had been indulgent enough, even so.

"Oh, well, here's a cheque for fifty. Run along and chuck it away if it amuses you!"

But that didn't satisfy her. Now, years later, he could remember how she used to stand for a moment or two, doubtfully, holding the cheque, looking at it, looking at him, as if there were some puzzle, some mystery she could not clear.

And after a time he had to put his foot down, because she had begun to make requests—almost demands, confound her—which were altogether preposterous. There had been a big area of bushland somewhere in the mountains—some wild, god-forsaken spot where no one ever went except a few crazy hikers, and she had actually worried the life out of him to buy it.

"Buy it? Good God, what would I do with a hundred acres of bush? Have some sense, Win."

"But it's the trees." She had been almost incoherent, in that impetuous way which he had liked at first, but which had quite deserted her now. "They're white gums —oreades—a hundred and fifty feet high. You must know the kind I mean—the straight, slender ones with trunks like silver. . . ."

He had listened then, thinking there might conceivably be a glimmering of sense behind all this, and he had said:

"Timber, eh? But what about access? And I'd have to find out what market there was for it on a big scale. . . ."

She had looked at him so incredulously that he had asked irritably:

"What's the matter now?"

And it had transpired that stray timber-getters were already felling the trees for pit-props, and she had wanted him to buy the land—*to save them*! To save a patch of trees—not even specimen trees, mind you, oaks or elms or maples or good imported trees of that kind, but just plain, ordinary gum trees! Simply to leave them standing there where perhaps twenty people might see them in a year! . . .

And another time she had got a bee in her bonnet about publishing poetry. He must provide the capital to establish a publishing house which would publish poetry. She knew a chap—a friend of that Bolshevik,

Roger Blair—who had some stuff in manuscript which she called "important!" Funny ideas of importance she had! The existing publishers wouldn't touch it. He had said comfortably:

"Well, old girl, if Roberts and Anderson won't touch it, you can bet your boots there's nothing in it."

But to satisfy her he had actually gone into it with a chap who knew about such things, and he had explained to Winifred:

"I tell you it's no good. I'd lose money on it."

And her answer had been:

"Would that matter?"

Would it matter? Sitting opposite to him, she had actually said that, in the voice he had since learned to know so well. Would it matter? He had asked with despairing patience:

"What do you think a man invests money *for*?"

It was an amazing thing how a woman lost her looks as soon as she began to mix herself up in things outside her own sphere. He had always said so. You wouldn't find a more womanly woman than Lorna, for instance, anywhere, nor a better-looking one. On that particular occasion, he remembered noticing, Winifred had suddenly looked almost plain in her intense seriousness.

"I should think," she had replied slowly, "that when he had as much as you have, it might be—sometimes—just to—to help."

"To help? To help what?"

She had made a movement with her hands which summed up, pretty accurately, the unpractical vagueness of her thoughts. "People," she said. "Ideas. . . ."

Well, of course, she was eccentric. He realised that now. Her bright-eyed enjoyment of life, her infectious laughter, the merry audacity of her conversation had deceived him, before their rather sudden marriage, into thinking her a normal girl, like Lorna, normally interested in dances and parties and charities and other activities proper to womanhood. But with that old crank of a father of hers he might have guessed. . . .

And lately, in the last few years when things had been so unrestful, so menacing, you would have thought she'd have realised the importance of people in their position—well, hanging together. Showing a united front. Class loyalty and all that kind of thing. But there was never a conversation in his house in which she did not disagree with everyone else. There were times when she talked, ignorantly, perhaps—he was willing to make allowance for the limitations of feminine understanding—sheer Socialism. Books which she brought home, and into which, with a kind of contemptuous apprehension, he dipped, had shocked and alarmed him. There had been one which actually linked and attempted to establish a common basis for Christianity and Communism. Whereas every fool knew that the Soviets had done away with religion altogether. He had said roundly, then and many times since, that such stuff should be censored; it was nothing more nor less than blasphemy. And at that she had flared out with a passion that staggered him, claiming that all censorship should be utterly abolished, that the limiting of social and religious and sexual propaganda was an indefensible wrong; and more in the same extravagant vein, so that at last, being rather tired of it all, he had shut her up with one brief sentence which he thought really pretty telling:

"Freedom, Winifred, need not necessarily mean licence."

And she had stopped in the middle of a word, and stared at him, and given a sort of half-hysterical laugh, and walked out of the room! Trust a woman to run away when she had been bested in an argument!

And she couldn't take it in a sporting spirit. Because he wouldn't buy forests, and finance a few shabby scribblers, and because he pointed out where she was wrong in all her crazy ideas, she seemed to think that he was no longer her husband, and she had no further duties and obligations to him. But, by God, he had asserted himself last night, and he was glad of it. All the same he wasn't malicious, and he didn't nurse a grudge as she so

21

often seemed to. And to prove it to himself he yawned audibly as if he had just wakened, and asked with an attempt at geniality:

"Hullo. Did you have a good night?"

She turned from the window and came slowly down to the foot of his bed. He realised with a spasm of irritation that, with her usual perverseness, she was going to treat his purely rhetorical question as one deserving a considered answer. And, treated that way, it was an awkward question. She said:

"You know what kind of a night I had."

He floundered over in bed, scowling. Yes, he knew. He had heard the sounds of her smothered weeping twice when he had wakened. It was years since he had heard her cry. He pulled the key from under his pillow and threw it on the bed. He snapped:

"Well, don't be such a fool again."

She picked the key up and stood looking at him, tapping it on the palm of her hand. He was astonished and a little suspicious to see a brief smile pass over her face like a sun-gleam across shadowed water.

"A key doesn't solve it, Arthur."

He was suddenly furious. She made him furious. She did it deliberately. He jeered: "Oh, I know! Stone walls don't make a prison, and all that!" She should see that it wasn't only herself and her highbrow friends who could quote Browning. "All the same you said you wouldn't sleep in this room. But you did."

"Strictly speaking," she said, with another of those fleeting smiles, "I didn't. But that's a quibble. I spent the night here. And the result is that this morning things are far worse between us, far more hopeless. . . ."

He hunched the bedclothes sullenly over his shoulder, and grunted: "Well, anyhow, you didn't keep your date with your friend next door."

He expected her to flare out at that, but she only walked across to the window again, putting her cigarette butt carefully down on an ash-tray as she passed the dressing table. Then, with her back to him, she said wearily: "You're being more stupid than usual, Arthur."

He sat up violently, and then, for a moment, he forgot all about her. Superimposed upon a pain which was at once piercing and rending, intermittent flashes of hot light, as from a furnace, burst inside his head, and he clutched it in his hands with an incoherent groan, thinking that these damned hangovers were getting worse lately, and he'd have to see a doctor. When he opened his eyes and lifted his head very cautiously from his hands, Winifred was leaning on the foot of his bed again, considering him.

She was thinking that in spite of his encroaching fat, and his bad colour, he was still a handsome man. When you looked at him attentively as she was doing now, in the cold morning light, you could see that his face was slackening; there was a looseness, hardly perceptible, about his mouth and jaw, and about the muscles which held his eyelids up, not quite alertly enough. She thought, with a little shiver, that Nature exacted payment for stupidity as ruthlessly as for deliberate viciousness. And it was fair enough. We're given nerves and brains, she thought, a whole highly specialised equipment for living vividly, for feeling intensely, for thinking deeply and intricately. You can't blame Nature if she doesn't like it when we live like—like worms, or grubs, or something with practically no nervous system at all. You can't blame her if she gets back at you slyly, subtly, working in spite of you on the nerves that you try to wrap about with placidity and inaction, tangling you in your own uncomprehended impulses, filling your life with vague confusions and despairs. . . .

More stupid than usual. The words had come, however calmly, from a deep and bitter anger. But now she found herself considering them dispassionately, and thinking that perhaps stupidity might be less a lack of intellect than a lack of perception. And then obtuseness was a better word for it. Ian, bless him, had no academic brilliance, no particular subtlety of thought or profundity

23

of knowledge. But he had a warm and intimate appreciation of life as a whole. He could meet you, instantly, in
realms which, for Arthur, existed not at all. He could
value things justly. But Arthur lived in a kind of half-
world—a world from which all but the obvious, the trite,
the conventional, was excluded. Among concepts which,
for her, for Ian, for all the people she cared about, gave
life graciousness and meaning, he blundered like a blind
man, irritated, uncomprehending, incredulous. They
weren't visible, these things. They weren't tangible. He
didn't believe, in short, that they existed, except in un-
balanced and eccentric minds. Life was perfectly simple;
these things served only to confuse it. Away with them!

But his every repudiation only strengthened them.
His every denial only brought them closer about him. . . .

He said loudly:

"Well, what then?"

She was startled. She had been hardly conscious of
him, but now she realised that he had been speaking,
and she asked:

"What did you say? I didn't hear you."

She thought:

"He looks rather queer. I suppose it's only last night's
carousing. . . ." He repeated thickly:

"I said you'd better be careful. Lorna might see you
go over next door one night when she's coming in late."

She pulled her dressing-gown closer about her, repressing a shiver. She must have become chilled, she
thought, standing so long at the open window. She said
slowly:

"You mean she might pretend to have seen me?"

He banged his fist down on the bed furiously, and
shouted:

"I mean exactly what I say! She might see you!"

"No."

She went over to the window again, trembling a
little, but whether with cold, or anger, or a creeping fear,
she hardly knew herself. It was nearly sunrise. She
looked across the groomed brilliance of their own garden,

24

across the low, dividing hedge, at Ian's, dim beneath its tangle of trees, and its great grey buttress of rock. The water was like glass this morning, the mist hanging motionless over it. From its breathless quiet and serenity she gathered a little reassurance, and she said, calmly enough, without turning:

"Arthur, this can't go on. There must be a divorce."

The incoherent sound of fury which he uttered made her turn, and she realised that discussion was impossible now. His face was crimson, a suffusion due, perhaps, less to anger than to pain and nausea, and he was still shouting:

"I tell you I don't want a divorce. I won't have it."

She said quietly: "Very well. That's that."

"I'm to give you a divorce," he raged, "so that you can marry that fellow Harnet. A fine fool you must think me!"

She retorted sharply, strained beyond patience:

"Why shouldn't I marry him?"

He looked at her as if unwillingly. In that glance there was something which really frightened her, and she thought wildly: "It's absurd—it's hideous—that he should dare—to *depend* on me!" He asked:

"Don't I come into this at all?"

She made a movement of desperation.

"Why should you? How can you? You don't care anything for me. We have nothing in common—nothing. I believe that you've been unfaithful to me at least three times."

"And you? How many times have you . . . ?"

Her interruption silenced him though she did not raise her voice.

"You know Ian isn't—never has been—my lover. If you know nothing else you know that."

He said sulkily:

"How should I know?"

She told him with the detached patience of a teacher explaining a lesson to some obstinately dull pupil:

25

"You know if I did that you might be able to take Brenda from me."

"Why should you think I'd take Brenda?"

She stared at him helplessly till her gaze narrowed and became intent. For a moment it seemed as if he were nothing, as if all she were looking at was a pair of striped pyjamas, grotesquely supported, grotesquely alive. Her moment of shock was not for that illusion, but for the knowledge, a moment later, that illusion may be the shadow of truth. For it was true. This man had no substance. He had no integrity, he kept no faith even with himself. He was nothing. She sighed and looked away from him to the window and to the wall of Ian's house, so close to it, and she thought: "How far? Twenty yards? Thirty? Thirty yards from misery to happiness! How queer that is! Life gets you bound so that you can't walk thirty yards to save yourself from—this. . . ."

The silence made her realise how he had been shouting, and she wondered, with sudden dread, if he had wakened Brenda. She passed him without a glance, unlocked the door, and went quickly down the passage.

Brenda's room was dim, its window shadowed by a huge loquat tree. Winifred, bending for a moment to listen to quiet breathing, realised that her legs were weak and her body aching as though from some intense physical effort. She sat down on the foot of the bed, her hands clasped round her knees, her heart thudding dully back to quietness. She thought ramblingly:

"This morning I'll take her down to the Cove. Denis and Jonathan will be there. They'll speak of Ian. We'll all swim, and lie on the sand, and then I'll take them up to the shops and buy them ice-creams. It's dreadful that the happiness of children has to depend on the untidy intricacies of adult life. This afternoon is George Hegarty's wedding. I won't go. *'Crowds waited outside the church to see a wedding which unites two of our best-known families.'* Oh, my God, what a silly life. . . . Would Lesley be dragged into it, too, if she married Sim? No wonder Lorna hates me! Ian might have heard Arthur just now. His bedroom window is always open. . . . Oh, darling, darling, don't mind too much. . . .

"How are the tides now? Full about half past eleven yesterday, wasn't it? Denis and Jonathan will know. It's prettiest in the Cove when the tide's full, poor little Brenda. . . . When the boys say 'Look!' her head comes up and she listens. Her little face, so happy, so eager. . . . But she can't hear the white sails of the eighteen-footers, and she can't hear the gulls swooping down for fish; she can't hear the seaweed the boys are pointing at, or the rock anemones that close over her finger, or any of the thousand little sights that make the morning's happiness for them.

"Yet she isn't unhappy. That's what one clings to, that's what one battles for. And she isn't helpless. That was harder to achieve. Not for her, for me, for me! To let her have a little tumble and pick herself up again, to let her bump into things, touch things carelessly so that they fell and broke. Not to help her when every nerve in my body strained to help her, not to protect her when that's all I live for. Not to snatch her back from small dangers she must learn to manage for herself, not to keep her always by my side when every minute she is out of my sight is agony—agony. . . .

"No, that is all foolishness. The little physical harms are nothing. There's the harm life can do to her when she's grown up; there's the danger of this house, the incredible silliness of the lives that will be all about her unless . . ."

She said softly:
"Hullo, darling, are you waking up? It's morning."

*　　*　　*　　*　　*

Lorna turned uneasily, half-opened her eyes, and thought irritably: "Damn Arthur and his rages!" She didn't want to wake yet, but it was not altogether weariness which dragged her back towards sleep. There was something angering, hurtful; some undeveloped, unacknowledged memory which she didn't want to face

27

just yet. But the more she thrust it back the clearer its outlines became, and the more she struggled towards sleep the faster it escaped, a black mist thinning, dwindling, receding, till at last it was gone, and she was staring at the silver-grey square of her window and thinking clearly of Sim Hegarty.

She had been a fool to stop. But seeing him so unexpectedly, standing there reading his paper under the street light, she had thought: "Here's a chance!" and the pressure of her foot on the brake had been almost reflex.

"Hullo, Sim!"

"Er—oh, hullo, Lorna! For a second I couldn't see who it was. This the new bus, eh?"

She had looked at him silently for a moment, smiling. It was a trick which, she had found, served her well with men. In that little silence they often blurted out things they would not have said in a briskly running conversation. And Sim's eyes were on her with a look she knew and had come to expect from all men—a helpless, fastened look, a look which returned and returned again to refresh itself upon her beauty. She said:

"Do you like her?"

"She looks fine."

"Can I give you a lift home?"

"Oh, no—no thanks, Lorna. I'm not going home just now."

"Isn't George having a last bachelor party or something?"

"George? Yes, as a matter of fact, he is. You'll be at the wedding to-morrow, of course?"

"I'll be there. Some of us are going on to dance at Manero's afterwards. How about joining us?"

"I'm afraid I can't manage it, thanks. Anyhow, I'll be a cot case by then."

"Why?"

"Nerves. My first stab at being a best man. Yes—really! George is jittering for fear I'll do something wrong."

She had laughed and tried her little silence again,

28

but it wasn't all coquetry this time. With surprise and annoyance she had found her heart beating too fast, and she had thought angrily: "What a fool I'm being!" Now, lying here in her big bedroom with its windows open on the garden and the harbour, she was railing at herself again for not "managing" the interview better, scorning herself for a brief surrender to one of the few genuine moments of emotion in her life.

She reached out to the bedside table for cigarettes, and lit one, frowning. For a moment Arthur's voice, which her own thoughts had blotted from her consciousness, returned, bringing a vague sense of pleasure. But in the next instant it was gone, and she was back in the car under the street light, and Sim was leaning his elbows on the lowered window and playing with the wheel, so that his hand was very close to hers, and she had asked him smilingly:

"Why didn't he get somebody more experienced?"

"I wish to God he had. Only brother mustn't be passed over, and so forth, I suppose."

That had given her a chance. Show her the man who didn't love a bit of flattery!

"Don't be so modest, Sim. You know very well you cast a glamour. Famous young airman, idol of the people . . ."

He had grinned at her, the cheerful, unembarrassed grin which won him affection wherever he went, and he had said lightly:

"Oh, there isn't anything in that."

And then she had made the worst blunder of all. The very thought of it made her sit up in bed so suddenly that the ash from her cigarette was jerked off on to the sheet. Good heavens, how had she come to make such a damn fool of herself? He had just refused two invitations —to drive with her, to dance with her—and yet she had offered him a third!

"We're taking *The Swift* out on the harbour on Saturday. Would you care to come?"

"Well, thanks very much, Lorna, but I'm afraid I

can't. I have an engagement for Saturday. Good of you to ask me."

And then he had looked up the road again and added:

"Here's the bus coming. Well, cheerio, Lorna—I'll see you to-morrow."

And he'd gone. She had started the engine up viciously, stalled it, looked across the road at the lighted bus pulling in to the kerb. And there was Winifred's sister, Lesley Channon, getting up and making her way along it, holding on to the backs of the seats. And then the bus had moved on, leaving them standing on the path together. . . .

Lesley Channon. Good God! She wasn't even as good-looking as Winifred, and Heaven knew Winifred was nothing very marvellous! But Lesley was almost plain. A pale, small face and a big mouth and weird, speckled eyes. And an Eton, which was something you simply *couldn't* wear unless your features were perfect.

Lorna looked up instinctively into the long wardrobe mirror which faced her bed. She moved her head a little from side to side, considering the fair and rather fragile beauty which, from babyhood, she had accepted as one of her many superiorities. While she looked her mind played idly with phrases treasured, stored: *"One of the loveliest debutantes was Miss Lorna Sellman, sister of Mr. Arthur Sellman. . . ." "At the Government House Garden Party we noticed the beautiful Miss Lorna Sellman. . . ." "That good-looking pair, Mr. Arthur Sellman, and his sister, Miss Lorna Sellman, entertained a large party at the Yacht Club dance. . . ." "For the Spring Meeting Miss Lorna Sellman chose a shade of blue which set off her fair loveliness to perfection. . . ." "A recent camera portrait of Miss Lorna Sellman, whose beauty is everywhere admired. . . ."*

She pulled her waved, ash-blonde hair back from her forehead, wondering what to do with it for a change. A fringe? That was an idea! *"You Can't Help Noticing Miss Lorna Sellman's fringe. . . ."*

She thought excitedly:

"I could dash into town this morning and have it done in time for the wedding. Of course I'd have to get a new hat—something off the face. . . ."

She lay back on her pillows and blew smoke-rings. It was one of her social accomplishments—she just had the trick of it as she had the trick of knowing what clothes to wear, and with whom to be friendly. And yet—she frowned again, thinking that it was really only luck that it had been Mariammne Gore-Herbert who had introduced everyone to that young Englishman who turned out to be a Communist. Of course she, Lorna, had said afterwards: "My dear, it was written all over him!" But here, alone, she could admit with uneasiness and anxiety that it hadn't been written all over him. That she, with her flair for picking the right people, would have been just as easily deceived by that well-tailored, well-mannered young man as Mariammne had been.

And that was another thing about Sim's friendship with Lesley Channon. Everyone knew what an old Radical her father was. Everyone knew that he'd resigned his Professorship just in time to avoid being deprived of it. But he was a man who really *did* have it written all over him. You had only to take one look at him strolling about the city in grey flannel trousers and a tweed coat, his round, wrinkled face burnt as dark as a native's under his shock of white hair, a newspaper parcel under one arm and a couple of books under the other—and such books! He passed them on to Winifred to read and Winifred left them lying about the house. . . .

General and Mrs. Spence had dropped in one afternoon, and he had picked up a book from the chair he was about to sit down in, and glanced at the title and then at Winifred looking a bit touchy. He'd asked:

"And what *is* the intelligent man's way to prevent war, Mrs. Sellman?"

Of course you could never rely on Winifred to cover up a slip like that. She said:

31

"I should be delighted to lend you the book, General, if you'd care to find out."

The poor fool! Like offering to lend a master butcher a book on vegetarianism! Naturally he'd been pipped; told her that unfortunately military men were kept too busy planning the defence of the country to waste time reading rubbish. And she'd answered in that infuriating double-edged way of hers that it was *most* unfortunate, and she was so sorry. . . .

No, Winifred was a dead weight. She was quite impossible. What in God's name had ever possessed Arthur . . . ? And not a bean. That mightn't have mattered so much if she'd *tried* to fit in. But she made no attempt whatever. She wouldn't sit on charity committees and she didn't play bridge, and she deliberately waited till the season was practically over before she went to Kosciusko for the ski-ing. She loathed golf, and only played tennis at the Channons' with Lesley and Ian Harnet (how much *was* there in that?) and the new and rather attractive doctor with the little frump of a wife who had come to live the other side of the Harnets'. And all the rest of the time she mooned about with Brenda and the two little Harnet boys, or read interminably or went with Lesley and her father to mouldy concerts and art shows and lectures.

Lorna yawned. She had been up late last night. When she had left Sim and come home there was a 'phone message waiting from Basil Smith asking her to have dinner with him. So she had rung him up and accepted, but when they were in his car they'd decided to drive out of town somewhere, and they had ended at the Hotel Bellevue at the foot of the mountains. Basil had been a bit of a pest. He'd had one or two aboard, and he'd even gone so far as to suggest their staying the night. What did he think she was? He'd been a good deal of bother on the way home, too; grass widowers with their wives away in England were often the very devil, and Basil, of course . . . well, everyone knew Basil. . . .

Another yawn became mixed with a smile. It wasn't

altogether an unpleasant memory. She was proud of her skill in preserving to her twenty-eighth year a technical virginity, and thoughts of that skill and the need for it were more soothing to her self-esteem than other thoughts to which she had reluctantly awakened. She turned, stretched, yawned again, and slept. The clear outlines and delicate colouring of her face against the pillow, the pale gleam of her hair, the lovely curves of her body under the single sheet, had a strange and moving beauty.

*   *   *   *   *

Afterwards Ian was to remember that in this pale November dawn the walk which he had taken so many times had seemed strange. He had noticed the sound of his own footsteps on the asphalt path which led him down to the beach, and he had found himself looking upward several times into the empty silver sky, as if some part of him were expecting an event, a happening so monstrous and cataclysmic and yet so utterly formless that there seemed no other place from which it might appear but the illimitable heavens. Only the salt-water smell of the harbour, that smell which had been in nearly every breath of his nostrils since boyhood, formed a link between reality and the dreamlike quality of this summer morning fugue.

For it was, in a sense, a flight. He realised that as he walked along the path beside the Bay, thinking with one part of his mind that it must have been a much prettier beach, a prettier Bay altogether, in the days of that Robert Watson after whom it had been named. Now the high-water mark was littered with rubbish—bits of coke, bits of orange-peel, driftwood, seaweed—all the flotsam and jetsam of a great harbour where ships came and went; and the gulls picked their way among it, or ran with little mincing steps across the sand.

Yes, it was a flight. One of those flights of the soul which drag the body with it. One of those outbursts of spiritual impatience which are abruptly translated into physical movement, so that one seeks and finds in new

33

activity and new surroundings, sometimes an illusion, and, rarely, the reality of peace.

Well, the reality did not seem to be for him; but here if anywhere he would find the illusion as he had found it many times before. He put his hand up to his left temple where a familiar pain was beating behind his eye, so that its lid twitched and burned. From force of habit rather than from inclination he stopped under the vast, dark roof of a Moreton Bay fig tree, to one of whose mammoth branches, thicker than a man's waist, it was his custom to lift Denis and young Jonathan so that they might bestride it like a horse. He looked at its trunk in whose crevices children hid, and at the tops of its giant roots sprawling and coiling over the ground, and wondered how old it was; but the image of his sons which it had roused in his mind stayed with him now, half a pain, half a pride.

He walked on more slowly to the pier, and stood before the memorial to Robert Watson, reading its inscription half-absently, worrying at the problem which was always present in his mind. His brows contracted sharply at the memory of the voice which had wakened him half an hour ago. It was a voice which he had hated, he reminded himself, long before he had learned to love its owner's wife. High, monotonous, it handled words as a miser handles coins, without thought or appreciation of their intrinsic value, but with an ugly gloating; with a mouthing of syllables, with a smug and tyrannical complacency. It was a voice, Ian thought, to enrage and repel at any time, but when you were wakened by the sound of it abusing Winifred—when you could hear not the words but the tone of it—shouting at her. . . .

He was staring at the path. Suddenly, under his blank, unseeing eyes a shadowy golden lacework spread itself, wavered, dimmed, deepened again to a pattern of sun and leaf-shadows. His eyes focussed on it, and the angry drumming of his blood eased a little. He looked up at the sky. The pearly haze of morning still veiled it, and in a second or two that elusive beauty at his feet would vanish. He looked down with an odd feeling of sadness and watched it fade, thinking how delicately life offered you, in the midst of your ugliest moments, its reminders of an enduring beauty. He glanced again at the memorial before he turned to cross the park, and as he walked his brain, to shut out the turmoil of present problems, began to speculate about Robert Watson, and to wonder if that *Quartermaster of the "Sirius," Pilot and Harbourmaster,* and *Keeper of the Macquarie Light,* had come at last to love the harbour which had been his charge, or whether he had felt himself, to the end, an exile in a barbarous and inhospitable land.

The grass was clover-starred, and the path which led across it was bordered by palms and clumps of tall bamboo. When Ian came to the other side of it and crossed the road where the trams ground noisily down the hill to their terminus, he was struck anew by the narrowness of this southern headland; by the fact that in two minutes you could walk from a placid harbour beach, where little children paddled, to the top of those grim cliffs at whose base there came crashing in the waves of that ocean so oddly named Pacific. And when he had climbed the few stone steps from the road and stood with his elbows on the fence and the ocean far below him, he was aware instantly of a slackening of tension, a clearing of thought.

He began to think of Winifred again, but by this time the illusion which he had come to seek had claimed him, and he saw a Winifred no longer captive in the big house and formal garden next door to his own, no longer quiet, dangerously quiet, with a quietness which held a paradoxical hint of violence. No longer with those lines of repression about her mouth, and that rather grim steadiness of gaze. Another Winifred. Winifred alone, wrenched away from all the people and all the circumstances which now encumbered her. But with this thought, this dream, came the relentless knowledge that though you could, in thought, rip her husband away from her, and her sister-in-law, and all the silly, futile life she shared with them, you could not separate her from Brenda without damaging something which was as essentially part of herself as her directness and her sense of fun.

He pulled his pipe and his tobacco pouch out of his pocket, staring across the wakening opalescence of the sea, watching the flash of the seagulls' wings as they skimmed and wheeled above it. God knew, he cried out silently, he didn't *want* to separate her from Brenda. He was a parent himself—perhaps more strongly a parent than most fathers because ever since his sons were little more than babies he had had to do the job alone. He understood—no one could fail to understand—her determination to do nothing which might further injure the already mutilated life of her little blind daughter. No one could fail to attempt—even if it meant a continual torment of self-discipline—to help her in that determination.

He lit his pipe, shielding the lighted match with his hands from the upward draught of air, and walked a little farther along the cliff edge to where the anchor of the wrecked *Dunbar* was set against a wall of rock, and he turned his back on the ocean and looked up the harbour, dull silver like a misted blade in this early light, winding and threading westward till it became lost in a vaporous nothingness, partly sky, partly distance; and for the first time he thought of it as the main highway of the city. Not the long, tortuous street which led between high canyon-sides of buildings, along the route where once bullock teams had plodded a bush track—but this gleaming waterway. . . . Not the noisy thoroughfare whose sea-smell was left behind so soon, to be replaced by smells of dust and petrol, fleetingly, for a hundred yards or so, of flowers, and then petrol again, and factories, and more petrol—but this long and shining finger of the sea itself. . . .

He remembered how his wife, May—pretty, practical May—had said to him just before Jonathan was born that she believed he liked his job more because it had to do with the harbour than because it brought them all a comfortable living. He admitted to himself now that she had probably been right. He did like his job; and he could think of no particular reason for liking it except the one which she had with such indulgent scorn proclaimed: that it had to do with the harbour. That it brought with it the smell of salt and seaweed which suggests adventure; that there was still enough of the boy in him to like ships as Denis and Jonathan liked them—from afar—seeing them with the eye of the landsman as things haloed with glamour and romance!

Yes, he thought, looking at his watch, he had no quarrel with the work which, presently, would summon him down from this high place to eat his breakfast, and catch his ferry, and walk across the swarming Quay to the weathered stone building on its outskirts. From his office on the top floor he could see glimpses of the harbour, and hear the ferry sirens, and the deeper note of the mail boats; and the salt-water smell was with him still, blowing in through his open window. He had gathered more than a material living there. Denis and Jonathan knew how much more! Was he not the answerer of innumerable questions which other boys' fathers boggled over?

"Dad, look! What's that mean?"

"They want the Pilot, Denis."

"Dad, there was a ship with a red flag . . ."

"They have oil on board. After sunset they'll show a red light."

"Dad, how far to Honolulu?"

"Four thousand miles, odd, Jonathan."

But the boys, he admitted, were only an excuse for his own interest in such details. He remembered now that the first time he had ever been attracted by Winifred· had been once in the days before he had sold his car, when she, missing her ferry, had come running impulsively up to his office to beg a lift home. He never looked up from his desk now without seeing her as he had seen her that day, standing at the window and looking down at the Quay and the ferries and the people, turning round to say to him eagerly: "How good it smells! The salt water—and there's a man down there selling brown boronia! I've missed it all dreadfully—I've been abroad you know. . . ."

And then she had found some printed lists on his desk. Even now his mouth twitched at the memory of her laughter and her infectious foolery.

" 'Bacon, bark, bones, butter. . . .' What *is* this all about? *'Single-stranded drawn copper wire, bar copper, drawn copper, copper ingots'.*" She had looked up at him with a shade of real anxiety dimming her laughter. "How dreadfully ignorant one is!" She bent her head over the list again. " *'Timber (sawn), Timber (rough), Timber (in shooks).'* Do tell me, Mr. Harnet, what *are* shooks? *'Charcoal, coconuts, coke, copra.'* I *do* know what copra is! *'Returned empties, bags in bales, and casks and cases in shooks.'* Shooks again! *'Rock salt, sand, sugar, sulphur.'* Such odd mixtures! *'Wool, per butt, fudge or bale'!*"

She had begun to laugh helplessly, and he had laughed with her, feeling the sudden stab of his own solitude, then still fresh enough to wound.

And with that lightning-swift perception of hers which never failed to startle his more methodically moving consciousness, she had seemed to feel his hurt, and she had looked at him for one moment with all the laughter gone from her face, and a strange, intent compassion flowering there instead.

"May I help you sometimes with your little boys? I like children."

He had been astonished by his own lack of resentment. He had been touchy in those early days about being "helped." There were too many blasted interfering females only too ready to be rather insultingly sorry for a pair of babies left to the care of a mere father! He'd provided a good nurse who also supervised the housekeeping and the activities of a succession of young "helps," and he considered that, on the whole, he was managing very well. He had refused violently when his own unmarried sister offered to come and "look after" him, and politely when May's mother had made the same suggestion. But when Winifred said: "May I help?" he hadn't minded. Perhaps because she had looked and sounded, in those days, so young and irresponsible—as if she might think she was being guide, philosopher and friend to his children when she was really nothing but a playmate. So he had only said: "That's very kind of you." And they had gone down in the lift together to his car.

*　　*　　*　　*　　*

His eyes, far-focussed on those memories, were attracted by two small, blue-shirted figures racing towards him across the park.

They must, he thought, have heard him go out, and he imagined them conspiring together in whispers to get up and follow him; struggling with their clothes, Jonathan helping Denis, for though Denis was eight and the elder by a year, he was not so clever with his fingers as Jonathan.

They rushed across the road and up the steps to him. It did not hurt him as it might have hurt a mother that they dived past him with no greeting but the bright glances of their eyes, and that, craning through the fence, they were instantly absorbed in the miracles of dawn, and ocean, and seagulls, and salt wind.

And another miracle. Denis saw it first.

"Dad, look, a ship!"

Ian looked where he was pointing; his own excitement took him by surprise. A speck, grey and ghostly on the horizon—what could there be in that commonplace sight to catch the breath in one's throat, to fill one with a wild elation? He watched it with his arms along the top rail, and the children watched it with their arms along the lower rail; it came up over the rim of the world, out of infinity like a wraith, as if it were something fashioned of the pearly insubstantial mist which made sea and sky into one, so that on the edge of this cliff one stood as on the edge of a gulf, a void. Was it because of this immensity that one felt a thrill to see so small an atom, human-wrought, emerging like a challenge? Yes, there was a challenge; the challenge of humanity to the dreadful, the implacable mystery of its environment, and across miles of ocean Ian felt a response in himself, a leap of pride. It wasn't, he recognised with some amusement, the cool, practical approval of an official whose business is with the port in which ships make their safe arrivals and departures. It was something warmer and less coherent; a pride which saw her not as so many tons of steel efficiently navigated across the ocean, but as something more abstract, more (again he must confess it!) romantic.

Perhaps as an idea of effort and of conquest. A product of man's brain, an expression of his courage and ardour, and of that endearing inquisitiveness which, of all his traits, binds him closest to his simian ancestry. Somewhere I can't go? Something I can't do? Something I mayn't know? Unendurable thoughts; unfailing goads and spurs! Out of them had grown so many marvels; out of them had grown that grey speck in a waste of sea and sky, chasing the sun up over the edge of the world.

"She's a collier."

"She is not, Jonathan, she's a mail boat."

"I bet you she's a collier! I bet you!"

"Oh, don't be mad! Anyhow, colliers don't come from over there, they come from up that way."

"Why do they?"

"Because they get coal from Newcastle, and Newcastle's up there. North. Isn't it, Dad?"

"Yes, but sometimes they come up from the South Coast, too."

"Dad, can we stay and watch her come in?"

Ian, looking at his wrist watch, shook his head.

"It would take too long. We must get back to breakfast."

"Can't we just wait to see what she is?"

"You'll see her go past up the harbour later on. Come along."

They followed him with backward glances. Once they were in the park again they raced ahead; they were waiting for him under the Moreton Bay fig, and he swung them, first Jonathan and then Denis, on to their branch. Denis peered through the leaves.

"Look, the *Captain Cook's* going out!"

Ian turned. The little pilot ship was moving slowly out of the Bay, and the mirror-still water held the imprint, the long graceful curve of her progress. Jonathan knitted his brows:

"That sort of statue-thing of Captain Cook on the front—what's it called, Dad?"

"The figure-head."

"Yes. Did they really have telescopes like that in the olden days?"

"It wasn't much more than a hundred and fifty years ago, Jonathan."

"But, gee, that's a long time! Was it him put the telescope to his blind eye, Dad?"

"No, that was Nelson. Captain Cook was out to see all he could."

Denis, still watching the pilot steamer, said:

"She's going to bring that ship in."

Jonathan proclaimed:

"When I grow up I'm going to be a pilot."

"That's nothing. I'm going to be a lighthouse-man."

Ian said:

"Come on, boys. Jump down."

"Can we paddle along the beach?"

"Yes, if you come quickly. I'll carry your sandals."

By the time they reached the road again the sun was shining, still pale, still partly dimmed by morning mist, but with the promise of heat in it. Ian slackened a little instinctively as they came in sight of his own roof and that of Winifred's home next door. To be near her was pain; to be far from her brought her closer in his thoughts. He began to wonder again, as he had wondered so often before, whether he should not go away, move to some other house, some other district. He said on an impulse to Denis, who was walking beside him:

"How would you like to live somewhere else?"

He added hurriedly:

41

"No, no! We're not going to! I was just wondering . . ."

But he was seized by a kind of desperation. That look
on the child's face, that startled upward look of blank
horror! You couldn't fight that. Nor could you go on for
ever enduring a physical nearness which forced you,
spiritually, farther apart than you need be. Far away
you could dare to love her; you could dare to sit and think
of her, to picture her, all golden-brown, eyes, skin, hair;
to remember her voice and her gestures and her trick of
sitting with her hands clasped round her knees. So close
to her, nothing but a strip of garden and a hedge between
you, your mind must repel her very image for fear of
goading your body too far. You must strive unceasingly
to shut her away out of your thoughts, and in doing so
something lovely and gracious in your life, like a welcome friend, becomes an enemy to be vanquished. . . .

A spasm of pain contracted his face, and he put his
hand up sharply to his left temple. For a few minutes
thought died and consciousness narrowed to the stabbing
torture behind his eyes. He walked mechanically, seeing
his own feet as blurs rhythmically appearing and vanishing. The children's arguing voices shook him into an
unaccustomed violence of exasperation. He said:

"What's the matter? Stop shouting, Jonathan. . . ."

They wavered before his eyes, blurs of light blue and
dark blue, misty ovals of faces. There was a glittering
oblong dancing about behind their heads. Jonathan
clutched at his hand.

"Look, Dad. It says: 'B.Sc., M.D., Ch.M.' What does
it mean? Doesn't the 'Ch.M.' mean Chloe Marshall?
Denis says it doesn't. . . ."

Denis added irrelevantly:

"Anyhow, why is her name Chloe Marshall when her
father and mother's called Denning?"

"Yes, why, Dad?"

Ian put his hand out, felt the stone wall, and leaned
on it. Wheels came gliding into his field of vision; trouser
legs and tan shoes appeared. A voice said:

"You're all out early. Hullo, kids!"

Ian's head cleared a little, and his eyes with it. The pain stopped thrusting and began a dull, subdued beat. Jonathan ventured:

"Would you tell us, Dr. Denning?"

Ian blinked and saw again. Oliver Denning was bending over his own brass plate, pointing with a leather-gloved forefinger.

"That one means Bachelor of Science."

"But—aren't you married, Dr. Denning?"

"Yes—this is a different kind of bachelor. M.D. means Doctor of Medicine, and Ch.M.——"

Jonathan implored:

"Doesn't it mean Chloe, Dr. Denning?"

"Doesn't it mean what?"

"Chloe. Chloe Marshall. Ch.M. Doesn't it?"

"It *should,* of course. Actually it's a title now obsolete——"

"What's that?"

"Not used any more. And it means Master of Chirurgery."

"What's Ch—what you said?"

"It's an old-fashioned way of saying surgery."

Again it was Jonathan who ventured.

"Dr. Denning, why is Chloe's name Marshall? Why isn't it——?"

Ian said with an effort:

"Come along, boys. Too many questions."

Oliver straightened up and looked at him.

"More neuralgia?"

"A twinge. It's easing off now."

Oliver nodded. Jonathan, with a sideways glance at his father, whispered persistently:

"*Why* is it, Doctor?"

"Why is what, Jonathan?"

"Why isn't Chloe's name Denning, like yours?"

"Because I'm her step-father. Her real father's name was Marshall."

43

"Oh." They looked worried and a little shocked. He asked:

"What's wrong?"

Denis couldn't tell him. Jonathan stuttered:

"Aren't they—I thought—step-fathers and step-mothers—aren't they—*bad* people?"

Oliver laughed, unlatching his gate.

"You've been reading Grimm's grim fairy-tales. Good-bye."

They turned from him to their father, more questions on their lips. But he was already at their own gate waiting for them, and they followed silently, checked by some suffering on his face which they could not understand.

*　　*　　*　　*　　*

From the top of the steep and winding path Oliver could see the harbour over the roof of his house, and he paused for a moment just inside the gate pulling off his driving gloves, watching its stillness breaking, quivering, disintegrating under the strengthening sunlight. He never stood facing westward like this in the early morning without remembering the eastward dawns he had watched from his balcony at Thalassa; and he never compared them without realising that there lay in the back of his mind the comparison between two emotional as well as two physical environments. He was gratefully aware of a stimulating mental activity which remained unaffected by emotional states. He had always enjoyed those idle meanderings of thought which supplemented so royally the pleasure of mere logical reasoning, so that the mind became a thing mysterious and infinite, retreating but never altering, as a reflected figure retreats down an endless succession of mirrors. That this should remain to you, he thought, through states of emotional happiness no less than through fogs of emotional gloom gave you a reassuring invulnerability. There was, deeply and securely locked away in you, that which no outward circumstances might touch. To be happy was a good thing, to be miserable was a bad thing; but to be at peace with oneself made misery a triumph, and happiness a miracle.

Thinking of his thoughts he walked slowly down the path and through the shuttered French windows into his consulting-room. He threw his gloves on the desk and went on into the dim hall, treading quietly. But for all his caution Chloe heard him, and called his name as he passed her door. He put his head in.

"Hullo, brat. You should be up and swimming in the Cove."

She demanded:

"Where have you been?"

He went in and pulled the sheet up round her pointed, elfin chin, teasing her.

"Don't you understand yet about professional secrecy?" But she only insisted, unabashed:

"Well, what have you been doing?"

He began to laugh, and sat down on the edge of her bed cautiously, because the mattress creaked. He told her, expecting her to laugh, too, and she did laugh, but it was laughter that faded suddenly into rueful pity. She sighed:

"Oh, poor thing! It must have hurt."

He rumpled her hair and stood up.

"Not much. I gave her a whiff of ether. Now I'm going back to bed for an hour and a half, and if you start practising before eight o'clock I'll do some heavy step-father stuff."

She said indulgently:

"I won't disturb you, darling." And added one of those apparently inconsequential remarks which occasionally sent Oliver's eyebrows shooting upward in startled amusement: "It must be fun for mummy being married again."

He went on down the hall and turned the handle of the last door noiselessly. The windows were wide open on the dark, rustling leaves of a palm which almost brushed the wall; on this side the house was high above the sharply sloping ground. Oliver, while he took off the few clothes he had put on to answer his telephone call, watched the curtains blowing, and thought of another view, an ocean view, which he had watched once while Lois lay sleeping beside him.

She was sleeping now, very soundly, curled into a tight ball. Her short, dark hair was thick and perfectly straight, and a kind of sheet of it had fallen across her face, and moved slightly with every breath she took. Her capacity for sleep was astonishing. Not only at night, but at odd times during the day she slept. He wondered if it were because she never resisted or attempted to resist or even considered resisting her normal impulses that she lived so vividly and slept so soundly, the living leading her inevitably to sleep, and the sleep renewing her for more living. She worked so hard, was so continually active, either mentally or physically, that a few moments' relaxation seemed enough to bring sleep suddenly, disconcertingly, to claim her. The room smelled faintly of turpentine. It had always amused him that this should be what fashion writers might have called her "individual perfume," and he remembered that he and Chloe had conspired last Christmas to give her some in an elaborate and expensive bottle of cut glass, with a spray. . . .

He got into bed very cautiously, trying not to waken her, but hoping all the same that she would wake. For he knew that she was still healing him of wounds whose dangerous depth he had not fully realised until he married her. He understood now that Helen's every involuntary recoil from him had been like a tiny injection of poison into his veins. He knew that the way she shrank no less from every thought of his mind than from even the lightest caress of his hand had been affecting him as a slow, insidious absorption of toxin affects the body, and he remembered that first marriage now as one remembers a bad dream whose details have faded, but for whose general unpleasantness one still feels a tremor of disgust. Of Helen herself he kept a clear and poignant memory. She, even more than himself, had suffered during their life together; she, even more surely than himself, had been saved by the desperate remedy he had forced upon her at last. That thought comforted him; his respect for her had survived the slow starvation of his love, and his own new-born delight could not have lived with a knowledge of her grief.

In the middle of a yawn he suddenly remembered old Romani in his black silk pyjamas and his dressing-gown of Oriental magnificence, with the fur rug clutched about his shoulders, holding the lantern aloft in the dark, ill-smelling shed, uttering incessant lamentations and rich Italian blasphemies, wiping tears from his florid cheeks, making strange clucking noises of endearment and encouragement with his tongue. . . .

He felt the bed shake a little under his sudden explosion of silent laughter, and Lois stirred sleepily, pushing a hand out towards him. He held it and her arm against his chest, feeling, not for the first time, an odd rush of gratitude, of a relief which had a certain uncharacteristic humility mixed with it. He remembered that on the day of the fire in Thalassa he had stared at himself in a mirror, wondering if there could really be something repellent about him, and he knew that Lois, in her instant and complete and utterly matter-of-fact acceptance of him, had checked the growth of what must have become at last a dangerous bitterness. He gathered her closer to him and yawned again. She said something into his shoulder, and he peered down at what he could see of her face and asked:

"What are you mumbling about?"

She sighed and said with careful distinctness:

"I said what were you laughing at?"

"Just a confinement job I've been doing."

She said reproachfully:

"They aren't funny."

"This one was. Though poor Romani was in tears most of the time."

She lifted her head sharply and blinked at him.

"Romani! Oh, Oliver, not—not one of his sisters? *Don't*, darling, you'll wake Chloe and Mrs. Trugg."

47

Oliver's shout of laughter subsided.

"No, not one of his sisters. One of his goats."

She repeated suspiciously:

"Goats?"

"Yes, a nanny-goat. I managed to deliver her of a fine male kid, and both mother and child are now doing well."

She began to laugh helplessly; he protested:

"Keep still, blast you! You're making cold draughts, and you're blowing down my neck."

She murmured consoling and repentant noises, and he felt another vast yawn taking possession of him. A heaviness, delicious and irresistible, weighed on his eyelids. He could tell from an intermittent silver flashing on the palm leaves, and from the golden ghost of their pattern on the opposite wall, that the first ray of sunlight had just struggled over the hill. His arms tightened for a moment and then slackened again with the swift oncoming sleep.

*   *   *   *   *

But Lois was still awake. Her attention was concentrated on her own hand where it lay imprisoned in both Oliver's on his chest, and she was seeing them, those three hands, in a detailed and detached way as they would look in a picture. Already in her mind she was painting them, and her brain, just now so indolent, was intensely, almost painfully, occupied with the problems of technique which instantly confronted her. Such mysteries as her own strange gift she accepted without wonder, for she had none of Oliver's more sophisticated intelligence, and none of his intellectual passion for analysis. The fact that she happened to have a genius which consisted of minute observation and rather childlike simplicity combined with great technical skill was one which she hardly realised enough to question it. It did not occur to her as it would have occurred to Oliver that her clear mental picture of the exact way that their hands were lying, and the exact manner of the interlocking of their fingers, was something which was being conveyed to her brain by a

thousand delicately adjusted sensations, and there impersonally translated into a picture by a part of her which
had nothing to do with the Lois whose fingers responded
warmly to his occasional unconscious pressure.

She never even realised how much hard work she
expended on such moments of creative ardour. For
every picture she had actually painted on canvas she had
planned a hundred in her mind, lavishing on them a fury
of intense and difficult thought, and then without regret
and almost without awareness abandoning them, unsus-
pecting that later, in one guise or another, those seemingly barren moments blossomed and bore fruit. She did
not know, as Oliver would have made it his business to
know, that it was this quality of generous extravagance,
of inspired wastefulness, this capacity for spending herself recklessly, which had been, years ago, shocked by her
first husband's economical storing of every thought, his
anxious fear that some intricacy of plot or situation, some
dexterity of phrasing, might elude him and be lost for
evermore. She did not think, as Oliver would have
thought, of comparing such extravagance to the extravagance of Nature, which flings down a thousand seeds that
one may grow—the hardiest, the strongest, the fittest to
survive. She would, indeed, have been puzzled to explain
exactly what the law of natural selection meant. She only
knew, vaguely, that of all her ideas some "worked" and
others didn't.

And now, carelessly releasing her mind from its flood
of mental energy, she found herself thinking, no longer
impersonally, of the scars on Oliver's hands and face and
body and of that lovely and dreadful day when he had gone
from her straight down to the fire where old Nicholas
Kavanagh's labouring heart was failing him at last. And
she felt again a now familiar little pang of irrational
jealousy that it was not herself who had waited for him
when he went into the blazing house to rescue Kavanagh's
poetry, but the queer girl who had been Sir Frederick
Gormley's mistress, and who had come stumbling into the
studio that night, her eyes bloodshot and her face black-

ened with smoke, holding out a package and saying: "He said to bring it to you. He's in the hospital."

She clutched convulsively at Oliver's hand, trying to blot out, with the peace and serenity of the present, moments whose turmoil and difficulty were still painful to remember. But that vividness of mental impression which so served her art, often victimised her emotions, and she could not stop the array of pictures which now marched relentlessly through her brain. She could not help seeing herself driving the car whose brakes needed mending along Gormley Highway, and nearly wrecking it on the sharp down slope at the hospital gates. She could not help remembering her own imbecilic surprise when she saw Oliver's wife, Helen, sitting beside the bed where he lay bandaged and unconscious. But more vividly than anything else she saw that wife, so lovely and so afraid, with the light shining downward on her gold coronet of hair, and throwing the shadow of her long lashes on her cheeks; and beside her, startled, gauche and miserable, her own small figure in a paint-stained overall, with untidy hair and hands blackened by that charred package which he had sent her. . . .

She could even hear the two voices, her own and Helen's, as she had heard them then, coming from a distance like the voices of actors from a stage:

"You're Mrs. Marshall, aren't you?"

"Yes—I—someone just told me—he was hurt. . . ."

And she could see on Helen's face the understanding of things which had long bewildered her, growing slowly and cruelly, so that of all her beauty only the fundamental structural beauty of line and form remained; and she remembered with inexplicable shame that, staring at that transformation with the ruthless, avid interest of any artist watching something which is material for his art, she had forgotten the suffering that caused it—she had even forgotten Oliver.

*　　　*　　　*　　　*　　　*

Lady Hegarty listened to Sim's quick footsteps going down the hall and to the opening and shutting of the front door. So early? She looked a little anxiously at the patch of sky which her window framed, thinking how fresh it must be outside, how sharp and lovely the sting of the water would feel on his back as he swam through it down to the Cove, and how good it must be to run as he was running now, down the long, curving road till he reached the track, and then to jump and scramble down the rocks on to the sand. . . .

How good to be young!

The smile which accompanied this thought veiled its sadness with a faint derision. It was one of the queer parts of the mother-son relationship, she thought, that Sim would never realise what a daughter would almost inevitably find out some day—that his mother had paid for this zest of his with some of her own early-morning vigour! So, in a sense, you might imagine that it was really yourself dashing off in that active brown body, swimming out with long, lazily powerful strokes to the little raft moored in the Cove.

Part of yourself. An absurd fancy, absurdly comforting. The other part—the fat, clumsy, elderly, weary part lying here in bed alone—could turn with a feeling of slightly mitigated boredom to the great happening of the day. But it could not hold your thought for long. You had never been able to worry much, or to wonder much about George. George was a dear, good fellow, amiable, sound —his father over again. George seemed—and again the sad and self-derisive smile gleamed and faded—actually more like a husband than a son, for he was Hegarty's Ltd., and you had been married for so long to Hegarty's Ltd. that when James died and George took it over there didn't seem to be any real change in the heavy, monotonous prosperity of your existence.

Only Sim made a life of it. And what was Sim? A belated reincarnation of your own youthful ardour which had been so painfully stifling in the long fifteen years between George's birth and his? Life was so odd, so unexpectedly ingenious, that it might well have said:

"There's something worth saving in this creature, but she's not equal to saving it herself!" And behold, Sim!

She made an impatient movement and rang the bell by her bedside. She spread her pudgy hands out and looked at them critically, thinking that no one would guess how work-worn they had been once. In fact, her mind added with sudden and disconcerting violence, no one would imagine that she'd ever been a useful person at all! There weren't many people who remembered Mary Wilmott, the schoolmaster's daughter, housekeeping for her father, bringing up the young brothers whom the war was to take and kill; and those who did weren't in her circle now. . . .

She thought:

"My 'circle'." She thought it soberly and with some bewilderment, wondering how she had got into it, but not even considering now that she might ever get out of it again. She twisted a fragment of ribbon on her night-gown, thinking: "I suppose it was just the money that did it; and the title. I used to think his name was attractive. I think I partly fell in love with his name. Jimmy Hegarty. Sir James! . . ."

She called:

"Come in!"

Maud pushed the door open noiselessly with her knee, and came in carrying the morning tea-tray. Lady Hegarty's face softened. This was a nice child! Something about her friendly ingenuousness, something about her naive delight in the unfamiliar luxuries and splendours which surrounded her, had made Lady Hegarty override the housekeeper's emphatic: "But she's quite untrained, Madam!" with a calm and final: "Train her, then."

Well, money and a title gave you that. You could command. In your own house, your little kingdom, you could play the despot, and if you had won nothing else from your long married life you had acquired a technique for that little bit of paltry authority! And God be thanked you could still see its paltriness, though you could never escape it now. There remained to you the common sense which saw the absurdity of this "circle" in which you moved, and you didn't conceal it from yourself though you concealed it from all the world, that behind your imperturbable: "Train her, then," had been an odd impulse of unwillingness to lose out of so silly and formal a life anything so fresh and friendly as this funny little Maud.

She sat up with an effort, for she had rheumatism in one shoulder-joint, and movement was often painful. She said:

"Good-morning, Maud."

"Oh, good-morning, Madam, it's going to be a lovely day for the wedding. I'm real glad. Jessie says . . ."

"You've forgotten a teaspoon, Maud."

"Oh, Madam, I'm sorry! I'll get it. I was that excited watching Mr. Sim racing Mr. Blair down to the Cove. . . ."

She vanished; Mary heard her running, light-footed, down the hall. She thought, turning her head to look out the window again:

"Blair. That's the man who runs that queer paper. George—well, of course, George wouldn't care for him. . . ."

A violent, impetuous sort of man with a habit of saying things which made people uncomfortable! And yet—she smiled grimly—not a man who could be altogether ostracised, even by her "circle!" A man doubly armoured in scholarship and good breeding, a man in whom the social solecisms of being in earnest and speaking plainly must be attributed, somewhat wanly, to eccentricity!

She looked at Maud, who had returned and was placing the spoon in the saucer, arranging it with infinite care so that it lay exactly parallel with the handle of the cup. She asked:

"Who won, Maud?"

Maud gave her a brilliant smile of conspiratorial delight.

53

"Oh, Mr. Sim did, Madam, easily! Does he swim real well, too, Madam?"

"Yes, he swims very well. Did he have his tea before he left?"

"Yes, Madam, I took it in to him, and four biscuits, like you said."

"Will you pour my tea for me, Maud?"

Maud poured; she continued cheerfully:

"I want to learn to swim, too. Up where I come from —near Gundagai—there wasn't no chance for swimming. Sunday afternoons when I'm off, I'm going down to the Cove, and my boy-friend's coming over from town to teach me."

Lady Hegarty asked:

"Have you a nice boy-friend?"

She thought, taking her cup, that the child looked a little puzzled by that question. As if it were one she had never considered. She said vaguely:

"He's all right. He's a bus-driver." She hesitated. "Will that be all, Madam? Will I get you the morning paper?"

Lady Hegarty winced. She didn't want to see, to read, the half-column of nonsense there would be about "To-day's Wedding." She thought suddenly of all the obscure young couples who had chosen this date for their obscure marriages—who would go unimpeded by avid crowds, undisturbed by imbecile curiosities, to some registry office or to some quiet church, and there be married as she herself had been married to Jimmy Hegarty forty-two—no, forty-three years ago. She said quickly:

"No. Not just now, Maud. What is it, child?"

Maud stammered:

"Madam, could I see your dress? Your dress for the wedding? I—you see, Madam, I'm off this afternoon—I won't see you before you go—I . . ."

Lady Hegarty looked at her. Was this a unit of the crowd she had just been hating in her heart? Avid? Imbecile? That pretty face flushed with embarrassment and a generous eagerness? She said sadly:

54

"Do you like weddings, Maud?"

"I just love them, Madam, don't you? Real pretty ones, I mean. Last week I went with my girl-friend to that one—you know, where Miss Ariadne Matheson got married to Colonel Miller that used to play golf with Mr. Hegarty. We got a real good view. We climbed up on a railing near the church and we only had to wait about an hour, and we had a *Photoplayer* to look at. Gee, she was lovely, Madam! Her dress was made with a cowl neck and long sleeves, and she had a little boy and a little girl carrying her veil and six bridesmaids, and they were dressed . . ."

She stopped. Crimson flooded her face again; she said awkwardly:

"Gee, I'm silly! I forgot you were there, Madam, weren't you? We saw you go in and I pointed you out to my girl-friend."

Lady Hegarty said:

"Yes, I was there." She thought:

"I was there. I was inside looking at lovely Ariadne and thinking of how she treated young Tony James last summer; looking at Theodore Miller and remembering the details of his divorce nearly ten years ago . . ." She said hurriedly to Maud:

"My dress is hanging in the wardrobe, Maud—you may get it out. It's grey, and I'm going to wear my pearls and . . ."

A moment which held the shadow of panic made her stop, frowning a little. Good things, even moderately expensive things, she thought, you could like and buy, gratefully; but there came a point where you found yourself stabbed by a fierce revulsion. There was a point where costliness became ugly, like idiocy. There was a point at which it began to revolt not your sense of economy, not your conscience, but a deeper pride in your own sanity, your conception of relative values. And now, watching Maud holding up the frock, reverently, ecstatically, she was aware not of its cost alone, but of the combined cost of all the splendours which would adorn this afternoon's function, and she felt a wave of humiliation and despair.

She remembered that she had tried once to explain her feelings to George when he had bought her a birthday gift of half a dozen handkerchiefs at five guineas each. Poor George! He had thought it was simply a protest against extravagance while others went hungry, and he had explained, just as his father might have done, about the necessity, almost, one might say, the holiness, of "creating employment." She had heard it all before, and though she hadn't argued because she didn't understand the patter of that masculine business world, she had remained calmly unimpressed, unconvinced. For, where her own self-respect was in question, she neither needed nor allowed a tutor. There remained, quite unaffected by George's harangue, the fact that the possession of five-guinea handkerchiefs violated that self-respect and offended that sanity by which she tried to live.

Maud was saying:

". . . don't you think, Madam?"

"I didn't hear you, Maud."

"I said it's like water, Madam. This silk. Like in the very early morning. Not now—the sun's up and it's beginning to look blue now. But when I get up it's grey, and it has sort of shiny streaks on it that seem to move— like this . . ." The silk swayed and shivered under her hands. "Oh, Madam, you'll look lovely! Me and my girl-friend are going, but I don't suppose we'll get such a good view as last time. I'll hang it up again now, Madam. Will I take the tray?"

Lady Hegarty said wearily:

"Yes, take it, Maud. And you may as well bring me the paper after all."

*　　　*　　　*　　　*　　　*

On the hill above the Hornby Light the barracks sprawled behind high fences, a record of those days when invaders did not swoop like hawks out of the sky. Here on South Head the barracks, on North Head the quarantine; for civilised man, bringing fear with him wherever

56

he goes, must hasten to raise at the very gateway of his new land defence against war, and against diseases which had never threatened it until the danger of them came like spectres in his train.

Wide new roads, tree-planted, wound about the Cove, but down here at the northern end of the Bay the streets were old and narrow. They twisted between buildings which stood now very much as they must have stood when most of the land between them and the growing city was bushland; when they, huddled near the harbour's entrance, made one of the scattered settlements on its still wild and virgin shores. Here the beach narrowed, too. The pier to which the ferry brought its passengers thrust out into the deep water, and the Bay was dotted with small craft moored close to the sandy shore. Dilapidated houses opened their rickety gates on to the path which skirted the beach, and here Jack Saunders, coming out on to his verandah, stretched his great chest under its torn singlet, and, sitting down on the step, began to roll his trousers up above his knees. When he had finished he still sat idly tickling with one finger a tiny kitten which came to roll and gambol in a first faint gleam of sun upon the step. He felt heavy and lethargic, and he scowled, thinking of Ruby still lying where he had left her on the disordered bed—asleep again, most likely. He moved his bare toes in the sunlight, his face closed and intent, his mind turning inward upon his own sensations. But it was a mere bewildered contemplation; he lacked that ability for mental gymnastics which could have translated sensation into coherent thought, extracted it for detached analysis, and he knew only that he was tired and yet restless, miserable and yet hot with a formless resentment.

He held his hands out before him, palms upward, his elbows on his knees. He opened and shut them, noticing absently how the veins along his vast brown forearm swelled; and, abruptly, in a flame of anger, the hands became clenched fists, and he leapt to his feet, shaken with fury because there was nothing to hit with them, nothing to do. . . .

Suddenly he remembered that it was his birthday That made him think of Sim Hegarty; twenty years ago, both nippers of eight, they had met in the Cove, swimming, and they had discovered that they were twins. Twins! An ugly amusement twisted his face. Twins! Well, at eight they'd been happy enough in that only true democracy of childhood. Sim could swim faster, but he, Jack, could stay under water longer. Sim had already a great deal of strange, worldly knowledge, but he, Jack, could counter with a different kind—a knowledge of tides and boats and fishes and bait, of childbirth, of splicing ropes, of how people looked when they were dead, of the best way to get oysters off the rocks, of how much beer it would take to make you drunk—yes, he'd held his own all right in those days!

Eight, nine, ten, even up to twelve he'd kept pace. They could still meet down there in the Cove where, with nothing but a pair of nondescript trunks to cover their golden-brown nakedness, you couldn't see any difference between Jack Saunders, son of Bert Saunders, fisherman and bottle-oh, and Sim Hegarty, whose father had just been knighted.

Knighted! Jack, without moving, spat scornfully over the gate on to the beach. Knighted—for what? For selling hardware! Well, if he sold it better than the other chap let him have his bloody knighthood! But what had Sim done that all his life the way should have stretched before him so broad and straight and smooth? That the money he hadn't earned should clear it of obstacles, smooth it into comfort, adorn it with beauty?

Hadn't they stood on that jetty not a stone's throw away when they were eleven years old, one bright February morning at about half past ten, straining their eyes upward to a speck in the sky, a plane making its ceremonial entrance through the Heads on the first flight from England? Hadn't he said, clutching Sim's arm: "Crikey! When I grow up I'm goin' to fly an aeroplane!"

And hadn't Sim's eyes come round to his, awed with the glory of that inspiration, and hadn't he cried: "I am, too! I'm going to have an aeroplane of my own, and fly from England like they did. . . ."

Well, the sky was lousy with them now, but he, Jack Saunders, had never been up in one yet. All day they were droning about over the harbour and the city, and no one bothered to gape up at them like they had that day; and flying from England was just a picnic. All the same, when Sim had done his solo flight he'd been a blasted hero, with his picture in the papers. *"Son of Sir James Hegarty."* And that was the bloody truth—that was the whole show! That was why he got what he wanted. Christ, a man don't ask to be spoonfed, but he can't compete with blokes that have twenty thousand pounds start of him. No, he'd given up that dream of flying years ago. A farm was more in his line. He liked to work with his body, to break hard earth, to lift heavy weights, to spend his strength against things that resisted it. But that dream was receding, too. . . .

He went moodily inside and passed down the hall, his bare feet padding softly on the uncovered boards. He stood in the doorway of the dark, stale-smelling little kitchen, and the kitten followed him and began to rub and wreathe about his ankles in an agony of hungry supplication. He took no notice; the old ukulele on the top of the safe had sent him off along another train of thought.

Now that young brother of his had gone and got himself into trouble. Once these kids of eighteen start getting black marks against their names they're finished. He should have stayed here at the Bay, but, hell, what sort of life was it for a hefty kid like Bruce? A bit of fishing and then loafing around. . . . And Ruby nagging at him. . . . You can't blame a kid when he's nearly a man for wanting to go off on his own. And what had he done, anyhow? Jack picked up a crumpled evening paper, spread it out, folded and turned and re-folded it till he found the tiny paragraph again: *"Bruce Saunders, aged eighteen . . ." ". . . stole some newspapers, the pro-*

perty of Southern Newspapers Ltd. . . ." ". . . valued at five and ninepence. . . ." Sold them and bought himself a square meal with the proceeds. The first he'd had for a week or more, most likely.

"There ain't any milk, blast you! Here, lick the plates and stop y' miaowling!"

What had that cost him, anyway? Three bob at the outside. Well, he, Jack, had put in a month as waiter at one of the swell pubs—until they kicked him out because he wouldn't crawl enough—"his manner wasn't right," they said!—and he had seen Mr. Gerald Manning-Everett, owner of *The Messenger,* Managing Director of Southern Newspapers Ltd., in the dining-room ordering soup at six bob a plate, and champagne at thirty-five bob a bottle, and liqueurs at a bob a mouthful he was too gorged to drink!

He spread the paper out on the table and took half a loaf of bread from an old biscuit tin. His face was dark and brooding; he sliced the bread with a strange, vicious concentration, as if any action, however trivial, which could employ his hands, became more precious to him than a mere action—became a rite by which some of his great, restless muscles could be solaced and employed. He opened a safe and felt inside it. He brought out a tin of treacle, and half a tin of plum jam. There was a cold chop on a plate, too, and he wrapped that in a bit of newspaper to keep it from the already swarming flies before he spread his two slices of bread thickly with the jam. His knife moved slowly, absently, smoothing and re-smoothing the jam. He was reading again—a paragraph in which the flash of a familiar name had caught his eye: *"The wedding of Miss Veronica Stewart, daughter of Colonel and Mrs. Stewart, of Point Piper, to Mr. George Hegarty, Chairman of the Board of Directors of Hegarty's Ltd. . . ."*

Jack's mouth moved slowly into a derisive smile. This germinating contempt, of which he himself was quite unconscious, lent to his dark face a menace which anger and resentment had never painted there. He was not aware of his great, bent shoulders supported on the columns of his rigid arms, or of the knife besmeared with blood-red jam still held in one hand, or of the remote and secret smile on his face; he did not know that, with the awakening of an unreasoned but deeply felt scorn, his bitterness had been purged of envy, leaving a hatred undiluted, concentrated, malevolent.

When his package was ready he stood for a moment looking blankly out the window. The littered yard, the broken paling fence half-smothered in blue morning glory, were too familiar to engage an attention again helplessly concentrated upon himself. As his vocabulary would have been too limited to describe, so his mind was too shackled by his environment to understand the increasing blackness of his mood. He was only aware of its results. Aware that a light-heartedness which long ago had coloured his life kindly, hopefully, was gone. Aware that the great physical strength in which he had once found pride had become like another self, a dark and violent stranger in his body. He moved uneasily. His thoughts went back to Ruby, asleep, exhausted. . . . But the dark and insatiable stranger was not stilled, he was not satisfied. He was full of a frightful and remorseless energy, fed by a frightful and remorseless hatred. . . .

He walked slowly out the back door into the lean-to where the washing was done, and took a coil of rope and a rope ladder down from a nail. But his movements were mechanical, his face still closed, the eye of his mind still confronting that shadowed turmoil of emotions which was driving him.

To be driven forward in the dark. Not to know where you were going, not to know when or where an abyss might open at your feet, but only to feel sure that nothing, not even death, could be worse than this agony of slow disintegration. That urge to violence in yourself —you have to drug it with promises of a time when all its dammed back and frustrated energy will at last find an outlet in some wild fury of destruction. To kill and smash and trample—Christ, how good! An ecstasy of relief, like the lancing of some long-agonising boil!

When the energy of your body is rusting you take your package of lunch and your rope ladder, your lines and your bait, and you climb down the great cliffs to the flat rock below the Gap. The cliffs are sheer and high, but they don't beat you; strong as you are the great waves are stronger, but they don't get you. Your body seeks this savage environment, and finds peace for a time in conquering it. But what can you do with a spiritual force which has no direction, no outlet? Hatred burns it up. Hatred uses it. Yes, like a fire, for it goes beyond your control. Yet you hardly know what it is that you hate so fiercely. It isn't your environment. Not the salt water, ocean or harbour, whose strong, clean smell is the smell of all your childhood. Not the gulls, swooping and turning against the vivid sky. For these things—for all the land to which you were born, and which yet has no place for you—you feel something too unrestful to be called love, only strong enough to stir a dim, uneasy sadness. Your hatred cannot fasten upon causes too tangled, too incredibly ramified for your shackled understanding, so you turn upon effects. Violent and bitter contrasts. Sim Hegarty, piloting his own plane. Bruce satisfying unlawfully the clamour of his young, desirous stomach. The big house of Arthur Sellman, the green lawns of its garden sloping down to its private swimming pool, the boatshed with its launch, the yacht moored to a float in the Cove. This dingy house, this dingy woman, this dingy life of your own. Sim Hegarty again, in dazzling cream flannels, a racquet tucked under one arm, striding round Circular Parade to play tennis at old Channon's, and waving a hand to you, Jack Saunders, doing a stray bit of relief work on the road. Pretty bloody condescending of him!

He laughed—a short, ugly sound, without humour. He thought:

"What are we for, anyhow? Just to stick around till we're needed for another of their wars!" He slung the rope and the ladder over his shoulders and vaulted the broken fence. He lifted his head and his eyes to the steep street, the cliffs, and a ray of sunlight lay warmly on his face and his bared breast. The cliff line stood out harsh, black, violently lovely against the milky opalescence of the sky, but he felt no warmth and saw no beauty. He walked fast up the hill, his bare feet soundless on the asphalt.

*   *   *   *   *

Roger Blair, pulling himself up on the raft, said, coughing a little, for he had accidentally swallowed a mouthful of salt water during his last dive:

"Of course, I'm a Socialist. The one unpleasant thing about salt water is the feel of it in the back of your nose. Everybody of any intelligence is a Socialist nowadays."

He glanced down at Sim, wondering why he found it impossible to despise or even to dislike someone who was, by every standard he believed in, so wilfully blind, so inertly complacent, so worthless! And not only that. The thought of Lesley, like the thoughts of so many other elusive unattained ideals which he cherished, twisted in his heart and brain like a goad, filled him with a vast, unendurable impatience, charged him with an over-flowing nervous vitality. His instinct, seeing what he conceived to be wrong, was all for action. Action at once, action at any price, an effort, an attempt . . . But when it was Lesley he saw, struggling with some feeling for Sim Hegarty whose depth he could only guess at, no action was possible. Chafing, furious, anxious, he could, at least, realise that intervention from himself would be not only inexcusable but useless. He was not sure how reliable women were when it came to a matter of principle. He was not sure (although he told himself with increasing vigour that he was) that she mighn't just abandon all her theories if she were really, or imagined she were really, in love with this rich and good-looking, likeable young man who now rolled over lazily, and supporting himself on his elbows answered with faint irritation:

"Oh, rot!" But his good humour reasserted itself,

and he added lightly: "I'm not. But perhaps you don't think much of my intelligence?"

He laughed, seeing Roger turn an intent and appraising eye upon him. Supported on his forearms he lay sprawled upon the raft, only a very shallow surface of his mind was occupied with what Roger did or said just now. He was far more acutely conscious of things which, if he had considered them at all, he would have thought to be of very little importance—the rough feel on his skin of the coir matting which covered the raft, the queer glow in his body which was compounded of outer cold and inner heat, the delicate, seductive warmth of the early sunshine, the lovely glittering leaves of the gum trees round the Cove. Roger, considering him with alert, blue eyes, said impatiently:

"You're too busy enjoying life to think about it."

Sim murmured with malicious complacency:

"Then I'm a darned sensible sort of bloke. Pity there aren't more like me."

Roger retorted instantly:

"There are plenty like you! That's the whole trouble!"

Sim looked at him out of the corner of one eye. Some streak of schoolboy mischief always tempted him to flippancy in any discussion with Roger, but a real interest, and a real groping after ideas, often betrayed him into an earnestness which left Roger openings, swiftly seized, for retaliation. Sim said dubiously:

"I do plenty of thinking at times—but it gets me nowhere."

Roger said, promptly:

"But, then, you have great possessions."

Sim grinned.

"Scripture, eh?" Roger nodded.

"Good stuff, the Scriptures. Logical, uncompromising. They'll be banned if ever our politicians discover them."

Sim said slowly:

"What of my 'possessions' as you call them? I use

them as decently as I can. I don't spend a third of my income on myself."

He stared rather moodily at the disturbance in the water where Roger had just vanished. Lately, he thought, the faint, aching restlessness of which he was now aware again had overlaid this spring and summer which should have been so happy, as a mist dims the brightness of a mirror. His feeling for Lesley Channon had astonished and disturbed him. It had not been his first encounter with a set of standards different from his own, but it had been the first time the difference had seemed to matter. It had always been so easy, he thought, when you met a chap—a jolly decent chap, probably—who didn't take the same view as yourself, to agree cheerfully to differ, to wring his hand in honest and unaffected tolerance, and part with the amiability of mutual indifference. But when you discovered fierce uncomfortable convictions— which you could not share—in a girl to whom you felt yourself quite seriously attracted, you were up against something which mere tolerance could not solve. These convictions of hers went too deep, attacking convictions of your own which resisted violently; they sought to undermine the very foundations upon which your life had been built. Worse, they threatened to undermine your self-respect, your peace of mind. . . .

That was why, he supposed moodily, they had found themselves lately avoiding conversation, checking abruptly, with fear, when a sentence seemed to be leading to some dangerous spot where they would confront each other as strangers, even as enemies. Turning to the safety of laughter and light-hearted fooling, and then, by slow, inevitable degrees, to silences and smiles and glances and tentative caresses, and from there . . .

He brought his fist down on the raft in a spasm of misery and impatience. From there, of course, the path had led them straight to last night, to hours of almost bewildered happiness in each other's arms. But it had not stopped there. It had led them through those hours to this clear daylight, and, incredibly, they were still the same people, and their difficulty still confronted them, unchanged.

No, not entirely unchanged. For there was a shadow of resentment now in his thoughts of her. He recognised it unhappily, but was not able to account for it. He did not know that in the world which he inhabited the majority of women, by the mere fact of their parasitic dependence upon their menfolk, came to be regarded by them as possessions in every sense of the word. Being good-natured and easy-going, he habitually accepted what he was told, and what he read in the newspapers: he was told that women were "independent," and he read in the papers that they were "emancipated." He saw them all about him, living luxuriously, quite as a matter of course, upon money provided by fathers, husbands, brothers, playing at work sometimes under the guise of charity, and it never occurred to him that this was a strange "emancipation," a hollow "independence." Instead, he absorbed the inevitable point of view. And his feeling for Lesley, which before had been a restless longing, was now, since last night, a slightly impatient possessiveness. She was his. That was his emotion, and out of it, dimly, came the resentment which he felt against that part of her which was not his, and would never be his.

He looked up the path which led from the road to the Cove, and wondered if she would be down for a swim this morning. Roger, emerging on the other side of the raft and supporting himself on it with his elbows, said:

"This is a quotation—I don't remember where it comes from: *'If the barricades went up in the streets and the poor became masters, I think the priests would escape, I fear the gentlemen would, but I believe the gutters would be simply running with the blood of philanthropists'.*"

He vanished again. Sim, thinking of the Cheshire Cat, and realising that the blackness of his scowl was being wasted on the water, waited until the head reappeared to say, good-naturedly enough:

66

"What would you? We shouldn't have it—we mustn't give it away. . . ."

Roger, scrambling on to the raft again, made one of his vigorous, impatient gestures.

" 'It!' 'It!' Money! Your 'great possessions!' Can't you see that it isn't the possession of your money that counts—it's the withholding of yourself."

"You've got to be very sure," Sim objected, "what you really believe in before you start giving yourself to it."

"Return to your Scriptures."

"Well, what of them? *'Go, sell all thou hast and give to the poor. . . .'* But when I . . ."

Roger, leaning over him with almost threatening emphasis, said:

"Nine people out of ten, quoting that passage, stop where you stopped. But that isn't the end of it. It says something about getting treasure in heaven thereby, and finishes: *'and come, follow me'.*"

"What of it? When I mention that I give away nearly two-thirds of my income you start making cracks about philanthropists."

"Because, you poor simp, you're so blinded by your great possessions that you can't recognise the *'follow me'* as the important part of that command. Follow any idea that you believe in. The 'give away' is only a necessary preliminary to seeing straight what you are to follow. Hang it all, if you gave away every bean you possessed to-morrow, it wouldn't be the little bit of 'philanthropy' that mattered; it would be the freeing of yourself."

Sim objected, heatedly:

"Freeing be blowed! I'm free enough. . . ."

But Roger had vanished again.

Physical action, at least, was always possible! Under the water his arms moved like flails, his legs threshed and his heart pounded, and the bursting, impotent fury of impatience which tormented him was faintly appeased. He thought, in time with the movements of his swinging, striving body: "The octopus! Money, the octopus! With its tentacles round everything! 'Render unto Cæsar the things that are Cæsar's, and unto God the things that are God's.' But the things of the Spirit are in the grip of the octopus, too. We, who care about them, we, who want to build and cherish them, must go, cap in hand, to people like George Hegarty! George Hegarty!" The name became the rhythm of his crawl-stroke, and he splashed out "Octopus! Octopus!" with his feet till he stranded in the shallow water, and lay there face downward, the first heat of his anger subdued by a pleasant and passing weariness. He looked back at Sim and called:

"I'm going. Kiss the bride for me. See you later."

Sim lay down on the raft again. The echo of his own last words haunted him, and he began to toy rather hurriedly with the conceit that when one's words, intended for other ears, did not reach their destination, they became like ghosts, like earth-bound spirits, seeking constantly to return to the body which had sent them forth. But under this idle flirting with absurdity his thoughts ran on darkly, a submerged current, cold and powerful.

" 'Withholding of myself.' What the hell?" He rolled over on his back, and with his arms crossed over his eyes went on thinking. "Well, I suppose we all have an idea—a sort of picture of what we want the world to be. Everybody happy, everybody well. Nobody in want, nobody humiliated, nobody suffering. Lord knows, we all want it, and Lord knows most of us do nothing to bring it about. Is that—withholding? . . ."

He did not know at what point his thoughts faded out into incoherence, and left him once more aware of nothing but the pleasant reactions of all his senses. It was the sound of a car-horn which roused him at last from this state of bemusement, and it made him think, sharply and suddenly, of Lorna Sellman. Funny. She had vanished completely from his consciousness at the moment when he had left her sitting in her car last night, but now he remembered her in rather startling detail—a fair, fragile little thing with palely gleaming hair and shadowed blue eyes—an appealing image called into

being by the horn of some hurrying milk delivery van!
People had chaffed him a good deal at one time about
Lorna. And he realised now, with some surprise, that if
it had not been for Lesley he would probably have proposed to her by now. Funny, that! He would have been
Lesley's—well, what in God's name *was* your relationship
to your wife's sister-in-law's sister? If any? From some
barely defined regret which he rejected almost before
he was aware of it, he passed sharply to other thoughts.
Talking of sisters-in-law, it was a bit of trouble poor old
George was laying up for himself to-day! Just two ideas
that fiancée of his had in her dark and handsome head—
just exactly two! To go to England and be presented at
Court, and, some day, to be Lady Hegarty! No rest for
George till she had achieved those two desires—and probably, from mutual force of habit, very little afterwards!

His thought of George slipped as idly out of his
mind as it had slipped in, but the thought of his mother,
which followed it, had more intensity. He wondered suddenly, grinning, what odd little trifle she'd have for his
birthday, and that thought, combined with smells and
sounds and physical sensations so potent to evoke the
past, woke in him a memory which made his brain begin
to work with sudden throbbing energy.

He saw this same Cove fifteen—no, sixteen years ago,
on just such an early morning as this. No shark net then,
and no raft, and no refreshment kiosk, but the same clear,
jade-green water, and the same Sim Hegarty.

The same? No, not the same at all! He admitted it
instantly, his eyes on the high rock which everyone called
the Pulpit, and upon which that other Sim Hegarty had
sat with Jack Saunders, relating exultantly the long and
glorious list of his birthday presents.

"Dad gave me a bicycle and a new tennis racquet, and
mum's going to take me in to town to-day to buy a wrist
watch. George is giving me a pair of skis for when we go
up to Kosciusko this winter. Aunt Mary sent me a bonzer
Encyclopædia in a little bookcase of its own with glass

doors, and Uncle Bruce has promised to get me boxing gloves and a punching ball. What did you get, Jack? . . ."

He could see now, behind his shut eyes, Jack's bent head and his avoiding eyes and the violent rush of colour to his face. He could hear a harsh and queerly jerky voice saying:

"Me? Oh, a whole stack of things. . . ."

And then Jack had leapt to his feet and run. Sim had stared after him in surprise, called out: "Hey, are you going? What's up?" But the brown, agile figure in the faded bathing trunks hadn't stopped; it had clambered up the rocks, dodged through the scrub, vanished from sight. And Sim, sitting alone, had suddenly realised what he had done.

No, it was a different Sim Hegarty, that twelve-year-old rushing home in a fury of misery, self-reproach, compassion, a maze of incoherent resentments! Jack had had a pocket-knife in his hand, a cheap little pocket-knife—the kind you buy for a bob, and he had brought it to show. *I told him about all my things. I'd give him half. . . . He could have the boxing gloves and punching ball if he liked. . . .* "No, Mother, it's nothing, I'm not hungry. . . ." *Why couldn't we give him some of our money? . . . We have heaps. . . . He was nearly crying. . . . I'd give him the bicycle. . . . Jack, Jack. . . . He won't want to go swimming with me any more. . . .* "Yes, Dad, they're all bonzer, thanks. . . . No, *nothing*, Mother! *Oh, Mother, Jack didn't get any presents except a pocket-knife. . . .*"

No, there had been no "withholding" then! All his soul had been one wild clamour of protest. "It isn't fair! It isn't fair! Mother, can't we give him some? Why not? I don't *want* things if he can't have them, too. *Why don't we do something?*"

And that morning, listening in misery and bewilderment to his father's attempts to explain to him, his mother's unhappy efforts to comfort him, he had had his first lesson in acceptance. Whatever is, is right. Accept it. Believe it to be wrong if you must, but accept it all the same. Don't make a fuss. It isn't done. Things are *so*. There is no way to alter it. Human nature . . .

Father saying:

"I set aside fifteen hundred a year for charities, Sim. One does one's best that way."

Mother, with some real distress of her own reaching out fumblingly towards yours, coming a little nearer to the mark:

"Darling, we'll always give each other very cheap little presents. Don't be so upset. I'll never give you a present again that Jack mightn't easily have, too."

Yes, it was nearer, though still so far astray. A poor distorted embryo of the right idea! Not that you should be ready to give out of your own plenty to them, but that you should be ready to take on your own shoulders a little of their need, a little of their lack. . . .

But at twelve one is being, quite helplessly, moulded by one's environment. The acceptance had begun on that morning when he had first realised that there was something to accept, and by his thirteenth birthday he had become already more philosophical about it. Through childhood that dangerous, artificial, well-meaning little compact he had made with his mother had been insidiously soothing, but it was time now—it had been time long ago—for him to reject its hollowness. It had been an honest enough groping after some standard which they could not clearly define, and as such, he thought, it had had, perhaps, a certain virtue. But it was no solution. It was less a gesture of love than a gesture of cowardice—a strategic retreat from an intolerable idea! Roger's word—withholding. Yes, it seemed clearer now. Not the *"sell all thou hast"*—not the "give to the poor"—but the "follow me!" But as long as you have these great possessions you are as a man bound and blinded. . . . You cannot follow. . . .

A sudden wave of resistance and revulsion shook him. Rubbish! Great possessions in the hands of a great man. . . .

But it was no use. Great men have had great possessions, he thought, and achieved nothing more than a little temporary and local alleviation. Great men have endowed hospitals, founded libraries, played patron to great artists out of their great possessions, and to their eternal honour —but the unarguable fact still confronts you that all these things could have been done even better by a community whose every member lived in comfort and contentment.

He sat up abruptly, listening, looking up the path. It had sounded like her laugh, and a moment later he caught a glimpse of her dark, boyish head among the trees. Her father followed, brown almost to blackness, gnarled and tough-looking like an old, storm-wrecked tree in his ancient bathing suit, which hung more loosely now than it had done when it was new. They hadn't seen Sim yet, and he sat quite still on the raft, hugging his knees and watching her as she climbed down the rocks and stood for a moment before jumping on to the sand, to kick off her rubber shoes and her white shorts.

Wondering if she, too, had taken a long time to go to sleep when they had arrived home, long after midnight, he heard her say:

"There's Sim, Dad—on the raft." A clear, high whistle and a wave of her hand greeted him. He watched her run across the beach, wade a little way through the shallow water, and then begin to clamber along the rocks of the opposite shore till she reached the Pulpit. There she stood for a moment, and laughed, hugging herself with both arms.

"Is it cold, Sim?"

"Like ice!"

"What a brute you are! I'm sure it isn't!"

Her father, wading up to his waist, called:

"Courage, my child! Watch me!" He sank out of sight for a moment and came up gasping, pushing his white hair back from his forehead. Sim tipped himself off the raft and swam across to the foot of Lesley's rock. He said, softly:

"Come on, darling! Don't be such a funk!"

Her body flashed through the air above him, shot,

with hardly a splash, into the water. He saw her for a second or two gleaming under it, her bathing suit a patch of moving emerald, her legs and arms dimly green, and then he lost her. He swam back slowly to the raft. When he reached it she was already there, and her father was paddling breast-stroke out to the net. Sim put his arm round her cool, wet shoulders, and said:

"I hoped you might come down—but I thought you'd be too sleepy."

She climbed on to the edge of the raft and sat there with her legs dangling in the water, and Sim, resting on his arms, looked up, smiling, into her eyes. She answered:

"I was sleepy. But I guessed you might be down here, and . . ." a queer pain and desperation crept through the laughter in her voice, the lightness of her words ". . . it was so long since I'd seen you . . . three and a half . . . nearly four hours!"

They still looked at each other, but suddenly there was no laughter, not even the remnant of a smile, left on either face. Sim said hurriedly, glancing over his shoulder at her father:

"I couldn't sleep after I got home. I kept feeling that I'd done a—a—rotten thing. . . ."

She looked a little bewildered and laughed nervously.

"Rotten? You don't mean . . . ? You aren't seeing yourself as a seducer, are you, Sim?"

He said, violently:

"Good God, no! What I meant was that—perhaps . . . Well, it has been so hard to—see our way, and perhaps this . . . may only make it harder. I don't know. I'm not much good at explaining."

She said slowly:

"I want so much to talk to you again." Suddenly she twinkled. "But you're going all Society Wedding to-day, aren't you? I have to go to the library this morning, but I have most of the afternoon free. . . ."

"I'll leave the first moment that I can."

73

"Won't you be dancing and carousing after it's over?"

"Well, I'll have to show up at the reception, of course. I'll hang round just long enough not to let mother down, and then I'll vanish. Lorna asked me to go on to Manero's afterwards, but I said I couldn't."

"Lorna Sellman?"

"Yes."

"Do you know she's in love with you, Sim?"

"Lorna? With me?" He looked startled, and she felt a little quiver of fear. Something said to her: "Don't make any more difficulties! You can't afford to! Such a fuss over a different point of view, a different way of life, a different set of values!"

She was a little shocked at the flood of fierce and unscrupulous possessiveness which swept her. Her momentary impulse, feeling danger in the person of Lorna Sellman threatening her love, had been recklessly all-inclusive. There hadn't been time to consider, to enumerate, but even now, on the ebb of it, she knew that she had been quite prepared to abandon everything to its clutches. Work, standards, beliefs, her interests, her ambitions, her whole habit of life and thought had been straws which that current could sweep away. She herself became helpless in it—willingly helpless—spun along in a kind of emotional drunkenness by a force that she didn't even want to resist. She thought:

"What have I done? You let this thing get hold of you and it's like a madness. I see what Sim meant. We have made it harder. You can train yourself to think coolly, but your body remains jealous,. and savage, and possessive. And you can't be sorry! You can't be ashamed! . . .

Sim whispered:

"Darling, what is it? You look so—so——"

"So what?"

"So distraught! What are you thinking?"

She sighed ruefully.

"I was thinking that there are more things in heaven

and earth and Lesley Channon than I realised yesterday.
Move away, Sim. I'm going over to dad, who's being
marvellously tactful, if you notice, never even glancing
this way! And then I'm going to swim across the Cove
and back. And then I'm going home for some breakfast.
Good-bye, darling."

"But when shall we meet? Where?"

She slipped into the water.

"Ring me up at the office, if you have time. I'll have
to go there after lunch to collect some typing. But after
all a wedding in the family's an event. I won't mind if
you discover you're too busy after all."

But as she swam back to the beach with her father,
as she rubbed herself down and put on her shoes and
shorts, as she climbed up to the path again and turned for
a last wave to Sim, she was thinking of Lorna Sellman,
fearing her beauty, resenting her very existence.

*   *   *   *   *

Roger, his hair sticky with salt water, walked home
through the curving, tree-planted streets of the Cove in
his bathers and his sand-shoes and his once-white shorts.
His fair skin, refusing tan, had settled down long ago to
a fierce brick-red, against which his short moustache
showed tow-coloured and his eyes a brilliant and imperative blue. He swung his towel in his hand and whistled
as he walked, not because he felt cheerful, but because
it was his nature at all times to do as many things at
once as was humanly possible. His thoughts, in spite of
the piercing melody which came so gaily from between
his lips, were turning and turning like wheels, manufacturing turbulent convictions into words which his mind's
eye saw already ranged in black, printed lines under the
word "Editorial." The next editorial of *The Free Voice*
—and probably the last. That thought and its accompany-
ing reminder of the sheer necessity for money, for the
Octopus, smote him so cruelly that he threw up his
clenched fists despairingly in the involuntary gesture of
the completely uninhibited, and his gaily coloured towel

blew across his face for a moment, so that he did not see Lesley, pulling on her bathing cap, come to the front door of her home across the street, and, seeing him, draw back again.

He turned down the side path which Ian, in a turmoil of far different emotions, had trodden not an hour before, but when he came to the beach he jumped on to the dry sand and ploughed through it, his head down and his eyes smouldering with unerupted wrath. That impulse to forsake the smooth and easy walking of an asphalt path for the heavy going of soft sand was not one which even touched his consciousness. It was merely a result, logical, if trifling, of an inherent faculty for combat, a chemical peculiarity of cell-tissue, perhaps, which endowed him with an inexhaustible energy and resilience. But the feel of the sand beneath his feet, the sight of it beneath his glowering eyes, wove themselves into the rhythm of his thoughts, and he trod it viciously, thinking: "Surfing, horse-racing, cricket! The Holy Trinity! Lying on the sand, doped with ultra-violet rays, or yelling themselves hoarse over a Melbourne Cup, or getting hysterical over a Test Match! If Bradman doesn't get his century the skies have fallen, but if Roger Blair doesn't get enough support to carry on his paper—who cares? Who even knows? Culture isn't news (one corner of his mind seized this phrase and put it aside for future use, docketed: "Heading—Culture isn't News!"). But his thoughts ran on uninterrupted: "A sordid murder's news, and an American film star's news, and a Paris-trained mannequin shedding the lustre of her presence on her native land for a month or two is Big News. But the fostering of a national consciousness isn't news, a magazine in which the nation can become articulate without having to compete with cheap syndicated trash—that isn't news! It's hooey. It's bunk. It's one of Roger Blair's queer obsessions. . . ."

He stopped for a moment, halted by the word "obsession," but instantly he took it in his stride, acknowledged it, embraced it, made it part of his armoury. Of course, it was an obsession—why not? What else could it be when you saw glaring wrongs about you and had the voice to protest? Your contempt for your countrymen might increase, but your love and your fear for your country went from strength to strength. You saw her doomed by custom and apathy to remain forever nothing but a vast producing machine of goods for export. Wheat, wheat, wheat, and wool, wool, wool, frozen mutton and sugar-cane; gold, fruit, opals, butter, skins. And people; singers who were not acclaimed till some other land had set the seal of its approval upon them. Scholars who fled to communities where scholarship was not an eccentricity. Writers, painters, musicians, preferring the struggle abroad to the slow starvation at home. Wealth, material and spiritual, pouring out of it—and what in return? *What?* The sand squeaked and scattered under his violently tramping feet. "Money—that false and arbitrary substitute for the real wealth of the soil, of man-power, of brain-power; money, and rabbits and black-berries and wireless announcers, and sundry other pests!"

He stepped up on to the path again, crossed it, and walked more slowly through the park. The cottage, one of whose rooms he inhabited in a discomfort which he hardly noticed, faced the clover-strewn grass and the dry rustling of the palms and the tall bamboo; as he entered and tiptoed down the hall to his own door he was mar-velling anew at the volume and sonority of his landlady's snores, and he stood just inside the door listening half-absently, till his eyes and thoughts were attracted by a letter lying obscurely on the floor. It must have been slipped under the door last night, he thought, stooping, and recognising Professor Channon's writing. He had come in late and had undressed in the moonlight that was streaming through his window, thinking of his chance meeting with Sim and Lesley earlier in the evening, think-ing of Lesley's brilliant eyes, and Sim's obvious exhilaration. . . .

He sighed, tearing the envelope open, and read, standing at the window:

"Dear Roger,

"Thank you for the copy of 'The Free Voice.' I sat up till very late last night reading it and thinking about it, and more particularly about your Editorial, in which you provoke and challenge controversy in your usual ebullient and inimitable style!

"One phrase you used sticks in my memory and supplies me with a text for the protest which I must make. 'The strange times we live in.' That has become a catchword—a kind of slogan—but actually all times have been strange, the whole history of mankind is strange, and always will be strange. Our times are ugly and dangerous. They are like a volcano in full eruption, flinging up terror after terror, spreading ruin and laying waste. But they have their own sombre and exciting magnificence—as a part of that history. They are full of conflict. It doesn't matter a twopenny damn if the eruption of the moment is called a nationalistic war, or a civil war, or an industrial revolution, or a Holy Inquisition. The combatants may call themselves by what names they please—the conflict is the same old conflict of Adam with his own spirit, the conflict of expediency, of temporal power or gain, with some sense of fundamental rightness which he dare not wholly deny. And there is no road to peace except through the heart of mankind.

"As for your immediate aim, I do sympathise with it. I understand your ideal, and I shared it once. Love of one's own country is, or has been, a natural emotion, but we must grow out of it. Its danger lies in the fact that it reaches a cerain pitch, it embraces a certain conception— and then it attempts to remain static. But love is a living thing, the most vital thing in man, and like every living thing it must grow or it must decay. It must deepen, strengthen, enlarge, until it embraces far more than one country, one people, one ideal. That is not an impossible aim. It is other aims which are impossible. *They can lead you nowhere but into renewed conflicts. Nothing short of a love which embraces all his kind can bring man to that*

78

pinnacle of human achievement where Christ still stands alone.

"I know how nebulous all this must sound to you whose energy and enthusiasm chafe at even half-hours of delay! Don't misunderstand me. Don't think that I am belittling your valiant crusade, your attempt to release the lovely maiden called Culture from the jaws of the commercially-minded dragon! And don't imagine that I think your ardours and your indignations are wasted. I find more joy than I can tell you in watching you tilt at ignorance and vulgarity and apathy and all the other ignoble qualities which are busily trying to stifle the things of the spirit in this country. But I can't share your fears—or your impatience. I'm too old! I know that the spirit, finally, is the one thing that can't *be stifled. I know that it is man's one 'immortality,' and that it is not national, or even international, but super-national. For there is already among men—and how vast an achievement it is!—a tremendously strong* intellectual *sense of brotherhood. The scientists and the artists, at least, are already from the very nature of their callings, from the deepest mainsprings of the spirit, super-national in their outlook and their creed. They, and not diplomats trained from the nursery to think in terms of 'my government,' can, and ultimately will, lead us into peace.*

"I have my despairing moments—but I believe that. Evolution is a slow and blundering old Ichthyosarurus with the slime of his primeval mud still thick upon him, but I shouldn't be surprised if it has always been such people as yourself, in the last six thousand years, who have prodded his tail and kept him moving! More power to you!

"Yours,

"H. J. CHANNON."

Roger folded the letter and began plunging about the room in search of clothes. As he kicked off his sand-shoes and rubbed sand from between his toes with his towel he was holding a vigorous mental argument with its writer: "That would be all very well if we had time!" An imaginary picture of the old man's wrinkles deepening with his smile as he answered: "Geologists and astronomers tell us that we probably have several million years. Isn't that enough?" made him so wild with impatience that he flung his sand-shoes against the opposite wall and swore with guilty apprehension when the snores ceased abruptly. "But why *should* we have these periodical lapses into barbarism? These intermittent wallowings? Haven't we progressed far enough yet to go on steadily rather than like a man climbing a sand-hill and slipping down a step for every two taken upward? Can't you see the chance we have here to do just that, if we do it *now?* We're losing the blessed isolation that has saved us so far; we've actually, God forgive us, tried to lose it! Clung to Europe and the festering diseases of its senility! Can't you see the chance we have, the glorious opportunity to build—if they leave us something to build with! Nearly seven million precious lives—give us time to breed from them as we could breed if we could feel security ahead. Yes, I know all about the birth-rate. But we must have security to breed. You can't expect women—it's all very well to talk of being international—who wants to rush forward and embrace his brother, the leper? The old world is *unclean . . ."* He stormed half-aloud, pacing up and down in his shirt and struggling with his back collar-stud, ". . . and unless we can awaken a national consciousness soon . . ."

A knock on the door sent him leaping for his trousers, and he called, struggling into them:

"Come in!"

His landlady's daughter entered, bearing shaving water. She was a complacent child of nearly sixteen, and the mere sight of her filled Roger with a sudden agony of hopelessness. He had enough—only just enough—worldly sense not to shout aloud to her: "Good God, you silly little fool, don't you know you're *beautiful?*" But he stormed inwardly. What could you do with, what could you expect of, what could you hope for a girl who knew

80

so little of her own subtly awakening loveliness as to obscure its lines with shoddily "fashionable" clothes, to torment the wide, soft folds of her red hair into the formal corrugations of a "perm.," to plaster her petal-smooth and sun-tinted face with greasy unguents, to spoil the free movements of not-yet-forgotten childhood with shoes upon whose stilt heels she could only mince and totter? A national consciousness! How were you to impose culture upon people of this mentality, concerned only with clothes, and the silly anæmic flirtations of adolescence, and the latest Clark Gable talkie? He said gloomily:

"Hullo, Mavis! Thanks!"

But when she had gone, her nose wrinkled with a contempt for him only less than his contempt for her, he sat on the edge of his disordered bed, thinking of bills. Office rent and telephone; stationery; printers; contributors. They, at any rate, wouldn't badger him. . . .

"What can I do now? Go round with a hat? Go to the sheep barons and the cattle kings and be told politely by supercilious secretaries: *'Sir Marmaduke Merino is not interested.' 'Sir Samuel Shorthorn has devoted his life to cattle and knows nothing of literature.'* Go to Society: *'Mr. Hegarty is sorry, but he has no available capital to invest in an enterprise of this kind.' 'Mr. Sellman has asked me to explain that he makes no speculative investments.'* Go to your friends—again? Ask them for tenners, fivers, stave off disaster just a little longer. . . ."

His spirits mounted with his mounting anger, and he felt his thoughts, released again from the brake of dejection, begin to career exuberantly before him, experimenting joyously with ideas and words with which to clothe them. The pen is mightier than the sword—and how much cheaper! What does it cost to equip a man for killing? Must look that up. A writer can get in a lot of deadly and potent work with a sixpenny exercise book and a penny pen and a threepenny bottle of ink! Hurrah for the pen!

He shaved hurriedly—finished dressing. He had no cigarettes left, and there were still twenty minutes before breakfast, so he went out again, and crossed the park to the little shop where, even before the official opening hour, a discreet knock on a side door would bring cigarettes or tobacco from a sympathetic fellow-smoker.

"There y'are, Mr. Blair. Thanks."

"Right, Paddy. Lovely morning?"

The unshaven face emerged, squinted upward at the sky.

"H'm. . . . Goin' to be a scorcher, I reckon."

Roger walked back across the park cheerfully. A scorcher. Good. He liked the heat. Already the "locusts" were shrilling in the trees.

PART II
THE COVE

"Indeed nothing can be conceived more picturesque than the appearance of the country while running up this extraordinary haven. The land on all sides is high and covered with an exuberance of trees. Towards the water craggy rocks and vast declivities are everywhere to be seen. The scene is beautifully heightened by a number of small islands . . . the view being every now and then agreeably interrupted by the intervention of some proud eminences, or lost in the labyrinths of the groves that so abound in this fascinating scenery."

From a letter written by Daniel Southwell in 1790.

"Some of these indentations in the land are designated coves . . . These inlets have all the same general physical aspect. They are bounded partly by beaches of fine, sparkling sand . . . and partly by natural terraces of sandstone."

From "Reminiscences of Thirty Years' Residence in New South Wales and Victoria," by R. Therry, Esq., 1863.

JONATHAN, his mouth full of bread and honey, shouted excitedly:

"Hurry, Dad! The boat's round Bottle and Glass!" Denis rebuked him:

"There's loads of time, silly—she stays five minutes at the Bay. Gee, look! I'm eating my bread and butter bare! Pass the honey, Jonathan. . . ."

Ian poured himself another half-cup of coffee and drank it, standing. He felt better now that he had had breakfast, but he was mistrustful of an urge to see Winifred, to speak to her, to learn from her own lips what had happened this morning, to be reassured that, ugly as circumstances might be, life, for her, still held some grace and beauty. He went quickly into his own bedroom, and, standing near the window, looked across the garden and the hedge at the window he knew to be hers. His forehead creased sharply, and he felt his heart turn over, for there was nothing on the sill. Nothing. He thought:

"This is ridiculous." But he went on staring. Nothing at all, for the first time since that last meeting when they had decided to meet no more alone. The utter blankness of the window gave, he thought, a very terrible impression of hopelessness—of a life completely drained, completely empty. But he fought that panic down with some annoyance. There might be a thousand reasons why she had left nothing there. They had never made any arrangement, never agreed upon any code or system of signals; the thing had evolved, it had grown out of their need, and, quite imperceptibly, it had become a custom. There was a small table at her window, and in the first misery and despair of their resolve not to see each other, he had matched the bowl of flowers in her window with a bowl in his own. It was not a message—not even a gesture—simply an obscure and imperative need for some

85

kind of communion, something which should serve as a symbol of his thought of her.

But in time the thing had become, by its very childishness, a saving gleam in both their lives. It had amused them to tax each other's ingenuity, and he thought it had bred in himself, usually rather slow in the uptake, an astonishing mental agility—an almost feminine proficiency in leaping about among flimsily associated ideas! They had found that in a way they could still share their life and thoughts. He left a book lying on his sill one day, and the next morning a pair of field-glasses on hers reassured him; a few days later a copy of the same book with a blue ribbon tied about it in a triumphant bow told him that she had liked it, too, and they had both felt, behind this childish game, this rather pathetic joking, a mental experience shared, some slight alleviation of solitude.

But there had been times when the window gave him tidings almost insupportable. A photograph of Brenda and a thermometer standing in a glass beside it told him of illness. It seemed to him now that during the following days he had seen and known nothing of the outside world at all. He had not been able to tear himself free of the agonising conflict in his own mind, and he had spent the hours—night hours, daylight hours—in an odd state of duality, looking inward, watching himself struggling with something so ugly that even now the memory of it sickened him. Into those sleepless nights and tormented days the vicious pain of his neuralgia had first come stabbing, and now, standing before his window, he found himself remembering his odd interview with Oliver Denning in the surgery next door.

"Any worries, Mr. Harnet? Financial difficulties, or anything of that sort?"

"Financial? Oh, no; no financial . . ."

His voice had trailed off while his mind, stupid with conflict and lack of rest, grappled with a half-formed idea which would not take on roundness or coherence. Worries—yes—but this was neuralgia—a pain in the head. . . .

86

"Well, anything else on your mind? Because you're fit enough, you know. People don't suddenly become sleepless, suddenly get neuralgia, suddenly subside into the state you're in, without some cause."

"No—no, I suppose not."

He had looked up from the doctor's square-patterned linoleum to the doctor's face, and there was the square-patterned linoleum printed all over it. He had laughed; and then, with a sufficient remnant of normality to stab him with shame and horror, had begun to sob helplessly, painfully, without tears. When he had drunk from the glass Oliver gave him, he became quieter but not more lucid. He began to talk, vaguely conscious that his words poured out of him of their own volition, and with no apparent effort of thought to form them into sense. He explained to the blurred figure listening silently with its elbows on the desk that he had children himself, and that he loved them, and that, strong as that love was, he realised that Winifred's love for Brenda was stronger still. He explained that with every nerve and cell of his body, with every thought of his brain, with every emotion of his heart, he longed for the child's recovery. He explained that for her sake he had submitted, and submitted willingly, to conditions which made his life a slow torture; that he, no less than Winifred, realised those conditions to be inevitable, unalterable. He explained that his anxiety, not knowing how the child was, not being able to comfort and reassure her mother, had robbed him of sleep, was driving him insane. . . .

And the blurred figure took its arms off the desk and said:

"You know, it's the most natural thing in the world for you to think of what the child's death would mean to you."

He had felt a moment of intense shock, and then a slow clearing. It was as if some blockage in a pipe had suddenly given way, and he found himself looking at a darkly sunburned face and saying: "Yes, I suppose it is."

Oliver offered him a cigarette, and said, striking a

match: "You've reacted too violently to a perfectly natural wish. It was a wish so abhorrent to you that you never even formed it into a coherent thought. You just hurled it back into yourself as if it were a snake that had tried to bite you."

Ian said slowly:

"It's an impossible thought to live with." But Oliver corrected sharply:

"No thought is impossible to live with. If you feel you can't live with a thought it has you beaten, because it'll live with you all the same, in disguise, as that thought has been doing. Working God knows what harm and havoc. A bit of mental arrogance is what you need to cultivate!"

Mental arrogance. Ian looked across the garden at the empty window and thought:

"She has that. It's a good description of her way of thought. Not an arrogance towards other people's ideas or other people's weaknesses—just a sort of 'I'm-boss-in-my-own-mind' attitude. A sort of 'Yes-I-see-you-but-don't-try-any-of-your-tricks!' to any thought of her own that seems to her unworthy. And now—to-day—it has all become so empty, so ugly, so despairing, that there's nothing she can say to me. . . ."

The sound of the ferry siren startled him. It must be just leaving the Bay; he would have to run. He looked hurriedly round the room. Something to leave there, so that later, coming to put her hands on her own empty sill and look across the garden, his love and his compassion would speak to her. He saw a little book lying on the top of his dressing table, and smiled briefly as he snatched it down. A little dull green book, bulging with maps; a book about flag signals and light signals, wharfage and harbour dues, pilotage rates, coal and bunkering, time, tides and weather, pumping and salvage plant, rates for swinging ships—the whole foundation, growth, trade and facilities of the Port of Sydney. . . .

Well, he couldn't give her anything that was more himself! She would know that, and achieve a smile—perhaps even a laugh—of loving and understanding amusement when she saw it lying there. She wouldn't need field-glasses to tell her what it was! He laid it on his window-sill, tilted slightly so that she could see it properly—snatched up his hat, and ran.

*   *   *   *   *

Lesley thought for the hundredth time:

"Thank God for my Eton!"

She could hear the ferry hooting at the Bay, and she called to her father as she collected her bag and gloves, and fastened a bundle of books together with a book-strap:

"Father, will you be home for lunch?"

He answered from the garden where he was adjusting the sprinkler on the lawn:

"I think so. I'm going in to see that Exhibition this afternoon."

"Well, there's some cold lamb and a salad in the safe, and you'll find some socks on the bed—I hadn't time to put them away last night. And leave a note for the baker, will you? One loaf will do."

She thought:

"Really this is very absurd. Father and I like to think we're sensible people. In theory he has his work and I have mine, but automatically, just because I happen to be a female, I become the housekeeper. The very thought of suggesting that he should darn my stockings is ludicrous—but I darn his socks as a matter of course. If I had been a son we'd have shared the housework. We'd each have darned our own socks, and we'd probably have taken it week and week about to arrange the meals and remember the baker. As it is we'd have a permanent housekeeper if we could afford it, but because our funds only run to a 'daily,' we both simply take it for granted that I fill the gaps. It's silly. It's irritating. . . ."

Opening her bag hurriedly to make sure that her ferry season ticket was there, she was conscious of an intense annoyance, not because she grudged an extra

89

expenditure of time and thought and energy on domestic details, but because it demonstrated the power of a long-established convention to affect even rational people. The right of a woman to her own mental life, and to a career not necessarily domestic, had always been so much an accepted axiom in her life and her environment that she was not able to discount such remnants of another age as unimportant. She could not say, never having known such an age: "How far we have come!" but only: "How far we have yet to go!" And irritation pricked at the back of her mind because some instinct warned her that in this particular matter she had best leave well alone. Father was always ready to discuss an abstract matter— abstractly; but to discuss this abstract matter with a view to its practical application would be a very different story. It, no less than any other question, would be turned, dissected and analysed with all his customary lucidity and wit, and he would almost certainly agree that in theory there was neither logic nor justice in the situation. And then he would probably assure her with bland regret that unfortunately many things which were sound in theory simply did not work. And he'd be right. That thought exasperated her so much that she almost forgot to pick up the box with his dinner suit in it which she was taking in to the cleaners, and the remembrance of it exasperated her still more. For why, in Heaven's name, *shouldn't* it work? It wasn't any use saying that he hadn't been trained for such duties. She hadn't been trained for them either, but she did them. Ninety-nine women out of a hundred hadn't been trained for domestic work, but they did it all the same. Mostly they did it very well, and sometimes they did it pretty badly, but at least they *tried!* They didn't stand round looking helpless, as most men so craftily did. in similar circumstances! She laughed at herself for her moment of cantankerousness, but it was a rueful laugh. For, twist it as you would, the very existence of such a question meant a left-over fragment of insincerity between men and women in their dealings with each other. It meant that underneath a professed equality

90

and comradeship women were still over-influenced by that queer sexual impulse to submission and service, and that men, recognising it, turned it to their own advantage. It meant that no matter how deeply a woman cared about her non-domestic work, no matter how greatly its importance, nor how real her ability, she must, in the vast majority of cases, either deny herself her sexual fulfilment, or accept, along with it, the extra burden of domestic cares.

That was bad enough, Lesley thought, frowning, but at least you did get some sort of compensation in the drudgery of married life. It was the parental enslavement of daughters which was the really ugly thing. It was the assumption that though son and daughter both worked all day away from home, it was natural and fitting that daughter should help wash up at night while son read the evening paper. That in week-ends daughter should attend to her own laundry and mending and quite possibly the son's, too, while son went to football matches, or spent the day on the beach. It was that kind of thing which made women shrewish and bitter. It was that kind of thing which bred in them the feeling that it was not much good being reasonable and honest with men, and expecting fairness—you were more likely to make your life comfortable by schemes and prevarications and sexual wiles which left you cynically disgusted with them, and with yourself, and with the whole relationship between you. . . . She thought miserably:

"Oh, Lord, is it Sim I'm thinking against now?"

For there had been a heat and hostility in her thoughts which, she had to admit, were born of an indignation more personal than general. There was the teasing resentment which had been at the back of her mind ever since she had begun to know him well, because he had that offhand way, which only the wealthy can have, of disposing in a moment of difficulties which other people spend time and strength and labour to overcome. There had been an impatient, an almost contemptuous feeling that life, for him, was too easy a thing altogether, and that she didn't want all the lovely and exciting difficulties in her own life, difficulties which to her energy and ardour seemed like friendly antagonists, laid low with a few strokes of Sim's pen in a cheque-book! All that had helped to form the background of resistance with which, until last night, she had met Sim's wooing, but it did not seem to account for the transformation of very mildly exasperated thoughts about her father into very violently hostile thoughts of Sim. For that last fragment of thought, though tacked so neatly on to a purely abstract argument, was nothing more than the bursting out of an emotion she had repressed in one dreadful moment last night when she realised that her body had betrayed her. Not all the honesty of her intention and the sincerity of her effort to build for them both, in the confusion of their differing values, a common meeting-place of thought, had brought them so close together as that dark, delirious communion of the senses. The despairing cry of her heart had been then: "He doesn't care! He doesn't want to know me—except like this!"

She swung round mechanically for that final, perfunctory glance in the mirror by which she reassured herself each morning that her haste had not resulted in any glaring faults of appearance. Her scrutiny was for her clothes, not for herself, and it had the impatient conscientiousness with which she attended to all those details of convention which one cannot ignore. She smoothed her skirt, gave her hat a little forward pull, and was turning away when she suddenly became aware of the figure in the glass as a reflection of herself. She was very far from lacking a right and natural vanity, and when the necessity for new clothes had to be met she met it with care and thought, and a natural eye for beauty. But the hungry and restless intellect inherited from her father, and constantly whetted by conversation and argument with him and with Winifred, had left such preoccupations in the background of her mind, and it was only as a background that she was in the habit of seeing them.

Now, for a few poignant seconds, that reflected figure

leapt forward to the very threshold of her consciousness. It became branded there like a picture—the picture of a figure arrested in mid-movement, a slender figure, almost too boyish for these days of reinstated curves, clad in a string-coloured linen frock with a dull red leather belt, and a small red hat shadowing one side of its face. A face of clear, sun-tinted pallor, red-lipped and dark-browed, with startled and rather puzzled eyes of brown-flecked hazel.

She knew when those seconds of shock were over and her thoughts began to work again that a realisation had overtaken her unawares. It had been as if the physical self, which she had so casually relegated to second place in her life, had suddenly made a peremptory bid for her whole attention. *"Look at me! I'm stronger than you think!"* And she had looked, frozen by the knowledge that it was this Lesley Channon, this visible and tangible body whose reflection confronted her, which had last night asserted itself with such recklessness and joy.

She was a little bewildered, a little anxious, but not at all regretful. She had that characteristic faculty of normal womankind for accepting the fundamental impulses of life, and, difficult as her brain might find it to reconcile them with cherished intellectual conceptions, that calm conviction of their inevitability and their ultimate rightness saved her from being lost in a panicky confusion of emotions.

The instinctive strength of sex-simplicity she had; but she had also the impatience of youth, and its sublime habit of demanding perfection. It was not enough for her that this physical self, which, up till now, had been kindly but casually accepted by her mental self, should suddenly have assumed command of her life. These two selves, she decided, must be reconciled—and immediately!

That enormous resolve which might have made her father smile, merely painted a slight frown of determined preoccupation between her brows as she turned away from the mirror. It did not occur to her any more than it has ever occurred to youth that there can be a rare spiritual fulfilment in the courageous acceptance of a compromise, and she would have been, very properly, revolted by such an idea. Her thought as she ran down the path waving to her father, and banged the gate behind her, was simply that when she saw Sim again this afternoon they'd have to come to a definite understanding. . . .

Gates were banging all along the street. A few doors farther down young Mr. Smith called over his shoulder to his wife: "What boat will you be coming home on this afternoon?" And she, standing at the fence with the new baby in her arms, and the sun on her hair, answered: "The five-twenty, I expect. We'll look out for you."

Lesley, hurrying past, said:

"Good-morning, Mrs. Smith."

But the young woman's eyes were on her husband's back, and, though she answered pleasantly enough, Lesley, through some channel of what she felt to be a new sensitiveness, was aware that she was thinking only of the moment which now came—the moment when, having reached the top of the steps which led down to the wharf, he turned to wave his folded newspaper, and she lifted the baby's plump and passive hand in reply.

Fat Mr. Mason was running. Lesley's own step quickened, for he, from his windows, could watch the boat leaving the Bay, and if he ran haste was clearly necessary. Twelve-year-old Bobby Younger's familiar footsteps came pounding up behind her and he said as he dashed by: "Give you a race?" His eyes and his teeth glinted cheekily, and his school-bag bumped against his leg as he ran. As she approached the steps, Lesley saw Ian Harnet in the scattered group nearing them from the opposite direction, and when they met at the top she said: "Hullo, Ian!" thinking with a pang of worry and compassion how tired and how depressed he looked. Side by side they hurried down the steps, and near the bottom he asked abruptly:

"Have you seen Winifred lately?"

"Not since Monday. Why?"

He shook his head. She looked at him sharply. He was a good deal thinner, she thought, than he had been a year or so ago, and his face had aged in a queer way which she could not at first define. There was no grey yet in his closely cut dark hair, and no lines on his face, except those wrinkles round the eyes which dwellers in strong sunlight acquire so early, but his expression was strained. It was something in the way he looked at you, or at anything, she decided, thinking of Sim's direct, zestful, healthily objective stare. Ian's eyes had a look of tense concentration—the expression one sees in the eyes of people suffering physical pain. She said quickly:

"Do you want me to give her a message?"

His gaze came round to her half-absently, waking by degrees to the sense of her words. He said:

"No, not that, Lesley. But—just find out if she's all right, will you? I—felt—look, we're going to miss this boat if we don't run. . . ."

They joined the last stampede. Mr. Mason, puffing, was outdistanced. The deck-hands had stopped shouting: "Hurry *on*, please!" The gangways were already down, and the strip of water between wharf and ferry was widening.

Lesley jumped, Ian jumped; Mr. Smith and Mr. Smith's friend, Mr. Bindley, for whom he had waited, jumped. Mr. Mason, in an heroic culmination of effort, grabbed the outstretched hand of a deck-hand and jumped. After the railing across the gangway opening had been shot home, three young bank clerks sprinted down the wharf and leapt on board like kangaroos. And finally Bobby Younger, sailing through the air, landed on the remaining three feet of attainable stern, having lingered on the steps so that he might fulfil a self-imposed vow of being always last on board.

*   *   *   *   *

Denis and Jonathan, high upon the great buttress of grey rock in the garden, gave a last wave towards the

95

ferry, just rounding Bottle and Glass on its return journey to the city. The white flicker of Ian's handkerchief answered them, and then, this daily routine over, they turned their attention to other things. Jonathan, restless and energetic, with his mother's dark eyes and her happy preoccupation with practical affairs, climbed down from the rock at once, by the steepest and most difficult route, but Denis remained there, lying on his stomach and watching the harbour. The sun was warm on his back now, and the rock was beginning to get warm, too. Down below him he could see moisture still gleaming on grass blades in the shadow of his rock, and the trees were full of the busy chirping of small birds. He could see the garden of Brenda's home on the left, and he thought how much nicer their own was. In Brenda's the steps curved down to the water-front smoothly and regularly, and an iron handrail curved beside them, and at the bottom there was a little wharf and a boathouse and a swimming bath, with strong bars and netting round it. But in their own garden the steps had been made very long ago, and the descent was a scramble. Sometimes there were two or three steps cut in solid rock, and then a few which were simply big wedged boulders, and then a gap where there was nothing at all and you just slid. Trees and shrubs and clumps of tall bamboo made a green tunnel of it, and when you came out from its shelter at the bottom you were on rocks. Big rocks which the high tide nearly covered; rocks with pools full of anemones and periwinkles, rocks whose crevices harboured sideways-darting crabs, rough rocks on which your bare feet gripped, and about whose edges your toes curled firmly. There you could stand and watch the water. There was every kind of green in it, and silver edges to the water, and it was clear—so clear—as clear as . . .

No, there was nothing else so clear. Under it the submerged rocks seemed to twist and sway as if they, too, were fluid; when you dangled your feet in it it ran over and about your skin with a cold, delicious prickle, swinging them to and fro as it came slapping up against the

96

rocks, bumping your hard heels gently against the peri-
winkle and oyster shells.

Yes, it was a good garden. Best of all this vast rock,
half-covered in ficus and staghorns. It was magnificent
for climbing, or for hiding, or for holding against siege;
or simply for sitting on as you were sitting now, watching
the life of the harbour go by.

There was always something to watch. There were
the great ships that went to America and to England,
and the colliers and the coastal steamers that went south
to Melbourne or north to Brisbane and Cairns; there were
island ships bringing in copra and coconuts from the
Solomon Islands, and ships from Suva and Rabaul, from
Sourabaya and Singapore. Although you had only just
begun to do geography at school you were really quite
good at it, and it was because of the ships. You asked
where they were going, or where they had come from,
and dad got out an atlas and showed you, and in a way
you understood, though it was puzzling that when you
stood on the cliffs and looked out across the ocean you
couldn't see anything but ocean—and yet on the map it
looked such a *little* way!

Sometimes there were tankers. They carried oil, and
they were sort of par—par—well, they were sort of avoided
by the other ships. Because they were dangerous, and
they might blow up, and anything near might get blown
up, too. And they were like ambulances or police cars, or
fire brigades—they were always allowed to go first, and
other ships had to give way to them. And if you were on
one you must simply never, never smoke, or even have
matches, and you had to wear rubber soles on your shoes,
because if you had nails they might make sparks and
blow everything to bits.

Yes, tankers were perhaps the most exciting of all.
Except battleships. Once in the very early morning when
you had wakened in your stretcher on the verandah your
eyes had opened straight on to a picture—a vision—dim
and pearly-pale, ghostly, silent, mysterious, so that you
hadn't stirred, thinking that it might be part of the dream-

world you had just left. Over there beyond the Sow and Pigs shoal it moved—a long, silver-grey shadow, beautiful, wicked, exciting, sky and ship and water all one colour, all one substance. It made you feel queer because you could see its beauty, and yet you could feel its evil; your heart didn't know which way to turn—to admire it, to hate it. . . . That was why you had not wakened Jonathan. Jonathan just plain *loved* battleships. He would have climbed out of bed and on to the rail, and shouted and pointed and asked questions, and yelled: *Boom! Boom! Boom!* pretending to be the guns. He wouldn't have understood that when, with your head still on your pillows, you saw it going by like a wraith you could just watch while it was in your field of vision, but you wouldn't move your head to see it longer, no, not an inch; and then you would shut your eyes and sleep again, so that when you woke it was as if it had been just another dream.

By then the sun would be up, and the mist beginning to lift from the harbour. Then there were gleams and streaks of silver on the water, and glimpses of veiled blue in the sky. You called Jonathan, and you both got up and put on your bathers and rushed down through the garden to your own swimming pool, which dad had made by piling rocks on each other. When you had swum and splashed enough you climbed out and sat on the rocks, and watched Ted Billings' launch chugging out from the Bay, fussing away up the harbour, cutting through its veil of stillness and silence, waking it up into the normal daytime world. Then you would see the funnel of the early ferry over the top of the Bottle and Glass headland, and you'd watch her come round, not knowing quite why you loved her so, and why, though you could see the same thing a dozen times a day, you still liked to watch her gliding into the wharf, the deep, glass-green water at the bow and stern suddenly pale and churning as she stopped, and the gangway rattled down for a handful of passengers. Then she'd come right past you, close to the shore—so close that you could see everyone and everything on her, so close that Jim, the deck-hand, who was a friend of yours, would call out: "Hullo, there!" and wave the great looped rope he was holding ready to throw over the bollard on the next wharf. But sometimes there wasn't anyone who wanted to get on or off at that wharf, and she'd go straight on round the next point, past the *Captain Cook,* out of sight into the Bay.

Yes, the ferries were the friendliest things on the harbour, even in the daytime, but especially at night when everything was so inky dark, so unfamiliar. There they were still, busy and confident, transformed now by the lights which made long pathways of shivering yellow reflection across the black water; and down the centre of each path blazed one long, magnificent streak of colour— green on the starboard side, red on the port. . . .

They were the friendliest, and tankers were the most interesting, and warships were lovely and dreadful, but the things which really belonged were the sailing boats. On Saturdays and Sundays all the eighteen-footers were out; they came racing down the harbour, their white sails fat and straining with wind, their crews leaning out horizontally over the water while they turned round the buoy and went skimming back again. Sometimes one capsized, and that was sad—not because it really mattered, but because those lovely, eager sails were flattened and crumpled in the water, and it was as if a bird had been injured, as if a seagull had come down to die.

When you grew up you were going to have an eighteen-footer. But Jonathan wanted a speed boat. When he saw them roaring past half out of the water, their great plume of spray following them, his face got very pink and he just sat and stared; it was the only time he didn't say anything at all.

But really there was nothing that was quite such fun as your own canoe. The girl next door, Chloe Marshall, had a canoe, too, and they had races. She was quite big, about fourteen, but he and Jonathan together could always beat her. Often on Sunday mornings and in the holidays she and they would paddle round to the foot of the Sellmans' garden, and Mrs. Sellman would bring Brenda down to them and lift her into Chloe's canoe, saying: "Here's your bodyguard, darling!" That was nice to be a bodyguard. Brenda was never allowed to go swimming with anyone else, and although she could swim quite well she wasn't allowed in even Chloe's canoe unless they were all there, all three of them, her bodyguard. Because, of course, it wouldn't be much use being able to swim if you weren't sure what direction to swim in. But down in the Cove you and Jonathan got one each side of her, and she put her hands on your shoulders and just swam with her legs and you all went out to the raft together. And there was the Pulpit, which was—oh, quite high, higher than a door out of the water, and you counted: *One! Two! Three!* and you all jumped from it together at the side where it was deepest, holding hands, Brenda in the middle. You wouldn't think anyone blind could be so happy. Sometimes you forgot and called out: "Look, Brenda!" and then you remembered that she couldn't look, and you were sorry—but she didn't seem to mind.

Suddenly his thought-world exploded. All the details of his daily life which had been reflected in it as the details of a room are reflected, rainbow-coloured, miniature, familiar and yet unreal, in a soap bubble, vanished as the reflections of the burst bubble vanish, leaving you contemplating plain windows, plain walls—the solid original of your nebulous imaginings. But Denis felt no sense of loss or disillusionment. Instead, he gave to his recaptured actual world an ardent welcome, and spared for the other only a hasty marvelling that he should have so wasted even a few moments of this golden day.

Calling: "Hi, Jonathan, where are you?" he scrambled down from his rock.

*   *   *   *   *

Brenda said, sedately:
"Good-morning, Daddy."
She climbed into her chair without receiving or

seeming to expect an answer. Winifred, taking her place opposite and glancing at the spread newspaper which concealed her husband, felt herself shaken, for the second time that morning, by a wave of rage and hatred. It was not preoccupation with the day's news, she thought, which had kept him silent. She wished that she didn't, in some ways, understand him so well. She wished that she didn't see so clearly the two motives which combined to make him ignore Brenda's existence—the desire to wound herself, and the unreasoning, almost superstitious repugnance which he felt when he saw that small face so like his own wearing the strange, still serenity of blindness. Those eyes whose colour was the blue of his own and Lorna's, looking at the world without seeing it, and yet expressing a joy in it which he had never been able to achieve.

Brenda's hand was feeling beside her plate for her spoon. She seemed, Winifred thought, watching her sadly, very far away, imprisoned in some world of her own which even her mother might not share. In an access of dejection and bitterness Winifred saw it as a cruel and ironical gesture of fate that the very tragedy which held her so close to her daughter that she must abandon hope and thought of her own happiness, shut her out of the child's mind through which alone real companionship might come.

She had been lonely before during her married life, but now that most agonising of all human trials, spiritual solitude, seemed to weigh upon her with an oppression almost unbearable. And yet in the midst of it she had a fleeting consciousness of the involuntary reaction to adversity with which the normal mind maintains its equilibrium. Some corner of her brain, invincibly aware of itself, saw in that instant rallying of moral strength against depression and defeat, a parallel to the prompt mobilisation in the blood of leucocytes to war against disease, and she thought, with a glimmer of amusement: "Really our home defences are very good indeed."

Grateful in a detached way for that automatic resistance in herself which had never failed her yet, and which now subdued the something in her which longed to tear her hair and beat her hands upon her breast in a frenzy of helpless grief, she continued to sit calmly in her chair, marshalling her long dark thought behind a quiet face.

It had been easy enough just after Brenda's birth, and before the awakening of the mind to which she must now remain a stranger, to lose herself in voluptuous depths of maternal preoccupation. For a blind baby was not so very different from any other baby. Those sad and fleeting delights with which motherhood consoles itself for glad and lasting sacrifices had possessed her, no less than happier mothers, and she still had memories which were not the less precious and poignant for their impotence to aid her now. There is a weight, a warmth, a scent about a baby in your arms, she thought, which make up an experience your senses never will forget. All your life afterwards you can close your eyes and feel that child cradled against your heart; the palm of your right hand still holds the sensation of a leg which your fingers could encircle, and a round knee, smooth as satin under the delicate roughness of knitted wool. The sole of the bare foot which rested in it is still innocent of the earth, and its toes lie together as freshly and compactly as a row of young peas in a newly opened pod. There is, in those few and quickly passed months during which a mother nurses her child, some conception, however elusive and uncertain, of a miracle which has happened. . . .

Brenda said:

"Have I finished all my cornflakes, Mummy?"

Winifred felt a pang of love and compassion. Such a *good* little girl! Above all the things denied her—beauty of sky and trees and ocean, Punch and Judy, Mickey Mouse, picture books, soap bubbles, rainbows, stars, moonlight, ships passing, Christmas trees a-glitter—it seemed to Winifred, in a second of agonised revolt, that the most cruel loss was the loss of her right to naughtiness. For her little bursts of petulance, her moments of almost frenzied temper, were not the spontaneous eruptions of normal childhood, but the nervous reactions of a mind struggling too constantly with an environment which could not but be alien. This bright world where people lived by seeing was not her element, bravely as she grappled with it. What was her element? Was there some world of the blind where the blind could be happy —alone? But she could not be alone, and all her existence was jagged with the intrusion of foreign words, foreign conceptions which she must toil to understand. No, in this anxious and difficult schoolroom which all life must be for her, the healthy naughtiness of confidence and self-assertion could have no place; and the happiness which so often shone from her face, and which you cherished, and by which you kept your heart alive, must be some unreasoned inner happiness whose very strangeness gave it the flavour of a grief.

She said:

"Here's your toast, Brenda, and the butter's just in front of you. Would you like jam, too?"

She thought:

"It was just when I was beginning to realise how far away from me she must always be, that Ian happened."

He had saved her then for a few swift and uneasily lovely months from the solitude which now seemed about to engulf her at last. She wondered, idly pushing her teaspoon round her saucer with one forefinger, whether it would not have been better if this hungry and imperious element of love had never invaded their friendship. It had been, for them both, so happy and satisfying a time. A time of books and thoughts and jokes exchanged, of long Sunday mornings playing singles on the tennis court in her father's garden, of happy picnics with Lesley and the children down in the Cove, of looking out for each other on the ferry and sitting together upstairs at the front, voyaging into the teeth of a salt wind, between a silver dazzle of water and a blue gulf of sky.

A strange thing, this love. An irresistible thing. For it was no use pretending that by not seeing each other you were resisting it. You might as well pretend that by stepping out of the path of an avalanche you were hindering its descent. The avalanche went on, your love went on, gathering strength, gathering volume—all you could do was to decide whether or not your physical self went with it. . . .

* * * * *

Arthur put his paper down and blew his nose loudly. Now that he had had his shower and a cup of strong coffee he felt better physically, but he was still conscious of a mental uneasiness. He liked, in a sluggish and indolent way, to live at peace with everyone; the effort of being at loggerheads was distasteful to him, and he glanced sideways at Winifred, weighing the chances of a reconciliation. Not that he was going to climb down. By no means! But he believed in burying the hatchet for the same reason that he believed in most other catchwords—that it saved him the trouble of thinking out each situation on its own merits. He said with heavy amiability:

"I'm taking the Packard into town this morning, Win. But Martin can drive you and Lorna in her car this afternoon."

For a moment she was puzzled.

"This afternoon . . . ?"

"George Hegarty's wedding. Hadn't forgotten, had you?"

Winifred's face closed, tightened, so suddenly that he looked hurriedly away, and then, with some uneasiness, back at her again. More often than he could remember that odd expression—as if a mask had covered her face, as if a blind had dimmed a lighted window—had plunged him into sloughs of incomprehensible animosity and discord. He never clearly understood what it was all about; he did not suppose that he would understand now, and his sudden rising was really a movement of escape rather than, as she construed it, a movement of impatience. Her words stopped him. She did not know herself why it seemed so important that she should stand by her resolve, casually made this morning. She was so exhausted by the sleeplessness and the misery of the night she had just spent that she felt all her resistant thinking dulled and confused, and the wedding became a symbol of the life which she hated, and which was, so emphatically, his and not hers. She felt, with the over-violent determination which sometimes flares out of intense fatigue, that she would rather die than conform any longer, even outwardly, to this life of his, and she said sharply:

"I'm not going to the wedding."

Here, at any rate, he thought, was a definite statement —something solid and understandable. From a safe vantage point, founded upon neighbourly courtesy, convention, social expediency, he demanded:

"Why not?"

Winifred lifted Brenda down from her chair and said: "Run out to Olive, darling; I'll come presently, and then we'll go down to the beach."

But while she stood with her back to Arthur, watching the child out of the room, she was not thinking of the small figure which her eyes followed, nor of Arthur, nor of Ian, nor of anything but her own rocking self-control. She was screaming inwardly: "I can't go on, I can't, there must be an end—any end—somehow—soon . . ." She turned back to the table, her voice taut:

"I dislike Veronica Stewart, I don't care a rap for George Hegarty, and I can't bear fashionable weddings, anyhow."

Arthur actually chuckled with relief. This, he decided, was just a plain feminine tantrum. Far from disliking such things, he felt that, in Winifred at all events, they were reassuring simply because they were not those frozen, incisive moods which so angered and bewildered him. He lit a cigarette and said indulgently, between his first puffs:

"Well, they aren't madly exciting, I admit. But one's expected to show up. Sort of social duty. . . ."

She said, bitterly:

"You have funny ideas of social duty! Are you going yourself?"

He eyed her, wondering if this might not turn out to be more than a tantrum after all, and he said:

"Well—no. I have a meeting."

For all his practice, he had never learned to lie with ease and assurance, and now, with ill-judged assertiveness, born of an uneasy sense of guilt, he added commandingly:

"But I want you to go."

She stared. Her voice became very quiet, edged and dangerous like whetted steel.

"I've told you, Arthur. I'm not going."

They faced each other across the table. Arthur's jaw hung a little, as it did when he felt himself at a loss, but there was a slow, up-creeping redness over his neck and face. His eyes, set in that deepening colour, had the bright opaqueness of china eyes, and suddenly Winifred, watching him, came back out of her blinding fury like one returning out of a fog on to the high-road. She thought with shame and self-disgust:

"I despise him. But the fact remains that he lives by his own standard of what's right, and I don't. I actually get a sort of shoddy pleasure out of goading him—even out of goading Lorna. . . ."

She looked at him searchingly, with an intentness almost pathetic, willing, in that moment of acute self-reproach, to see his good qualities, and to forget or ignore his bad ones. But she acknowledged a moment later that it was no use trying to separate people into "qualities." The pernicious doctrine of dualism, always trying to divide the indivisible! To rend apart that closely knitted, intricately woven, delicately adjusted entity called man. To make him into "mind" and "matter"; "soul" and "body"; "god" and "beast." To endow him with "good qualities" and "bad qualities," when every quality in him drew its vitality from a common source, as every leaf of a tree draws its nourishment from a common root-system. No, all you could truly say of anyone involved a mystery more profound than any dissection and analysis could yield you. Here is a human being—unique. There has never been one exactly like him, there will never be another exactly like him. That is his one "quality"—his only "significance." What was it, that something so inherent in you that all your words and deeds, the shape of your thoughts, the very movements of your body, were dictated by it? An attitude, a conception? And what determined it? What made you friend or foe to life? What made you one with it so that its rhythms flowed sweetly in your blood, and your eyes saw its beauties? Or what made you outcast, tuned to some different key, so that your whole existence was a discord, and your eyes saw nothing but corruption? Or what, again, made you such as Arthur, neither friend nor foe, existing torpidly, a mere mass of functioning flesh, seeing nothing?

He was saying:

"Lorna's in bed, I suppose?"

She blinked her eyes back to focus on him, and, still chastened, answered rather confusedly:

"Lorna? Yes—I suppose so. Why?"

His face was still very red, and his eyes looked slightly protuberant in their fixedness. His voice had the same note of hoarseness which she had noticed in it last night, and she realised with a sense of nausea and fear that when an unimaginative man has won what he conceives to have been a victory, he is ripe for further essays in intimidation. He said:

"I'm going in to tell her that you'll be going to the wedding with her in her car this afternoon. And I'm going to ask her some questions."

"Questions?"

She saw darkness opening in front of her. It was there very suddenly, a pit of her own digging, inescapable.

"Lorna might see you go over next door one night."

"You mean she might pretend to have seen me."

But he hadn't meant that. Her own sharply leaping brain, her own uncontrollable, contemptuous tongue, had shown him the way to a form of coercion he was quite incapable of thinking out for himself. She thought wildly: "It serves me right for deliberately making Lorna hate me so. It serves me right for giving way to that cheap impulse to score off her all the time. For being irritated

107

by her complacency and trying to prick it. . . ." She asked with an effort:

"What kind of questions?"

But he did not answer that. He was looking at her very intently, and she realised that his mind would inevitably construe her obvious agitation as alarm—guilt. If she cried out now the thing that was tearing her heart: *"I'm ashamed of myself!"* he would regard it as an admission of adultery and as nothing else.

She watched him walk out of the room, and then she went across to the wide bay window overlooking the harbour, and sat down limply on its semicircular seat. She shut her eyes for a moment—several moments—she did not quite know how long, nor whether she had actually slept in the dark little interlude between thought and thought. But when she opened them again they opened on to blue, sparkling water, and she heard the sound of the ferry going by.

It came into her field of vision, and she watched it quietly without moving, studying the rows of people, mostly men at this hour, who sat along the outside seats downstairs, pipe and cigarette smoke drifting up over the tops of their outspread newspapers into the still hesitant morning sun. She could recognise one or two of them— portly Mr. Mason, who lived in one of the brick bungalows on the other side of the street, and young Mr. Smith, whose wife had had a baby recently, and the man whose name she had never been able to discover, but who had once saved Brenda from a fall on the wharf by moving swiftly out of her way a basket of bait which a small boy had left there.

She couldn't see Ian. He always sat upstairs at the back, and behind the solid barricade of newspapers it was impossible to identify him. Still, he was there. That thought gave her a queer comfort, linking her, however precariously, with the sober and humdrum but solid life of work and routine which that boatload represented. From different bays all over the harbour, she thought, just such ferries as this one were setting out to converge at

last, and release their crowds upon the city. For an hour
or two the Quay would be like an ants' nest intermittently disturbed, and the clanging turnstiles and the
tramp of feet along the wharves would make a noise so
familiar as to be unnoticed unless you had been away, as
she had once, for a long time, and then returned. . . .

She watched the ferry till it rounded Bottle and Glass,
and a handkerchief fluttered suddenly from its top deck.
Winifred smiled, thinking of Denis and Jonathan,
perched upon their rock and watching it, too; and then,
with a feeling of actual physical sickness, she remembered
that she had left nothing in the window.

Nothing.

Her reaction to that realisation was the same as Ian's
had been. They were not messages which the windows
framed, but symbols. Fragments of their lives, as though,
denied a complete intermingling, they might still say:
"Here is some of myself for you. This was my thought
to-day, this was my mood, at this I was working, this is
what I saw, or felt." But to-day, nothing.

Frozen, she walked down the hall to her bedroom,
and across it to the window. That omission had, for her
as for him, a dreadful significance. At last she had been
swallowed up, at last she was downed, and beaten. There
remained untouched none of the real Winifred, and she
had now not even a fragment of an inviolate self to offer
him. In this mood, she looked across the garden and saw
the little green book, bulging with its maps, lying on his
window-sill. She did not know, standing with her
clenched hands against her mouth, whether the blinding
of her eyes with tears meant grief, or joy; gratitude, or
fierce rebellion.

*   *   *   *   *

Lois asked without turning:

"Well, how about—beef? And we could have it cold."

She was leaning on the kitchen window-sill which
faced east, and the sun was shining on her bare arms and
hands. She was very interested in a patch of grass in the
shade of a big stone in the garden. It looked absolutely

mauve; not that purplish darkness which some shadows have, but a mauve as clear and pale and definite as if the grass were strewn with fallen jacaranda flowers, and there was a silvery, cobwebby surface to it which must be the effect of dewdrops still in shade. The really odd thing about it was . . .

Mrs. Trugg's chuckle, rich and breathless, sounded again behind her.

"Go along with you, Mrs. Denning, I don't believe you know so much as the name of any sort of meat besides beef!"

Lois protested, wrinkling her brow a little in the effort to detach her thoughts.

"Of course, I do, Mrs. Trugg. There's mutton and veal, and—that nice indigestible stuff—pork. How about pork chops, then?"

The really odd thing about it was that although the grass, except where the stone shaded it, was quite green, you could not, look how you would, see where it became green and left off being mauve, and when you looked at the mauve for a long time it stopped being mauve and became green like the rest. Now was that because you *knew* it was green, and your knowing was strong enough to bully you into seeing what you ought to see instead of what you did see? Because . . .

"Well, it upset Miss Chloe last time we 'ad it. Meself I don't think she's too strong in the stummick. All that there sitting at a piano and practisin' scales. . . ."

Lois said hastily:

"Oh, well, not pork, then." Inspiration visited her. "Brains! They're very digestible because they give them to invalids. . . ."

Mrs. Trugg made a sharp noise of disapproval.

"Now, Mrs. Denning, don't you remember the doctor won't *touch* them! Don't you remember 'e says: 'Anything on God's earth,' 'e says, 'except brains,' 'e says. And any'ow, they're not nice done over."

Lois said, rather forlornly:

"Not brains, then."

110

Because when you looked away from it for a moment and then suddenly back again it *was* mauve. And if your knowing could bully your eyes over a thing like that perhaps it bullied them over all sorts of things? When you were painting? Did you perhaps only see things truly for the one flash of sight before your mind had time to get to work on them? . . .

"Well, what would you think of a nice steak and kidney pie, then? That's something they both like, and we 'aven't 'ad it for a week or more. . . ."

Lois took her arms off the window-sill and turned round. After the sun-dazzle of the garden, she seemed to see Mrs. Trugg looming out of the darkness, the vast spread of her apron making a patch of white behind which everything else receded into semi-obscurity. Lois found herself thinking suddenly of her husband's ice-blue eyes, which were the first impression you always had of him, and which, she thought, in their keenness and directness, and rather startling lucidity, seemed like symbols of himself set in his darkly sunburned face. And of Chloe's restless, expressively moving hands. And of Lorna Sellman's magenta-lacquered finger-nails. And of the back of Lesley's Channon's head, shapely and strong-looking with its austerely clipped Eton and its compact, close-lying ears. And of her own absent-minded, slightly anxious expression. And she wondered if perhaps all human beings bore or acquired some one feature, trick, expression, garment or adornment which, with merciless truth and accuracy, summed them up? Symbolised them. A portrait of Mrs. Trugg, for instance. Wouldn't it be an amorphous semi-darkness from which emerged a vast and comfortable expanse of white apron? Wouldn't further details be worse than unnecessary? Mightn't they be actually misleading—distracting your attention from the whole essence of cheerful and ignorant and good-hearted servitude which that apron instantly suggested?

"Well, that's the first course we 'ave. Now what would you say to just some stewed peaches and a nice jelly? Then you'll only 'ave to 'ot up the pie."

Lois asked, tentatively:

"Wouldn't the pie be nice cold, too?"

Mrs. Trugg pursed her lips a little in indulgent disapproval. Of course, this Mrs. Denning was one of those artists with 'er 'ead in the clouds most of the time, but artist or no artist the doctor must 'ave 'is good 'ot meal at least once a day. A man needed an 'ot meal after the day's work. It was all very well for artistic people that just played around with a box of paints and some brushes to nibble at a bit of fruit and a lettuce leaf, but a man was different. If she, Mrs. Trugg, didn't see to it that she left something ready in the larder on 'er afternoon off, like as not all the doctor would get would be a cup of tea and a biscuit. No, you could be an artist if you 'ad to—no one could say that Aggie Trugg wasn't broad-minded—but if you were married your duty to your 'usband came first, and an 'ot meal was not more than your duty. So she said, firmly:

"Now I'll cook it for you this mornin' and make a crust, and you just tell Miss Chloe to put it in the oven say about a quarter to five, and it'll be real nice. But she must mind and not leave the gas full on like you did last time, or my crust'll get burnt to a cinder. Well, that's all settled, and I'll go up to the butcher's straight after breakfast. Now, there's one other thing . . ."

Lois, half-way to the door, turned patiently.

"Yes, Mrs. Trugg?"

"Well, this afternoon I was thinking I'd go to the Zoo, not 'aving been since the old days when it was out Moore Park way, and I thought it would be real nice if I could take Mr. 'Arnet's two little boys, and that poor little blind thing of Mrs. Sellman's might come, too."

Lois said eagerly:

"Why, they'd love it, Mrs. Trugg. But what about coming home? Weren't you going to the pictures in town to-night?"

"Yes, I'm meeting my married daughter at 'alf past six. But I could put them on the ferry and they'd be all right. Most likely their dad'll be on it, too."

Lois nodded. She felt an oppressive but not unfamiliar sense of shame and inferiority. People like Mrs. Trugg, she thought, really did seem to find their own happiness in a wide, generous, utterly spontaneous benevolence. She was a terribly fat, terribly ignorant, terribly superstitious old woman who could only look back, if she looked back at all, upon a long and difficult life of poverty, of misery with a drunken husband, of continual and futile child-bearing; and now the hard work, the small wage, the increasing precariousness of life as a "general" was all her reward. But she could offer, with real joy, her "afternoon off" for the entertainment of two little boys. Her great bulk, lurching on weary feet and purple-veined legs, would struggle after those two lean and agile children up and down long, steeply winding paths; her face, crimson with heat and shining with perspiration, would still smile at them, and, panting, her only protest would be: "You and Jonathan look at the seals for a few minutes, love, while I get me breath."

Lois said:

"I expect that would do splendidly. I'll ring Mr. Harnet up at his office later on, and ask, and I could run in and see Mrs. Sellman."

But she was thinking as she went out the back door into the sunshine and began to walk slowly down the garden path, that she herself, because of a compulsion in her which she had never attempted to discipline, could not even remember that her husband disliked brains, or that pork didn't agree with her daughter. That even such a little practical duty as putting a pie in the oven and remembering to turn the gas low irked her almost beyond bearing.

She leaned her arms on the low stone wall which shut off the garden from the twenty-foot drop on to the rocks below, and watched a ferry passing Middle Head on its way to Manly. Calm as the water looked, you could see her dipping ever so slightly in the long ocean swell which came in through the Heads, and as she dipped her windows gave back a silver flash from the sun. Lois found

113

herself thinking that no matter how soberly you lived on the shores of this harbour, no matter for what dreary purpose you travelled upon its glittering water, your life could never be entirely unaffected by its happy air of adventure and of holiday. It would not really matter, for instance, if you had to go to Manly every day to serve behind a shop counter—the beginning and the end of your day were still voyages in miniature, lit with glamours which had also attended the journeys of Marco Polo and Diaz, Vasco da Gama and Magellan, Christopher Columbus and Captain Cook! You had the strange movement of the sea under your feet, and the salty breath of it blowing into your lungs; you saw gulls and heard their wild crying; for a few minutes as you passed the Heads there was nothing between you and the edge of the world but blue ocean. Even when you disembarked you were only on a mere shaving of land; the quiet water of the harbour lapped it on one side, and the vast breakers of the ocean assaulted it on the other, and something of their magic blew over the place like a spell, so that people discarded, not only their clothes, but their haste and their problems, too, and took on, instead, an air of eager expectancy. Men, women and children walked the streets in sunburned semi-nakedness; merry-go-rounds spun madly; in the aquarium vast captive sharks swam endlessly in terrible and sullen longing for the sea; white capped and coated men in doorways spun pink cobwebs out of sugar and piled them in twists of paper for eager-handed children; along wide, tree-shaded roads the whole population succumbed to the nostalgia of an ocean-faring race, and went down to the sea again with surfboards and bright towels and toys of gaily coloured rubber. . . .

You couldn't blame them, she found herself thinking; and then wondered, with that vagueness which always attacked her mental processes when they ceased to be instinctive and became deliberate, what it was that you couldn't blame them for? Oliver's hands came down on the wall beside her, and she looked at the dreadful scars on them, the whitened, shrivelled skin and the two per-

manently bent fingers, and then up into his face, smiling.
It occurred to her that he would almost certainly be able
to explain her own thought to her, and she said:

"I was thinking about all the people who live here"
—her arm swept the harbour and the distant city with an
embracing gesture—"and I discovered myself saying that
you couldn't blame them. Now what did I mean by
that?"

He wrinkled his brows at her amusedly.

"How should I know?"

She sighed.

"I just thought you might. I was thinking how happy
and holiday-ish they always look. It seemed to have something to do with all the salt water. I suppose I was just
dithering."

He sat on the wall and looked down at the rocks,
considering. He wondered if what she had meant was
that you couldn't blame them if they preferred the easy
and exhilarating joys of the body to the difficult and elusive joys of the mind; simple, physical triumphs of the
moment—the winning of a Test Match or a Davis Cup,
the coming of a Phar Lap—to those laborious and unspec-
tacular activities whose laurel wreaths would be bestowed
by a remote posterity! You couldn't blame them, in
short, if their heroes were men of deeds rather than men
of thought.

He explained, adding:

"Was that what you meant?" She nodded.

"Yes. And really to me it seems better that way. I
like it. To begin with. It makes a sort of—background.
Or do I mean a foundation? All that physical joy and
health. All that vigour and—and——"

"Gusto?"

"Yes, that's it. It's—oh, I don't know . . ."

But Oliver, looking across the water, thought that
perhaps he did. He wasn't an artist, but he had felt all
the same the invigorating stimulus which came from an
environment so abounding in rude physical enjoyment.
Before the seed can germinate, he thought, the soil must

be prepared, and here was the preparation going on. And a soil of what richness! What exotic and unique and gorgeous blossoming might it not produce—in time. If it got the time. An incoherent and involuntary prayer forced itself sharply up in him that it might be given the time, that it might be spared a further holocaust of precious lives which it could so ill afford to lose. If it were spared, he thought, children not yet born would work without honour or reward in the generation which had bred them, and they would die as old Kavanagh had died, unlamented; and their work would live on as his was living, quietly, obscurely, till the day came for its liberation.

Yes, a great poet like Kavanagh, a great artist like this odd little person at his side, could draw endlessly upon so inexhaustible a store of vitality. His thought strayed through space and time to Will Shakespeare, living upon the crude and rich and colourful materialism of his age, sucking his strength from it as a parasite sucks the life-blood of its host. Genius, he reflected, does not need circles or self-conscious intelligentsia; talent grows there; wit flourishes, and epigram, and the grisly cleverness of decadence. Genius asks only to feel the thrusting urge of growth about it—a clamour and a flood of life. . . .

He sighed and said:

"Well if man's first duty is to be a good animal I suppose we aren't wasting time if we devote a few generations to it!"

"Do you really think that, or are you still only saying my thoughts for me?" He laughed.

"I'm not sure. I only know that it's a good morning and I'm glad to be alive, and unless too much work piles up we're both going down to the Cove for a swim before lunch. Does that put me among the Goths and barbarians?"

With an effort, a definite moment of self-discipline, he closed a door of his brain upon unexplored byways of

116

thought diverging from that question, and turned to answer Chloe's call from the house.

"Did you say breakfast?"

They walked back across the lawn together, their hands loosely joined by interlocking fingers, while Chloe studied them with benevolent interest from the dining-room window. This sudden remarriage of her mother's still intrigued her; her own competent and methodical habits had bred in her, since babyhood, an oddly protective attitude towards so unpractical a parent, and it amused her now to see Oliver acquiring it, too. It was lucky, she thought, that he really cared about mother's work only less than he cared about mother herself. Otherwise he might have missed the ordered perfection of his former home in Thalassa. And when he saw mother looking plain and untidy and sometimes rather cranky in her paint-stained overall, he might have missed the lovely, serene, golden-haired wife whom, from a distance, she, Chloe, had once so passionately admired.

When they were out of sight, going up the path at the side of the house, she turned her attention to the harbour, thinking that when she had done another hour's practising after breakfast she'd go down to the Cove for a swim. Or perhaps she'd better do two hours as she would be minding the house and answering the 'phone this afternoon while mother went over to see her pictures in the Exhibition. She turned round to see Lois and Oliver sitting down to the breakfast table, and she slid into her chair between them. Lois looked up from her grapefruit and said instantly:

"Have you been doing something you shouldn't, darling?"

Oliver, reaching for the toast, decided after a glance at his step-daughter's face that she did look rather wickedly gleeful. She began pouring herself a cup of coffee before she answered:

"No, of course I haven't. But I was talking to Mrs. Trugg just now, and I asked her how many children she had had, and—listen, Mother, because this is very interesting—she said she had had six, *'not counting odds and ends!'* Now what do you think she could have meant by that?"

Lois' spoon paused half-way to her mouth while she gave this a moment's surprised consideration. She shook her head.

"I can't imagine, darling. I mean to say, either you have children or you don't. I never heard of anyone having anything you could call odds and ends. Did you, Oliver?"

But Chloe cried excitedly:

"I believe I've got it! She must have meant miscarriages and contor—oh, shut up, Oliver—what *are* they called, anyhow?"

Lois said admiringly:

"How clever of you, Chloe! She must have meant that. Don't you think, Oliver? You mean abortions, darling. Do eat your breakfast. How many of those had she had? You know people like Mrs. Trugg are really very wonderful. They just don't seem to *notice* what they're having."

"Did you ever have any of those, Mother?"

"Which, darling?"

"Abor—I don't believe that *is* right. It sounds silly. What are they really called, Oliver?"

"Abortions," he said, wondering irrelevantly what Helen would have thought of this breakfast-table conversation, "is correct."

"Well, those."

"No. I never had anything at all except you."

"You aren't really very experienced, are you. Considering your age, I mean. Never mind, though; now that . . ."

Oliver interrupted:

"She's never going to have any experience of odds and ends, my child, so don't look bright and hopeful. Pour me out some coffee and pass the butter."

But he had not finished his first cup before the waiting-room bell rang, and as his second was being poured out it rang again. Saying ruefully: "God help my digestion!" he swallowed it and made for his consulting-room, and the day's work.

*   *   *   *   *

Professor Channon, having seen Lesley's boat out of sight, went into the house and washed his hands under the bathroom tap. Then, still hatless, he returned to the garden, picking up the morning paper from a chair as he passed. He went down the path and stood with his hand on the gate looking up and down the road.

A certain appearance of joviality, due to the roundness and rosiness of his face and the genial lines about his eyes, seemed oddly mixed to-day with an intent gravity. In the weeks since he had last seen Oliver he had thought interminably, and rebelled against his thinking as he had never done before. They had been weeks of incessant and disconcerting revelation. The realisation, to begin with, that a knowledge of approaching death made violent alterations in one's mental attitudes. Caused you, in fact, to recoil from the mere idea of mental attitudes. And yet, because you were yourself, because your mental life had always been the very focus of your existence, you were not able to achieve a simple physical enjoyment of the fragment of that existence which remained to you.

He made a movement as if to open his paper and stopped. He thought: "It doesn't matter to me any longer."

On that thought, as if on a gigantic pair of wings, he seemed to feel himself lifted away from the earth—to be seeing it from an incredible distance, and with an incredible, an all-embracing comprehension. If all men could be, for a little while in his position, facing certain death—and then suddenly reprieved! Wouldn't they have learned as he was learning, from the facing of a common enemy, something to bind them together? Might they not, under that sentence of annihilation, return to the simple knowledge that for mankind there are two elemental states, life and death. And for dealing with them

119

two elemental qualities, love and courage. In life to love —one's world, one's work, one's fellow-man; and to meet death with courage. Such things, he thought, have been said so often that they mean nothing any more. Man, bullied by the restless ingenuity of his brain, longing for problems to worry as a dog worries a bone, cries: "It isn't as simple as that!" But when he knows that death is near, the Professor thought, putting his hand for a moment against his side where the faint, creeping pain stirred suddenly like a living thing, he begins to understand that it is just exactly as simple as that. "Though, God knows," he acknowledged, spreading his paper out with a sigh, "a thing needn't be easy because it is simple!"

He read:

"Failure of Peace Talks." "Committee Adjourns for One Month."

And he saw the globe of the world spinning beneath him, in sun and in shadow, with calm oceans and stormy oceans, with long wastes of white at either pole, and the lush green of tropical growth about its middle like a bright sash. That was all; from this vast distance humanity and its little preoccupations were not even visible. There was, perhaps, here and there a greyness, clinging and unwholesome like a mildew; the patches where parasitic man had lived longest and most densely, where he had built and torn down again, where he had tilled and then laid waste, where he had fought, and toiled, and learned and fought again, spawning endlessly so that at last the soil to which he was born could no longer support him and he went out to infect fresh lands. . . .

Failure of Peace Talks. Well, presently perhaps, that greyish patch which was Europe would burst into smoke and flame. And what then? A little breathing space for the rest of the world in which to rebuild its health and sanity? Was there any hope of that? But whatever happened the world would go on spinning, half in sun, half in shadow, with calm oceans and stormy oceans, with white wastes at either pole, and the bright sash of tropical green about its middle. It was even conceivable that the tenacious parasite which had infested it for thousands' of years might vanish quite away. . . .

He found himself struggling against this thought even as his brain formed it. From the terrible and solitary heights in which impending death held him captive, he saw a great island continent alone in its south sea, and he knew that somewhere in it there was a street and a house at whose garden gate there stood the shell of an old man with a newspaper in his hand. Godlike in his aloof omniscience, seeing all the world spread out below him, he desired nothing but to return to that shell of humanity, old as it was, doomed as it was, to return and be part of it as he had always been, struggling with the complications of its communal life, part of that life, whether it marched to survival or to death.

He did not want to be a detached and dispassionate observer of its fate. He did not want to see it as a trivial manifestation of one form of life, which would endure for a moment of eternity and then vanish, leaving no trace. *We are such stuff as dreams are made of* . . . Dreams of an achievement which might have been and which failed. Like Peace Talks. Failed, like them, because the first principles of life were so much too simple to be taken seriously by creatures who had developed a sophisticated intelligence at the expense of a fundamental wisdom. So our little life—our little life which we have so loved and so maltreated—is rounded with a sleep. . . .

We were not worth it. To inherit the earth. So the earth flings us off, and we perish. . . .

To inherit the earth. That, he thought, is a big phrase—a phrase spacious and noble and worthy of the man who first uttered it. A great and arrogant phrase, expressing a great and arrogant conception of man's destiny. And with a sudden narrowing and intensifying of his thoughts, the Professor felt his incorrigible brain, like a dog hot upon a trail, begin to nose out a hidden significance in a word which had come unbidden, unsought, to his mind. He thought: "Arrogant. Yes, yes, a good word,

121

accidentally used! *Arrogantia*—the disposition to arrogate. I claim! But not enough! This little bit of the earth, that little bit of the earth—mine, thine—how poor and trivial a conception has this vast intellect evolved! How far from the vision of a Galilean carpenter, that man should at last inherit through love and unity, not a small land, or a great land, or an empire—but the earth. . . .

Despair seized him. He thought: "I can't stop it, this brain, this thinking machine running on the power of my life-spark. It won't stop till I stop. Once, perhaps, we knew how to switch the power off from it, to divert the power—to remain quietly just living, just glorying in life. But now we can only think, and think of our thoughts until we go so deep into the mystery and darkness of our minds that we see the lunatic hidden in each one of us peering back into our fearful eyes. For the delights of intricate thinking, of making patterns with ideas, of building words and forms and sounds into triumphant structures, of playing Peeping Tom to our own wild hearts, that is the risk we have to face, and the penalty we sometimes have to pay."

He came back wearily, as one might return with relief and gratitude to a shabby home, to the consciousness of his own humanity. His hand moved almost lovingly on the sun-warmed rail of the gate, and he turned his head so that the faint breeze from across the water ruffled the hair back from his forehead. All his mind fastened eagerly on to the trivial details of his daily life.

Now that Lesley had gone and the coast was clear, he must stroll along and see Denning. The X-rays would be there probably, but there wasn't much doubt of the verdict. And he thought suddenly: "I hope I don't hang on till the winter. Summer; that's the time to die, when the sun's hot, and the earth warm to receive you and turn your useless body to account again."

He walked along the road slowly, noticing how a cloud of gulls rose and screamed and settled again over the Bottle and Glass rocks.

"Some fisherman must have left bait about," he thought, and then stopped dead, half-turning as if to escape. But it was too late, for Winifred, coming out of her gate with Brenda, had seen him already and waved. He sighed, responding with a lift of his folded newspaper, and went to meet them.

He thought, looking at her pallor and the sharply drawn lines about her mouth, how oddly satirical it was that both his daughters, with their deep mistrust of riches, should have happened to fall in love with wealthy men, but he only said, with his hand on Brenda's fair head: "Are you off to the Cove?"

Winifred answered:

"Yes. Where are you going, Father? Won't you come down, too?"

He answered her second question.

"I've had my dip. Lesley and I went down before breakfast. We had it all to ourselves except for Sim Hegarty. Perhaps I'll join you later."

Brenda turned her face up to him.

"Why don't you lift me up on your shoulder any more?"

The suddenness of the question disconcerted him a little, and in the instant of hesitation before his reply he felt Winifred look at him quickly. He explained:

"You're getting so big, Brenda. And when people grow old they get rheumaticky in their joints, and can't lift heavy little girls." Winifred asked him:

"Rheumatism, Father? This is the first time I've heard of it." He laughed.

"Just a twinge or two."

"Oughtn't you see a doctor?"

With a flash of relief he answered:

"That's just what I'm going to do, dear. I'm on my way to see Dr. Denning now. It's nothing much, but he may be able to stop it going any farther. Go on down to the Cove, and when I've seen him I may follow you."

He watched them walk off, hand in hand, towards the little reserve about the Cove. He thought, half-closing his

123

eyes, that they looked so decorative, so completely one with their environment of bright light and warm, strong-scented air, that it was difficult to remember that one of them was blind, and the other despairing.

He crossed the road slowly, and paused for one second of involuntary hesitation before he opened the gate with the brass plate on it.

*   *   *   *   *

When Arthur had gone Lorna reached for another cigarette and lay back on her pillows, her heart beating a little faster than usual. She hadn't meant to go quite so far, to lie to him quite so definitely. When he had come in and she had seen what he was working up to, her intention had been merely to shrug and make a few ambiguous remarks as she had done often enough before. But somehow she had been all on edge this morning, and words had burst from her for which, even as she uttered them, she had felt only half-responsible. It was Arthur's fault, anyhow, for bothering her while she was having her miserable excuse for a breakfast. She did not mind the stringent rules she had laid down for herself at other meals, but at breakfast she longed for oatmeal with cream and brown sugar, for a poached egg on buttery toast, for coffee with more cream, for hot rolls and marmalade. Her glass of orange-juice and her two dry rusks always filled her with a murderous rebellion, and for nothing on earth except her beauty could she have cared enough to make so irksome a sacrifice. But she knew what no one else suspected, that the least indulgence sent the scales up ominously, blurring the long, graceful lines of her body, spoiling the picture which she carried always in her mind of Lorna Sellman, the beautiful, the soignee, the seductive. . . .

But her mind, this morning, was haunted by another picture, the picture of a boyishly slender figure with a boyish Eton crop, stepping out of a bus, standing beside Sim in the lamplight. Very slender, her thoughts repeated and insisted—very slender, and only twenty-three.

Winifred's sister. Winifred never had to diet, and she was over thirty. . . .

It was a funny thing, Lorna thought, sitting up again, frowning with the effort of memory, but since she had said that to Arthur—just in these last few moments—an elusive impression had been flickering at the back of her mind that it wasn't a lie after all. It was too shadowy to be called a memory, and yet it persisted. Herself coming down the steps in the early hours of the morning, and seeing a figure stealing through the garden. . . .

That *négligé* of Winifred's—the very pale green one, almost silvery, with the wide sleeves—hadn't the figure been wearing that? Wasn't it, most likely, true after all? Might it not have been some occasion when she herself was—well, not exactly shot, of course, but pretty sleepy, and just wuzzy enough to see—and then forget? Until Arthur's questions roused an imperfect fragment of memory which lent to her words a conviction which had surprised herself.

She put both hands up to her cheeks, yawning. Her own state of mental confusion meant nothing to her but an annoying, an incomprehensible mental discomfort. She did not know, and would not have believed, that anything so mundane as the irritation of frustrated hunger this morning, or anything so vulgar as the irritation of frustrated desire last night, could have laid the foundations of so black and dangerous a mood. Jealousy of Lesley, who, last night, had captured Sim from her, was ridiculously merged with jealousy of the girl who was younger than herself, and could eat what she liked for breakfast. Dislike of Winifred became intensified, with illogical fierceness because she was Lesley's sister, and because she, too, had no need to diet. Round and round her resentments travelled—from her glass of orange-juice to Lesley, from Lesley to Winifred, from Winifred back to the glass of orange-juice and instinctively, seeking the only comfort and reassurance that she knew, she jumped suddenly out of bed and faced her reflection in the long wardrobe mirror.

125

Once there, standing close against it, she became completely absorbed in the picture which it showed her. She forgot Winifred, Arthur, Lesley, even Sim. She stared hungrily, anxiously, as a woman stares into the face of a lover by whom she fears to be forsaken. Underneath her eyes the skin showed a faint criss-cross tracery of lines, and she thought, with a shrinking worthier of threatening death, that perhaps after all she might have to give in and wear glasses as Dr. Moore had advised a year ago. Headaches, yes, you could endure those with the aid of aspirin and medinal, but lines—wrinkles—age . . .

She turned away from the mirror, her arms clasped across her breast, and her body shaken by a little goose-flesh tremor. She went across to the window and pulled its curtain back with an impatience which sent its rings clattering along their wooden rod, looking absently and then with sharp attention at the corner of the Cove which was visible—at the raft, and at a figure lying face downward on it. Sim? Narrowing her eyes, she peered. It looked like Sim, but she was not sure until he lifted his head from his folded arms and waved a greeting to some-one farther up the Cove. She felt her heart give a sudden uncomfortable thud, and she thought viciously: "I'm behaving like a flapper!"

She sat down at her dressing table, and her face settled into a kind of rapt concentration. She opened a low cupboard under its mirror and studied its contents for a moment. There were all kinds of creams—cold cream, tissue cream, vanishing cream, bleaching cream; all kinds of powders—talc powder, dusting powder, face powder in various shades, with rouge and lipsticks to match. There were eye-shadow, and mascara, and eyebrow pencils. There was a setting lotion for the hair, a soothing lotion for the eyes, a bleaching lotion for the hands, and an astringent lotion for the skin. There were cuticle remover for the finger-nails, and polish remover, and a magenta lacquer. She studied them all sombrely, thinking what unpleasant stuff salt water was, and wondering if, after all, it might be better not to see him till this afternoon, when all the varied contents of these jars and bottles would have reinforced her beauty, and she could face him in her own environment, and with the knowledge of an immaculate and sophisticated loveliness to discipline the dangerous turmoil of her heart. She looked up into the mirror at her own reflected face, and, horrified, saw her eyes fill with tears. Tears, the arch-enemy of beauty! She snatched a handkerchief and dabbed them away, the unbidden emotion which had produced them instantly quelled by anxiety. She decided, examining her face closely and critically, that they had done no harm. There was still the faintest pinkness and wateriness about the whites, but that would pass in a moment or two. She seized cream and cleansing tissues and began to work feverishly. When she had finished she took a hand mirror to the window, and studied her skin in the bright light. It wasn't so bad, she thought with relief. She might risk it. No good using powder, but a touch of lipstick would be all right.

When she had put on her bathing suit she studied herself again in the long mirror. The fair skin which was so greatly admired, and which looked so dazzling in evening dress, was not, she knew, exactly right on the beach. But it was no use trying to sunburn; several seasons of trial and failure had convinced her of that. So she had decided at last to make capital of what she could not avoid, and her brief black bathing suit emphasised the milky whiteness of her arms and legs, her graceful shoulders, and her really lovely back. This, she had found, worked very well, mostly because, to preserve that whiteness, she had to keep herself swathed most of the time in an all-enveloping breach wrap, so that her emerging won the flavour and the excitement of the unfamiliar. Other girls, in bathing suits even more sketchy than her own, were, nevertheless, clothed in their smooth brown sunburn as in a garment, and no one turned a head to look at them. But the whiteness of her own seductively

127

moulded body proclaimed its nakedness, and men's eyes turned to follow its rare and brief unveiling.

She had always enjoyed that, as she enjoyed homage of any kind, but now, for a moment, she was aware of a shrinking as abrupt, as inexplicable, as swiftly passed as those unwelcome tears—a fluttering of purpose, sharply and contemptuously overridden.

She snatched up her black bathing cap. It fitted her head snugly like a helmet, and the strap under her chin completed the dark framing of a face strangely lovely in this unaccustomed severity of setting. Even to herself, who missed and regretted the soft waves of ash-blonde hair about her forehead, and the delicate colouring of lips and cheeks, the faint blue shadowing of the eyes, the skilful emphasising of brows and lashes, there came a moment's uncertain and rather bewildered appreciation of a beauty unfamiliar because unaided, a beauty of shape and contour, of bone and muscle, a beauty which, for a startled second, she recognised as actually her own.

She thrust her bare feet into rubber sandals, and swung a multi-coloured beach wrap over her shoulders. The thought that she hadn't really time to do this, that she should be dressing to go into town and have her hair done if she wanted to get through the day without rushing, was beaten down with a kind of sulky and fatalistic obstinacy. She went out the back of the house into the bright sunlight, and unconsciously her eyes wrinkled against it, and the faint tracery of lines, which she had just been so assiduously massaging away, deepened and settled round them. She ran up the winding stone steps to the street level, and stepped out on to the hot concrete footpath. When she reached the top of the track winding down to the beach, she could see two or three groups of bathers already lying on the sand or splashing in the water, and she noticed, with a spasm of annoyance, that Winifred was already sitting on one of the rocks on the far side of the Cove, reading, and glancing up, now and then, to watch Brenda wading about with the two little Harnet boys.

For a moment Lorna thought she wouldn't go down after all. There was an echo of her own voice saying: "Well, I didn't want to bother you, Arthur, or make mischief, but as a matter of fact one night I did see . . ."

She said half-aloud, and with a trace of hysteria in her voice:

"Oh, *damn!*"

For it had occurred to her that Winifred and Brenda were a very good alibi. A family party. Her derisive smile shook and faded. Suddenly she'd see Sim and be *so* surprised! . . . Her thought did not take her the farther step beyond awareness of herself into an awareness of Sim which would have told her he was far too unself-conscious a person to attribute her sudden appearance in the Cove to anything but a desire to swim. She went down the path and crossed the beach towards Winifred without a glance towards the raft.

Winifred looked at her silently for a moment and then said:

"Hullo!"

Lorna sat down on a nearby rock and drew her wrap closer about her. She thought with a sense of injury that if only Winifred would have quarrelled with her openly sometimes she wouldn't have been driven to telling Arthur that lie this morning. But there was something about her sister-in-law's attitude towards her which roused a fighting hatred she was quite unable to suppress. An attitude of casual amiability. A stare, not without admiration, sometimes, but quite without envy. Sometimes a trace of amusement, and quite often more than a trace of pity. . . .

"Arthur wants me to take you in my car this afternoon. You'll have to be ready early, because I'm picking up Julie and Bing."

Winifred answered:

"I'm not going to the wedding. Be careful, Brenda, that rock's slippery."

"Not going?" Lorna looked round at her sharply.

129

"Why not? Too superior to mingle with the vulgar rich?"

"You can take out the last word," Winifred said lazily, "and leave it at that." Lorna's sudden fury made her voice sound odd even to herself.

"I suppose that's a dig at our grandfather."

Winifred shook her head.

"It wasn't meant to be. I think vulgarity's a matter of behaviour, not of birth."

"Then it was meant for me—and Arthur—and George Hegarty, and Veronica, and all our friends. . . ."

Winifred murmured judicially:

"Not *quite* all."

Lorna stood up. She had decided that now she could become aware of Sim, and she did not know if it were that decision or fury with Winifred which was making her shiver as if she were cold, and catching her breath unevenly. She said:

"Why, that's Sim on the raft, isn't it?"

She looked down at Winifred, and Winifred was looking up at her with that intent, considering expression, as if she were examining some rare specimen upon which she would presently have to make a report. She answered after a moment:

"Yes. Didn't you know?"

Lorna said furiously:

"Why should I know?"

Winifred opened her book again. "I just thought you might have seen him when you came to your window a little while ago. He's been down here since before breakfast."

Lorna's curiosity got the better of her rage, and she asked:

"What on earth for?"

"Perhaps," Winifred suggested, "he likes being here."

Lorna, with an exclamation of impatience, stepped off her rock into shallow water. Winifred, her eyes on her book, her mind struggling between self-contempt and the malice she could never quite suppress in her dealings with

Lorna, thought: "It will dawn on her in a minute. . . .
I don't know why I bother . . . it's ugly and cheap to
torment her . . . they do that to me . . . no, it's myself. . . ."

Lorna asked abruptly, turning:

"How do you know?"

Winifred looked up from her book again. The tone
was the tone she had expected and provoked—apprehensive, resentful, the mere sound of it roused her antag-
onism, edged her own voice with a deliberate, hurtful
triumph:

"Father told me. He and Lesley were swimming with
him before breakfast." Her voice became suddenly a
different voice, the voice of another woman: "Brenda,
stand still, there's some broken glass there. Wait till I
move it."

Lorna left them and waded slowly out, shivering a
little, till the water came up to her waist. Her anger
changed from a shaken temper to a cold and implacable
determination. It might have been caused by Sim's
brusqueness or by her own thoughts, her own fears for
the fading of youth and beauty which must begin some
day; or it might have been a result of Winifred's implica-
tion that she, Lorna Sellman, was in love with a man
who loved someone else. Or perhaps it was an overwhelming fusion of everything—Sim's unresponsiveness,
Winifred's barbed politeness, Lesley's youth and slender-
ness, her own lie which was perhaps not a lie after all,
the threat of glasses, the threat of age, the bleakness of
rusks and orange-juice, the stirred and frustrated emotions
of her evening with Basil Smith. . . .

Rebellion rose in her, and hardened into resolve.
Her whole life became filled by one aim—to "get" Sim.
It was, quite unself-consciously, the word which her
thoughts used. "Of course, I'll get him." Of course. All
the hitherto unassailed security of her life flowed round
her in a warm tide of reassurance. She had never failed
yet to get anything or anybody she wanted. For things
there was money; for men there was beauty. Sometimes

she had needed them both, but separately or together they had never failed her, and they would not fail her now.

She leaned forward and let the water take her weight. Slowly, so that she did not splash her face, she swam out to the raft.

*   *   *   *   *

When Oliver opened the door of his consulting-room to let a patient out, and saw Professor Channon sitting in the chair near the waiting-room window, he had one of those rare and almost uncontrollable impulses, which attack most doctors at one time or another, to run away. Not a literal and physical flight, but a violent mental recoil from an impossibly difficult task.

The old man was reading a magazine which he had taken from the littered table, and he looked up as the door opened, over it and over the tops of his spectacles, so that his smile had a quizzical air which was made the more poignant by its unconsciousness. He stood up, the magazine still in his hand, and said:

"Good-morning. Have you ever seen one of these six-foot long specimens in the flesh?"

Oliver looked over his shoulder.

"Goanas? No. Horrifying looking things, aren't they? But harmless enough. Come in, will you, Professor."

He stood aside to let his patient pass, and, when he had closed the door of his consulting-room, pulled forward a chair which was not normally the patient's chair. There were times, perhaps, when you did not want the light to shine too brutally upon a face. The old man was chuckling as he sat down.

"Harmless? Well—it depends. A chap I knew was out in a vast paddock one day with a couple of dogs and they startled one of these things. Normally they make for the nearest tree when they're attacked, but there wasn't a tree or a stump within a couple of hundred yards, so it made a bee-line for this chap and swarmed up *him*. Clawing at his head—bald, he was, too. And the dogs leaping and snapping about him, mad with excitement. He was taken to hospital in a nasty mess, I believe . . ."

He stopped rather abruptly. He thought:

"This extremely healthy-looking young man is about to put on the black cap. And he doesn't like it." He spoke the rest of his thought aloud:

"Nature does some damn silly things at times, Doctor, but it's a fact that somehow as you get older you mind the thought of dying less and less."

It was true, he told himself. At all events largely true. Your shrinking when you were old was not the violent, horrified reaction of flesh and nerve which it was to youth, but rather a regret for things undone which now you would never do, and for a life all too inadequately enjoyed and soon to be taken from you. For himself, he would have liked to finish his book. . . .

He asked: "I suppose you have some news for me?"

Oliver answered, opening a drawer of his desk:

"The rays came yesterday. They confirm what I had already told you—what I had deduced from your symptoms. I should suggest—and advise—an operation."

Professor Channon sighed briefly. Funnily enough, he thought, his body did shrink from that, where it accepted the prospect of death quite calmly. And yet, perhaps, not strange after all. For an operation meant effort—the effort of ageing cells to heal and restore you. An operation was a fight, and death a quiet surrender. He said dubiously:

"Would I stand an operation? I'm seventy-one."

"There's no reason," Oliver replied, spreading the dark negatives out before him, "why you shouldn't stand it."

He looked down at the pictures he had studied yesterday with a sinking heart. Even now, as they lay flat upon his blotter, he could see the ghostly shadow of the vertebræ and the two downward curving lower ribs, the smooth light curve of the barium-filled stomach, its clarity of outline broken by the dark, sinister invasion of the carcinoma. He said without looking up:

133

"An operation gives you a very good chance, you know."

"And without it?"

Oliver thought: "Confound it, why can't I look at him?" He did so, and answered: "Without it the end is quite inevitable. And you'll have increasing pain."

"How long . . . ?"

"That's impossible to say, Professor. Doctors do sometimes give a time limit, but I think it's unwise. You see, with all the data one can get—X-rays included—the condition remains very largely guessed. Only an operation can show for certain how far the trouble has gone."

"And if one has the operation," the old man said thoughtfully, "and it has gone too far, one has wasted a good deal of valuable time and still more valuable energy."

He stood up, and suddenly sat down again. He met Oliver's troubled eyes with astonishment. For his brain had been functioning calmly, his only emotion had been one of resignation and regret, but his legs had been afraid! He was slightly annoyed, but deeply interested. The flesh, then, even at seventy-one, could still quail before impending dissolution! He said:

"I must think a little about this operation." Oliver offered him an open box.

"Of course. Will you smoke?"

"Thank you."

His hands were steady. Perfectly steady. Nothing had panicked but his legs! He lit his cigarette from Oliver's match, and said, glancing at a book lying on the end of the desk: "You're a student of economics, Doctor?"

Oliver shrugged.

"Hardly a student. One's almost driven, these days, to hunt for something that promises even a glimmer of stability. You've read this, I suppose? Your daughter lent it to me."

"Lesley?"

"No—Mrs. Sellman."

The old man nodded.

134

"Yes, I've read it. It's sound—as far as it goes. There are hundreds of books like it being turned out now—all sound, all sincere, all true—as far as they go. But you won't find your stability in any of the 'systems' they dissect or advocate. The germ of self-destruction is in every one of them. The older I grow the more I become convinced of that. Years ago—may I have that ash-tray?—thanks—years ago I began to write the things I was not allowed to say. I found myself writing things it would never have occurred to me to say. And in time I found that I had gone full-circle—from the conventional, unquestioning religious faith of childhood, through the rebellious, assertive atheism that attacks one in adolescence, through the more rational and tolerant agnosticism of middle age, back to a definite faith."

Oliver's revolving chair swung him round to face his patient, and a rich, familiar appreciation of life's unexpectedness stirred in him. He asked:

"A faith? Yes? A religious faith?"

The old man went on thoughtfully, as if speaking to himself:

"More than a year ago I began a book. I need at least six months to finish it. It is, actually, merely the amplification of notes I have been making for years. Are you interested in religion at all?"

Oliver admitted ruefully:

"I'm interested in so many things that I seem to get no time to study any of them properly. What exactly do you mean by religion?"

"I mean the sense that man has and has always had of some power to which he owes reverence and obedience. I mean his moral reaction to that sense, his acceptance of it as a guide to behaviour."

"I see. And your book?"

"My book is an attempt to demonstrate that nothing on earth can save mankind but the universal acceptance of a religion."

Oliver asked:

"Isn't that just the difficulty? To find something universally acceptable? Unless . . ."

"Unless what?"

"I was wondering about the theory of the composite man. The man who might evolve in a few thousand years if we broke down all barriers. Or if they broke themselves down, which is more likely. A completely unrestricted mating—black, white, brown, yellow, all the racial characteristics blended, all the resulting generations coming into the world free of the handicaps that are hung round the necks of half-castes now. Of course, that silly superstition that the worst qualities of both races are represented in the half-breed is almost dead now. It's accepted that the conditions into which he's born, and the treatment he's subjected to, are quite enough to account for the fact that he's often a failure—always an Ishmael. After all, it stands to reason that if race were abolished utterly there would remain only man." He added after a slight pause: "And then, perhaps, there would come your universal religion."

The Professor nodded agreement.

"It's a theory now, in the infancy of mankind—but it will be a fact. It must be. Everything points to it. We've destroyed distance already—that's the beginning of the end of race. These madnesses we're going through— these insane outbursts of racial hatred and jealousy— they're only instinctive gestures of fright from minds without vision or serenity. From minds incapable of grasping the universal religion."

"Which is?" Oliver felt himself seized by a strange, expectant eagerness, but the old man shook his head, smiling.

"You keep me alive long enough, Doctor, and I'll try to express my idea of it in my book. In the meantime, I can hear another patient in your waiting-room. I'll come again in a day or two and see you about this operation. . . ."

Oliver reluctantly crossed the room to open the door for him, protesting:

136

"You have such a gift for leaving off in an exciting place that I think you should be writing serials."

On that laugh, the laugh that spontaneously follows the most trifling joke between people mentally in harmony, they parted. Oliver, turning from his last glimpse of the Professor's back silhouetted against the brilliant green and gold of the open doorway, found himself looking into the sullen and mistrustful eyes of Jack Saunders. He said:

"Good-morning. Will you come in?"

Watching the young man stand up, one clumsily bandaged hand nursed in the crook of his other arm, he thought that he had seldom seen a finer physical specimen. But as he closed his consulting-room door and went back to his chair, he was conscious of the faint weariness and depression that some of his patients instantly awakened in him, and against which he was constantly struggling. He thought: "Here's a robust young giant with a sore hand that will heal up in a week or two—but the old man with the incurable cancer is the one who carries hope and inspiration with him." He asked, as his patient still sat dumbly:

"What's the trouble? Hurt your hand?"

Jack began slowly to unwind his bandage. The anger, which all the morning had lain like a heavy weight in his brain, had made his feet clumsy on familiar rocks not more than twenty feet from the bottom of the cliff, and betrayed his fingers in handholds they had found without error or hesitation for years.

He did not see his fall as a result of his mental turmoil, but as another gratuitous insult of fate, and he had hardly known, during the few moments when he lay winded on the spray-drenched rocks, whether it were pain or rage which most tormented him. Bruised, trembling still with the shock of his slipping foot, and the atavistic fear of falling which has haunted man since his arboreal days, he had struggled to his feet and burst into frenzied blasphemies, shouting against the noise of the waves and the screaming of the gulls. And, suddenly, down here on this semicircle of flat rock, hemmed in by high walls, the vastness of the ocean almost at eye-level and the ominous glass-green depths of it showing intermittently as the veil of spray and foam was momentarily withdrawn, he had felt fear added to his pain and resentment, so that life became not only an enemy, but an enemy invincible and without pity. . . .

In that moment, divorced by emotion from his usual habit of stolid thinking, he had a flash of perception, a violent, irrelevant functioning of an imagination almost atrophied by long disuse. Coming down he had seen the old anchor of the wrecked *Dunbar*, as he did most days of his life, without conscious thought of it. But now, in the shock of over-stimulated mental activity, he saw day-light engulfed, and this ill-omened spot upon which he stood drowned in the storm and the blackness and the driving rain of a wild night eighty years ago. His impression was not the less vivid for being inaccurate; his conception of the wreck was the popular one, and it was here, actually in the Gap, in fleeting gleams from the Macquarie Light, that he saw the ship come in, riding the breakers till they overwhelmed her and flung her against the cliffs; saw the topmasts go over at the first impact, heard thinly above the clamour of the storm the cries of doomed men and women being swept and sucked down into the gulf of waters. The place where he stood, and had stood so many times from boyhood, became suddenly a graveyard. Bodies which had been, in fact, washed up upon harbour beaches were in his wild imaginary picture flung here at his very feet, and he became himself the one survivor, huddled on a ledge of rock through thirty-six freezing winter hours, while the sea tossed back at him contemptuously the corpses of his shipmates, and the wreckage of his ship.

It was nothing but a moment in which emotion had worked mysteriously upon a subconscious mental image, and it passed as suddenly as it had come. But it had left fear in him. Physical fear, something he had never known before. Fear of the water, fear of its terrible power which

now, for the first time, he realised. His body, whose
strength and endurance he had come to regard as illimitable, unfailing, could be whirled about in it like a straw,
sucked down by it into dark green, glassy silence. . . .
Had it happened? Every nerve and muscle in him *knew*
it with the certainty of experience. Knew the wild rebellion of helplessness, the despairing recognition of impending death, the instant of godlike detachment before its
fierce descent. . . . But it was as an experience divorced
from time that he knew it, as an unplaced incident in
some monstrous void which did not know the friendly now
upon which one stands so firmly between dead events and
events unborn. His mind, wrenched from that conception
of a present moment, floundered and struggled as the body
might struggle, wrenched from firm earth to quicksands;
only the insistence of physical pain drew him slowly back,
sweating and bewildered, to a day, an hour, which he
could name and know. He lifted his hand stupidly and
stared at it, and at the blood dripping from it into a
rock pool and staining it crimson. He tried to move his
fingers and found three of them inert and he thought,
looking at them with astonished curiosity: "They're
broken!" Nothing else, though he stirred gingerly, testing
with cautious experimental movements his arms and legs
and the fingers of his other hand, seemed to be harmed.
He looked up with the sudden wildness of a caged animal
at the rock wall above him, wishing himself safely at the
top. He began to climb. That route, so simplified by
rope ladders, by iron stanchions concreted into the rock,
but above all by years of practice, could not offer any
serious difficulties even to a man with three broken
fingers. He did it without mishap, but slowly, retarded
by the backwash of fear and pain, the spending of nervous energy, the accumulation of resentment against a
life which added, in sheer devilishness, broken fingers to
unemployment, and then, as if that were not enough,
pierced the blackness of his mood with something that
was near enough to a vision to alarm and infuriate him.
That fury swung round upon itself, like a snake biting

139

its own tail, and he spun with it helplessly, resenting his anger, angry with the formlessness of his resentment, fighting himself all the way up the cliff till he sat at last on the top, nursing his injured hand, struggling with a monstrous desire to fling himself face downward on the ground and weep with rage and pain as if he were a child.

When he had reached the house, Ruby had been gossiping over the fence with their next-door neighbour, and they had both cried out shrilly at the sight of him, because during his ascent of the cliff his face and his white singlet had become smeared with blood from his hand. Ruby had followed him into the house, tearful, and he had given her a push that was almost a blow, because to attack something gave an obscure momentary relief, and she happened to be handy. But she went without resentment when he told her, and found him another singlet, torn and unwashed, but at least not bloodstained, and she brought rag and helped him bind his hand. This rag with the remnant of a cheap lace edging on it, which he was now slowly unwinding under the doctor's disconcerting eyes. Oliver said, taking the wrist in his left hand and gently moving the inert fingers with his right: "Made quite a mess of it, haven't you?" And then felt his brows contract a little involuntarily, because of a suspicion that his remark might apply not only to the hand but to the whole life of this silent and gloomy-looking young man. He glanced up at his patient's face as if seeking confirmation of his first impression, and found the sombre eyes which had made him wonder, fixed not on the hand he was tending, but on his face. He asked, to cover up the hasty turn of the young man's head:

"Hurting?"

"It's nothin'."

"How did it happen?"

"Climbin' down the cliff at the Gap. I must of fell on them."

There was a pause while Oliver worked, but while he bathed the hand, and dressed the cuts with glycerine

140

and perchloride, one corner of his mind was still busy with that intent stare which he had surprised.

*   *   *   *   *

The young man said suddenly, and with what seemed to Oliver a total irrelevance:

"I'm on the dole."

"Bad luck. Married?"

"No." There was a pause in which Oliver realised with another involuntary contraction of his brows that this information had been the man's way of saying that he had no money for medical fees. His eyes, still fixed on the hand he was tending, took in, also, the bare arm attached to it, an arm so massive, so tanned, so hard and bulging with muscle, that the mere thought of its being idle seemed as painful as if a great artist were to waste his gift for a mere lack of material or instrument. He asked: "Been out of work long?"

"Two years. Get a bit of relief work now and then."

Jack raised his right arm and wiped a sweat of pain from his forehead on the sleeve of his singlet. He had stood outside the waiting-room door, the hot sun on his back, and read the legend on the small, glittering brass plate: "Ring and enter." He had been thinking rather disconnectedly because of the throbbing of his hand, that never before in all his twenty-seven years had he visited a doctor. Once in his childhood when he had caught whooping-cough from the next-door children a doctor had come to visit him, and once he had been taken to the outpatients' department of a hospital to be vaccinated, but this room which now, in obedience to the brass plate, he entered, was the first waiting-room of his experience. He sat on the edge of a seagrass chair and looked about it; it was filled with a queer, shifting, golden light from the sun which came through yellow and white checked curtains blowing in the open windows on either side of the door. There was a nondescript but highly polished linoleum on the floor, and a collection of chairs such as the one he was sitting on, and there was a round, dark

141

table with a bowl of marigolds the colour of oranges in the middle, and magazines scattered round it. There was nothing, he recognised, of the slightest monetary value in the room, and yet somehow by its cleanliness and order, and by the strange effect of sunlight through the yellow curtains, it became a room in which he felt himself uncouth, in which the stained sand-shoes into which he had thrust his bare feet seemed to stand out shamefully, their size disgracefully doubled by reflection in the polished floor.

His misery increased. His resentment widened to include this room so different from the dark and squalid rooms of his own dwelling; the man who owned it, elderly and prosperous (as he imagined him, unconsciously drawing upon childish recollections of the one doctor who had attended him), slightly corpulent, with a red, well-shaven face and rimless spectacles. The knowledge lay like a small burning spot in his mind that he had no money to pay for this treatment which he was about to ask; there was a small bitter voice perpetually accusing him from within himself, and he answered it with the truculence which was his only weapon of defence or attack: "What the hell do I do, then? Get around with three broken fingers? What d'you think a man is . . . ?"

When the door had opened at last he looked up. He heard the doctor's last remark, saw his smile and the smile of his patient, felt here some freemasonry from which he knew himself debarred as from all the other good things of life. But because that sense of an intellectual comradeship beyond his own attainments was something too nebulous for him to formulate to himself as a grievance, his mind, with the symbolism of all primitive and unsophisticated minds, fastened upon the doctor's drill coat, and passionately resented that. In the gloss of its well-laundered whiteness, stretched taut across the shoulders, the golden light was delicately reflected; as the door opened and closed behind the old man, a streak of sun, rainbow-coloured, touched it for a moment with a subdued mother-of-pearl version of itself. Jack's eyes, observant, sullen, saw these things, his mind made nothing of them but a crude sense of contrast between the coat which could reflect such splendour and the dingy unresponsiveness of his own limp singlet.

And this chap was not old. Hardly middle-aged, in spite of the touch of grey in his dark hair. He was young enough, near enough in height, size and obvious physical energy to make it inevitable that Jack's contrasting of their garments and their rooms should not stop there. He was aware of qualities in Oliver as a near-blind man is aware of the brilliance of a sunlit day. A certain easy directness of gaze, a certain alert confidence of movement, an air of being utterly at home in his environment struck upon a consciousness not equipped to analyse such things, as the sun-gold scene would strike upon eyes unfit to translate it into its component parts. Not thus, something said in him, could you look and move and be if you were on the dole. He looked down at the hands working on his hand, and he noticed that they were both marred by wrinkled whitish scars like the scars of burns, and that, on the left, two fingers moved awkwardly. His eyes travelled up the white sleeve, creasing crisply with the movements of the elbow, across the bent shoulders, upward again, considering the narrow bluish-grey line of a soft collar, a neck as well tanned as his own, and better barbered, a cheek and jaw smoothly shaved, but, like the hands, marked by pallid scars, and finally a remembered impression of the eyes whose lids only were now visible to him, a sense that their complete preoccupation with their work was somehow the crowning point of this man's well-being. He didn't have to worry! From this definite thought, which was all he was able to evolve out of his scrutiny, he passed to clumsy conjecture. In something there must lie the secret of this obvious rightness. In what? He found himself blundering among impressions of a house much finer than this quite modest bungalow, wealth far greater than he had any reason to suppose Oliver master of, sensual delights—of food, of clean clothing, of hot baths, of some woman, wife or

143

mistress, whom his imagination painted in colours whose opulence would have astonished Oliver and humbled Lois —and yet he knew, uneasily, that he was astray. Something else, something far different, gave a man that air of assurance. He thought sharply, his eyes on the splint which Oliver was binding to his forearm: "It's 'aving a job. It's 'aving a job and being your own boss. . . ."

Oliver, who had been thinking, too, asked suddenly: "What was your job—when you had one?"

The question, a natural enough one to follow his own last remark, seemed, however, so uncannily a response to his thoughts that Jack was startled, and said sullenly:

"I was on the wharves—up at Glebe Island part of the time. . . ." His mind turned inward again, sombrely, in a mingling of thought and memory. It wasn't just having a job that mattered—you had to like it. It had to seem important to you. He had hated the wharves. They came back to him in a medley of impressions so poignant that he seemed for a moment actually to smell hessian, dust, sweating horses, petrol, and through them, struggling, the smell he loved of the salt water lapping darkly under the wharves, gleaming through their diagonally running cracks. Up there it was imprisoned and polluted, not like it was down here near the Heads. Up there in the middle of the city, he thought, you see the ships spewing out their dirty water into it, stewards emptying their buckets of garbage, tourists throwing the bottles of their last carousal out of the portholes. . . .

Well—that's commerce. . . . Wool on Glebe Island. . . . And at other times other wharves, and other cargoes. His nostrils moved slightly in an involuntary spasm of nausea at the memory of the molasses casks from Cairns, piled under the hot iron roofs, giving off their potent, sickening odour. . . . The ear-splitting rattle of loaded trolleys going to and fro . . . and the blasted tourists. . . .

His mind shied again as it had shied before from the thought of the tourists, the blasted tourists, dressed up and mincing down the gangways, picking their way among the bales and casks and saying petulantly:

"Wouldn't you think they could keep these wharves a bit tidier?"

Oliver was saying:

"No chance of getting back now things are a bit easier?"

Jack made a queer sound—an abortive laugh.

"Not me! I talk too much!"

Interested, Oliver prompted him:

"Talk?"

There was no answer. He glanced up, and then down again at his work, wishing that the minds of his patients could be as easily examined as their bodies. Some bitter memory, he could see, was working, but he could not guess the dark satisfaction with which Jack was thinking:

"Well, I gave her a shock all right, the old bitch!"

Sixty if she was a day, fat and waddling, dressed up to kill. Powder lying like snowdrifts in her wrinkles, scarlet framing her false teeth obscenely, and enough diamonds on her crimson-tipped talons to have bought him his farm twice over! Her voice calling from the top of the gangway to her boy-friend on the wharf: "Get a taxi, Bobby, I just have to wait for my mail!" That was how he had seen her, while he sat with his mates in the shade during the midday spell, munching his sandwiches and drinking strong black tea from his billy. Asking idly:

"Who's the duchess, Steve?"

Steve, fat and lazy and ironical, answering:

"Doncher read the Society columns? Doncher know Mrs. H. B. Merivale-Brown, O.B.E.?" He spat. They watched her receive her letters from an obsequious steward, and come tottering down the gangway on her high heels. One of the men farther up the wharf called to her: "Not that way, lidy," but she gave him a withering glance and went on till she found her way blocked, just behind where Jack and Steve were sitting, by a trolley loaded with molasses casks. She called imperiously to Jack:

"Will you kindly move this away; I'm in a hurry."

Jack pointed laconically down twenty yards of sun-scorched wharf:

"That there's the way out, lidy."

She snapped:

"Nonsense! I'm certainly not going to walk all that way in the blazing sun when there's nothing to stop me going through here except this trolley. It's ridiculous to have the whole wharf blocked up like this, so that the passengers have to walk . . ."

Jack, his face several shades darker, said:

"Good for the figure, lidy."

She stood before him, shaking with fury.

"I shall report you if you don't move this thing at once."

He said, shaking Steve's restraining hand from his arm with sudden violence:

"I'm 'avin' my dinner-hour. Why don't y' call y' boy-friend to move it for y'?"

Well . . .

He became aware that he had drawn a deep breath, which Oliver, glancing up at his face again, mistook for one of pain. That, as far as he cared to remember it, was the story. Its sequel, his dismissal, his outburst of fury to his mates, standing on an overturned box and haranguing them upon an injustice which had widened in his own mind from the particular to the general, was nothing but a dark confusion in his memory; a confusion out of which emerged with sudden clarity the words which had been on his lips when he was arrested.

"She and 'er sort's the kind that makes wars. We and our sort's the kind that fights them. Not me!" Suddenly, to his own surprise, he found himself repeating aloud to Oliver the end of his ill-fated speech: "I got up on me 'ind legs and says to them: ' 'Ere in me own country I'll fight if some other fellow tries to butt in. But they can shoot me before they'll ever get me out of it for one of their bloody European wars!"

Oliver said briefly:

146

"Same here." And added: "What's the matter? Did I hurt you?"

But Jack said confusedly: "No—it's nothin' . . ." staring down at his hand, now neatly bandaged, its injured fingers lying straight along the splint, and then again at the bent head of the man who had just uttered those astonishing words. His jump had been one of sheer revelation. All the contrasts which had been tormenting him were welded into one sharp contrast of two individuals—himself, idle, embittered, all his mental and moral vigour turned inward with the dangerous unawareness of a mind not naturally introspective. And this alert and self-confident man in whose busy and active life self-investigation took its rightful place as a pastime, a stimulating exercise of the intellect and the imagination. Yet in both their minds thought processes had flowered into the same resolve. In one darkly and chaotically, struggling unreleased through mazes of personal resentment, retarded or deflected by a thousand of those well-worn clichés from which the undeveloped intellect escapes so hardly. Building itself into a final and unalterable conviction only by virtue of these fundamental senses which together make the sense so justly known as "common." Common to all normal men and women, persisting deeply and tenaciously, with an integrity never wholly smothered by the faulty conceptions of their bewildered brains. The sense of justice, the sense of a purpose in life to be fostered by the arts of peace and constantly imperilled by the threat of war. The sense that in the affairs of mankind, no less than in the body of the individual man, health must mean tranquillity, and disease must mean conflict and disintegration.

And in the other, a process more painful because always under a white light of an unrelenting self-awareness. A process in which every emotion must bear the scrutiny of a detached, observant brain, and every thought must be turned and turned again. A process of disciplined reasoning; of contemplating without panic a long array of ugly facts, of horrifying alternatives, of revolting greed and still more revolting callousness; of fear run mad over the face of the earth like a pestilence. Of final retreat into the last, the only unassailable stronghold, the retreat which is not a flight, but a withdrawal into that one freedom of the spirit which no outer forces can dismay.

Some dim conception of that last triumphant power which he shared with Oliver and with all mankind had shaken Jack, and he repeated "Not me!" with a fervour which so startled himself that he lifted his stiff arm with its aching fingers and demanded sulkily: " 'Ow long do I 'ave to wear this?"

Oliver, already rapidly emptying basins and putting things away, answered:

"Three weeks at least. Come and see me, say, next Thursday. You didn't tell me your name."

He went to the door and held it open. Jack moved towards it slowly. Pain, which he endured as an animal endures it, as a thing of the body alone, not to be thought about, had taken greater toll of his vigour than he realised. Now, attempting the words which he had known that he would have to say at last, fatigue crept into his voice:

"Saunders, Jack Saunders. I live down by the beach at the Bay. I 'aven't . . . I can't . . ."

Oliver thought desperately:

"Good God, we're a long way from decency yet! There's no such thing as 'give' any longer—nothing but 'sell, sell, sell'." He said hastily:

"That's all right—it only took a moment. Keep your arm up till you get home and then put it in a sling."

He watched the dark, powerful body silhouetted against the brilliance of the outer door as it opened, and then went back to the desk for his visiting list.

*   *   *   *   *

The front door closed behind Lady Hegarty with a gentle and conclusive click. She stood on the porch at the top of the long flight of steps and thought with astonishment: "How easy it is to rebel!"

The astonishment remained, but fastened itself on to a different thought, as she began to see a picture which familiarity and habit had hidden from her for years as effectively as if they had been a black curtain before her eyes. How sad it was, she reflected, that one could grow accustomed to beauty—how dangerous altogether, perhaps, that tendency to "get used to" things! For obviously if they were evil they should be endlessly resisted, and if they were lovely they should be an unceasing wonder; but what happened was that beauty and ugliness alike could become, by the mere passage of time, so welded into one's life that one no longer regarded them at all. She herself had got used to playing second fiddle to Hegarty's Ltd. She had got used to the life in which it had involved her. She had got used to being rich. And now, with shame, she realised that she had even got used to the view from her front porch. She smiled to herself walking down the steps, thinking in self-justification that the people whose nervous systems would stand the strain of living in alternating moods of rebellion and adoration must be very few; and yet those ordinary mortals, whose nerves craved long intervals of bovine acceptance as the body craves an armchair, probably never achieved the fullest enjoyment which life had to offer, and she mixed a sigh with her smile as she opened the gate.

Crossing the road she noticed an empty car standing in front of the house opposite, and as she stepped on to the footpath beside it she noticed Dr. Denning being shown out the front door by Mrs. Moran. From the corner of an observant eye she watched her neighbour's rather over-effusive farewells, and was pleased to catch, or to imagine that she caught, on the doctor's face, as he turned away from the closing door, a hint of her own amusement. She thought with a flicker of contempt for her own sex: "I suppose the good-looking ones get a lot of that sort of thing," and felt a surprised and unregenerate chuckle struggling to escape as she realised that she herself was purposely lingering so that he might reach the gate before she passed! When he had first come to the neighbourhood, she remembered, a year or so ago, she had met him at some bridge party, and afterwards George had said, with a touch of his odd, old-fashioned prejudice, something about a divorce following a scandal—some affair with a woman artist—a dim mental picture of a lank and untidy female in a smock, a vague impression of jade earrings, cubist furniture, bare feet in "arty" sandals, a preposterous cigarette holder, had made her think: "What a pity!"

Looking at him now as he emerged on to the footpath beside her, she thought it again, and said:

"Good-morning, Doctor."

His absent glance focussed hurriedly on her face. She saw him thinking: "Now who . . . ? Oh, yes, of course!" He answered:

"Good-morning, Lady Hegarty. Are you going down the hill? Can I take you anywhere?"

Her hesitation was momentary. She had run away, pretending to herself that she wanted a walk. She had left a hundred trivial details of the ordering of her household to the housekeeper who was, after all, paid to attend to them. She had left half a dozen letters unwritten, she had not made at least four telephone calls which she should have made, and she had cancelled her appointment with the hairdresser, who was to have coaxed her rather wild grey hair into a coiffure suitable for the importance of this afternoon's occasion. Now, ostensibly wanting a walk, she accepted a drive, and gave Oliver a smile in which there flashed for a second so youthful a gleam of defiant amusement that he returned it involuntarily, thinking: "This is rather a jolly old person!"

She said:

"It's very kind of you, Doctor. I thought I'd go down to the beach for an hour or so. My son is there. Will that be out of your way?"

"It's on my way. I've only a few more visits to do and then I'm going to play truant, too."

She glanced at him as she struggled into the front

150

seat and waited for him to climb in beside her. A young man, she decided, of perspicuity. A valuable quality in a doctor. She said:

"Truant? How did you know I was playing truant?"
He laughed.

"You looked defiant. Are you?"
She considered this, and replied seriously:

"I believe I am. I even suspect myself of wishing I didn't have to go to my son's wedding this afternoon. Such a confession as that," she added dryly, "must be regarded as a professional secret."

He looked at her quickly, and then back at the road. He liked driving along this particular strip of concrete; its curves were long and sinuous, repeating themselves with an almost rhythmic regularity; on the right the hill rose to the ridge upon which the lighthouse stood, and it was bright with a patchwork of red roofs and gaily terraced gardens. Mauve lantana spilled itself in almost breath-taking profusion over walls and fences, and jacaranda trees repeated more ethereally its lovely note of amethyst. Below the road the roofs were shrouded in trees, and the hillside dipped to join the harbour whose blue and silver lay there as the background, the strange, unchanging background, of the changing land. The gleam of a physical enjoyment in the car's smooth response to the alternate slackening and tension of his muscles was interwoven with the thought: "How many kinds of unhappiness there are! How seldom a human being fits perfectly into his environment, comfortably, snugly, like a kernel in a nut! Progress. But to what, in Heaven's name, should we progress if not to happiness? . . ."

He found himself saying rather lamely, because he realised that his silence had already lasted too long:

"I thought all womenfolk enjoyed weddings."
She shook her head.

"There's just one wedding one is completely sure about—one's own. And then one's mistaken. You can put me down here, Doctor."

He stopped the car, protesting:

151

"Are you always as cynical as this?"

She did not reply at once, for getting out of the car was a business which demanded her whole attention. He was at her side to help her, and when, panting a little, she stood on the footpath again, she looked up at him and said:

"When you know me better you must decide that for yourself," and held out her hand hurriedly, finding herself strangely embarrassed under the amused speculation of his curiously light blue eyes. When she had turned away he watched her for a moment, walking with her slow and rather waddling gait down the asphalt path, leaning on her stick, looking round her with quick enquiring movements of her head. He did not know that it was the first time for nearly five years that she had been down to the little beach which lay almost at her front door; that she was sniffing with conscious enjoyment scents which took her back to childhood, and which she had, almost since then, forgotten to enjoy—the scent of ti-trees and young gum saplings mixed with a fugitive breath from the Cove of salt water and drying seaweed. He did not know that more than forty years ago she had scrambled about those rocks down there with young Jimmy Hegarty, climbed through dense scrub over this hillside down which his car swooped now on a curving concrete road, and cried: "Here, Jimmy! We'll have a house here some day!"

She had achieved her house—and got used to it. The loveliness at which she had gasped that day had been hers for years now, to feast her eyes upon, but she had got used to that, too. Only to-day, for some strange reason, life had become intense again. It had a sting and an edge like a frosty morning—the challenge and welcome which it has for the very young. The wedding, she thought. For the marriage of one of your children had a tremendous significance, after all. It was, potentially at any rate, though with these modern girls you could never be certain, the beginning of another generation. And you yourself, pushed on by that new generation a step

152

nearer to death, were reawakened rather belatedly to the preciousness of life.

How one wasted time! But even familiar phrases took on a new flavour this morning, and she found herself objecting: "No, no, that isn't possible; time isn't just another of our commodities that we can waste it, like money—or food. We waste ourselves *in* time. Waste, waste —and suddenly it's too late. . . ."

She stopped on a flat rock overlooking the Cove, and her forlornly meandering thoughts were halted by the sight of two little boys, whom she recognised presently as Denis and Jonathan Harnet, just below her in the pale green water over the yellow sand, darting and turning like fish, shouting, laughing, spluttering defiance at each other. How odd it was that of all humanity only its young—and its very young at that!—knew how to live with completely unstinted zest. Not one fragment of themselves were they wasting, she thought; not one of the myriad cells of their small brown bodies but was functioning at top pressure in its appointed task, manufacturing and consuming the tremendous, the awe-inspiring energy which they were devoting simply to being alive.

She watched them, absorbed, admiring, even a little nervous now and then. Surely they would hurt themselves scrambling out of the water over those oyster-covered boulders? Over that green and slippery seaweed? They were, after all, quite *little* boys—were they safe on those very high rocks over the deep water? Of course they could swim, but . . .

Suddenly she uttered aloud a sharp exclamation, for Jonathan had climbed craftily up one side of the Pulpit where Denis was standing absorbed in his clockwork boat, and pushed him off backwards into the water. The lean, small body somersaulted through the air and hit the water with a smack. Jonathan, standing on the edge of the rock, jeered and exulted, and Denis, coming spluttering to the surface, yelled:

"Come on in! You daren't! Funky, funky! See what you've done, you mutt—you've made me lose the boat!"

Jonathan sobered instantly.

"Gee, has she sunk? Hey, get out of the way, Denis, I think I can see her. I can see a bit of red. I'm going to dive."

When he did so the surface of the water hardly rippled, and from her rocky height Lady Hegarty could see his body under the water, dim and distorted and spiderish, groping about on the sandy bottom. Denis, too, with one practised movement, and with one flash of bare legs above the water, turned himself upside down and joined in the search, and she, amused at herself for an alarm so obviously unnecessary, looked farther up the Cove to where a crescent of white sand lay out of reach of the full tide.

Young Mrs. Sellman, in her white bathing suit and vast green hat from beneath which there came a wisp of cigarette smoke, was helping her small daughter to dig a hole with a ditch leading down to the water. There were two or three other groups on the beach. She recognised that unutterably boring woman, Mrs. Mason, who hounded and waylaid her on every opportunity, who invited her, with a persistence quite unaffected by constant refusals, to her stodgy tea-parties, who had literally wrung out of her an invitation to George's wedding—all because she was Lady Hegarty! And sitting on the rocks as far away from everyone else as they could get, were Mrs. Cameron and her daughter, Jean, who avoided her like the plague for exactly the same reason! She laughed with real amusement. Two kinds of snobbery—the grovelling and the disdainful! The vulgarian who kowtowed to you because you had a title, and the aristocrat who despised you because that title was a purchase and not an inheritance! And which was the sillier? She did not know, and it did not seem worth bothering about, anyhow, so she scanned the beach again, looking for Sim.

Farther up, where the sand was hot and dry, she saw him at last lying propped on his elbows talking to a girl. What girl? The all-enveloping beach wrap with its hood drawn forward over the face made certain recognition

154

from this distance impossible, but Lady Hegarty thought rather grimly: "Lorna Sellman," and then smiled to herself, because of Sim at least she felt that she could be warmly and reassuringly confident. She liked the little Channon girl with her honest and critical eyes and her youthful ambitions, and it was not without a touch of satisfying malice that she made her way down the path and across the beach to where Sim and Lorna lay. Sim said genially:

"Hullo, Mother. Oughtn't you to be praying and fasting or something?"

But Lorna's annoyance, Lady Hegarty thought complacently, was almost as great as her surprise, and she said amiably to Sim:

"Lower me down on to the sand, dear. My shoes are full of the wretched stuff. How are you, Lorna? Oh, must you run away?"

Lorna answered: "I'm very well, thank you." Sim's mother paid her an ironical mental tribute for the brief glimpse of her lovely body which she allowed to Sim as she jumped up and readjusted her wrap about her head and shoulders. She asked:

"Have you the time, Lady Hegarty? I left my watch at home."

It was nearly eleven, so Lady Hegarty, shaking sand out of her shoes, told her that it was half past, and added, lifting her lorgnette:

"How charming dear Winifred looks in her white bathing suit with her lovely brown arms and legs! They must take after their father, those two girls. Must you go, Lorna? Well, good-bye, dear; we'll meet again this afternoon."

Sim's answer to Lorna's casual good-bye sounded off-hand enough to please his mother, who was struggling with the buckle of her shoe, so that she did not see the expression with which his eyes followed, for a moment or two, the slender, white-shrouded figure. By the time she looked up he was face downward again, his forehead resting on his arms, and for the second time that morning she gathered an obscure comfort from the thought and sight of his physical strength and beauty. She might be old herself, but her son was young; she might be fat and tired and elephantine of movement, but her son was lean and full of vigour, and moved with an effortless grace. An illogical compensation, she thought, watching Lorna, who had paused to speak to Winifred on her way off the beach, but no doubt it was just as well that mothers were able to discover such comforting illusion, for their actual rewards seemed often few and meagre! How very intense Lorna looked, and with what a startled intentness Winifred seemed to be listening! And presently Lorna shrugged her shoulders and walked off, her cape swinging, and Winifred sat for a moment or two very still, her face invisible behind the brim of her huge hat, the smoke of her cigarette wreathing gently into the air.

Lady Hegarty shrieked:

"Good gracious, what's that?" and ducked her head under a shower of sand. Denis, apprehensive, stopped a dozen yards away, and Jonathan stood on one leg, and said rapidly: "I'm sorry, but I meant to throw it at Denis."

She bent her head and brushed at her hat with her folded gloves.

"You don't throw very straight, do you?"

Jonathan explained gravely:

"You were in the way."

She raised her lorgnette, examining him.

"In the way?" With her stick she drew a circle round herself in the sand, and Denis, edging closer to Jonathan, whispered loudly:

"What's she doing?"

"This," she explained, "is *my* bit of the beach. You can have all the rest. *All* of it." She made a munificent gesture, and Denis, seeing that she expected a reply, answered politely:

"Thank you very much, but it belongs to the Council."

Sim said sleepily: "Snub for the Duchess!"

She asked: "Aren't you Mr. Harnet's little boys?"

They said "Yes" in chorus, and, teasing them because she could see them itching to be off, she plied them with further questions.

"Do you go to school?" Denis answered:

"Yes, only we're having holidays for a week because we had our tonsils out." Jonathan added hurriedly: "Mine were the biggest."

"Are you good at your lessons?"

They looked at each other as if silently debating this point, and then Jonathan said:

"I am. But I don't do so many things as Denis. He does geography. That's about continents and islands and . . . and bays and gulfs and things like that. But I'm good at spelling, and sums, and writing. . . ."

"And conduct?" she asked nastily. He answered with untouched serenity: "I don't do conduct."

Denis volunteered shyly:

"I'm up to sums with feet and inches in them."

"How many inches," she demanded, "in this stick?"

Startled, Denis stared at it, his face going pink with embarrassment. He ventured with valiant carelessness:

"Oh—'bout a hundred."

There burst out immediately a noisy and violent dispute: "Ar! You're mad, Denis! There's about a thousand!" "Bet you there's a hundred!" "Bet you there isn't!" "Anyhow, I'm a better incher than you, and I bet there's only about a hundred. Or two hundred."

Sim sat up, and said suddenly:

"Look here, Mother, you like Lesley, don't you?"

Lady Hegarty said:

"Good-bye, little boys!" And watched them scamper down the beach and through the shallow water in a spatter of sand and silvery spray. She answered, gladly:

"Yes, I like her. Why? Are you going to marry her?"

Waiting placidly for his "Yes," she prodded holes in the sand with her stick, but his answer when at last it came slowly and sombrely shocked her so much that she turned with a movement which was almost violent to look at him.

"I don't think so. I'm in love with her all right, but . . ."

She said sharply:

"What are you talking about? Don't be so ridiculous! You don't mean that she's turned you down?"

He shook his head.

"Not exactly. But she's never been sure that it would work. She—she's a queer sort of girl—serious—has all sorts of ideas that most girls don't bother with. They mean a lot to her. It makes me feel uncertain, too. I think we're too different. . . ."

She felt something happen to her. A kind of slumping, as if some unusual mental and physical alertness which had been sustaining her had given way, as a supporting rope might break and let its burden fall. She actually felt her face change, felt it settle into its lines of age and weariness, felt it become inert as her thoughts were becoming inert, robbed of the audacious and enterprising independence which had so briefly enlivened them. She murmured:

"Different?"

He said moodily:

"I've been down here all the morning trying to worry it out. She came down early for a swim, and after she'd gone I felt—well, I felt I had to get it clear in my own mind—somehow . . ."

She said sharply, and instantly regretted it:

"And Lorna's been helping you."

He said shortly:

"We didn't discuss it. I can do my own thinking."

She thought rather wildly:

"But you can't. Not any longer. You were thinking for yourself on your birthday years ago when you wanted to give Jack your presents. And we stopped you—your father and I. You can't think for yourself any longer. You can only think in terms of the life you've always

158

led—the silly life I brought you into, the perilous life of an unvarying comfort and security. . . ."

She said awkwardly:

"It's so dangerous to be safe, Sim . . ." and then stopped, dismayed, because the truth of the thought seemed spoiled, somehow, by the paradoxical clumsiness of the words. She added, lamely, with an instinctive retreat to the mundane sphere in which, alone, she could now feel herself at home: "You didn't come home to breakfast."

"I didn't want any breakfast. I just wanted to make up my mind. For her as well as for myself. I couldn't bear to make her miserable. I couldn't bear to see her hating marriage like Winifred hates it. Look!"

He sat up and locked his arms round his knees, watching the figure in the white bathing suit slowly cross the beach to the rocks where her book and her beach wrap were lying. Some suggestion of defeatedness, of an almost intolerable weight of misery, seemed to express itself in the way she walked, idly, slackly, with bent head and swinging arms, and he felt a chill, an uneasy apprehension, an inexplicable fear that life with Lesley would be difficult, full of problems, complex. . . .

Just to be with her forced you into action. Not physical action, but rather something which made you disturbingly conscious of yourself as an individual, with an individual's choice of thought, of belief, of behaviour. You lost the comforting sense of being merely a member of a system, you lost your background. She had the same effect on your existence, he thought, that a stereoscope has upon a picture; she made it leap forward, stand out, rounded and real and dramatic, something violent, to be reckoned with violently, and perhaps with pain. He thought desperately: "How could we? How could we?"

He flashed out with a bitterness which surprised himself:

"She thinks I'm a useless sort of person. Worse than useless. Vicious. Because I have money. How the devil can I help it? If we shut down Hegarty's to-morrow three thousand people would be out of jobs. She can't see . . ."

Lady Hegarty said in a small voice:

"That's what they call creating employment, isn't it?"

He glanced at her in surprise.

"Yes. Why?"

"Nothing. I've heard your father speak of it. And George."

He said gloomily:

"We could get married, I suppose. But inside a year she'd be hating her life with me as Winifred hates hers with Arthur Sellman. Or we could make paupers of ourselves—and I'd do the hating. Those girls are both . . ."

He dropped his forehead on to his folded arms.

"Oh, I don't know," he said hopelessly.

*   *   *   *   *

Winifred lay face downward on the sand after Lorna had gone. She could feel her heart pounding against it. She rested one cheek on her folded arms so that she could see Brenda and began to fight an increasing panic with obstinate and unavailing determination, as the victim of poison gas fights for breath against its irresistible fumes. She tried to tell herself that Lorna had been lying, that she was in a rage because Sim was indifferent, that it hadn't happened, that she had heard or understood wrongly. She thought: "Goodness, how melodramatic. She actually hissed at me!" and tried to laugh, an attempt hurriedly abandoned because she could feel that it was a nervous laughter which might turn to weeping—dreadful, hysterical weeping which one couldn't control. And it would frighten Brenda. She shut her eyelids over an ominous burning and suffusion; shut them tightly and kept them shut till she felt she could without danger open them again, and all the time she was thinking wildly:

"Did she see me? Did she really see me that night?"

For there had been a night last winter, a cold, wild night when the little harbour waves became breakers

160

against the rocks, and the southerly buster had the smell of rain in it, and all her resistance had suddenly given way. Jonathan was ill. Brenda had told her that, for it was after her compact with Ian that they would meet no more, and she had seen Oliver going in the next-door gate more than once. The second time she had stopped him, asked with a deceitful pretence at mere neighbourliness:

"How is Jonathan to-day, Doctor? My little girl misses him so much."

In the moment before he replied she wondered, having the naive belief of all lovers in their invisibility: "I wonder how he knows? I wonder who told him?" For there was obvious comprehension and sympathy in his eyes, though his words and voice were a faithful answer to her own.

"He's on the mend now, Mrs. Sellman. He should be about in a week or so."

She had gone home with her worst fears allayed, but with her love for Ian blazing, its flames fed by pity and the longing to help him in his anxiety and solitude. For she knew and loved in him the quality which made him take his parenthood very seriously. She knew that not the housekeeper, but he himself would answer Jonathan's midnight wails, carry his drinks and his doses, empty his basins, turn his pillows, soothe him again to sleep; the impulse which made her snatch a dark overcoat suddenly and fling it round her, which sent her groping across the garden to the low stone wall, was one for which she had never been able to rebuke herself—an impulse of unmixed service and devotion. But she got no farther than the wall.

She heard Lorna banging the door of the garage shut, saw her coming running down the steps, a dim shape, a grotesque shape in her widely swinging fur coat; saw her disappear into the porch, heard the front door open and shut.

She crouched there against the wall shivering, not only with cold. She had hidden from Lorna. She had turned the white, betraying oval of her face away, clutched her dark coat about her, huddled back into the shadows of the vast hydrangea bushes, and now she was sick and furious with a humiliation quite new to her, and quite unendurable.

This was what it would mean. Hiding from people you despised. Lying and contriving. A continual assault, even if you were never found out, upon your self-respect —and his. She had stumbled back across her own wind-swept garden to the verandah and let herself in by Brenda's door. She had sat on the edge of the cot looking at the sleeping child, holding her numb hands beneath the warmth of the bedclothes, thinking: "I must not . . . I must not . . . I must not . . ."

One long prohibition. That was her life now. One long effort for self-control to deny herself, and him, their happiness. "That's all right!" she told herself fiercely as she had done a thousand times before. "We aren't individuals any longer, Ian and I—we're just parents! The minute you become a parent your life ceases to belong to yourself. That's obvious." She thought rather wildly: " 'Hostages to fortune!' Good old Bacon! What happens now? Did she really tell Arthur that? Did she really see me? What would be the good of telling the truth to a man with a mind like Arthur's? They say you might as well be hung for a sheep as for a lamb. . . . We're going to be hung, anyhow. Brenda . . ."

She saw the bare, brown legs of Sim and the grey-patterned skirts of Lady Hegarty go by, and she shut her eyes in case they should speak to her, taking refuge in a pretence of that devotional abandonment to sunshine in which one may remain as undisturbed as if one were at prayer. But her frightened thoughts went on in the reddish darkness behind her closed lids:

"What will he do? What shall he do?" She felt the baffled helplessness with which one confronts a mind lacking both intelligence and standards. It was utterly impossible to say what Arthur might or might not do. Would he follow some tortuous mental process which he would call reasoning, or perhaps only some obscure impulse of jealousy and revenge? Finding himself able to hurt her would he not do so with the same ugly, intent, tortured enjoyment which she had read in his face last night?

She leapt up, scattering sand about her. The movement had been, like Ian's walk earlier in the day, an instinctive impulse toward escape. She thought: "How silly! You're morally helpless and you make the same movement that you'd make if you were trying to shake off a spider or a wasp. To move your arms and legs, to go from one place to another—your body never learns that that's only an illusion of being free. . . ."

But she was still tense, her muscles alert as if for flight. Physical action might mean nothing, but they demanded it all the same. Shaken with a rigor of remembered humiliation, her body cried out in angry panic for exertion and more exertion, violent movements to burn up energy like a flame in her, consuming and rebuilding till every nerve and cell was exhausted and renewed, exhausted and renewed again, the memory of its abasement and disgust grown mercifully dim. She said:

"Brenda, I'm going in again. Are you coming?"

Brenda, feeling carefully about her hillock of sand, replied:

"No, Mummy, I haven't finished my garage. Where's my car, Mummy? I can't feel it."

Winifred half-stooped for it, and straightened again.

"It's behind you, darling, near your left foot. No, nearer than that. Yes, that's right. Will you stay here while I have a swim?"

"Yes, I'll stay."

"Here are Denis and Jonathan coming back. They'll help you if you want them to."

She threw her hat down, ran across the sand and splashed through the shallow water. She swam out to the net, going all out as if she were racing, and then along it to the rocks. She rested there, holding on to the net, a little disturbed because she was trembling more than

163

her burst of exertion justified, and her eyes turned to the beach again, searching automatically for Brenda. Not only Denis and Jonathan were with her now, she saw, but a man and a woman whom she recognised presently as Dr. Denning and his wife, and the children, standing in a row, wore the unmistakable alertness of excitement.

Winifred swam slowly across to the raft and clambered on to it, wondering half-absently if she would ask Dr. Denning about her father's rheumatism if he came within speaking distance. She watched him thoughtfully as he crossed the sand with his wife, giving them her whole attention now, allowing them an importance as living examples of a satisfactory marriage; wondering if her own life of perpetual frustration surrounded her with a shadow and a chill, as their obvious well-being surrounded them with an almost visible warmth. Mrs. Denning, she thought, was a pretty bad swimmer, just as she was a pretty bad tennis player and, if rumour could be believed, a pretty bad housekeeper, too. She was not even good-looking, though there was a certain piquant charm about her, and she always dressed as if she had just become aware of the fashion of the year before last, and was anxiously trying to catch it up. Watching her slow and splashing progress, Winifred thought that it seemed odd that those strange pictures which she had admired long before she knew their author should be the work of this silent, shy, and otherwise rather inept young woman. Dr. Denning, swimming lazily on his side, reached the raft first, and Winifred said: "Good-morning . . ." and stopped abruptly, because she was shocked to see that the burns which scarred one side of his face and neck extended over his shoulder and chest and were lost to view beneath his bathing suit; she had a sudden mental picture of him, now so lazy and relaxed in the water, battling in some dreadful unknown circumstances with that other element which had so brutally and irrevocably marked him.

Lois, panting, clutched the edge of the raft with both hands and gasped:

"Mrs. Sellman—would you let Brenda—go to the Zoo with Mrs. Trugg—this afternoon? She's taking Mr. Harnet's two little boys, and she'd like—to take Brenda, too. . . . Help me up, Oliver, I'm puffed."

Winifred said doubtfully:

"It's very kind of her. I don't quite know. . . . Would she be bringing them right home?"

Lois explained:

"She'll put them on the ten-to-five ferry. I rang up Mr. Harnet, and he said he'd be on it himself most likely, so they'll be quite all right, Mrs. Sellman. Are you coming up, Oliver?"

Winifred said, slowly: "I see."

She thought:

"He'll be on the ten-to-five ferry."

Her gaze, absent with this thought, crossed Oliver's as she looked unseeingly round the Cove, up the hillside; a strange, wandering, absorbed, restless look, Oliver thought, the look of one spiritually adrift, searching all the time either consciously or unconsciously for some anchorage, some haven. Thoughts went round in her mind with the dreamlike quality of thoughts in fever or delirium. They had shape and colour, large lazy wheels of iridescent light. "He'll be on the ten-to-five ferry. It's his usual one. The children will be on it. Why shouldn't I be on it, too? Why shouldn't we sit with our children and talk to each other for a little while? There is no sense in this torment of solitude. Things are coming at us, things are going to happen to us . . . what things? Arthur and Lorna are dangerous people. Dangerous to Brenda. It is absurd not to tell Ian when Brenda is in danger, it is absurd that we should not be together to give each other strength. . . .

The wheels spun faster and faster. There came a sudden, terrible tightness in her head and a sheet of silver, like falling water in the sun, shut out her vision, scalded her eyes. One sharp, coherent streak of knowledge darted arrowlike into her consciousness, an incredible but indisputable knowledge.

"I'm going to cry!"

Tears, silver and blinding, shut out sight. She heard Lois say in sharp distress:

"Mrs. Sellman! What is it? What . . . ?"

The coir matting felt hard and nobbly under her forehead. Helpless, shaken by a paroxysm of weeping utterly beyond her control, she yet was aware that it was lucky people did lie face downward on the raft; it was lucky that this thing had happened to her when there was no one about but the doctor and his wife, who were now sitting with their backs to her, their legs dangling in the water, screening her from the conventional, well-behaved world whose code of behaviour she was so disgracefully violating.

Her body was driven and possessed by this weeping. It seemed so little of herself, and so malignantly an alien force which was temporarily inhabiting her, that she made no conscious effort at resistance; her relief when she felt its violence abating was akin to the relief with which one might watch a man-eating tiger walking away from one's place of hiding.

Exhausted, she lifted a blotched and smarting face. Oliver glanced over his shoulder, asked:

"Better?" She nodded.

"Yes, I'm all right. I—I don't make a habit of this sort of thing, Mrs. Denning. I didn't sleep too well last night—I suppose I'm tired, or something. . . ."

Lois looked at her seriously, a strangely searching, impersonal look, of which she seemed herself to become suddenly aware, and blushed, turning away again. She said awkwardly:

"I'm sorry. . . . Would you like me to—to do anything. Would you like to go home and leave the children with me?"

Winifred slid off the raft and dashed a few handfuls of water over her face. She met Oliver's considering eyes, and said with a touch of defiance:

"I suppose you have me all diagnosed, Doctor?"

He answered sharply:

"It doesn't take a doctor to recognise unhappiness. Are you going home now?"

"Yes, but I promised to take the children to get ice-creams on the way. Is my face presentable?"

He smiled at her.

"It'll do. It has coir matting printed all over one cheek, but that will soon fade."

"Good-bye, then."

She swam ashore and went across the sand to the children. They were still absorbed in their building, and she got her green, shadowing hat on before their gimlet eyes had time for scrutiny. She asked, on a convincing note of cheerfulness:

"Ice-creams, children?"

Brenda said:

"Hullo, Mummy. I thought you were someone going past. Mrs. Denning asked if I can go to the Zoo with Denis and Jonathan this afternoon. Can I go, Mummy? Mrs. Trugg is going to take frightful care of us."

Jonathan objected:

"What's the good of her going to the Zoo, though? She can't see anything."

Denis said fiercely:

"Shut up! She can hear, can't she? Seals make an awful noise, and birds, and monkeys. And sometimes the lions roar. And she can ride on the elephant and the train. And we can tell her what the things look like. . . ."

Brenda cried eagerly:

"I know the shape of lions. And elephants. I had some toy animals in a house called a Nark. I know lots of animals. Are we going for our ice-creams now, Mummy?"

Winifred answered: "Yes, come along," and Denis and Jonathan ran ahead of her up the track. Holding Brenda's hand, she followed. All the morning her brain had felt clogged, heavy with misery. Her thoughts had pushed through an obstructing despair, and emerged shapeless, drained of vitality. But that storm of tears, like flood waters released, had surged through it, emptied

167

it of all emotion, left it swept and garnished for the knowledge which now so calmly and radiantly possessed it.

This afternoon she would see him. There seemed to be no room and no reason either for any other thought. She had come through a tormenting labyrinth of intellectual efforts into a clear acknowledgment of need and essential rightness; she felt oddly light-headed, as if the fears and resolutions and prohibitions and careful reasonings, which had been swept from her brain, were an actual, a material load of which she was now intoxicatingly free. Her only mental comment upon a situation so ineffably simple was one of mild surprise that she had been so long in accepting it. She saw it with the stark, mad clarity which belongs to all mental aberration, from mania to that temporary exaltation which now possessed her. She saw it as reason never sees, sharp, brilliant, a picture without a background, a word, "joy," snatched from its context, a single event, divorced from surrounding realities, short of inevitable consequences. Herself, Ian, their children, together. That, the inmost springs of her being told her, was right. That made sense, and harmony. Reason, rocking and afraid, reason already shamefully routed once this morning by its dark enemy, emotion, remained silent, stunned, and she walked behind the children lightly, a little smile on her lips, not knowing herself possessed.

She gave Denis the money for the ice-creams; a shilling so that she could have one, too. "A chocolate one for me, Denis." She hummed softly to herself, swinging Brenda's hand while they waited in the sun outside the shop, and Brenda joined in, so that when the boys came out with the four tapering cones they all set off down the road, singing together:

"Once a jolly swagman camped by a billabong
Under the shade of a coolibah tree,
And he sang as he watched and waited till his billy boiled
'Who'll come a-waltzing Matilda with me?'
Waltzing Matilda, waltzing Matilda . . ."

But you couldn't sing and eat ice-creams at the same time, so they stopped singing and went on down the road towards the cornflower-blue of the water again, and Winifred's thoughts, building up to a reckless gaiety and inconsequence, planned what she would wear this afternoon, this lovely afternoon, this glittering gold-and-silver afternoon, when she would go to her hour of happiness as to a festival. And she planned for Brenda, too; the little frock of pale yellow linen with the tiny green and white animals printed all over it—she would like to wear that when she was going to the Zoo, and the boys would compare it with the real animals and she would feel important, not inferior or alone. . . .

She would not ring Ian up. She would just go. She would go up in the wheezing lift, and along the dark old passage to his office, and knock on the door. He would say "Come in," and look up, expecting a clerk, or a typist. . . .

Suddenly, with the instinctive care and detachment of normal womankind, she became Ian, looking at Winifred in the doorway. What would he see? Her mind fastened with an intentness and a tenacity, which not even Lorna could have excelled, upon the details of her appearance, and she worked upon it mentally until, with Ian's eyes, she was satisfied, and became Winifred again, walking down the sun-baked asphalt, nibbling at the last half-inch of her ice-cream cone.

The hard, bare feet of Denis and Jonathan made no sound on the footpath, but Brenda's sandals pattered sharply. Jonathan had finished his ice-cream and was running on ahead, but Brenda still had some left, and Denis, holding her hand and walking soberly, was licking at his with a restraint almost religious in its intentness. Brenda asked suddenly:

"What colour is cold, Denis?"

Denis, his tongue protruding, looked at her in surprise for a moment, and then lingeringly ran it round the dwindling surface of his cone before he answered:

"Cold isn't a colour, it's a feel."

She said, puzzled:

"Some feels have colours."

"No, they don't. There's pink ice-creams, and brown ice-creams, and white ice-creams, but they all feel cold just the same. Yours is a pink one."

"What's yours?"

"Mine's brown."

"Let me have a lick of yours, Denis."

He put it grudgingly against her offered tongue.

"Only one lick. There you are."

She said:

"Pink has a nicer taste than brown."

Denis was silent for a moment, his brows drawn down in thought.

"Pink," he said at last, "hasn't got any taste. Or brown either."

"Denis, that's a story, they have. I tasted them. I've finished mine." She opened her mouth widely and breathed inward. "They make the day feel hot inside my mouth. Have you finished yours, Denis?"

"Nearly."

"Where's mummy?"

Denis looked back. Winifred was walking down the path behind them, looking up at the sky. Denis could hear her humming to herself about the jolly swagman and the jumbuck that he shoved into his tucker-bag, and he thought that her face looked unfamiliarly beautiful against the vast green circle of her hat brim. He answered Brenda:

"She's just behind. She's smiling."

*   *   *   *   *

Oliver banged on the bathroom door.

"Let me in, darling. I have to do a visit before lunch."

Lois answered in a harassed voice:

"Oh, dear! All right, I'm just out. I'll leave the shower running for you." The lock clicked. "There you are, you can come in now."

He opened the door, and stared down at her in amazement.

"What on earth are you doing?"

She lifted a heated face from the bath-mat.

"I've lost one slipper. I think it's gone under the bath. The floor's dreadfully wet, Oliver—I *can't* have a shower tidily."

"Who can? Have you got it?"

"It's there. I can see it right against the wall. I'll have to lie down, and I'll get wet again. Blast. I've got it now. . . ."

She scrambled to her feet, holding her towel, her bathing suit, her cap, her eye-shade, her sponge and her wrist watch in one hand; standing on one leg she tried anxiously to clutch her wrapper about her, and at the same time to put on the recovered slipper.

Oliver caught her suddenly in his arms. Her sponge squelched wetly between her face and his chest, and they were both a little surprised by their kiss. He had an exultant sense of relief and release. He was still swayed by these abrupt and violent ardours, the wild uprisings of a desire goaded into over-urgency by too long and bleak a restraint. He recognised it, and knew with an almost incredulous joy that with Lois it didn't matter. She, too, had been alone for many years; her love embraced that part of him which his first marriage had flawed, and promised it healing. She minded the scars of moral battle in him no more than she minded the scars of fire on his face and hands and body.

When he lifted his head and looked down at her upturned face her eyes were closed. It was an odd little face, he thought, studying it with an emotion not spoiled but enriched by a tinge of amusement, and when her lids lifted slowly, blinking with a touch of bewilderment, he said:

"You look like a dishevelled little owl."

She answered with spirit:

"You dishevelled me. I thought you had some work to do?"

He sighed:

"I have."

"Let me go, Oliver; I'm dropping everything, and I'm standing in a puddle, and the sponge is dripping down my front. Not," she added politely, "that I didn't like it."

He released her, and said, stooping over her fallen paraphernalia:

"If you'll hold out your ten fingers I'll hang something on each one for you. For God's sake don't try to open the door or you'll drop everything again. There you are. Good-bye. You've made me frightfully late."

He shut the door on the beginning of her outraged protest, and peeled off his bathing suit, scattering sand on the wet tiles. A memory of this morning's encounters returned to him. Harnet, tormented by his neuralgia; the Professor, condemned; the young chap with the sullen eyes and the broken fingers; the old lady who did not want to go to her son's wedding; young Mrs. Sellman, weeping helplessly on the raft; half a dozen other patients, drearily struggling with sundry illnesses! With his eyes on the dazzling scene which was visible through the high, open window, he felt a pang of something near to despair, and a poignant sense of incongruity. He tried to reassure himself, thinking that it was his job, after all, to see the misfits. In his day, any day, they must predominate. But the scientist in him, coldly aware how few and how simple are man's needs for well-being and fulfilment in his rich and fruitful world, refused to be placated, insisting: "There should be none. There need be none at all."

PART III
THE CITY

"I have the honour to enclose your Lordship the intended plan for the town. The Lieutenant-Governor has already begun a small house which forms the corner of the parade, and I am building a small cottage on the east side of the cove. . . ."

Governor Phillip to Lord Sydney, Sydney Cove, July 9th, 1788.

T HE bump of the ferry against the wharf, and the rattle of the gangway, roused Jack from sleep. He blinked, forgetting for a moment the helplessness of his arm, which lay in its white sling across his chest, and remembering it with a throb of pain as he tried to move it normally. He sat up, yawning. The unroofed ends of the top deck were flooded with sun, and he had had the stern to himself. When the ferry left the Bay he had stretched out full length on the slatted seat, his head pillowed on his sound arm, and he had slept blackly during the forty-five minutes of its voyage to the city.

He stood up now, stretching, wondering whether to go ashore or to stay where he was and travel back to the Bay. He had had no particular reason for coming to town. It was just to kill time, to occupy an afternoon which now, with one arm useless, stretched out incredibly into a horrifying boredom. He pulled a few coppers, a threepence, and a couple of sixpences out of his pocket and looked at them sourly. He had had nothing to eat all day but a slice of bread and treacle and a cup of strong, milkless tea, for he had forgotten the parcel of food he had taken down the cliff with him, and left it lying where it had fallen on the spray-drenched rocks. He grudged the turnstile money, but he was hungry and he was thirsty, and on the other side of the turnstiles there was beer, and perhaps a meat pie, so he went along the deck and heavily down the stairs. He paused on the gangway peering over at the deep, jade-coloured water and the fringe of dark, vast-leaved seaweed swaying under it along the edge of the wharf, and he was conscious of an uneasiness, a half-memory, something like the remnant of a dream. He walked up the sloping ramp of the wharf and lingered for a moment in front of the bookstall, picking his teeth with a match and reading what was visible on the front pages of the sporting papers, smelling, without at first being conscious of it, the city smell of dust and hot pavements drifting through the turnstiles to join the salt smell of the harbour. When he did become conscious of it he moved towards it, drawn by the fascination which gregarious humanity feels in any city. His coins clinked, rolled, vanished; he came out on to the footpath and walked slowly along to a cheap restaurant where he bought a pie and stepped out into the sun again, to stand on the kerb, his shoulder against a post, eating slowly, without dropping a crumb, and staring up and down the Quay.

He was full of unaccustomed lethargy, heavy-eyed, rather stiff from his long sleep, content to stand for the moment with sunlight beating down on him, and watch the people. The men came and went, hardly more distinguishable from each other than ants, but the women held his eye, an eye hungry for excitement, variety, and finding a shred of it in colour, in the flutter of a skirt, in a bunch of carnations in mauve tissue-paper, in an armful of red gum-tips and pink boronia flinging a breath of bush fragrance at him as it passed, in the sudden surprise of a face momentarily upturned from the shelter of a hat-brim. In voices, too; in fragments of conversation, in half-sentences, mysterious and intriguing:

"... the bushfires came up to his fences ..."

"... good-bye then, darling. Take care of yourself ..."

"... 'ad the face to tell me there was no such thing as brain fever! Doctors! I ought to know, I says, I've 'ad it three times!"

"... you get a man like Lenin once in ..."

"... same place, same time, eh? Don't be late!"

"... yes, I've read it. Decadent stuff. Defeatist. But if you want ..."

"... so shut up, will y'? I tell y' I'm not comin' back!"

"... there's goin' to be somethin' doin' in the Domain this afternoon. Fatty's got 'em boilin' ..."

"... hold y' noise, Perce, or we won't go to Manly, so there!"

Jack's half-closed eyes flickered and opened, his mind just beginning to consider words indifferently gathered

176

by idly listening ears. Somethin' doin' . . . in the Domain. . . .

He straightened and turned to look for the man who had made that remark. He could not be sure who it was among the crowd which straggled sparsely but incessantly past him, and he slumped against the post again, wondering, chewing the end of his match, thinking that perhaps after he had had a drink he would stroll up to the Domain and see . . . just in case . . . there might be some fun, something to watch . . . "somethin' doin' " . . .

Excitement, movement, things happening. Other men round you, a sense of being one with them, a place —any place—in some scheme or plan—any scheme or plan. . . . Anything but this isolation. Anything but this idleness, day after day, week after week. For it began to get you, to do to you . . . something . . .

He began to move slowly along among the crowd, and half-visible to his mental eye and half-obscured was the knowledge that lately when jobs cropped up, odd jobs here and there, a bob's worth, five bob's worth—he didn't want to take them. A kind of dull inertia was beginning to possess him, an apathetic weariness and disgust. What's the good of it! Keeps body and soul together—for what? Where do I get? Give me something with an end to it, something to make, to build, something of my own. Chopping a bit of wood here, digging a flower-bed there, cleaning a car somewhere else. . . .

He crossed the Quay, looked at a tram going up the hill, decided to walk. He loafed along, pausing at street corners to read the newsboys' placards, loitering past shop windows, hesitating, fingering his money, before tobacconists', walking on again. He stood at the end of the long canyon of Castlereagh Street waiting for a chance to cross, and an amorphous thought formed in his mind that in all the activity, the enterprise, the wealth, the industry which the city represented, it was strange that there should be no use for the restless strength which he could feel consuming him. He found himself remembering a map he had seen somewhere of this country of his, which could engulf

177

twenty-nine European countries and still have a good many thousand square miles to spare, and with that cold common sense which defies and defeats intellectualism, he thought: "You don't tell me there ain't jobs to be done! You don't tell me this ain't just bloody muddlin' . . . or worse. . . ."

On that sinister thought he began to move again. And at a cross-street, waiting for a stream of traffic to pass, he saw a small crowd gathering, a little farther up a fat man talking, people stopping to stare, a few policemen unobtrusively converging on the spot. Quickening his pace, warmed by an obscure stirring of excitement, he went to join the onlookers.

* * * * *

Inside the great steel helmet the air was hot and rushing, and Lorna moved her head impatiently. She said: "This thing's burning me. Switch it down, can't you?" But the girl in the white overall had her head half out the window, and the noise of the drier combined with the dull roar of traffic below drowned Lorna's voice, and she did not turn.

Exasperated, Lorna manœuvred her head out of the helmet and, leaning forward, prodded the girl with a comb. She turned hastily.

"Oh, Miss Sellman, I'm sorry. Is anything the matter? It wouldn't be dry yet."

"I know it's not dry, but you're burning my scalp off."

"I'm awfully sorry, Miss Sellman. Just a minute while I switch it down and then I'll hold it while you get your head in again. It's a lot cooler now. There, is that all right?"

"That'll do. What's happening out there. Did I hear shouting?"

"It's a crowd. And a chap talking. I suppose they're unemployed, or something."

"Oh, is that all? I thought there must be an accident. Where's Miss Mills? I'll have a manicure while my hair's drying. But I want her and nobody else. And listen . . ."

178

the girl turned at the door ". . . bring me a magazine to look at, will you?"

Lorna stifled a yawn. This hair business always made her sleepy and quite often gave her a bad headache into the bargain, and she looked at her watch, thinking that when it was over she would only just have time to rush round to Claire's and see if she could find a hat that wasn't too utterly awful. Lunch was out of the question; it was almost lunch time now. She'd have to make for home, and Heaven send there would not be too much traffic on the road or she would be too late to have her sacred half-hour's rest before dressing.

And she wasn't sure that this fringe was going to be a success after all. The trouble was, her thoughts said abruptly, taking a dark and disconcerting plunge, you never knew with a man like Sim what effect a scandal would have. She stirred uneasily, pushing at a hairpin which was pressing uncomfortably on her scalp, wondering why it was that she felt so uncertain, so astray in calculating her own influence over Sim, and whether, in the event of Arthur divorcing Winifred, his attachment to Lesley, which she had triumphantly felt this morning to be wavering, might not become stronger rather than weaker. For she saw that attachment only as one of the odd and temporary failures of judgment to which men were prone. She did not seriously believe that she could fail to rescue him from it, and her complete confidence in herself and her power was less vanity than a steadfastness of faith.

That it was a limited and a limiting faith did not occur to her. It was the only one she had ever known. Blessed are they that have anything over five thousand a year. Blessed are the beautiful. Blessed are they that wear the right clothes and know the right people. Blessed are they whose names are constantly in the society columns, and whose photographs adorn the Sunday papers. And thrice blessed are they that have titles, no matter how they got them. She said Amen to it all quite sincerely.

Only lately, when her thoughts turned to Sim, she

found herself struggling with an unfamiliar, moody in-
decision. She did not know that for the first time in her
life another human being had become real to her. She
was used to thinking of people as names followed by a
kind of inventory. She knew their appearance, their more
superficial habits, their incomes, their social standing—
and that was all she knew, or cared to know. But Sim
had become real. He had become a person like herself,
full of incalculable impulses and intentions, and she was
afraid. She stretched out her hand as Miss Mills settled
down beside her, and said crossly:

"Hurry, will you? I'm going to have an awful rush."

She wondered idly, looking down at the picture of
a bride in full array in the magazine on her knee, what
sort of a show Veronica Stewart would put up this afternoon. Funny that she and Veronica would be sisters-in-
law some day! Her own wedding dress, she thought, sinking into a trance of voluptuous reverie, would be plain—
sensationally plain! Not even the gleam of satin; some
kind of silk, heavy, dull, with a sort of nun-like headdress framing her face, and no· jewels at all except her
engagement ring, which would be a vast single sapphire.
And no flowers. An old ivory-bound prayer-book like
that one which had belonged to Winifred's mother would
be just the thing. And she would use no rouge, and only
the least suggestion of lipstick, and a good deal of the
bluish eye-shadow which always made her look frail and
rather weary. And she would have six bridesmaids all
in close-fitting *décolleté* bodices and vast bouffant skirts,
and she would see that they were all brunettes. . . .

And for her honeymoon. . . .

The sharp, involuntary movement of her hand was
very slight, but she had to explain it to Miss Mills' enquiring upward glance by snapping: "You hurt me—I've
a sore thumb—do be more careful!"

For she had found that the thoughts, which had been
for years her favourite method of passing an idle hour,
had been swallowed up in a dreadful and urgent cry from
some hidden self whom she scarcely recognised. "Sim,

Sim!" she cried miserably in her heart, terrified of her own uncertainty, resentful of his reality which made him so intractable, "Sim—oh, Sim—Sim! . . ."

There was an uproar in the street below. Miss Mills called to one of the other girls: "What's happening, Marcia?" And Marcia, running in from the passage, put her head through the window again, and exclaimed: "Gosh!"

Lorna said sharply:

"Wait a minute, I want to look. My hair's dry now."

What she really wanted was to escape from an unfamiliar world of doubt into her own world again; from a treacherous thought world into this familiar, material, recognisable city where she reigned as one of the rich, the beautiful, the privileged. To look down from a high window upon some vulgar turmoil in the street was not only a physical but a comfortingly symbolic action, and she stood leaning against the sill, her white, black-fringed lids drooping over her eyes, her red mouth with its full and delicately coloured lower lip just touched with the suggestion of a smile. There was nothing much to see after all. There had been a crowd, but the police were dispersing it. They had arrested someone; she could see him being marched away. A fat man with a beard was shouting something. He seemed to be exhorting others, and as Lorna watched a handful of men emerged from the crowd and gathered round him, and they began to move away up the street. She was turning with a faint shrug back to the more pressing business of her wave and her manicure when she noticed a shabby young man with his arm in a white sling standing on the footpath, watching. Her brows wrinkled for a moment. Then she remembered him.

The virginity which she had so conventionally cherished had not been preserved without cost. The cost, though she had never recognised it as such—had never, indeed, recognised it at all—was the development in her of a kind of submerged and unacknowledged lust which made men, in her eyes, mere vehicles, more or less desirable, of sex. It was a current of emotion which ran darkly and continuously like an underground river, and it so coloured her thoughts that they seemed to her mere bodies, and the discovery that they were also human beings came always with a faint impact of surprise or of alarm upon her consciousness.

That man with his arm in the sling had done some repairs to their launch once. She remembered going down to the boathouse and seeing him there in a torn singlet and a pair of grubby khaki shorts, bending over the dismantled engine. She remembered standing for a moment watching the movement of muscles under the brown skin of his huge arms and shoulders, studying his powerful neck and his vigorously curling dark hair, and then going away up to the house again with a feeling of frustration and annoyance which she really believed to be due to the fact that his presence there had spoiled a solitude she was expecting.

He must be, she thought now, from the Bay. Her mind skimmed the notion of a walk down there one afternoon, and a well-exercised mental censor, with the watchful assiduity of a highly trained servant, sprang forward to remind her that it was a very pretty walk, and one she had not taken for a long time. But when she saw him step down from the kerb and push his way through the crowd to a little group round the man with the beard, she shrugged and turned away from the window, relegating him in only half-conscious thought to that plane impossibly remote from herself, inhabited by people who were disciplined and not protected by the police.

But he had served his turn. The mere sight of him had deflected the tempestuous current of her emotions back into more familiar channels. His physical magnificence had made it possible for her to snatch Sim down from the preposterous pinnacle to which he had won; to be able to make a comparison between him and another man, which was even slightly to his disadvantage, gave her back that sense of detachment, confidence and power which was the very breath of her life. It was not her

182

métier to worship, but to be worshipped, and, restored to it, she smiled at Miss Mills, holding out an exquisite hand for her ministrations.

Emboldened, Miss Mills ventured:

"It ought to be a lovely wedding this afternoon, Miss Sellman."

Lorna smiled. There was, of course, of all the weddings which to-day would see, only one which mattered. Only one in which the combined incomes of bride and groom added to a really impressive total. Only one at which society would gather in force, only one which would attract a crowd of hundreds round the church door so that arriving in one's car, exquisite, perfect to the last costly detail, one would feel a warm and pleasurable superiority at being a guest and not merely a gaper. Neither to her nor to the humble Miss Mills, enmeshed in dreams of luxury and glamour, did there come, even fleetingly, a conception of a wedding as anything more than a show, a kind of elaborate charade. They saw it as an act of Social, but not social importance. Beyond it, into its potentialities for good or evil, happiness or misery, they did not look, being occupied with satin and diamonds, rose-petals and orange-blossom, and the Voice which may have breathed over Eden, but would certainly never breathe o'er the nuptials of George Hegarty and Veronica Stewart. The organ, however, would do just as well, and Lorna, serene again, secure again, replied amiably to Miss Mills:

"There'll be a frightful crowd."

"What are you wearing, Miss Sellman?"

It was not Miss Mills' admiration, but Sim's, for which she hungered; she imagined that, however, the more easily under Miss Mills' rapt and wistful stare, and her description of her frock and its accessories was so lively and so detailed that her hands and her hair were finished before her story. She laughed, putting on her hat, gathering up her parcels, her bag and her gloves, thinking with a little thrill of excitement that this afternoon she would play her cards less clumsily. This afternoon, in white which she frequently wore to weddings because she knew that in it she could outshine most brides, she would continue the good work which that stupid old mother of his had interrupted this morning. Perhaps he would come on to Manero's after all? If she could, just once, make him cut an appointment with Lesley Channon. . . .

She said gaily:

"I must fly. My hands and hair will try to do you credit, Miss Mills. Good-bye."

Miss Mills, gazing after her, said to Marcia:

"She's sweet, isn't she?"

*   *   *   *   *

Lesley looked up suddenly from her book. She thought: "That's funny!" For nothing had disturbed her, and yet her movement had been a startled one. The long reading-room of the library was quiet with a companionable hush; her pencil poised over her closely scribbled pages, her left finger still marking absently her place in the book from which she was reading, she looked about it, along its book-lined walls, up to the richly coloured glass in the end window, trying again to trace in her own mind the impulse, the gleam of thought or instinct which had been responsible for her involuntary movement.

The man next to her wrote without stopping. For nearly an hour while she searched, and read, and made such notes as seemed likely to be useful for the short story she was contemplating, she had been conscious of the soft, irregular murmur of his pencil across the pages, and of the faint flutter of paper as the woman at the opposite side of the table turned a page of her volume of newspaper cuttings. No, Lesley thought, disappointed, there was nothing in the room which could have broken so abruptly into her absorption, and she sighed, giving it up, looking down at her book again.

And there it was! Her eyes skimmed the paragraph she had just read:

"The spot chosen . . . was at the head of the Cove, near a run of fresh water which stole silently through the very thick wood, the stillness of which had then, for the first time since the creation, been interrupted by the rude sound of the labourer's axe, and the downfall of its ancient inhabitants; a stillness and tranquillity which, from that day, were to give place to the voice of labour, the confusion of camps and towns and the busy hum of its new possessors."

And suddenly, as if conjured out of the very words, the confusion and the busy hum were there. Her ear had caught them, carrying the message to her still absent mind: *"Listen! There they are!"* Noises—the strange, incoherent, ominous noises of a city; she had lifted her head sharply, not knowing what it was she tried to hear. She thought now, looking down at the words again: "He probably wrote that not a mile from this spot. . . ." And then irrelevantly, with a flicker of amusement: "How pompous they always were!"

She looked in front of her, trying to imagine the "Sydney Cove" of those not so very far off days. But the words she had just read dimmed rather than illuminated. *"A run of fresh water"* struck no chord of familiarity; *"the very thick wood"* brought her only a mental image of some pale green twilight beneath the spring foliage of elms and beeches. With an involuntary frown, she reached for one of the books beside her and hunted through it until she found a drawing inscribed *"Sydney Cove, 1790."* She stared at it with wrinkled brows, searching for something in it which would link it to the land she knew, but she realised at last that between her and any conception of that scene, the drawing, like the words, of one who had been alien and not native born could only hang like an obscuring veil. These were men talking the language of their own homeland, describing in terms of their own countryside, even drawing, by some odd convention (or was it a nostalgia not to be suppressed, and thus finding an unconscious outlet?), oaks and elms instead of gum trees!

She thought suddenly: *"A creek in the bush. . . ."*

185

Immediately, as if the words had been an incantation, she saw it. It was a place intimate and real. All her senses, so obstinately unresponsive to unfamiliar imagery, woke now to a sharp memory of remembered ecstasies. Yes, she thought, although you had never seen it, and that artist and that writer had, your own imagination must give you a far juster picture of it than any they could have contrived by line or word. For, by the grace of a hundred and fifty years you were, not wholly, but a little, admitted. By the grace of something which those years had worked to implant in you, you could recognise in the austere stillness of the bush not "tranquillity" but a watchful and dispassionate waiting. You could see, over the whole landscape, the glitter of a natural and savage cleanliness. Water, clear as glass, changing its colour but never its limpid purity over rock and sand and seaweedy depth; silver tree-trunks, cool and satin-smooth to the touch, gleaming faintly above their downward stripping bark; leaves fluttering high in the sunlight, reflecting it from their polished surfaces like thousands of tiny mirrors; rocks grey with the weathering of unaccountable ages.

And when the invaders landed they felt a soil beneath their feet whose very texture was alien; a hard earth, which smelled not of grass and flowers and hay, the reassuring, familiar odours of man's long habitation, but, strangely, of an age-old solitude. Shrubs, ankle-high, waist-high, sombre in colour, hard-stemmed, armed to the very leaves, defied them, barred their way, tore at hands accustomed to a green and sappy growth. The scents of strange flowers were strong and heady, but not sweet to nostrils which knew sweetness as the breath of the violet, the hyacinth, the rose. An inhospitable land. they said; a barren, hostile country. . . .

Lost in her thoughts she shook her head. Hostile— no. It had never descended far enough from its majestic aloofness to be hostile. There it was, here it is still, untouched. Not it, she thought, but we, its invaders, have changed. We have built cities and roads and railways over it, we have torn gold and coal out of it, we have pastured sheep and cattle on it, we have spread fields of wheat, fields of maize, fields of sugar-cane across it like a bright carpet—and we have not altered it by one iota. It has altered us.

As she formed this thought she felt a gladness, which she had often felt uncomprehendingly before, take on a new significance. She thought of places where she had been years ago as a child with her father and Winifred; caves on thickly timbered hillsides where they had camped, sheltering, perhaps, where no other human being had ever sheltered; sandstone boulders upon which she had lain with warmth beating up into her body from a rough surface which, conceivably, had never before known the touch of any mortal hand; a sense which had come to her dimly, sometimes, of living in a place incredibly fresh, unstaled, hopeful; and she knew now that her childish acceptance of these good things, her unthinking sense of unity with them, were the measure of its influence and the test of its mysterious power.

*   *   *   *   *

Cheered and subtly reassured, she began writing. The lines of her story took stronger contours in her mind, the characters became clearer, like people advancing out of a fog, but she knew all the same as she wrote that it would be just another example of deft literary architecture, another neatly fitting mosaic of words. . . . Still scribbling, she sighed. She had taken to writing stories with this "period" background several years ago. They had sold well, and that had seemed a sufficient reason for exploiting the vein until it ran out. By now, fed by necessary research, her mental picture of the city in its infancy had grown so familiar to her that she had often felt when she had stepped out again from this quiet room into the daylight, and looked up and down Macquarie Street, surprised to find it no longer that city, no longer the straggling settlement of a handful of colonists, its streets no longer traversed by carriages and bullock waggons, its womenfolk no longer picking their way delicately upon tiny feet beneath gigantic crinolines.

At such times her eyes always went instinctively to the harbour. That had hardly changed, and it gave her some guarantee of permanence, some impression of an abiding character that nothing could destroy. More than once upon her expeditions about the city and its suburbs she had felt a sudden startled recognition of its ubiquitousness; down there near the Heads, she thought, you lived at its very source, but when your tram or bus plunged out from between some tangle of shops or houses in Mosman or Cremorne, a glimpse of it below you took you by surprise. When Sim's car whisked you off for long drives you were always meeting it somewhere, crossing it by one bridge or another; you had seen it from the window of a cottage in Middle Harbour, from the top of some dingy street in Woolloomooloo, from the roof of flats in Darlinghurst, from the balcony of a house in Drummoyne. It was so vitally a part of the city, so entangled in one way or another with the lives of its inhabitants, in so true a sense their highway and their playground, that its permanence seemed to promise them, too, security and anchorage.

She finished the passage she was copying, and began soberly to draw patterns in the margin, her mind returning again to her story. She had begun to suspect that her tenacious use of this period as a setting for her tales might have its roots in her own limitations. A careful attention to historical facts, an accuracy of historical detail—these were matters right into her hands; and if the stories had a dim unreality, a decorative air as of a formal design, perhaps it seemed not altogether unnatural in stories of a time and place so unfamiliar to their readers? If the characters moved and spoke with a slightly stilted air, might it not be attributable to the odd conventions of their period? And if they remained, for all the minuteness of description which she lavished on their clothes and their appearances, lifeless, was that not after all inevitable, for were they not indubitably dead?

She made a little sound of impatience and disgust. It had none of the frustrated despair of the artist to whom the faculty for seeing but not the technique for interpreting beauty had been given, for she had no illusions about her lack of literary ability, and no real regret. The proceeds of this free-lance journalism, added to her typing fees, made just the difference between an uncomfortable poverty and a poverty with occasional alleviations, and it was nothing but financial stress which kept her at it. Armed with a natural perseverance and a dozen pen names, she scattered through the weekly and monthly journals stories, paragraphs at whose fatuity she scowled or giggled according to her mood, brief articles, household hints, gardening hints, dressmaking hints and even, upon one occasion, when she felt impish, mothercraft hints, and earnest advice to wives upon how to retain their husbands' waning love. She had a flair, too, for innocuous verse of that convenient two-inch length which so comfortably fills the odd corners of a women's paper, and which, at sixpence a line, paid her quite well for the ten minutes spent in its composition.

The impulse of depression which had just prompted her exclamation was less the result of a knowledge of the essential worthlessness of what she was doing than a conviction that the time and energy which she was using so badly could be used well. But how?

The complicated maze of black patterns crept down the margin of the page. Sim was impressed by her stories, and thought them "jolly good." Roger laughed at them. He said: "You have the critical, not the creative, mind. Why don't you leave all this alone and do something you *can* do?"

But she was not ready yet, she was not sure. . . .

She scribbled suddenly all over her careful lines and circles, tormented by the ruthlessness of her intellect which would not allow her to divorce her personal problems from the vast, the bewildering, the menacing problems of all humanity, with which they seemed so alarmingly entangled. For she could not, having a devastat-

ingly direct and logical habit of thought, embrace one
creed and live another. Even less, being full of the normal
ardours of youth, could she dismiss the emotion which
last night had flared to its natural consummation; and an
overwhelming recognition that these two loyalties were
utterly irreconcilable filled her with a wild and dreadful
despair. It brought with it, as a temporary collapse of
morale so often does, awareness of intense physical
fatigue. Her few hours of restless sleep had hardly
touched the outskirts of that spent, black weariness in
which she had fallen into bed, before her father's summons to their early-morning swim had dragged her back
to consciousness again. The sting and exhilaration of the
water had braced her, sustained her up to this moment,
but now, with her arms folded across her scattered papers,
her eyes fixed unseeingly upon her scribbled notes, she
felt herself assailed by the same sense of spiritual solitude
which had so tortured Winifred earlier in the day.

What could one do, she thought hopelessly, but use
one's eyes and ears and then bring such intelligence as
one had to bear upon the strange things which one heard,
and saw and read? And yet the dogmatic sureness which
had once been genuine, and which she sometimes simu-
lated still, was really only a curtain now to hide a quak-
ing uncertainty and irresolution. It had been easy enough
to hold theories so long as they remained pleasant mental
abstractions. She was used to those. She had been
brought up on them. Her earliest recollections were of
lively debates between her father and any one of a dozen
friends who haunted their home to talk to him. She
thought, with a faint bitterness: "Fathers with a gift for
conversation lay up a peck of trouble for their children!"
Ideas, and the words with which to express them, had
been toys of her childhood along with books and dolls.
Dissections, ruthless and witty, of creeds, motives, conventions and superstitions had formed a background to
her life, made a deep and lasting impression upon a mind
consciously occupied with more childish affairs; and the
habit of never accepting any dogma upon trust had been

instilled into her along with the habit of brushing her teeth. She remembered her father saying once: "There's only one thing on earth you must accept without question, and that's the weather."

So that by now questioning was part of her. She could no more accept without question than she could breathe without air. But to live in this world, to read as she had always read, voraciously, and to be unable to accept, was a continual torment. Hard enough, ugly enough, even before Sim had come along to add a closer and more personal note to her perplexities; and now so hard that even her tough and resilient youth quailed before it.

There was no place in her mind for superstition, but one thing, all her life, had touched her with an irrational chill. When anyone asked her the date of her birth, and she replied: "August 4th, 1914," there was a pause. It might be so brief that it was hardly discernible, or there might be a glance with it, or even a remark. But it never passed unnoticed. It was not an ordinary date, it was a date of legendary ill omen; she had been born into a world of chaos. She had always felt herself obscurely tied by coincidence to the horrors of that time, so remote, so unreal to others of her generation, and she had read with a dreadful, uncontrollable curiosity book after book dealing with the events which had been born with her. People upon whom death was advancing at a time when she was advancing upon life—Tisza, Kitchener, Jean Jaures, Edith Cavell, Czar Nicholas, a line of figures luridly illumined by the glare of war—were poignantly real to her, and her knowledge of world events in the years before and immediately following her birth was probably more accurate and more detailed than that of many people, now middle-aged or elderly, who had lived through them. For by the time she was old enough to be interested and to hunt for information, the heat and hysteria of combat had given place to a more detached attitude of mind. Books were being written by people who, already, had emancipated themselves from the reek

191

of prejudice and hatred, and were hunting sincerely and without bias for the truth. Hunting with an undercurrent of desperation which impressed her, for in all their writings she felt the same fear beating: *"If we don't find the true causes of this thing and destroy them it will happen all over again."*

She felt her way through their arguments, she explored their analyses and weighed their remedies. She was astonished and angry and alarmed when she became convinced at last that the world was not run by people of integrity—not even, for the most part, by people of intelligence. The faith of the child in the adult dies so hard that she persisted, well on into her teens, in the naive belief that if a man held a high position it was because he was fitted to hold it. The jargons of finance and diplomacy at first impressed her. They sounded so complicated and so extremely wise that she was awed; but the habit of non-acceptance, firmly rooted, drove her on to investigation, to questioning of her father, and long hours of silent listening when he talked to his friends, to argument and discussion with Winifred and with Roger, and to still more determined reading. She found, to her amazement and dismay, that her own childishly simple and completely unlearned ideas, of which she had been so humbly ashamed, and which she had been so anxious to improve, were the ones which emerged unshaken from any test to which she could put them; while at ideas expressed in print by the great ones of the earth she could often only stare in unbelieving horror.

The natural gaiety and light-heartedness of youth worked hard to push such dark preoccupations from her mind; she often forgot, dancing and swimming and tramping in the bush with groups of her contemporaries, that such problems existed. But she had been for far too long her father's housekeeper and constant companion. There came a moment, always, when she felt an envy which was almost hatred for her carefree young friends—boys and girls who just *might* have heard of the Treaty of Versailles, but had certainly never read the Covenant of the

League of Nations; to whom struggles in Manchuria and Paraguay and Abyssinia might have been struggles in Mars for all they felt themselves concerned or affected. To whom Lenin was a name vaguely connected with Communism, and Karl Marx someone who had had some kind of doctrine. Who had never heard of the Kellogg Pact or the Locarno Treaty, and who would probably have guessed that the Statute of Westminster was something to do with Charles I. . . .

And they were happier than she was. So much happier. So much more free, so much more contented without scruples and indignations to perplex their minds and hamper their actions. If she could be like them she would marry Sim. There would be no need to hunt, with increasing panic, for some common standard of thought or behaviour, no need to fear the material wealth he was so eager to lay at her feet, as if it carried with it some obscure contamination. . . .

She shivered a little. The anguish of revelation which had accompanied her surrender last night overwhelmed her again. Your body could give itself with joy, but your mind, like a small, bright, constant flame, like a lighthouse beam over a turbulent sea of passion, stood aloof. Saying: *"This has nothing to do with me."* Saying: *"All this sort of thing is no good, you know, unless I'm satisfied, too."*

And it wasn't satisfied, it wasn't . . .

She stood up so abruptly that her papers scattered on the floor, and she bent, groping under the table, to pick them up. She took longer than was necessary, because tears had filled her eyes and rolled down her cheeks before she could stop them. She gathered her notes together and stuffed them into her old music case. She left the room, walking fast and blindly, and came out on to the steps in the sunlight, looking over the tree-tops in the Gardens to the water beyond. She ran across the road; her hurried glance as she skirted an oasis of green, clipped grass in the middle of it, showed her a figure in Elizabethan clothes, with quill poised over his tablets, and as she went

193

through the iron gates into the Gardens some chain of association was leading her thoughts to words:

>" *'Let me not to the marriage of true minds*
> *Admit impediment. . . .'*

He says '*minds*.' '*Let me not to the marriage of true minds . . .*' "

The asphalt path was hot through her thin-soled shoes, and she stepped on to the grass, her memory still groping for half-remembered lines.

>" *'. . . it is an ever fixed mark*
> *That looks on tempests and is never shaken.'*

That was almost what I was thinking in the library. A light over a sea of passion. But he means love, and I meant . . . I was thinking of the mind. . . . Is it the same thing? '*The marriage of true minds. . . .*' "

She came to a seat and sat down on it, fumbling in her bag for a cigarette, and thinking: "Of course I can't marry him. Of course I can't. This dreadful feeling of being in love with him, this helpless feeling of being tossed about by something too· strong for you . . . '*looks on tempests and is never shaken. . . .*' " She gave an involuntary and half-hysterical laugh, inhaled a mouthful of smoke, and began to cough, mopping tears from her eyes which were only partly due to that sudden paroxysm, and thinking wildly: "Poor Sim, darling Sim, I think you must be nothing but a tempest! . . ."

*   *   *   *   *

Ian said into the telephone on his desk:

"Yes, Mrs. Denning, thank you, they would enjoy it tremendously. Yes. Did you say Brenda was going, too? It's very good of Mrs. Trugg. Yes, I'm sure she will. I'm usually on the ten-to-five myself. but, anyhow, they'll be all right if she will see them on to it. Thanks very much. Good-bye."

He hung the receiver up, but kept his hand on it. He was not sure yet what that unexpected voice from next door to his home had done to him, but he was conscious that his day was shattered. He thought: "When you know something is inevitable, when you have accepted it as a fact that there's nothing you can do about it, that acceptance makes a sort of foundation for you to build walls about you. Protective walls of work or routine; perhaps of losing yourself in sensuous enjoyments, music, books, lovely places. You can make yourself a life of sorts, and nearly every bit of you can forget the thing you're starving for. . . .

"But it's precarious, a house of cards; some breath of a reminder, some trivial association hitting your consciousness suddenly, and it falls flat. You're exposed again. . . ."

He looked at his hand still resting on the receiver. To call a number, to ask a question, to hear her voice. To say—what?

He stood up violently and went to his open window, thinking restlessly that he would like to go to the Zoo himself this afternoon, and realising with irritation immediately afterwards that his wish was not really a wish for the Zoo, but for a return to the restful and carefree joys of childhood. It was a day, he thought, filling his pipe, his eyes absently on the busy Quay below, for being out of doors, and he decided on an impulse to walk up through the Gardens and lunch at the little kiosk near the Art Gallery.

Alone. Not the word, but the conception smote him, and he found himself with his back to the window, staring at the telephone again. He felt a kind of despairing anger that the small pleasures of his daily existence should be dimmed by the mere fact of being solitary experiences, and in a momentary reaction of defiance he determined that not even Winifred's absence should spoil his walk, his hour in the sun, his difficult appreciation of a day which Denis and Jonathan would take so effortlessly to their hearts. That resentment with which the normal person realises that he is behaving abnormally made him turn again to the window, and study with conscious deliberation the crowded street below. He had almost instantly

195

his reward, for he saw Roger Blair walking across the street with an elderly man, hatless, a bundle of magazines under his arm, his fair hair roughened by the sharp breeze from the water, his hands moving in rapid explanatory gestures, his whole body alive with the earnestness of debate. Ian, as they passed beneath his window, screwed a small piece of paper into a ball and dropped it at Roger's feet. A dozen passers-by turned, startled at his shout of recognition and salutation as he looked up. He disposed of his companion with a word and a clap on the shoulder which made him stagger a little, and dived inside the entrance below Ian's window.

Ian puffed soberly at his pipe, thinking that by now he should be used to Roger's impetuosities. It was, he reflected, the man's peculiar charm that you did not get used to him, that it was not possible, in fact, to get used to a person from whom you could only expect the unexpected. Even his knock, Ian's thought went on as an exuberantly rhythmed rat-tat-tat sounded on his door, was something which you had not anticipated, and yet which you recognised once it had happened as inevitably Roger's. You could picture him as if you had been there, pressing the bell of the old-fashioned lift downstairs, pressing it again, pivoting on one heel, peering up the lift well, whistling, pressing the button again, and finally, just as the lift was beginning its deliberate descent from the top floor, losing patience and dashing for the stairs, taking them three at a time, arriving breathless at your door to hammer out that knock in answer to which you were now calling: "Come in!"

But he was in already. And breathless. Ian's smile, begun as one of amusement, camouflaged itself tactfully as one purely of welcome. He asked:

"What have you got there? The new *Free Voice*?"

Roger, already fluttering pages, said with enthusiasm: "The best number yet. Magnificent stuff. Look here . . ."

But Ian, although he looked, saw nothing. His head was beginning to ache again, not violently yet but with

196

a sly, subdued menace which sent his thoughts back painfully to problems which he longed to forget for a little while. With his eyes blindly on the turning pages of Roger's magazine, his ears, unheeding, filled with the sound of Roger's voice, it was really Winifred's empty window-sill which he was seeing, Arthur's voice, high with abuse, which he was hearing. He said abruptly:

"Where are you lunching? I want a walk and a bit of fresh air. What about coming with me up to the Art Gallery kiosk?"

Roger, he thought, never seemed to need a moment for reflection. His "Yes, rather, splendid idea!" came promptly. He was ready. He was at the door waiting before Ian, more deliberately moving, had tidied away the papers on his desk, and assured himself of matches and tobacco in his pocket.

Once he was out of the room and walking down the stairs, he felt calmer, as if he had left a danger behind. He suspected the telephone—that insidious link stretching so temptingly, and yet with such futility, between himself and Winifred. Now, free from its black and subtle glitter, he went out into the sunlight beside Roger, and they walked across the Quay, dodging taxis and pedestrians, and up the less frequented street past the small, stone building of the Water Police. As they emerged from it into the long, palm-fringed street which crossed it at right angles, Ian found himself thinking with some amusement: "Macquarie Street, Macquarie Place, Macquarie House, Macquarie Range, Lake Macquarie, Port Macquarie, Fort Macquarie, Macquarie Falls. To say nothing of the Lachlan River. And probably half a dozen more!" And he said to Roger as they crossed the road and entered the Gardens:

"This chap strewed his name about, didn't he? Macquarie?"

Roger shrugged.

"The importation of place-names," he said, "along with the importation of rabbits, blackberries, prickly pear, convicts, sheep and traditions . . . isn't that Lesley over there?"

"Looks like her."

"It is. Do you mind if I don't lunch with you after all, old chap? Right! Here, take one of these. Take two. See you again soon. Cheerio!"

He strode across the grass, waving his bundle of magazines, and Lesley, watching him, stopped telling herself that she wanted to be alone and thought with a faint shrug and a smile: "Oh, well, Roger's nothing if not stimulating. . . ."

He said, throwing himself and the magazines at her feet:

"Hullo there! I thought you were examining bones in the Morgue."

"I was. Where were you off to with Ian?"

"Lunch or something I think. Yes, lunch. Have you had some?"

"I don't want any. It's too hot."

"You've been crying."

"Well, what of it?"

"It's stupid, that's all. You mustn't sentimentalise things. Either you get what you want out of life or you don't. If you don't you haven't tried hard enough. In either case . . ."

"Oh, shut up, Roger. It so happens that I felt inclined to cry."

"Heat, nerves, hunger, or perhaps—no, you were swimming this morning, weren't you?"

She laughed in spite of herself.

"You haven't an inhibition to bless yourself with, have you? Anyhow, it doesn't affect me like that. I . . ."

"God be praised. I had an elder sister, and whenever . . ."

She interrupted impatiently:

"Blow your sister. Have you got a cigarette? I've smoked all mine."

"Loads. Here you are. Three. What's the matter?"

"Oh, Lord, Roger, I don't know exactly. I'm all mixed up. Life's pretty darned difficult."

He lay on his back on the grass and locked his hands behind his head. He said comfortably:

"You don't mean life, you mean marriage."

She retorted swiftly:

"Once you're married your marriage *is* your life. It's silly to pretend otherwise. You can fill your time up with outside interests as much as you like—your life is still 'married life.' Everything you do, everything you think, has got to be fitted into it. . . ."

He made no reply. This, in a man so given to swift and impulsive speech, caused a little surprised check in the flow of her thought, and she looked down at him, wondering if it were only the angle from which she was seeing him which made his face seem unfamiliar. Two sharp lines ran vertically between his eyes, deepened now by the contraction of his brows against the strong sunlight, and his mouth in repose, as one so seldom saw it, had a set which spelt doggedness and tenacity. She was startled to realise that for years she had thought of him with a kind of affectionate amusement as a voice which could be relied upon to make unconventional statements and propound unconventional theories in a manner which people, according to their various tastes, found entertaining, stimulating, controversial or merely irritating. A voice which was one—perhaps the most voluble—of a dozen voices which had formed her intellectual background, expressed a set of ideas which blended with but did not dominate the incredibly diverse sets of ideas which other voices had expressed. She had never doubted his sincerity or his enthusiasm, but her own painfully developing standard of belief had remained unaffected by them; and now, with a faint sense of wonder, she realised that to him they were important enough to demand and receive sacrifices.

With an uncomfortable sense of humiliation she evoked deliberately a memory of him when she had first known him—when he had been brought to their house by Judge Merriman and introduced as a young scholar with a distinguished academic record, and an indubitably brilliant future. From there, she thought soberly, he had thought it worth while to sink—or perhaps he would say rise—to a life devoted solely to the advancement of culture in a country where culture was almost sublimely disregarded. Shorn at last of everything but his energy and his conviction, he was still crusading; and, she thought, whether you shared his conviction or not, whether you approved of his methods or not, you could not fail to respect his courage and his tenacity of purpose. You could not help feeling rather grateful for a demonstration that there was such a thing as a conviction. And that it was a powerful and sustaining thing to have. And you could not help wishing that, uncomfortable as its results might be, you could have one, too, as clear-cut, as compelling as his. . . .

She asked lamely:

"Or—don't you think so?"

He sat up cross-legged, gripping his ankles, his head back so that the smoke from his cigarette drifted upward clear of his eyes.

He said:

"It depends on the marriage. If it's the right sort of marriage it does the fitting. There's nothing irrevocable about an environment, a habit of life. But there's something absolutely irrevocable about a habit of thought."

She was very tired, and her mind, usually swift and sure, fumbled clumsily at his meaning. She asked doubtfully:

"You mean the marriage . . . ?"

He interrupted with his usual impatient vigour:

"I mean it may be possible to adjust a marriage to fit your conception of life, but it's utterly impossible to alter your conception of life to fit your marriage."

"Which means," she said slowly, "that two differing conceptions of life can—never marry."

"No more," he said cheerfully, "than two parallel lines can meet."

Paint was peeling from the wooden bench, and she made a heap of tiny flakes in the palm of her hand and stirred it with her little finger while she spoke again.

"You're always dead sure of everything, aren't you? It must be nice."

"I'm dead sure of my own job—not much else. But there's no question about that. This thing has to be done. It will be done. Your father says: 'Wait, have patience, and it will do itself.' But there isn't time to wait. A national culture isn't a luxury, a toy of the intelligentsia—it's a necessity. If people don't realise that they must be made to realise it. They must be made to see, to begin with, that a country can't go on indefinitely exporting its talent and its ability any more than a human body can go on indefinitely losing blood. The psychology of the *émigré.* . . ."

Lesley stroked her circle of paint flakes into a pile, leaning back against the seat, her eyes half-closed. She felt her lips move involuntarily into the smile with which she usually listened to Roger's dissertations—a smile which was not so much for the matter as for the manner—and with that smile and the sound of his voice and the heat of the sun on her bare arms, she was able to feel again that unhappiness was a part, and not the whole, of life. She listened to, but made no effort to consider, his words. She was too tired, too sleepy. An aftermath of passion still held her tranced, as lethargy succeeds delirium, and she heard him as one sees familiar objects when fever has abated, incuriously, recognising them with detachment as parts of a world to which one must presently return.

But Roger's were not words you could hear for very long with indifference. The quality of his conversation lay in the sudden assaults which it made upon preconceived ideas. Her sluggish consciousness was subjected intermittently to shocks as abrupt and rudely stimulating as the spanks with which a new-born child is jolted into life and breathing. From words which flowed with comparative smoothness through her mind there suddenly emerged: ". . . because, quite obviously, the natural capital of this country is Alice Springs . . ." and, blinking, she felt her reluctant attention drawn, pinioned, challenged into awareness. She thought: "It's rather like being smacked violently first on one cheek and then on the other. . . ."

". . . *the Sahara Desert was once good grazing land, now it's the Sahara Desert. That's a lesson for us. There's not the slightest doubt that of all our imported pests the merino sheep is the most deadly and dangerous. . . .*"

She protested:

"Oh, Roger, don't! Not now. I can't keep up with you to-day. Couldn't you say something nice and—sedative? Like a leader out of the *Messenger*?"

"That," he objected, "would be emetic, not sedative. What's the matter with you, anyhow?"

"I don't know. I feel jittery."

He asked abruptly:

"Are you and Sim engaged?"

Her heart gave a sudden bound against her chest, and in her astonishment she forgot, for a moment, to reply. The mere sound of Sim's name, the mere suggestion in words of that which some part of her so ardently desired, had the power to alter or check the flow of her blood, to dislocate the smooth working of her heart, to cause that thump, that blow, as if some prisoner within her were trying wildly to answer: "Yes! Yes! We are!"

She said wearily:

"I—I'm afraid we're—parallel lines, Roger."

He said in his matter-of-fact way:

"Of course. I hoped you'd find it out in time. Now you and I are definitely converging."

"Con——?"

She stared at him for a moment and then began to laugh.

"Are you proposing to me, Roger?"

"Certainly I'm proposing. What's wrong with you? I've never known you so dull. Do you want children?"

"Yes, in moderation."

"What do you call moderation?"

"Oh—I suppose three or four."

"Four's all right. Three isn't enough. Allowing for the sterile and the unmarried it leaves the population static. This country must be populated. We must have at least ten million . . ."

Lesley's nerves betrayed her into a half-hysterical shriek of laughter.

"Roger, I'm not a microbe."

His thought interrupted, he baulked for a moment and then joined her in a shout of laughter which frightened the pigeons away. He scrambled up from the grass and sat beside her on the seat, and suddenly, with his physical nearness, panic assailed her, and she felt her precarious laughter trembling on the verge of tears. She jumped up, brushing at her eyes with her handkerchief, and said crisply:

"This is a perfectly imbecile conversation. I'm hungry."

He reminded her: "You said you weren't."

She looked at him for a second in speechless irritation, and then replied with deadly restraint:

"Well—I—am."

He collected his magazines from the grass and asked with obvious good-humour:

"Where shall we go? Follow Ian to the kiosk? Give me that bag."

She moved her shoulders in a faint shrug. She was not really hungry, but she was alarmed and annoyed by her near abandonment to "nerves," and she suspected that food and strong coffee might restore normality to a world at present curiously distorted. She walked beside Roger down curving paths and across green lawns and under widely spreading trees. She paused for a moment to look at the cloudy pink of the vast Cape Chestnut in full flower behind the Conservatorium, and another moment beneath a flame tree whose fallen blossoms already made a vermilion carpet where pigeons moved, convulsively pecking; and though she noticed that Roger was unaccountably silent she was both too tired and too uncertain of her emotional equilibrium to question him. The dull tension which she could feel in herself puzzled and exasperated her. It was as though, struggle as she might, some fine invisible thread stretched between herself and Sim, not drawing her to him, but simply holding her, denying her a complete liberty. She thought wryly: "I'm going all D. H. Lawrence! I suppose you have to go through this before you realise how terribly accurately he paints—one side of the picture!"

Roger had stopped. She looked in some surprise at the statue he was studying. *"Mars."* A very innocent and infantile looking Mars, she thought. An obviously pre-war Mars. She glanced from it to Roger's intent face. He said:

"One day when I was about eighteen and the war was just over I was sitting up there on the grass waiting for someone, and a returned soldier came along on crutches, his left leg off at the knee. I saw him stop and stare at this thing for quite a while, and then he came close and did something to it. When he had gone I was inquisitive enough to come down and have a look. He had scribbled a thick black pencil mark round its left leg at the knee."

He peered closely and then straightened with a laugh.

"Of course, there wouldn't be a sign of it now. That was nearly twenty years ago and he's been all nicely scrubbed and whitewashed many times since then. But it made a great impression on me at the time. I'd been just too young for the war, you see, and I'd felt pretty bitter about it. I'd had all the usual dope pumped into me. Flags and glory, King and Country, war to end war—all that stuff. That pencil mark was the beginning of my disillusionment. I mean I had my first vivid realisation of war as destruction. Life destroyed, limbs destroyed, happiness and work and faith destroyed. I remember standing here on this very spot and getting what was the most staggering thought to me in those days: *'And what the hell did it have to do with us, anyhow?'* It came, but it went again, pretty quickly. We were all very effectively doped. You come out of that kind of anæsthesia just as you come out of chloroform—with struggling and nausea and vomiting and relapses. We only saw things in flashes, when something startled us. Ten minutes later I was up to the neck in King and Country again. And that shows you what a catchword can do to your intelligence. How can we, here, be for 'King and Country'? At a time like that your choice is King *or* Country. This is our country, crying out for population. How did we serve her? Sent away three hundred and thirty thousand of our finest sires to be killed or mutilated. It had taken us a hundred and thirty years to build up a population of nearly five million, and in four years sixty thousand of them were slaughtered by which, at a conservative estimate, a hundred and twenty thousand more were denied their existence. Like hell we served our country!"

She looked at him thoughtfully. Her eyes moved from his face to his collar, which was slightly frayed, to his suit, which was slightly shabby, to his feet. . . .

"What size shoes do you take, Roger?"

"Eh? Shoes? Eights. What on earth . . . ?"

She flushed.

"Goodness knows. I just wondered."

She stood looking down at the hot asphalt, the edge of the grass, the white pedestal of the statue. It was no use trying not to compare Sim and Roger. When two men wanted you you had to compare them, to weigh the qualities of one against the qualities of the other. You had to evoke, deliberately, a mental picture of Sim's lean, long-legged body, his sun-tanned face and his engaging white smile, the casual perfection of his tailoring, the easy and charming authority of his manner. You had to set beside it Roger's massive solidity, his utter lack of self-consciousness, a concentration so intense that his really lively sense of humour remained for long periods buried under the weight of his preoccupations. You had to face, unwillingly, a dispassionate estimate of Sim, and you had to bring a dispassionate estimate of Roger to confront it.

205

You had to compare a man whose weapon was a conviction with a man whose weapon was—a cheque-book.

So violent was her emotional recoil from this conclusion that she said aloud: "No—not . . ." and then stopped, embarrassed, seeing Roger scowling down at her. He asked relentlessly:

"Not . . ."

She admitted desperately:

"I was thinking of Sim. He really is a fine person, Roger, I mean he could be. I was thinking that his only weapon was his cheque-book, but that isn't fair. He's really generous, really clever, really courageous, and kind . . ."

Roger interrupted:

"Good God, Lesley, a cheque-book isn't a weapon. It's a pair of handcuffs. Of course, Sim's all you say. He's a great chap. But it's in spite of his cheque-book, not because of it. He'd be a darned sight finer without it. The trouble is you can't just throw handcuffs away. You haven't got them—they've got you. He's been struggling against that cheque-book of his ever since I knew him, but he'll never get away from it now. You know the saying about fire—a good servant but a bad master. That's even more true of wealth. If you earn it yourself you can, if you're one in a million, stop earning when you've got enough, you have to be one in ten million to know when you've got enough, by the way. But if you're one of those poor devils born, as the saying goes, with a silver spoon in your mouth, God help you! And He won't. It's no good crying, Lesley. . . ."

"I'm not crying."

"No, but you want to. I know you're in love with Sim. I don't blame you. And as far as I'm concerned if you hadn't said what you did about parallel lines I wouldn't have butted in at all. But once you've seen that for yourself there's no way back. Whether you marry me or not, you can't marry Sim. Unless you want a life like your sister's. . . ."

She flared out angrily:

"That's not true, Roger! Sim isn't Arthur Sellman."

He said reflectively:

"No. But when Arthur married your sister he wasn't so very different from Sim. I'm only a year or so younger than he is, you know. I remember him well. He was less intelligent than Sim, a good deal better-looking, equally good-natured, equally generous, equally rich. He hadn't Sim's sense of humour. He wasn't essentially as decent a cove as Sim. But he wasn't the mess he is now. Nor—listen to this—need he have become such a mess if he hadn't made a miserable and bewildering marriage. Be quiet. I know you think all the time of the wrong he has done to Winifred. You just think for a change of the wrong she has done him. Not intentionally, of course. But if he had married someone of his own kind his life would still have been stupid from our point of view—*but not from his*. It would still have seemed to us a rather ugly and meaningless sort of existence, but it would have satisfied him. He'd have still been a lazy, smug, parasitic nonentity, but he wouldn't have been a drunkard and a sadist."

"Sim . . ."

"Sim's subject to certain laws of Nature like everybody else. Parallel lines won't meet. Can you see me married to Lorna Sellman? The capacity for murder is latent in me just as it is in everybody. Look here, consider this—do I talk too much?"

"You know perfectly well you do."

"I always have. Pity. However, certain conditions are necessary for the healthy growth of plants—sun, rain, chemicals in the soil and what not. For the health of human bodies, proteins, fats, carbohydrates and sundry vitamins. You can't recognise that and then sling your whole mental and moral life into an unsuitable environment and say: 'I'll make it do.' You can make it do. If you try you simply get distortion. People floundering in an impossible marriage are guilty of things they'd be utterly incapable of normally. Cruelty, vindictiveness, spying, pettiness, hatred, deceit . . ." He stopped, breathless, and then added with a note of urgency which startled her: "Don't get yourself into that kind of mess."

She said flatly:

"Come along. We won't find a table. That place is always packed. Why haven't you ever married, Roger? How old are you?"

"I'm thirty-seven. I suppose until I was thirty or thereabouts I was too busy. And since then I've been waiting for you."

She looked at him unbelievingly.

"Since I was sixteen?"

"Certainly."

"Are you pulling my leg?"

"Why should I? I've done other things, too, you understand. To fill in the time. Waiting isn't my long suit."

She walked beside him silently, her head bent. It seemed queer somehow, she thought, that after waiting the Biblical seven years he should have proposed marriage to her on this day of all others. She wondered if he would mind much about Sim. Men, on this particular point, were often still incomprehensibly feudal. She did not want to hurt him. Already there was stirring in her a protective impulse towards him, an odd, warm, amusing sensation of being responsible for him, and she said with an uncertain laugh:

"You know, Roger, you arouse my maternal instincts. I want to—to mother you, but I'm afraid that's all."

He answered with cheerful confidence:

"Naturally it's all at present. You're still sensually, at all events, in love with Sim. Besides I've been making love under difficulties. I manage much better indoors. I haven't had a chance yet."

She said maliciously:

"So it has been love-making? I wasn't sure."

He grinned at her.

"You will be."

They passed, side by side, through the gate leading into the Domain.

Steam went up in a fine wavering column from Arthur's untouched coffee-cup, and smoke in another column, denser and more compact, from the cigarette in its saucer; slumped in a deep leather armchair he watched them morosely, hypnotised by their movement, so that it seemed to him as if his thoughts, too, were a vaporous emanation beyond his own control, weaving up to the softly lighted ceiling of the hotel lounge.

Gordon and Freeman, who had lunched with him, had gone. They had all begun their meal late and lingered over it, and he supposed lethargically that he, too, should be getting back to his office, for it was nearly three o'clock. He had left his car parked up in Macquarie Street when he had called for Freeman at his consulting-rooms, and they had walked down the two blocks to the hotel to meet Gordon. Now the thought of walking back up the hill in the heat filled him with a heavy and sluggish apprehension, for the task of digesting oysters and toheroa soup, sole, duckling with green peas, a good deal of gruyere and a couple of lagers was still claiming most of his energy. Besides he did not really want to go back to his office. He knew, and the knowledge pricked rather than reassured him, that he was not needed there. So long as he turned up now and then to sign cheques. . . .

Storey did the work. That was fair enough. He was handsomely paid for it. But there persisted in Arthur's mind the knowledge that although his own office was larger and more luxuriously appointed than Storey's, although Storey consulted him with a rather pointed meticulousness about everything, Storey was really "Sellman's," and "Sellman's" could more justly be called "Storey's."

There was something about Storey, he thought, that you couldn't put your finger on, but that was, all the same, offensive. He was big and ugly and nonchalant. He dressed badly and was beginning to go bald, but he had only to grin at one of the typists or say a genial word to one of the departmental managers to have them at his feet. He would come into your office with his hands full

209

of papers and find you reading the *Sporting Times*, and
he would say: "Are you busy, Mr. Sellman? How about
these estimates for the new restaurant?" And there was
just the shadow of an inflection in his voice, just the ghost
of an expression on his face which suggested the obvious
fact that he could see very well that you weren't busy.
That he understood you to be perfectly well aware that
all he wanted was a formal consent to his already per-
fected arrangements!

Arthur said to a passing waiter:

"Bring me a whisky and soda."

But when it was brought he did not drink it. He
looked at it gloomily several times, wondering if it were
worth the trouble of rousing himself, of hoisting himself
erect in the chair in whose comfortable depths he was
submerged, and he decided that it was not; it was not
worth while making any kind of effort at all. His head
was aching, his stomach queasy, his mind restless, roving,
active with a goaded and unwilling activity which hid
ugly depths of thought as a rippled surface will hide the
bottom of a pool. He told himself wretchedly that he was
not well. He must be sickening for flu or something. He
felt rotten.

Misery engulfed him. He drowned in it, went down
and down to the bottom where rage against Winifred was
strangled by his dreadful need of her, a need by now
so complicated that he did not know himself whether it
had its origin in love or hatred.

To-day she had haunted him. He had not been able
to get out of his mind the picture of her silhouetted
against the wakening light; he had not been able to subdue a sense of bewilderment so strong that it was alarming—for to meet something entirely outside rational explanation, entirely beyond understanding, was like meeting a ghost, taking part in some supernatural event. . . .

It had carried him back through the ten years of their
marriage, sullenly exploring, sullenly remembering, sullenly and increasingly confused, as events piled up,
remembered moods intruded, remembered ecstasies

flashed and faded, remembered furies started again a pulse of excitement and elation.

The failure of their married life, he maintained with stubborn conviction, was her fault, not his. And yet somehow she managed to make him feel guilty. That was the theme which, in all its myriad variations, formed his mystery. What the hell had he done that he should feel guilty? He had given her luxury, devotion, a social position, a child, what more could she want? He would be a fool if he didn't know that he was considered, at the time of their marriage, the catch of their social world. He had a pot of money, all the Sellmans were good-looking, and he was an easy-going, good-natured sort of chap, too darned easy-going as things had turned out!

He had been disappointed—what husband wouldn't be?—when he had found that she would not share his life, which meant, really, his amusements. He had tried, for instance, to interest her in racing. Most women loved a day at Randwick if only to show off their clothes, but after two or three attempts she had laughed and said she would play tennis. He had given her jewels and a fur coat which had made Lorna green with jealousy. She had thanked him, admired them, worn them occasionally, but she didn't really care about them. It was not natural. By degrees she had dropped out of everything. Within three years, except that she lived in his house, their lives no longer touched. But she owed him something.

His thoughts shifted to another plane. They ceased to be progressive and became static. They ceased to state a case and began to show him pictures. Winifred had been very lovely as a girl; her body was still youthful though her face had acquired an unbecomingly settled, almost grim look in the last few years. But he had grown out of the habit of looking at her face long before that. Its expression after the first year or two had disturbed him too much. She was his wife; that was simple enough, wasn't it? They might have rows now and then, most married couples did; they might not have much in common, though that wasn't his fault; they might feel differently about most things—no sane man could share *her* views—but they were still husband and wife. Nothing, as he had pointed out to her, affected that. It was simply silly to go on and on saying: "No, Arthur," and "Please, Arthur," and "Arthur, I'm tired . . ."

He had been perfectly good-tempered about it.

"Don't be ridiculous, Win. What's it got to do with a bit of a tiff this morning?"

"Arthur, I can't . . ."

"Look here, old girl, you're just being hysterical."

"No."

"What's that scent? Something new?"

"Scent? No—I suppose it's soap. Please, Arthur, don't . . ."

"For God's sake, Win—have you been married three years or three days? Don't be childish!"

"Arthur, I mean it. Don't make me hate you. . . ."

"You don't hate me, sweetheart. Come here. . . ."

Of course, she didn't hate you. Why should she? It was a sort of fad to resist. Some women were like that. The fact was they enjoyed a siege and repelled it as long as possible to sharpen the pleasure of capitulation. That was all. You had only to keep your temper and laugh at her pretended reticences. It wasn't possible that she could still be angry afterwards; it wasn't possible that the generous ardours which had thrilled and, yes, perhaps very faintly shocked you in the first year of married life should have genuinely altered to this silent and weary submission.

For it had always ended, at first, in submission. There had come to be, for him, a kind of added excitement in breaking down her preliminary resistance, and she had seemed to sense that, and had resisted no more. Then it became dull, and he was angry. What husband wouldn't be? One night he had called her names just to arouse her from her infuriating passivity, and he had succeeded so well that she had struck at him in a blaze of fury, and he had carried a bruise on his cheek for days

212

afterwards. But no names he had ever called her since had moved her. She did not seem to hear them.

It was because she had made him so miserable that he had begun to drink a bit more than was good for him. It was because even then the mystery had begun to tease him with nebulous stirrings of a shame he could not account for, and only when he was just a little bit lit up could he ignore them and re-establish the confidence with which he had always faced the world and which was rightfully his by virtue of his wealth.

And now in his thoughts he was back at a night about seven years ago when he had stood at her door saying sheepishly:

"May I come in, Win?"

He could remember very clearly what his feelings had been then. He and George Hegarty had had dinner in town together, and afterwards George had invited him along to the flat where he kept that blonde who had been his typiste. She had had a friend there, a fetching little bit, too, with red hair, and deep in his resentment against Winifred, Arthur had thought: "Well, serve her right! She's asked for it!"

But then, quite suddenly, his need for her, his maddening, agonising need which he had never been able to subdue, had overwhelmed him again, and with his head bent to kiss the red-headed girl it was Winifred's face that he saw, and all his desire was for her presence, to be near her, to hear her speak kindly. He had gone home, ignoring George's chaffing. He had driven furiously, full of an unreflecting sense of optimism. He had stood outside her closed door, and she had answered his knock and his call:

"Yes, come in."

She was always reading. She had a lamp at the head of her bed, and under its soft greenish light the shadows of her lashes were incredibly long, and the skin of her bare arms and shoulders warmly tinted against the pillows, the skin of her breast fading into darkness beneath the sheet. He sat on the edge of the bed, wondering whether to tell her about the red-haired girl or not. After all, what was the good of abstaining if your wife didn't know, didn't commend you, reward you with a kiss, with a little kindness. . . .

Desire stirred in him. Like alcohol, it would bring him a temporary peace. He felt the misery of his craving for her as a companion giving way step by step to the familiar ecstasies of anticipation. She had put her book down and smiled at him.

"Hullo. Are you just home?"

"Yes."

"Had a good day?"

"Oh, the usual. . . . What have you been doing?"

"I went round to see father this morning, but as a matter of fact I've been reading nearly all day."

"You'll spoil your eyes."

She rubbed them with the back of her hand.

"They are rather tired. I'll stop now."

He looked down at the book and was shaken by a storm of resentment. Her reading symbolised her estrangement from him. There she lived in a different world. There she went without him, and found, he knew, some solace which was denied to him. He read the papers, the magazines, a novel now and then. He liked a good story of travel or adventure, or a mystery yarn. They rested a man's brain after the day's work. He had looked at Winifred's books sometimes, read a page here and there, thrown them down. Bosh! Or worse. Words, words, words! But words which filled him, all the same, with an aggrieved and superstitious uneasiness, because he felt that behind them, as behind a barricade, there walked a Winifred he did not know, and could not know.

There remained, obviously, a Winifred he did know. A Winifred he could see and touch. Because he felt some part of her to be inviolate, beyond his reach, beyond the restless and stunted emotion which he called his love, he knew a keener satisfaction in his one unquestionable mastery. He bent over her and felt her stiffen, but she returned his kiss quietly, and her hand, cool and kindly, rested on his cheek. She asked:

214

"What's the matter?" He lifted his head; it was throbbing, and his eyes felt hot. He asked:

"Don't you love me any more, Win?"

She said painfully:

"We don't really seem to get on very well now, do we? I—I am fond of you, Arthur, but I'm afraid—it was a mistake. . . ."

He asked angrily:

"What do you want? Don't I give you everything?"

"Everything you can, I know. . . ."

He sneered:

"Oh, of course, I know I'm not a highbrow like your father and his friends. . . ."

"Arthur, don't talk like that. Do you *want* to go on? Wouldn't you rather . . . couldn't we—quite sensibly and as friends—arrange a divorce?"

He looked down at her, put his lips suddenly against her throat.

"Why should we have a divorce? I love you, Win. You love me too, really, don't you?"

She cried unhappily:

"No, no, Arthur. It's not being kind to lie about a thing like this. I don't love you any more. You—you can't love someone who speaks a different language, who hasn't one thing, one thought in common with you. . . ."

He said thickly, his mouth still buried in the curve where her neck met her shoulder, and where he could feel a small pulse throbbing:

"If we had a child it would be something in common . . ."

She pushed his head away in a panic which roused and angered him anew.

"No, no! It—it would be worse—worse than ever— *Arthur*—Arthur . . . !"

Well, this was all you got for remaining faithful! He said, with a half-hysterical anger:

"Don't be a fool! I've had enough of this. You married me, and you've done nothing but torment me ever since. I've been too patient, that's what . . ."

She had said in a dreadful voice of controlled desperation:

"Arthur, I'll scream. I warn you. I'll scream at the top of my voice."

He had called that bluff. "Go ahead, scream. Who's going to hear you but the servants, and I'll settle them!" But she hadn't screamed. He had known that she would not. She had the devil's own pride, and she hated a scene, a scandal, worse than anything on earth, but she had fought as if she were mad. She had seemed mad for days afterwards. When Brenda had been born blind he had wondered. . . .

But, of course, there was no scientific reason for that. Ridiculous. But she had never so much as looked at him from that day if she could help it. More than seven years. She had demanded, coldly and dispassionately, money—large sums—and she had consulted doctor after doctor without avail. Then she had taken the child abroad, to every eye specialist, to every clinic of repute in Europe, in England, in America. She had spent a fortune, and had returned at last, without hope. Her voice had an edge when she spoke to him, her contempt was like something tangible enmeshing him, but stranger than anything else was the mystery. There was a law, blast it all, a law of cause and effect. Hit a man on the head and he falls down. Overbid someone at an auction and he loses the article he wants. Win a couple of quid at contract, and someone else must lose it. Victor implies vanquished. It is so. But here in this domestic battle the law had failed. He had won. How could you get away from that? He had broken down her resistance, and he had imposed his will upon her—and she was not subdued. She had acquired somehow, instead, the most terrifying moral ascendancy over him, against which, until a year or so ago, he had struggled helplessly. He did not know what her weapon was, he only knew that he had none to meet it. And then she threw it down.

She began her affair with the fellow next door. Going up to town just so that she could come back on the ferry with him. Playing tennis with him round at old Channon's. Lending him books, borrowing books from him, standing on the footpath outside their gate talking endlessly, making herself conspicuous. . . .

She had put herself in the wrong. He had begun to feel again, solid and comforting, those conventions which were the foundations of his life. They supplied him with the only standard he knew, and they said, quite unequivocally, that a married woman must not fall in love with another man. Slowly his confidence returned; he nourished a righteous anger, sustained by the customs of the world he understood. And at George's party last night he had drunk a good deal and he had remembered the red-headed girl. That long ago abstinence, from being an involuntary impulse of recoil, had become transmuted by time into an act of splendid and heroic self-denial. Against it, he had set this new picture of Winifred, false Winifred, admitting and glorying in a sinful love.

Could you be expected to go home and put up with her airs? Could you let her look at you as if you were dirt? The strange inhibition which had held you for so many years was suddenly destroyed, you were free again, and you had another power, another weapon. You had only to say "Brenda," and she was finished. You had her now, at last you had her.

But on the very day of your triumph, in an outburst of rage, you had made a false move. There again, it had been her fault. Fault or intention? She was as wily as the devil. He would never have thought of asking Lorna if she hadn't put the notion into his head that Lorna might lie about it. He had not realised that even if she were lying, Lorna, now, had the whip hand. He had thought of it only as a weapon for himself against Winifred, but he could see now that once having admitted Lorna to the heart of the quarrel he would get no peace till he had divorced Winifred. And the curse of it was that, really, if it came to the point, he did not want to be bothered with a blind daughter. She was a pretty kid— took after the Sellmans in appearance—and if she hadn't

217

been blind he could have been proud of her. Introduced her into the life that was hers by right, and which her mother pretended to despise. But blindness made people —queer. No, he didn't want the responsibility of Brenda. Winifred might suspect that, but she wouldn't risk it. If his hand were forced now by Lorna, he would have to choose between sparing himself the encumbrance of Brenda and inflicting upon Winifred the misery her unfaithfulness so well deserved.

He did not, for one moment, suppose that the mere disgrace would worry her. She had, towards all such matters, an attitude which was positively callous. She displayed at all times an irreverence for the things he held sacred, and an exasperating respect for things quite obviously of no importance. Nothing held her but Brenda— he knew that. No sense of morality, no regard for her reputation or his, no proper deference to public opinion.

So if he just stood firm—didn't allow Lorna to bully him—held the threat of divorce and separation from the child over her head. . . .

His breath came out in a long sigh. It was all right after all. Somehow a man must preserve the sanctity of his home and his own good name. Somehow he must guard himself and his household against scandal. But it was hard, he thought wretchedly, when one had been, one could honestly say, a model husband; when in spite of everything there still remained, like a tormenting irritation in one's heart, love—even forgiveness. . . .

He was tired. He thought:

"Hell! This business has knocked me up!"

He stretched his legs out more comfortably, and settled his head into a dent in the leather. One waiter said to another:

" 'E's off. 'E's been noddin' there for 'alf an hour."

*　　　*　　　*　　　*　　　*

From the back seat, Bing said:

"My God, Julie, just get an eyeful of the proletariat, will you?"

Julie answered something, but Lorna, sitting in front beside Martin, made no reply. She was already looking at the dense, dark crowd, jostling good-naturedly, giving way good-naturedly, as the police moved through it, keeping a way clear for passing cars.

She liked crowds. But, unaccountably, as they had swung round the Queen Victoria statue and come face to face with this one, she had felt for one second a spasm of something which was almost fear. So foolish a reaction could be only transient. It must be, she thought irritably, the heat; or perhaps she was a bit run down, needing a tonic, or a holiday, or a sea trip or something. Nothing had gone right all day. From the first cloudy waking to an unwelcome memory, up to this absurd tremor of fear, it has been full of painful thoughts, unpleasant interviews, anxiety, uneasiness, anger.

That stolen hour on the beach with Sim had so dislocated her time-table that she had been forced to rush the search for a hat, which was an impossible thing to do; you could *not* buy a hat as if it were a pound of butter. And then she had reached home too late for a rest, and too late and too hot and too cross to do more than make a pretence of lunching. She thought now, clasping her gloved hands in her lap: "I couldn't be more nervous if it were my own wedding!" The day stretched behind her like the memory of a few miles of shocking road to a nervy motorist. She was still conscious of jolts and bumps, of sensations which pitted the usually smooth routine of her thoughts as potholes mar the surface of macadam; her spirit had ridden them precariously, and was now weary with the strain of its manœuvring. She heard Julie say in her high voice:

"You know, I think the police should move these people on. Why should they be allowed to stand and gape at us?"

Bing answered airily:

"Bread and circuses, my child, bread and circuses."

"What? What do you mean?"

Suddenly, startlingly, rather terrifyingly, as if the car

219

had found a voice, Martin said sardonically over his shoulder:

"And not so much of the bread!"

There was the silence of sheer astonishment from the back of the car. Lorna, her cheeks flaming, looked at Martin, her lips parted for a crushing rebuke. When you had had a chauffeur for a long time he might consider himself privileged to make a remark sometimes—but a new man—a man—and in such a tone. . . .

Her thoughts checked, faded. She had helped Arthur to decide on Martin because he looked well. She liked a tall man who could do credit to his uniform. She regarded him as part of her equipment, her background, and now, staring at him with eyes sharpened by amazement, she dimly apprehended another life which he lived behind the life which was devoted to driving her car, opening gates and doors for her, carrying her parcels. His eyes were on the road, his gloved hands moving skilfully on wheel and gears, for the car could only crawl here in the crowd and the congestion of other cars arriving at the church. For a few seconds, her lips still parted for the unuttered reproof, she studied the lean, long-jawed, leather-coloured face, the thin, firmly shut mouth where a hint of the sardonic tone of its last utterance still lingered in the downward twist of its corners. She felt confusedly that she had seen it before, not once, but a thousand times. It was, now that she came to look at it, a face almost as familiar as her own; tram-guards had it, ferry-hands had it, grocers and bakers and milkmen and postmen had it. Why, yes—in a way—Sim had it. It was not exactly the features. It was more the colour and texture of the skin, the way the bones showed under it, the quick way the head moved, the impression of a dry, good-natured humour which masked some disturbing quality which she almost feared to guess at—an independence— a pride as fierce and dangerous as fire. . . .

Her lips closed without speaking. She looked in front of her again, through the windscreen, her thoughts going back to the little brush she had had with him before they set out, and to which at the time, in the turmoil of other preoccupations, she had hardly given a second thought. Well, if she had been sharp with him he had deserved it. And she had had enough to worry her, Heaven knew, getting dressed in such a hurry, without his being late as well!

When she had come to the business of make-up she had realised that in spite of all her care and the cowl-like headdress of her bathing wrap, there was the faintest tinge of sunburn on her nose, and it had taken her a solid twenty minutes before the mirror to discover the blending of creams, powders and rouge which would disguise it. Even so she had to put more colour on her cheeks than she liked. She had sent for her maid to help her, and the girl had been so stupid and clumsy that, in a rage, she had sent her away again, and all the time Winifred was whistling out in the garden, gathering flowers and putting them in a basket which Brenda carried, trotting behind her like a little dog. All the time she was struggling with her hair, her face, her frock, that whistling had gone on with a pause here and there, the murmur of Winifred's voice, the clear treble of Brenda's—and then the whistling again. It had got on her nerves. She had thought: "So she really isn't coming. Arthur's a fool. Blast! That's too much—I look like a milkmaid. She's making him ridiculous. Perhaps the Rachel—no, that's worse than ever. Oh, hell, I'll have to start all over again!

" 'And he sang as he watched and waited *till his billy boiled*
"*Who'll* come a-waltzing Matilda with me?"
Waltzing Matilda . . .'

"Now she's set me off! I don't really like this fringe. Still it's new. He won't notice the fringe, but he'll realise there's something different. That's important. Something to fix his attention. Ah, that's better. How's the time going? Lord, I must hurry!

" '*Down came a jumbuck to drink at that billabong,*
Up jumped the swagman and grabbed him with glee,
And he sang . . .'"

221

Eyelashes were the very devil to do. In the agony of her concentration the haunting little melody had died from her lips, but not from her brain. When she stood at last, perfect to the last delicately, almost imperceptibly, tinted lash, to the last curl straying with an artless abandon which it had taken her ten minutes to achieve, it was still there. Winifred and Brenda had gone inside. The house was quiet. In that silence, that sacramental hush, she had stood before her long mirror, and her scrutiny of her reflection was curiously impersonal. She was still searching for flaws. Until she could tell herself with certainty that there were none, no emotion would invade her mood. She studied the slight, small figure as if it belonged to a stranger. She moved her head and her hands, took a step, turned, smiled, as if she were rehearsing gestures for a play. A streak of sun came through her window now, and the room was brilliant with its light. Her eyes, the soft sky-blue of forget-me-nots, and fringed with starry lashes, looked back at her intently from the mirror; her skin was as clear and as delicately tinted as porcelain. The tendency of her brows to lift at their outer corners had been skilfully accentuated; darkly, with the smooth upward rhythm of spread wings, they soared above her eyes to where the fringe, under a hat-brim which revealed, and then, with a swoop, shadowed her face, made a glimmer of silvery-gold across her forehead.

Her tension relaxed, and the smile which touched her lips, and which she did not pause to notice, had the unrehearsed charm of complete contentment. She picked up her gloves and her bag from the bed, threw a light coat over her arm and went out of the house, humming softly. Julie wouldn't be ready, she never was, so it was as well to leave a little early. Bing would give her a drink and a cigarette and say, in the midst of commonplace remarks, just one or two outrageous things. . . . Casually, with that wicked look which appeared like a miracle on his placid and rather chubby face. . . .

222

"Up jumped the swagman and sprang into the billabong,
'You'll never catch me alive!' said he,
And his ghost . . ."

Winifred and Brenda were going out the gate. Winifred was still in the shirt and slacks which she had worn at lunch, but Brenda had on her new yellow linen frock with the animals on it, and she was hugging Burrendong, the toy koala which she always took out with her. Lorna paused at the top of one of the short flights of steps by which the path mounted through the terraced garden. Nothing ruined your appearance like heat, she thought, and hurrying up the steps would be fatal. So she lingered a moment and then went on very slowly, until seeing Winifred alone at the open gate she realised that the car was not there, Martin not standing at attention.

Annoyance ran through her like a chill. She reached the gate and said sharply to Winifred:

"What's happened to Martin? Why hasn't he got the car out?"

Winifred was leaning against the gate-post, her hands in the pockets of her brown slacks, her eyes quite frankly wrinkled against the beaten-silver glare of the water. Lorna, true to her own strange gods, could not fail to recognise elegance when she met it, could not fail to see, with eyes trained by long habit to see little else, that where she with labour and long hours of sacrifice had achieved her own very exquisite effect, Winifred, with no trouble and very little thought, had achieved another —different, inferior of course, but not negligible.

Brown—there was something about that casual blending of brown—skin, eyes, hair, the silk shirt blouse finely striped in two shades of it, light and dark, the slacks, tobacco-coloured, the low-heeled sandals on bare feet. . . . There was an undisturbed harmony about the idle figure, a repose, a hint of some strange inviolability.

She had said irritably:

"Have you seen him?"

Winifred had straightened, taken her hands out of

her pockets and leaned her elbows on the half-open gate, swinging gently to and fro.

"Have I seen who?"

"Martin. I told him to have the car. . . ."

"He's just taken Brenda down to the boat. She's going to the Zoo with Mrs. Trugg."

Lorna's mind had formed into thought, then, a grievance which for a long time had been nothing but an emotion. All the servants adored Winifred. They jumped to do her bidding. She let them be too familiar, that was what it was, she laughed and joked with them as if they were her equals. After all, she had married a Sellman, which gave her a certain position and prestige to uphold. And standing there at the gate an hour ago, staring at Winifred's unchanging, absent smile, she had said furiously:

"It's like your cheek interfering with my orders. I told him to be here. . . ."

And Winifred, still with that silly smile, had interrupted as if she were deaf:

"Your frock looks beautiful, Lorna."

Of course it looked beautiful. It had cost enough, and she, Lorna Sellman, was wearing it. Why shouldn't it look beautiful? But Winifred's eyes had not matched her admiring words—they had been full of a gentle, absent-minded amusement, the expression you might see in the eyes of an adult looking at a Christmas tree. She had added idly:

"Here comes Martin now."

Yes, there he was. He had burst up on to the footpath with a bound which showed that he had taken the steps three at a time. He came striding along towards them, his leggings and his buttons flashing, his peaked cap in his hand, and he had said friendlily to Winifred:

"She's all right, Madam. Mrs. Trugg was there with the next-door youngsters, and she went off with them as happy as Larry. She says to me going down the steps . . ."

Lorna had felt her cheeks flush hotly. It was absurd.

He had hardly glanced at her. He had not seemed to realise. . . .

She had said with cold fury:

"Why isn't the car ready, Martin? Get it out at once. I'm late as it is."

His expression, she remembered now, had altered queerly as he looked at her, his eyes narrowing, his mouth snapping shut into the line which changed his whole expression, gave it some subtle, indefinable air of insolence. His cap had gone on to his head and his finger to its peak —a gesture in which, even then, she had irritably suspected irony. Winifred, still detachedly smiling, had said:

"You'll have heaps of time, Lorna. Thanks, Martin."

And as she strolled away down the garden, Martin, with that queer expression still on his face, had brought the car out, blue, glittering like a jewel, opened the door for her with a flourish just too pronounced, held it with an attitude just too deferential, creating, in some way she did not entirely comprehend, a ceremonial atmosphere which had made her departure just a trifle ridiculous. . . .

Bing, behind her, said: "Well, they *have* left us a way in, anyhow. . . ."

The car was drawing up to the kerb now, and Martin, brisk and efficient, was out of it, round it, opening doors. His behaviour was wooden, exemplary. Stepping out she heard her name whispered, repeated, heard the indrawn sigh of admiration which was usually music to her ears. But to-day, with a strange feeling which she imagined must be something like the "stage-fright" she had heard of but never experienced herself, she did not look at the crowd, tried not to hear it, hurried across the footpath and into the church.

                *   *   *   *   *

Hydrangeas. Well, they didn't look bad. But these misty blues and pinks and mauves and greens were not like Veronica. Your wedding should express you. The austere simplicity of her own imagined wedding gown, the ivory prayer-book, the sheaves of lilies which she would have for decoration were only the right, the artistically right setting for her own Madonna-like beauty. If Veronica had had any sense, which, Lorna thought with satisfaction, she hadn't, she would have used scarlet gladioli, stately and spear-shaped. . . .

"Hullo, darling—yes, it's dreadful, I'll be married in winter, won't you? . . . My dear, how are you, I haven't seen you for ages! Hullo, Jerry, where *does* one sit? Lead me to it, like a pet, I'm just ready to swoon with the heat. Oh, good-afternoon, Lady Burton, how is Sir George? Thank you, that's sweet of you, but I've had such a rush it's a wonder I didn't arrive in my nightie! Hullo, Bob. Isn't Mildred with you? Oh, poor dear, she's *always* having headaches, isn't she? Yes, my dear, I had it done this morning. Do you like it? Is this it, Jerry? But how *foul* of you, I can't see a thing! Never mind, there'll be nothing much to see! No, I'm not really—*I adore* Veronica. . . ."

God, it was hot! Now, for a time you must relax, rest. All this isn't important, but afterwards . . . If you can get Sim to go to Manero's, if you can . . . But of course you can! That murmur of admiration like a sigh from the mob outside. That whisper from Lady Burton: "My dear Lorna, how charming you look!" Jerry Winterleigh's eyes. Bob's eyes. Well, Mildred was a dowdy little thing, anyhow. Eyes everywhere. You could feel them on you; you often caught them when you turned, just looking away. Tram-guards, porters, taxi-men—it was always the same. You were used to it now—that quick second glance that remained and became, furtively, a stare.

Sim. There he is now. Just his back. How beautifully his clothes always fit him. But he should not stand like that with his hands behind his back and his face tilted upward, and his weight shifting rhythmically from one foot to the other. Before their wedding she would have to drill him a bit. There was something rather—well—perverse about Sim. She would alter that by degrees. He only wanted a wife with the right social gifts to rub off the corners, the disconcerting little roughnesses, to suppress those occasional wayward refusals to conform.

Here was Veronica coming now. Good *heavens,* what a mess! All fluffy and girlish! *Veronica!* It was incredible how little sense of dress and background some women had. It was just downright stupidity, just sheer lack of brains. And lily-of-the-valley! Really, this was a silly wedding. There was old Lady Hegarty. There was something about her, too. . . . Perhaps that was where Sim got it. A troublesome sort of mother-in-law. Oh, well, they need hardly ever see her. She looked a bit pale. Heat, or perhaps maternal emotion, though it was hard to imagine anyone feeling maternal over George; they say even a skunk smells good to its mother, and perhaps George had curls and chubby legs and dimples once that she can brood over now. . . . Really this maternity business. . . . Thank God you weren't born in the dark ages before contraceptives! It was nothing short of tragic to see what it had done to girls who were at school with you—ruined figures, ruined skins, ruined outlook. Nothing left but a stodgy domesticity and the beginning of a middle-aged spread!

There's Bob edging into the pew just behind. Did he wangle that? Goodness, how Sim is fidgeting! Funny how bridegrooms always mumble the "I will" and brides speak it clearly! I wonder where Sim and Lesley Channon went last night! I wonder . . ."

Her hands gripped the back of the pew in front of her, and for the first time in her life she felt the fear which is behind real jealousy run through her like a fire. It mounted and mounted, shaking her, fed by an imagination suddenly run riot and coloured by her own desires, so that for a moment she saw the church and the congregation through a mist, heard the minister's voice through a drumming in her ears, felt the thought flicker through her mind again: "What's wrong with me to-day?"

But there was nothing wrong. How could there be? She was Lorna Sellman, doubly armoured against all misfortunes. She could have anything she wanted. Things that other girls longed and struggled for in vain, were hers for the asking. She and some others of her set had appeared, for the fun of it, as extras in a film recently. Afterwards she had been offered a part, a leading part, with a good salary. Beauty counted—and a name, and influence, and money to buy shares. Laughingly, charmingly, with an air which said: "My dear man, this was just a *whim*! I don't want your jobs!" she had refused. When she was in London a few years ago she had turned down a title—certainly he was only a baronet and there had been a bigger fish nibbling—but if she cared to try again . . . But she didn't want to, she only wanted Sim. And, of course, he could get a title if he really wanted to. And then there was his flying. He might do a record solo flight or something. . . . Anyhow, title or not, she wanted him, she would have him. . . .

Let us pray. "Bob's eyes will be glued to me. His eyes are like a dog's—brown and limpid and wistful. Thank the Lord for a good profile and long lashes, and it's lucky he's on the side where my hat-brim turns up and not down. *Our Father which art in Heaven, Hallowed be Thy Name.* The reception will be utterly ghastly. I must try and get Sim alone, somehow. If he comes to Manero's I'll say it's too hot for dancing. We might take the car . . . I could send Martin home . . . *and lead us not into temptation but deliver us from evil* . . . I'll turn round presently and smile at Bob—poor devil, it's the least I can do! It's nearly over, thank Heaven. *Amen.* Goodness, what's happening over there? Lady Hegarty—what's the matter with her? She's fainting or something—there's Jerry to the fore. It'll take three of them to carry her! I will *not* get fat! I'll die rather than get fat. . . ."

*   *   *   *   *

Sim ran a handkerchief round the back of his neck under his collar before he followed George out into the murmurous church. It was crowded, of course. Packed. And the heat, heavy with the scent of powdered and perfumed women and of flowers, was something in which one seemed to wade, like something which one had to push away as one advanced. His body, tormented by a memory

228

of semi-nakedness, of faint breaths of sea air running over his bare shoulders, of deep water flowing round him, fretted in the brutal constriction of formal clothes; the palms of his hands felt sticky, and he knew that the rim of sweat which he had already mopped a dozen times from his brow was there again.

He locked his hands behind his back and stood restlessly, his eyes wandering, his mind ranging among aimless and scattered impressions, an odd idea disturbing and confusing him that with the passing of the long and idle morning some opportunity had passed him, too. With the coming of this crowded afternoon something else had come and had finally possessed him. This was not a thought, but a sensation which lay behind his restlessness. It made him fidget and strain at his locked fingers as if they were bound, and glance sideways at his brother's florid face as if looking for an answer without even knowing exactly what his question was.

George was as jumpy as the devil. What, Sim wondered idly, would be the reaction of his inmost self if Veronica suddenly sent a message to say that she had changed her mind? Underneath the shock of being made to look a fool, underneath his chagrin at losing a wife at once wealthy and handsome, underneath all the conventional agitation of the jilted lover—what would he feel? This question, almost aimlessly formed in his mind, took on a sudden urgency, and his roving gaze fastened, concentrated for a moment as if by intense stillness and observation the answer would make itself apparent. To his surprise it did. He knew with startling certainty that George would be unutterably relieved. What, then, had brought him here? What kept him waiting, what would lead her presently to stand beside him, and what would carry them all through the ceremony, quiet, well-behaved, well-rehearsed, smiling, hypnotised? . . .

Sim blinked rapidly, jerking his head a little, for the heat was making him sleepy. The organ pipes, he thought, were like huge copper pencils, and his eyes, staring absently at their long thin line of brightness, had almost closed. The thick fragrance of the church was stifling, and his jaws ached with the suppression of a yawn. He thought: "I was a fool not to get some sleep this morning."

With the thought there came a memory of the long summer night he had spent with Lesley, the queer, light-headed hush of the early-morning hours, the drive home through deserted streets with cocks crowing, and stars fading in the sky, and her head against his arm. The memory shone for a moment and then shook, glimmered, lost its outline, as a bright object flickers and fades distortedly, sinking in clear water. It was something which had happened only last night, and yet it had the legendary character of long, long ago. It was something in his life but not of it, eluding his comprehension as a drift of smoke eludes a grasping hand. A violent spasm of impatience shook him, and his head moved with a suggestion of desperation unnoticed by anyone except his mother. He made a deliberate and tortured effort to return in emotion as well as in memory to the dark-shadowed hillside where they had watched the long night out from the back seat of his parked car, and for a moment on the crest of his effort he did recapture a strangely blended mood of peace and exaltation, a momentary vision of light in long paths across the black water. Yellow lights, fixed and shivering, red lights winking intermittently, a dazzle of lights moving; Lesley's voice in a waking dream: "There's the last ferry, Sim. We must go." His own voice, bewitched: "Yes, darling. . . ." And long hours passing again, with the sound of lapping water and the smell of seaweed, and lights going out one by one and all the world sleeping but themselves.

Remembered scents, remembered darkness, remembered ecstasy—they are only remembered. Senses, avid for the present, bring you the fragrance of lily-of-the-valley in a wave. Veronica is there. White in satin-gleam, veil-cloud, diamond-glitter, things real and based on daylight. She is there, and George is not being jilted. They are being married. Well, why not? They stand securely

230

side by side in the same world. They have not struggled and struggled to reach each other, afraid, whirled apart by strange forces in themselves as deep and dangerous as currents in a storm-swept surf. Nor sought at last, reckless and desperate, the one union which is so easy, so complete, so poignantly lovely, so wildly sad—and so useless. . . .

"*. . . For God created man in His own image. And the Lord God said: 'It is not good that man should be alone. . . .'*"

Sim moved restlessly. Last night it had not seemed, in the fulness of his contentment, that he could ever be alone again, but to-day, increasingly, the feeling of solitude had come upon him. Why, having possessed her, did she now seem farther away than ever—irrevocably far away? He felt his understanding to be wavering and incomplete, a light like those paths across the water, revealing a little, fading a little, fading into darkness again. His life could borrow some beauty of it; enough to show him glimpses of a heaven attainable—not enough to light him there.

"*I charge you both as you shall be answerable in the Day when the secrets of all hearts shall be disclosed. . . .*"

The day of judgment. That is plain truth. There is .a day of judgment. There are thousands of days of judgment. Any day upon which you examine your own heart is a day of judgment. But that is an uncomfortable thought. If you think of it as being so remote as to be mythical—something belonging with the Last Trump, you can evade those days of judgment which crowd upon you.

"*. . . love her, honour and keep her in sickness or health, in prosperity or adversity . . .*"

If that were all! George mumbling: "I will." Again, why not? It is all very simple for them—all except the "prosperity and adversity," and of course they don't take that seriously. They will not ever come in the midst of some innocent conversation upon a chasm between their ideas and their beliefs. They will not find themselves

231

looking into each other's eyes in sudden fear, saying: "But don't you think . . . ?" "But can't you see . . . ?" Words failing, thought itself failing, hopelessness rushing over them, weariness engulfing them. . . . No, they would not come to that. They knew how to accept. It is not to be trifled with, this power which has filled the church with silent, beautifully mannered people, faintly rustling like trees, giving out perfume like flowers. So quiet, smiling, no thoughts running amok, out of control, dynamic, destructive, threatening. It is a power to be reckoned with. It is shackling the group of men outside with their notebooks and their pencils and their observant, disillusioned eyes; cool, cynically appraising eyes, adeptly framed questions, glibly scribbling pencils. Word-spinning, "conditioning," repressing this, emphasising that; frocks, flowers, presents, bridesmaids. Reception, speeches, honeymoon plans. Yourself, Sim Hegarty, deftly displayed to advantage, polo, yachting, air record, younger son of the late Sir James Hegarty. Not Sim tormented and betrayed by yourself, not Sim bewitched and released by passion to a transient bliss, not Sim thinking incoherently, insanely, fruitlessly. But Sim unlocking damp hands to feel nervously for a ring, Sim swallowed by environment, conditioned beyond all capacity for freedom, but not quite beyond a recognition and a desire. . . .

"Almighty God, the Father and Creator who did first . . ."

Father and Creator. You could never escape this giving and creating creed, and the ugly implications of its reverse. Taker, accepter, withholder. Words are dangerous to play with, like crackers, fizzing, big with eruptive ideas. You must throw them away, reject them quickly before they bang, before you are forced by the noise and the glare of their explosion to admit their potency, their ability to burn your fingers. . . .

Yawns crowded up behind his clenched teeth, making his eyes water so that the bit of blue carpet at his feet blurred and wavered, and his desire to sleep became a craving. He thought: "Buck up, you fool, there's plenty more of this show to be seen through yet!" Food and drink and speeches; the murmurous still crowd changed to a crowd vociferously chattering. "Once we get out of the church," Sim thought, "it won't be so bad." Those vile little white flowers of Veronica's, so heavy and oppressively sweet! More words. But his voice isn't bad, this chap, better than the monotonous mouthing of most parsons. . . ."

"Your adorning let it be the inner adorning of the Heart . . ."

More words, dangerous with the beauty of sound and of some meaning perilously compelling. But it is over now, thank the Lord! The stirring, the rustling, the breaking up of tension, the organ. Sim turned in a fury of impatience, thinking: "Only let me get out of here and breathe some fresh air again. . . ."

"What's that, Jerry?"

"Your mother. She's a bit off colour. She fainted just now."

"Good God! Where is she?"

"We took her into the little room out there off the vestibule or whatever they call it in a church. Dr. Matthews is with her. He says it's just the heat. Look here, Sim, shall I tell George, or not? It's nothing serious. Perhaps . . ."

"No, don't say anything. She wouldn't want a fuss. I'll go to her."

*　　*　　*　　*　　*

When Lady Hegarty opened her eyes she was lying on a couch in a small room whose light was so hotly and crudely yellow that her first instinctive action was to look behind her at the window. She could see from the shape of it that she was still in the church. It was, she thought, with oddly disproportionate amusement, a very ecclesiastical window, but glass of that colour was far from restful, far from soothing, and she shut her eyes again as she answered the question of Dr. Matthews, who, with Sim and Mrs. Stewart and Lady Burton and two or three others, made a crowd in the tiny room which was hardly less oppressive than the crowd in the church itself.

"Yes, Doctor, I'm all right, thank you. It was nothing but the heat."

Her eyes opened again. Sim, so dear, so handsome, with a carnation in his buttonhole; Mrs. Stewart, fussy, worried, with one ear on the sounds of departing guests outside; Lady Burton, thin and elegant; Dr. Matthews, Mrs. Peel, all the rest of them in their festive attire.

She added wearily:

"I'm so sorry for causing a commotion like this. I should have slipped out quietly when I first began to feel it a little—close. But I thought I should be all right. I'll get up now. . . ."

Dr. Matthews pushed her back on the green-covered couch. He said grimly:

"You lie still. Perhaps in half an hour or so . . . Drink this."

She sipped obediently, and said:

"But the wedding . . ."

"The wedding's over, and the celebrations can go on without you for a while. I'll send my wife in to stay with you."

She protested:

"No, no. Please, all of you, do go. Mrs. Stewart, do make them go. We mustn't spoil Veronica's wedding. I shall be perfectly all right when I've had a little rest."

They went, murmuring condolences. Dr. Matthews said to Sim: "You see that she stays there for a bit," and followed them. Sim sat on the edge of the couch and held her hand. She shut her eyes again. This moment, a moment of escape and peace. Outside all the clatter and gabble of the life she hated, and here, strangely and unexpectedly alone, herself and Sim. She felt curiously tired and inert, but anxiety had been nagging at her like a faintly aching tooth ever since Sim's despairing "I don't know!" had startled her on the beach, and she felt with misery and bewilderment that she should have some help to offer him. She *had* some help. She had the knowledge which was the outcome of her long, lonely married life, she had the bitter, hard-won wisdom of experience, but . . . She groped in her mind for an explanation of their uselessness, and it showed her, with freakish aptness, a tram-ticket. "Not transferable." That was it. She moved slightly, her brows contracting, and Sim asked:

"What is it, Mother? Are you all right?"

"I'm all right, dear. I only want to keep still."

Not transferable. She felt the frustration of the naturally inarticulate, big with emotions she could not express. The dreadful perils of security which already she had tried so clumsily to indicate were all about them at this very minute. For herself it did not matter now. For him . . .

She opened her eyes. He was looking absently at the window.

She knew that his thoughts were not free; customs dragged at them, and conventions and false conceptions of duty, and false standards and false ideals. She knew the sincerity of his bewilderment, she could foresee the slow and unutterably painful process of his emancipation. She herself, in her own period of bewildered acceptance, had helped to fasten this burden on him. He, probably, before he freed himself, would help to fasten it on to his children. But she knew, and the knowledge was her only comfort, that there survived in him somewhere, however feebly, that germ of independent thinking which at last would save him. That, at least, she had given him, even if she had, in ignorance, injured rather than fostered it. She said uncertainly:

"Sim?"

He patted her hand. "Yes?"

"When you said this morning . . . who is that at the door?"

It was Lorna. Lady Hegarty looked at her with a tinge of unwilling admiration. Her unformed thought was that no woman can entirely withhold from another acknowledgment of efficiency in that art of captivation which is the first biological function of their sex. One

235

must admire technique. Lorna's was perfect—masterly. . . .

Not a glance for Sim, jumping to his feet as she entered, his eyes upon her face; her lovely face, all concern and sympathy, her charming voice:

"Oh, Lady Hegarty, I'm so *sorry!* Someone just told me you weren't well. Is there anything I can do?"

What was the good? Poor Sim, how helpless men are! Beauty! They turn to it as incorrigibly, as inevitably, as moths to a flame. There's nothing to be done about it. Women like Lorna hold all the cards. You can't defeat them, you can only leave them to defeat themselves when the inexorable years come upon them, and their beauty fails and they have no other strength.

"No, Lorna, thank you. It was nothing but the heat. I'm just going to rest a little longer. Sim will stay with me."

Now, at last, she looks at him. An upward glance, a smile at once hesitating, appealing, anxious; no trace of coquetry. What is it that makes the charm of a smile. You can't blame him, you can't wonder when even to yourself it seems born of some fundamental graciousness of character. She will get him away from me. How will she do it?

"Sim, Mrs. Stewart was asking for you. I'll stay here with your mother while you go on to the reception. After all you're one of the performers. I won't be missed."

"I suppose I'll have to go soon, but . . ."

"I'll promise to take care of her. Really, I think you should go. Don't you, Lady Hegarty?"

It's too tiring. You can't fight any more. You can't live his life for him or save him from his own mistakes. You might as well say what she wants you to say. It's up to Lesley—if she wants him. If she wants him.

"I don't need anyone, Sim. You go on with Lorna and send the car back for me in about half an hour. I'll be rested by then, and I'll follow. Run along."

"But are you sure, Mother? Would you like to go

straight home? Lorna could take me to the beanfeast in her car."

"No, no, certainly I won't go home. I'll follow you later. Good-bye, Lorna."

"If you're quite *sure*, Lady Hegarty?"

"Quite sure."

"All right, Mother. I'll look out for you. Have a good rest, now. Good-bye."

His hand, again, between her own. Safety! How simple it is in childhood! *Take my hand, Sim! Hold my hand, dear.* Imperceptibly, so that you do not feel it happening, their safety becomes something you can no longer ensure; they have gone beyond your protection and your care. . . .

"Good-bye, Sim."

He was gone now. Beyond your protection and care. She closed her eyes again.

* * * * *

Professor Channon crossed the Quay and walked up Loftus Street towards the Education Building. He moved slowly, for lately he had found hills fatiguing, and he could feel faintly the pain which was now a constant and sinister reminder to him that his life was nearly over. And yet, even in the compulsory slackening of a stride which had once been brisk and full of purpose, he had found compensations. Walking slowly, looking about one, life and the scene against which it was enacted displayed myriads of tiny facets, details trivial but rich with the freshness of discovery. In the leisurely amble of age and infirmity, he thought, your eyes observed and your mind had time to grasp and consider such matters as the obvious ill-health of the Moreton Bay fig across the road in the tiny park which enshrined the Obelisk, and the comical little anchor of the *Sirius*. Was it not getting enough nourishment, he wondered, or did it hate the hot crust of city pavement which tried, not always successfully, to hold underground roots which loved to coil partially above the surface. How old was it? Not old enough, by a long way, to have seen the day when a couple of logs thrown across the creek down there had christened Bridge Street for all time, but a good deal older than himself, most likely! He felt the sudden revulsion against civilisation which comes intermittently to all those in whom the primitive still lives strongly. He felt his failing body mystically identified with the failing tree which stood at night in the naked glare of street lamps instead of in a darkness its ancestors had known, a darkness lit only by stars and the distant flicker of camp fires; he hated for its sake the brief, stark silence of nights which had once been long and intimately alive with the noises of the bush and the strange sounds of corroboree. The whole illness of humanity, the whole insanity of civilised life, the whole long, bloody history of mankind, rushed over him with a force which caused, or was followed by, or was blended with a sudden stab of physical agony, and he stopped on the street corner, leaning heavily on his stick, looking blindly down at the pavement, struggling.

Struggling for enough faith still to look forward, enough strength of purpose to resist the almost overwhelming urge to look back to a land still uncontaminated. Struggling not to yield to a rage senseless and useless, at the manner of its contamination, struggling to think, without fruitless bitterness, of a people dispossessed and murdered, and a last strangely surviving harmony of Nature sacrificed to the urgent discords of human progress.

"Age," he thought. "Illness. Defeat. That's all it is. But I should have liked not to go now. I should have liked to live to see some suggestion that it was worth while. To go out of life at a time like this is—is to die with the sound in your ears of all humanity raving."

He crossed the street slowly, thinking: "Well, you pessimistic old fool, it's just as well you're going to see some pictures. It's just as well you're going to be reminded that in the middle of this lust for destruction there's still an urge towards creativeness, too." But his mind jerked back convulsively: "What *is* this lust, anyhow?" A universal neurasthenia? A hatred of life with queer offshoots, queer, unconscious manifestations? War, of course. And suicide, and murder. But birth control? Euthanasia? A blind, instinctive movement against life. . . .

"Heaven help women in such a world. . . ."

That thought turned his mind to Winifred, towed it back from the deep waters of universal problems to the shallows of personal affairs. He felt a little guilty and a good deal worried about his elder daughter—guilty that he had not kept his half-promise to join her on the beach, worried because he could see no escape for her out of the ugly tangle which her life had become; and still oppressed, still thinking heavily and with reluctance, he found himself wondering if her intelligence, which he had so proudly and lovingly fostered, had been a help or merely an added torment to her in the collapse and distortion of her emotional life. Might it not even be true to say that eight out of ten girls of her age would have married rich, handsome, easy-going, stupid, indulgent Arthur Sellman and remained perfectly content?

It was he, their father, who had fostered in both his daughters the urge for thought and enquiry, analysis and deduction. It was he who had encouraged Winifred and later Lesley to play in his study where, wreathed in smoke, he sat talking to Marsden and O'Neill, and Peter Manning. To old Nicholas Kavanagh, of whom there remained now only the poetry which Denning had rescued from the fire, and rich treasure in the memory of his friends. To Mary Nott, and young Gerald Avery. To all kinds of people, whose one common possession was the intelligence to express their incredibly diverse and opposing views. There had been old Tories like Moore, decent, rigid, sincere; there had been artists and poets, novelists and journalists and churchmen. Scientists, prim and academic—little Tupps, for instance, knowing everything about the heavens and nothing whatever about the earth; doctors like Merryweather, specialists, buried beyond redemption in the narrow grave of their specialities; lawyers, bound and bewitched by "hereinbefore" and "inasmuch as"; barristers like Bill Jones, talking with the glib facility of habit; Roger Blair, violent and dynamic; old Judge Harding, mellowed and benign.

The children, he thought now with rueful amusement, must have sat there listening to voices from above the smoke-clouds as the mortals of mythology listened to Jove and the other gods thundering upon Olympus. And the time had come, of course, imperceptibly, when they discarded their toys and sat on chairs to listen. And later still they began to question or to comment. And still later the smoke from their cigarettes contributed to the blue, convivial haze, and they became members in their own right of whatever group assembled.

Was it coming to their aid now, that bright intelligence, whetted by years of reading, years of contact with the best intellects of their sphere? No, he thought, depression swamping him with another twinge of pain, love and its mistakes, its difficulties, its disillusionments, had claimed them too young. All her brains, all his own brains, could not rescue Winifred now from the bondage of a responsibility which life had fastened on to her.

He sighed, entering the building and holding up a hand to stay the just departing lift. He glanced at his wrist watch. It was nearly half past three. He had meant to catch an earlier ferry, but after lunch, lying on the grass with a book, he had dozed off for a little while. Old people, he thought resentfully, fall asleep so easily, waste so much precious time. . . .

There was only one passenger in the lift, a small woman whose hat shadowed her face, but as they reached the top floor and he stood aside to let her out she looked up at him with a shy glance of acknowledgment and recognition. His face creased deeply into its network of wrinkles as he smiled, and he thought she looked relieved. He said:

"I didn't know you at first, Mrs. Denning. In fact, I couldn't see you under your hat." She answered:

"I always wear a big hat when I go to see my own

pictures. It's almost as good as an umbrella for hiding."

He shook his head at her.

"Why should you hide?"

She said unhappily:

"People ask me questions and I don't know what to say."

"Is that why you never came along to tennis with your husband? Were you afraid we'd ask questions?"

He bent his head a little to see beneath the brim of her hat, for he had caught, before her head went down, an impression of colour running up suddenly in her cheeks. Blushing? Yes, quite definitely blushing. Intrigued, casting about in his mind for a possible reason for her embarrassment, he remembered that there had been some sort of scandal about her and Denning—at the time of the fire in Thalassa, and old Nicholas Kavanagh's tragic death. His wife had divorced him or something. Could she, he wondered, be sensitive about that? But she was explaining awkwardly:

"I'm not much good at tennis. And when I just sit still in the sun I—I—go to sleep. I've done it several times at tennis parties."

He said: "I see," quite gravely, restraining his amusement because he could see that she was evidently abashed, and they paused at the entrance to the Gallery while he paid and she rummaged in her bag for her member's ticket. He asked:

"What's your system? Do you go straight round or make for your favourites first?"

"I go straight round very fast, and then come back to the ones I like best. Only somehow there's never a seat in front of them. What do you do?"

"I just mooch along, ruminating, until I find it's time to go, and I'm not half-way round. It's always . . ."

But she was not listening to him. She was looking up at a picture, and suddenly her face was mature, settled, intent. Thinking: "She doesn't really feel at home with people, only with pictures," he left her, and began to prowl along the wall.

241

A seascape, conventional and uninspired. A picturesquely ruined shed with a pear tree blossoming over it; pretty, but uninteresting and unimportant. *Early Morning, Tweed River.* Yes, yes, this was better! He acknowledged, without much regret, that his interest in pictures as in other forms of art was less technical than sensual, and what he liked here was a suggestion of that warmth, that faint promise of the tropics which lies like a benediction on the North Coast, the dark opulence of the trees, the gloss on their leaves, the vigorous green of the grass, the chocolate richness of turned furrows, all expressing a fertility, a springing urge of growth. *Mount Warning.* Poor Wollumbin! Only the old inhabitants now remembered or used its rightful name. There it was, though, quite faithfully done, with its head in the clouds as usual, and Murwillumbah at its feet, and there it would remain, quite unaffected, whatever you called it! Northward again. *Bougainvillea, Townsville.* He looked at it with a poignant stab of recognition. It was, of course, an orgy. It was an abandonment to a lust for pure colour. It was flagrant, incredible, it was breath-taking, because you knew that the artist, tormenting his ingenuity, robbing his paint-box, must have still known when he had finished that he had achieved only an apology for that flaming, challenging cascade of colour.

Suddenly the Professor thought: "I'll never see it again."

For he had seen it a year or two ago, that very wall of rock, and he had stood still, rooted, on the other side of the street, staring and staring. He had walked on at last, reluctantly, turning his head from time to time for another look, leaving it at last with some hardly formed but comforting resolve to return some day and look at it again. He had carried away from there, he reflected, memories of much that was lovely; of vast rounded boulders, smooth and glittering, warm to the touch, of water coloured like a peacock's tail, of the gold-dust tipping on the mango trees' dark foliage; but more than a memory—a sensation almost—had remained of that riot-

242

ous deluge of scarlet and magenta and vermilion clothing the cliff-face, with the wild blue of the tropical sky behind it. Nowhere, he thought, shaking his head at the picture, except possibly in the robes of saints in cathedral windows, could you reproduce that brilliance, that poignancy, of light-behind-colour.

He moved on sadly and rather uncertainly to the next picture. His shoulders had sagged a little, and the alert enjoyment of life which kept his face young had vanished, leaving the deep-set creases to tell of defeatedness and age. He was aware of capitulation in himself, and he thought wryly: "That sort of thing's too strong for me now. Too heady. Those glorious crudities, those violent emotional audacities of Nature are for the young." But at the back of his mind was the stabbing thought that here, through the eyes of a handful of artists, he was seeing his native land for the last time. Feeling a faint eye-strain, he fumbled for his glasses and peered through them at the picture now before him.

Ah, this was good! *In the Path of the Westerly.* He thought: "Thank God so much of our work is still—what do they call it?—representational? I'm glad I'll be dead before it isn't!" Yes, there were places in the Blue Mountains where you found gums just like that. Bleak ledges half-way down the sandstone cliffs where the crumbling belt of red shale matched their rose-red bark, and their rounded, strangely spreading branches, knotted and swollen like the bulging muscles of a strong man, seemed flung out in defiance of the tearing gales. Did artists anywhere else in the world, he wondered, make such a habit of painting trees? As backgrounds, naturally—as parts of a composition. But just single trees, alone? Poplars, maples, sycamores, elms, beeches? He searched his memory. Not much good going among the moderns, he thought sourly, their trees were generic trees, decorative, unrecognisable—the tree idea.

He stood before the picture, his eyes on it, but his mind still searching. Lois came up to him and asked:

"Are you ruminating already?"

He nodded, and explained his thought. She said:

"Gum trees have drama."

He prompted:

"And other trees?"

"Well—let's say *most* other trees haven't. A chorus on a stage, for instance, can be lovely, but it depends on a kind of mass effect on the senses. But the solo dancer is an individual because you have room to see him; his movements and his costume and his expression suggest things to you. You think about him, whereas a chorus simply dazzles you. There's no poignancy about it, no passion. Most trees are a chorus, so they're used, like a chorus, as a background. But some trees, including gums and banksias, are born soloists." She paused, reflecting, and added: "It may be just a matter of being able to see them properly. Line, pure form, is always dramatic. And now I come to think of it, I believe all the other trees are—shall we say featured—much more when their branches are bare. They say you can't see the wood for the trees, and in most cases you can't see the trees for the leaves."

He laughed. "You may be right. Certainly no one could accuse gum trees of being what nurserymen call 'fully furnished'."

She looked a little shocked.

"Do they say that? Don't people invent dreadful phrases? Palms have drama, haven't they? Or had," she amended, sadly. "I'm afraid they only have melodrama now. Shall we go on?"

"Where are yours? I want to look at them now. I must get up to the Public Library to change a book, and I want to get the five-twenty boat home. I haven't really very much time."

She pointed.

"They're over there." A little laugh escaped her, and she answered his enquiring glance:

"They've put me among the moderns this year, but I'm afraid I'll look just as funny there as I did among

244

the conservatives last year. They find me rather a trial, I'm afraid—I just don't seem to fit."

No, she was right—she did not fit. He stood in front of *The Moonbeam,* half-smiling. The moderns, he thought with the prejudice of age, were other-worldly in the sense that their works were foreign to all human conceptions; but the other-worldliness of Lois' work lay in her capacity to present a new, an entirely fresh and original conception of familiar things. Everyone had seen moonbeams, but no one had seen a moonbeam in quite the way that she presented it. And yet, paradoxically, she had a quaint matter-of-factness which saved her work from a sentimentality which might otherwise have damned it. The moonbeam lay along the sand and touched the black water with a tracery of silver. The imprint of small, bare feet, running feet, danced ecstatically across it and vanished into darkness, the protruding tinfoil of an empty cigarette packet glittered with a transcendent splendour, a ginger beer bottle shone with a green and secret light, a little froth bubbling, iridescent, marked the line of the last retreating wave.

He thought:

"What is she doing? Practising? Most likely she doesn't know herself. These things of hers are like dreams, as if she's not properly awake, flashes of vision disconnected from reality. I wonder what she has done since her marriage to Denning? What effect will it have on her work?"

He turned away from the picture abruptly and went to sit down on one of the chairs arranged down the middle of the room, wearied, resignedly conquered by the returning thought: "I won't be here to see."

* * * * *

Four o'clock. Miss Benson with his cup of tea. Ian, yawning, took it, stirred it, leaning back in his revolving chair.

"Sugared, Miss Benson?"

"Two lumps, Mr. Harnet."

"Good. Did you finish that letter?"

"Not quite. Are you in a hurry for it?"

"Well, it must go to-day. Jimmy can deliver it."

"I'll finish it straight away then. Jimmy says there was some excitement up in the Domain after lunch. Did you see anything, Mr. Harnet?"

Ian nodded over his tea-cup. It must have been the same mob, he supposed, which had been pretty lively and vociferous while he was having his lunch. When he was leaving the kiosk he had seen Roger and Lesley come up from the Gardens and stroll across the grass to listen to the fat man with the great voice and the dramatic gestures. He had paused himself for a moment on his way back across the Domain, and had walked on at last reluctantly, saddened and depressed. For the man was worth listening to; he was not just a ranter, an iconoclast, a windbag. He had thought and he had read, and he believed the gospel that he preached. His words ran about the silent mass of his listeners, flickering, searching like tongues of flame, so that they came to life under them, stimulated, bewitched for the moment from the inertia of acceptance, seeing farther than the next meal, farther than the week's lodging, farther than their own lives.

He said slowly:

"There was a bit of a crowd, and some chap making a speech about unemployment. I hadn't time to wait."

He handed her his empty cup and felt in his pockets for cigarettes. When the door closed behind her he tried to work again but gave it up at last, and leaning his arms on the littered desk he shut his eyes. He tried to remember how it had felt to be at peace, even happy, as he had been once, and he wondered if peace and happiness were ever again to be known to his generation. For he knew that not only his own personal miseries and maladjustments were beating him. To live in a world weighted with anxiety, sickened with disgust, one needed, if one were to preserve one's sanity, some shred of personal happiness and security. To be a unit of a humanity taut with barely suppressed hysteria, living on its nerves, menaced

246

beyond endurance by a growing conception of itself as insane, helpless, past redemption, there must be at least one personal love, one personal loyalty, one personal union in which to find renewal.

A knock on his door made him lift his head impatiently.

"Come in."

She was there on the threshold, smiling at him. Even in the whirling and chaotic gladness of the moment he noticed that uncertain smile, with the beginning of fear in it, and tried with half a dozen lightning flashes of thought to explain it to himself. Had she been hurt? Physically hurt? Frightened? Had anything happened to Brenda? Had Arthur done something—said something— to drive her here, to him? To him.

That thought engulfed, obliterated the others. He hardly knew how she came to be in his arms, clinging to him with a feverish strength, saying nothing, her face hidden against his shoulder. He heard sounds from the outside world with a vague, stupid wonder that life should be pursuing, in this rocking moment, its everyday routine. He heard cars hooting, trams clanging round the corner, the churning of water as a ferry came in to the nearest wharf. He pulled her hat off, put his cheek against her hair, and asked:

"What has happened? What made you come?"

She was so still in his arms; her immobility and her silence seemed welded into a power which enclosed them like a fortress. She was feeling the terrible fragility of this moment, trying to preserve it with stillness, with held breath, even with a suspension of thought. That was not like her, he thought in anguish. It was a form of self-hypnotism foreign to that "mental arrogance" of hers; it could only mean panic and despair. He held her away from him, shook her a little so that her closed eyes opened heavily.

"What is it? Tell me!"

She moved away from him and sat down in his chair,

her arms along its arms, her hands dropping limply. She said:

"Suddenly it got too much for me. I feel as if I've been in a sort of dream all day. Ian . . ."

Leaning on the opposite side of the desk, he asked:

"What happened this morning? I heard him. . . ."

She looked up sharply. His voice, his face, frightened her. It came to her like a suddenly revealing blaze of light that she was treading dangerous ground. She thought: "This is how headlines begin." Angers, jealousies, miseries, goaded beyond control. Rage working in a mind wearied by long conflict, a mind not capable of resisting normally an anti-social impulse. Newsboys shouting: "Murder!" Horror upon horror engulfing her life, and his and the children's. She told herself with a sudden shocked steadying of thought: "I should not have come. I knew it. Why did I do it? It shows how one can be governed, and driven by emotions. For a little while. But in that little while one can do God only knows what harm. This is no way out. To go on from here leads . . ."

But her imagination baulked, looking at his face. The unendurable need for comfort and support which had driven her to him was swamped by a more imperative need—to protect him from himself, and from those wild impulses she could see reflected in his eyes. She made a little gesture of indifference.

"Oh, that. He was just raging about something to do with business. I wasn't listening, really. He does it so often."

She stood up, looking at him forlornly.

"I shouldn't have come, Ian. But it just didn't seem possible to—to go on without seeing you. It was stupid and wrong of me. Oh, darling, no. . . !"

But in his arms again some instinctive wisdom quelled her resistance. Looking at him, seeing the transformation of his expression from hatred to tenderness, from a dark desire which she hardly dared to name, into another which, in her heart, she could not condemn or

248

deny, she felt that something had been achieved—some evil averted and some good invoked. He said:

"Anyhow, you're here. You mustn't leave me again just yet. This morning it—nearly got me down, too. I almost rang you up, and then . . ."

"I mustn't stay here, Ian."

"No. But . . ."

"The children have gone to the Zoo."

"With Mrs. Trugg. Yes, I know, Mrs. Denning rang me up."

"They'll be on the ten-to-five. We—we could . . ."

"That's only about forty minutes. Listen, darling, we'll get a taxi, and drive somewhere, out to one of the beaches—we'd just have time. And we'll catch the ten-to-five ferry home with the children. Good God!" he burst out with sudden bitterness, "no one need grudge us that!"

She said sadly:

"No."

"Will you come?"

She was thinking of the evening, the night advancing upon her. Arthur would be furious that she had not gone to the wedding. Her tired brain fought away images that assailed it as a tired body might resist the suffocating tentacles of an octopus, and she turned hungrily to the promise of a half-hour's joy for the renewing of her strength and purpose.

"Yes, I'll come."

He snatched up his hat and they went down the stairs together, walking side by side, not touching, and came out into the mellowed sunlight of afternoon. Ian hailed a taxi and they got in. She heard him say "Coogee" to the driver, and leaned back in her corner, hugging an illusion of sanctuary, looking down at her hands folded in her lap, smiling faintly to herself because they were trembling.

* * * * *

Roger, resting on one elbow in the shade, looked at his watch and then at Lesley, face downward on the grass, her cheek on her folded arms.

249

"It's nearly four. Do you want to get your typing?"

She looked up, startled.

"Nearly *four*? Are you sure?"

She looked at her own wrist watch and sat up, smoothing her skirt.

"It is. I don't know how it happened, but it is."

"Do you want some tea?"

"Tea? I feel as if I had only just finished lunch. What are they up to over there now?"

"I don't know. I thought all the fun was finished an hour ago, but they seem to be gathering again. Shall we go and listen?"

"Is the fat man talking?"

"He's just going to."

"All right. But you know, Roger, I always feel—a fraud. . . ."

"Why should you?"

"I want to help—understand—but you can't really—from the outside. You can't if you've never actually *been* there. You feel that they resent you because you've never been hungry or without a bed to sleep in. It's all just a sort of academic problem. And you can't *get* there, because even if you were utterly destitute you'd still have—resources—in yourself—oh, I'm not saying it properly."

Roger said practically:

"There's no need to. And it has to be an academic problem. It's no good sentimentalising it. Every reform that was ever undertaken hurt somebody. When enough intelligent people begin to examine it without bias as an academic problem, it will be solved. Unless the victims get tired of waiting for that. Come on."

She pulled her hat on, but did not take the hand he stretched out to her. It had been, she thought, a queer afternoon. That was probably the effect of seeing, hearing everything through a haze of sleepiness. They had strolled across the grass from the Gardens and stood for a while listening to the orators, but she realised now that their words had been only a blurred background of sound to her confused and uneasy thoughts. At last, almost

irritably, she had refused to think any more of the perplexing situation between herself and Sim, and the still
more perplexing complication which Roger had so
abruptly introduced. She had surrendered herself to her
own hazy weariness, retreated into a stronghold of
blunted awareness and monosyllabic answers. She had
eaten her lunch slowly, relaxed and comfortable on the
shady side of the kiosk, almost empty by the time they
arrived. She had smoked three cigarettes, listening idly
while Roger talked, until the obvious impatience of the
waitress had sent them out again into the shimmering
heat, and the black shade of the Moreton Bay fig had
enticed them.

She might even have slept a little. There had surely
been moments when her dozing had slipped into complete
unconsciousness, for she had vague recollections of coming up out of some enveloping darkness to see Roger,
cross-legged on the grass, scribbling in a little red notebook. She said:

"Wait a minute, Roger. Sit down again. Do you
really want to marry me?"

"Of course. Didn't I say so?"

"In that case it's only fair to tell you that Sim and
I have been lovers."

He looked at her thoughtfully, remembering his
chance encounter with them last night, the tenseness and
excitement of youthful ardour which had unmistakably
surrounded them, and he thought that perhaps it had
taken that knowledge of passion to release her. His words
were reflective, rather than questioning.

"Last night, eh?"

She nodded, drawing a deep breath. Last night. It
still held her, still had power to shake her body and dim
her mind with ecstasy. She said, in a rush:

"And I still don't know, Roger. I still can't feel convinced that it's really impossible. It seems as if so strong
a feeling *should* be able . . ."

He patted her fraternally on the back.

"My good girl, use your head. Of course, it's a

251

strong feeling; it's a biological urge. It's concerned with nothing on earth but reproduction. So far, good. Reproduction's fine. I'm all for it. But you don't want to spend your whole life at it. Or do you?"

"Oh, don't be silly, Roger!"

"You don't. What are you going to do with your spare time then, if you marry Sim? Read books that he doesn't read, make friends he doesn't like, think thoughts he doesn't share, make plans for your children that he doesn't agree with . . ."

She said desperately:

"Yes, yes, I know. I know all that. But there *are* things we could do together, tastes we have in common. Places we both like; amusements, surfing, camping, tennis. He was going to teach me to ski. And to fly. I've always wanted to get my pilot's licence. You're always saying how important aviation is here. You talk as if I wasn't fond of Sim—as if it were all nothing but sexual attraction. . . ."

He shrugged.

"Of course, you're fond of Sim. Did you ever know anybody who wasn't fond of Sim? I'm fond of him myself. But that's not marriage. However, if you must find out from bitter experience you must. I'll be ready for you the day you get your decree nisi."

She laughed half-unwillingly, and stood up, brushing her skirt.

"That's very sporting of you. Let's go and join the revolution. Why—look, Roger, they're going somewhere. Let's follow them, shall we?"

"What about your typing?"

"It's too late. I'll get it to-morrow."

They set off side by side, walking briskly to overtake the straggling but quickly moving procession ahead.

*　　*　　*　　*　　*

The core of it advanced with purpose and intensity, but its outskirts were mere idlers, onlookers, full of chaff and banter, out to see some fun. People on the steps of the Gallery paused a moment to shrug or grin, people on the footpaths turned to stare, loafers on the warm grass looked up from their siesta and then lay down again with newspapers over their faces. Some rose and followed. Urchins drinking at a street fountain waved with hoots of joy, and fell in behind.

Jack Saunders, filled with an obscure excitement, strode along beside a man with a couple of bottles of beer under his arm, and more than one inside him. In twos and threes, urged by curiosity, the crowd swelled, so that from being on its edge Jack found himself at last near its centre, part of the closely welded nucleus which had formed about the fat man. He said to his neighbour with the beer bottles:

"Where they goin'?"

"Parliament 'Ouse."

"What's the idea?"

The man, eyeing him owlishly, launched into a description, vivid, detailed and obscene, of what they proposed to do to the bloody politicians, and the crowd about him raised an appreciative laugh. Jack thought darkly: "It ain't funny!" Someone jolted his injured hand, and an undercurrent of rage brought so savage a look and so bitter an imprecation from him that for fifty yards or so he walked alone, as if some quality in him made a charmed circle of malignancy into which others dared not venture.

They swung round the corner. A whisper ran through the vanguard of the crowd. " 'Ere come the cops! Beat it!"

But they could not beat it. People and traffic were piling up behind them, and ahead even the footpaths were blocked by another crowd. A different crowd. They stopped uncertainly, their objective barred from them, confronted suddenly by something unexpected. The police, they saw now, were not there to suppress a disorderly, but to shepherd an orderly, crowd. Long, gleaming, opulent cars with uniformed chauffeurs were gliding in to the kerb before the church, receiving people no less gleaming and opulent, and moving out again, slowly; approaching.

The two crowds, involuntarily, began to merge. Moving and manœuvring cars pushed them this way and that. Curious people behind pushed forward, and nervous people in front pushed back. Wedding guests, waiting near the entrance to the church for their cars, were engulfed, not suddenly, but slowly, almost unawares. They were forced apart, helpless, by a mob which, so far, was merely confused, quite good-natured, but already faintly infected with the ominous germ of excitement.

Lesley, near the back and standing on tiptoe, caught Roger's arm and said sharply: "Let's get out of this, Roger. It's the crowd from George Hegarty's wedding." He answered, glancing over his shoulder at her: "We can't get out yet. The crowd's packed solid behind us. Hang on to me and don't get off your feet. There's going to be trouble if I'm not mistaken. This parade of the Idle Rich is right into Fatty's hands. The police are trying to clear a way for the cars."

Yes, she could hear them, though she was not tall enough to see. *"Stand back there!"* *"Hey, you, stand back!"* There began a murmur, faint and indecisive, fading to silence, swelling again, a little louder. The crowd in front and a little to the left of them parted. Lesley, staggering with the sudden pressure of its yielding, saw a glimpse of a green, glittering car moving slowly, a glimpse of the people in it. For the first time in her life she found herself included in a look—an expression. . . . It might have been on her own face sometimes. . . . Slightly, but calmly amused, only mildly interested, only mildly curious. The look which people safely sheltered from a thunderstorm give to people still scurrying for cover. This has nothing to do with us. The look which people with reserved seats give to people standing in a queue. Not an unkind look, not a contemptuous look, not even, really, a superior look. Just a look of utter and irrevocable detachment. How odd! How uncomfortable! How sad! But it is not our affair. . . . Our world is different. . . .

For a moment she closed her eyes. That car was not Sim's, but it might have been. Our world is different. . . .

Roger said with sudden urgency: "Hang on!" and she felt his arm press her hand against his side. Simultaneously a terrible wave of excitement ran round her like an electric current, a terrible pressure of bodies filled her with panic and fury, her hat was knocked off, and nothing but her grip on Roger's arm kept her on her feet. For perhaps ten seconds she saw nothing, heard nothing, all her attention fiercely concentrated on the people immediately surrounding her. She fought them recklessly, and they fought her. A man's elbow hit her sharply on the breast; dimly astonished at her own blinding rage, she kicked him savagely, wild with fear of going down under the feet of men who were no longer kindly creatures who, seeing a woman fallen, would assist her chivalrously to rise. Once she was almost dragged from Roger's side. Her right arm ached intolerably with the strain of gripping his; she was reassuringly aware, all the same, that it was as hard as the branch of a tree, his body as strongly immovable as its rooted trunk, and that far from sharing her panic and revolt, he was deeply and exultantly interested in the whole affair. She caught a glimpse of his face now and then. He was acting as anchor for her in this mad sea of humanity, but his attention was elsewhere. His height enabled him to see over most heads, and the impression which her occasional upward glances gave her was of a man forgetful of her, forgetful of himself, oblivious of discomfort or even of danger, in his insatiable desire to observe.

She was suddenly grateful to him for the words of encouragement and reassurance which he did not utter, and ashamed of her own surrender to panic. There was something faintly irritating and yet, at the same time, intensely *right* about Roger's attitude to herself. She was physically smaller, physically weaker, than he, therefore his arm, his bodily strength, was at her disposal. The rest was up to her. Not only here, in the stress of physical conflict, but at every turn, in the stress of mental problems

255

and spiritual anguish, his air of friendly detachment, his matter-of-fact assumption that she had enough intelligence and enough moral stamina to rely upon herself, was heartening, bracing.

She saw through the press of bodies about her a glimpse of another car following the first, and then a third, and she thought:

"Once the cars get away it will be better." They were moving now, in a slow but continuous stream, through a laneway of human beings, and she felt herself and Roger being pushed by degrees nearer and nearer to it. She did not resist, but to the best of her ability aided this eddy which was sweeping them to the front of the crowd. There at least, she thought, one will be able to breathe, there will be a clear space in front of one, not this struggling, sweating, suffocating wall of people. There might even be a chance to work down the laneway and get clear of it all.

They were there at last; her hat was gone for good, her jaw aching from a blow she had hardly noticed at the time, and she discovered that a button had been torn from the front of her dress, and her collar ripped away half round her neck. Still gripping Roger's arm with her right hand, and only half-aware of the slow procession of cars moving past her, she tried with her left to repair some of the damage. Not till his car was abreast and something of familiarity in the lines and colour of its mudguards made her look up, did she find herself looking into the startled eyes of Sim, and the hostile eyes of Lorna Sellman. The car was almost past. She saw Sim lean across and try to open the door, making unmistakable gestures to her to get in.

She never knew quite what the emotion was which flamed in her, nor whether it had gathered added intensity from the fact of Lorna's presence. She was too practical, too logical, to be habitually swayed by emotional symbolism, but she felt a conviction at that moment which nothing in her attempted to deny, that here and now her choice must be made. The easy escape into Sim's moving car, the blessed physical relaxation into upholstered comfort and security were also, in a cold light of revelation, another kind of escape. Here, as always, Sim had that to offer—the easy way, the good things of life not battled for, not striven or sweated for, but just handed to you for nothing. The heat and turmoil about her, the reek of humanity, the ugliness, the endeavour, the fear and the hope, the brutality and the lusty humour were all translated into parts of another struggle in which, whether she liked it or not, she was involved. The escape Sim offered was an illusion. Roger's arm, solid, hard like the branch of a tree, was a symbol, too; Roger's eager stare, his uninhibited welcome to life in any one of its beautiful and terrifying forms, was the real escape, the only escape, by endurance and achievement, into peace.

Not calmly, as a profession of faith, but with the wild rush of an incoming breaker, this knowledge swept her, and she shook her head violently in repudiation of Sim's half-open door, gestured him onward, saw his car moving out of sight.

She heard Roger's cheerful voice: "Poor old Sim." For a moment she thought that his condolence was for a man finally and irrevocably rejected by herself. Then, with a chagrin which was quickly swamped by amusement, she realised that he was pitying the man—any man—who was *there*, and not *here*. . . .

* * * * *

Jack was in the vanguard of the Domain crowd. He had pushed and fought his way to the front because the agony of continual bumping and jolting to his injured hand was almost unendurable. His great size and strength, his dark and menacing expression, the efficacy of his sound arm and fist, had soon won him his present place of comparative ease, and he stood there with his head a little bent, breathing hard and looking upward out of his sullen and observant eyes. The man with the beer bottles, by clinging to Jack's coat, had followed in his wake from the heart of the crowd to its outskirts, and he stood now unsteadily beside his convoy, talking to himself and shouting now and then some drunken witticism which, ominously, the crowd received in silence. Jack watched with a strange, hungry intentness. He saw Sim Hegarty, his twin, get into his car with the Sellman girl. She was a good-looker all right—trust Sim to get the best of everything, even women! He saw their car move off down the laneway, followed by several others. He saw a Rolls Royce slide into the kerb before the church to pick up two men and two women. He knew one of the men by sight—the fair bald one who sat in front beside the chauffeur; his eyes narrowed, and his face flushed darkly.

The chauffeur was nervous. He brought the car out too sharply, so that a sudden wave of movement ran over the crowd as it pressed back to avoid the long, square-cut bonnet, the vast wheels. But Mr. Gerald Manning-Everett put his bald head out of the window and shouted: "Get out of the way, can't you? How d'you expect a man to drive? Stand back! Stand clear there, you!"

There was no sound from Jack and no movement, but when the low mutter like distant thunder ran through the crowd again he smiled. He was utterly absorbed, not in thought, but in an orgy of observation; drinking in a situation where, for the first time, he saw the established order, which had no place for him, opposed by something in whose latent, undirected power he saw his own bitterness, his own frustration, his own resentment multiplied a thousand times.

Someone threw a peanut. It bounced grotesquely from the dead centre of Mr. Manning-Everett's bald head, and a shout of laughter went up. But Mr. Manning-Everett was not amused. He was not equal to the grin, the gesture, the glint of a responsive humour which averts catastrophe and turns bitterness to mirth. Instead, his face red with anger, he tried to summon a policeman with the crook of an imperative forefinger. His words were lost in a roar of derision. The policeman, contemptuous, too busy with traffic to concern himself with peanuts, turned a deaf ear and a blind eye until a shower of small missiles compelled his attention. Mr. Manning-Everett's head was withdrawn abruptly into the car, and a glass window slid up, against which an empty cigarette tin clattered, and a banana-skin smacked wetly. The policeman, with upraised hands, admonished the crowd: " 'Ere, now! Stop that! Stop . . ." But some things cannot be stopped. The long, relentless march of associated events, the endless march of thought and memory, the ominous march of misery quickening to resentment, resentment quickening to hatred, hatred quickening to the wild onrush of action. . . .

Ever since a day years ago when Mr. Manning-Everett ordered a plate of soup for which he would pay, indifferently, the price of two square meals for a hungry man, through a day last week when, in his name, a starving lad was arrested for a youthful impulse, through these last moments when he had displayed not only a Rolls Royce and an unearned authority, but a mean spirit and a poor nerve, this moment which was now upon them had been building and evolving to unite him with Jack Saunders in their common downfall. A beer bottle swung for a moment in a powerful arm about a dark face suddenly distorted; it flew through the air, and there was a crash, a scattering of broken glass, a woman's scream, a glimpse of blood spurting, a figure sagging down into its seat.

* * * * *

The crowd opened to receive him. It may have been sympathy, it may have been fear of his tortured face, his great strength and his desperation. Farther back they had not seen who threw the bottle, and they were too busy fighting for their own safety in the sudden pandemonium to obstruct the violent young man with his arm in a sling who went through them like a machine. He fought his way out on the other side of the street, cursing with the pain of his hand, and looked back for a moment.

The wall of humanity was his protection. Swiftly, looking neither to right nor to left, he made for the

Domain, keeping with small groups of other people. He realised at once how conspicuous his white sling made him, and when he reached the outer Domain he made for the shelter of a group of trees and worked his arm free of it. He stuffed it in his pocket and struggled out of his coat. He was not sure if his arm in its splints and bandages would go into the sleeve, but sweating with pain, excitement and apprehension, he forced it in. After a few agonising seconds he had his other arm in, too, and, with his bandaged hand in his coat pocket, his injury was, to all intents and purposes, disguised. He set off again across the grass, noticing with one corner of his mind the peculiar limping, hurrying gait of a girl in front of him. Overtaking her, he saw that she had lost a shoe, and that she was carrying a hat whose brim was crumpled, and from which a flower hung forlornly by a couple of threads. It flashed into his mind that the police would be after a man with his arm in a sling, and a man alone. Some instinct of self-preservation made him see this hurrying girl as an added safeguard to himself, and he said, as he overtook her:

"You been mixed up in that roughhouse, too?"

She darted a frightened look at him and said: "Yes." He could see that she had been crying. She had a pretty little face, round and smooth and petal-pink, and her eyes were grey. She looked anxious, innocent, respectable. He asked:

"Lost y' shoe?"

She nodded.

"My foot's sore already. I got to get down to the Quay. Have you got the time on you?"

"No. It's round about half past four, though. Perhaps a bit later. What boat y' gettin'?"

"The ten-to-five to Watson's Bay. I work near there."

Luck! Even so faint a glimmer of it revived him to whom it had been so long a stranger. He said:

"Go on! I live there, too. Look 'ere, you 'ang on to my arm and we'll get along quicker. No, not that one, I'll get round the other side of y'. . . ."

"Did you get your arm hurt?"

"Got knocked down and hurt me wrist a bit—nothin' much."

"Gee, I've never been so scared. Me and my girlfriend went to watch the wedding. I work there—at Lady Hegarty's, I mean. What do you keep lookin' back for?"

"Nothin'. I 'ad a cobber with me, too, but we got separated. I thought 'e might be followin'. You work for Lady 'Egarty, eh?"

"Yes. She's real nice. She talks to me when I take her tea in of a morning. But Mrs. Lane, that's the housekeeper, she's an old cat. Will we get that boat, do you think?"

"We'll get it if we keep the pace up. We'll duck down through the Gardens, the grass'll be easier on y' foot."

More cover, he thought, if it came to a pinch and he had to run. He began to feel more confident. There was no reason to think that he had really been noticed, his description taken. He had only got to lie low for a bit. The exhilaration of his mad action, which had hitherto been buried beneath the urgency of his need for escape, flared out suddenly. He'd got even with the . . ."

"What did you say?"

He started, glancing down at her sharply, aware that the viciousness of his thought had forced it, if not actually into words, at least into a little explosion of sound, and he said hurriedly:

"Me wrist gave me a bit of a twinge. Can y' go any faster?"

She mended her pace valiantly, but it left her no breath for speech. When they reached the lower corner of Albert Street they could see their little ferry already at the wharf.

*　　*　　*　　*　　*

Arthur woke with a start, the sound of a chiming clock in his ears. He sat up slowly, rubbing the back of his neck, which was stiff from the position in which he had slept, and opening and shutting his lips with little

261

clicking noises of his tongue against his palate because there was an unpleasant taste in his mouth. Except for a man and a girl smoking in a corner and a waiter standing in patient boredom by the door, the lounge was deserted, quiet, cool, remote from the day whose hot yellow sunlight was just visible in a fierce and uncompromising streak through the drawn curtains. Arthur looked at his watch, blinked, and looked at it again. That must have been four o'clock striking; he had slept almost an hour!

He made a movement to rise, and then sank back in his chair, fumbling uncertainly for his cigarette case. It was empty and he beckoned the waiter.

"Get me some cigarettes. Country Life."

"Yessir. And a drink? Or some tea, sir?"

"No, nothing else. I'm going presently."

He sat morosely, thinking. If he went up now to get his car he'd run straight into the wedding, most likely. He did not want to admit even to himself how afraid he was that Winifred would have kept her word not to go; how anxiously eager he felt that she should, by going, have made a gesture which might lead even at this late hour to a reconciliation. He thought: "I'll go up and see if she's there and drive her home. We'll come into town again for dinner, and see a show or something. I'll order some flowers for her. I'll . . ."

"Your cigarettes, sir, and the change."

He took the cigarettes and waved the change away.

"Bring me some paper, and get a boy to take a note down to Julian, the florist."

He smoked nervously, refusing to confront the one lucent corner of his mind which told him that Winifred would not be at the wedding. The world of illusion and compromise in which he habitually lived made it possible for him to deny unwelcome and to encourage welcome thoughts, and, by the time the waiter had brought him his paper and departed again with a lavish order for roses, he was deep in an imaginary scene of marital repentance, forgiveness and ardour.

Thus pleasantly occupied, he went to the cloak-room

for his hat, washed his hands, and came out at last into the daylight. It struck him at once as he turned towards King Street that there was something happening. The wedding, of course. People always rushed these society weddings. It had been the same at his own and Winifred's—she had almost been mobbed as she left the church to get into the car. He turned into King Street, and found himself, with some astonishment, part of a steadily moving and excited stream of people, all making up the hill. He felt slightly mortified, a little annoyed. There had been nothing quite like this at his own wedding. Before he had gone a block the crowd about him was solid. Crossing Phillip Street, it was reinforced again. His annoyance deepened. After all, what was Hegarty's compared with Sellman's? Sellman's had always been—would always be—the *distinguished* shop. You bought with pride at Sellman's. Hegarty's was vast and cheap and amorphous—the Mecca of the lower middle class, but Sellman's stood for quality, distinction, good taste, the last word in modernity.

Suddenly he became aware from fragments of conversation heard about him that it was perhaps not the wedding after all which half the city seemed hastening to see. He thought: "Wait a bit now, I'd better find out what's doing before I go any farther." He tried to stop, to turn back, and found, with a faint twinge of alarm, that he could not. So he moved reluctantly, thinking that once he got to the church he could go inside, and all would be well.

But with every step his confidence ebbed. At the top of the hill he saw incredulously that the old Queen, plump and serenely oblivious of change, was looking down, her sceptre extended as if in rebuke, over a mass of turbulent and undisciplined humanity which moved, swaying, round her pedestal. He knew now that this was no mere crowd of wedding gapers. That crowd was always mostly composed of women, for one thing, and this one was almost exclusively male. But the tide, for the moment, was carrying him where he wanted to go—along

Macquarie Street—and he could see by standing on tiptoe that already the guests were leaving the church. He thought angrily: "Disgraceful! What the hell are the police about to allow such a thing to happen! I'll bet George is furious!" He was breathless from being pushed and jostled, and on the first step of a flight leading into a building he noticed a niche where he could stand for a few minutes to watch and recover his wind. He saw the police, after a good deal of trouble and several nasty-looking incidents, form a way out for the cars which now, banking up on the far side of the church, were adding to the confusion. He saw a fat man with a beard trying to exhort the people around him to do something or other, and he thought: "That's the chap they want. Gaol's the place for him and his kind. Disturbing the peace, obstructing the traffic, inciting to sedition. . . ."

The phrases ran through his mind with the well-oiled smoothness of cliches and catchwords. He said to a policeman shouldering through the press below him: "There's your man, Constable. He's the ringleader."

But the policeman either did not or would not hear him, and glancing round he met, disconcertingly, the eyes of several men in the crowd which hemmed him in. They said nothing. They only looked at him, studied his face and clothes, considered his voice and bearing. Placed him. And then looked away. Arthur glanced covertly at their now averted faces. They were so impassive, and the shape of bone and the pull of muscle showed so clearly under their tanned skin, that he was reminded for an instant of childhood pictures of lean-faced Red Indians. His eyes moved downward over their tall, loose-knit bodies in shabby clothes, and though they looked at him no more, and he, now, averted his eyes from them, he was still conscious of glances they had given him from appraising, intelligent eyes; eyes which lacked utterly any suggestion of deference. No thought formed in his mind from that momentary spiritual contact with men who acknowledged no tradition, which told them that a man's virtue was in his possessions or his lineage and not innate

264

within himself. But, confusedly, he felt danger; not only personal danger, but danger to all his jealously guarded world, and he stepped down on to the footpath and began to fight his way through the crowd again.

Suddenly he saw Sim and Lorna in Sim's car, and he waved his hat and called to them to stop. But they were intent upon something or someone on the other side of the laneway; Sim had the door half-open, and was beckoning. In a moment they would be past. He called again, and began to struggle through the crowd so recklessly that people rounded on him resentfully, with protests: " 'Ere! Who're y' shovin'?" "Keep y' feet to y'self, Cedric!" "Garn! Don't tease 'im! 'E wants ter play with 'is friends in the Rolls Royce!" And suddenly a big man with the white dust of the demolition job he had just left still thick upon his battered hat and his half-bared chest turned upon him, and said: "Oh, 'e does, does 'e? I'll 'elp 'im! . . ." and gave him a push which would have knocked him off his feet if it had not been for the press of people about him. He said angrily, his voice rising as it always did when he was excited: "I'll give you in charge for assault! I'll . . ."

But he said no more. No one struck him. He would have no injuries beyond, possibly, a bruise or two to show. But for a few moments the crowd played with him as if he had been a sack of straw. Several times he was off his feet, struggling and shouting, but there was so much struggling and shouting going on that he knew he was not likely to be noticed. It was after the crash that it stopped. His persecutors lost interest in him. He stood uncertainly, settling his disordered clothes, trying to see what it was they were staring at. There had been a crash—a sound like breaking glass, and almost instantly a strange, shocked lull, a suspension of movement, a breathless waiting.

Someone near him said:

"It was that bloke with 'is arm in a sling. Did y' see? Copped 'im fair on the 'ead with it."

"Is 'e badly 'urt? The cove in the car?"

265

" 'E'll be lucky if 'e isn't cold."

And then, through a row, half a dozen deep, of intervening bodies, Arthur caught a glimpse of a car he knew well. Manning-Everett's Rolls. Mrs. Manning-Everett in it, and Maurice Dart and another woman. And on the front seat—someone—whom they were supporting . . . a revolting, an incredible glimpse of a bloody face, a crimson-stained collar.

Arthur began with a ferocious desperation to fight back the way he had come. The thought of Winifred crossed his mind. She might be just leaving the church, too. But he found, as usual, the answer which would give him peace and reassurance. "She wouldn't be there, of course. She said she wouldn't. She can't blame me if she went when she said she wouldn't. . . ."

He struggled on doggedly, not too violently, saying: "Excuse me, please," and "Would you mind?" The heat was suffocating, and his progress very slow, but while he fought his way, inch by inch, his mind was busy with plans. "I can't possibly get to the car—that's certain. Shouldn't be surprised if those hooligans have damaged it. I'll get a taxi home, and send Martin in for it later." He reached the corner of King Street and found that here, though the crowd was not less dense, there was a stream of it moving his own way. Near Elizabeth Street it thinned, and he stood still, breathing heavily, streaming with sweat, and looked round for a taxi. There was none to be seen, but, suddenly, moving at a snail's pace through the disorganised traffic, a tram came abreast of him, making towards the Quay. Some impression of freshness, and quiet, and isolation, and a cool sea breeze, stirred him to impulsive action; almost before he knew it, he was aboard, falling heavily, exhausted, into an outside seat, watching the crowd jostling, thinning, disappearing behind him. He drew a long breath and looked at his watch. He thought: "I've missed the four-thirty. I'll get the ten-to-five. . . ."

*　　*　　*　　*　　*

266

Mary Hegarty, lying on the green-upholstered couch in the little glaringly lit room, hardly knew when she became aware of the sounds of confusion outside as something more than the normal confusion of departing wedding guests. She had been lying with her eyes shut because her head ached and the light hurt them, but she was not asleep, and through her troubled thoughts she was conscious of the sounds before she detached her mind sufficiently from Sim to consider and interpret them.

She supposed first, wearily, that it must be only the vociferations of an unusually admiring and enthusiastic crowd. That satisfied her for a little while because she was not really interested. She was old-fashioned enough to know a pricking of guilt at the indifference she could not help feeling for her elder son and all his activities, but too honest to deny it; her momentarily disturbed thoughts returned hungrily, anxiously, to Sim.

Shouts? A strange, swelling murmur like wind in pine trees or distant rushing water. She lifted her head to hear better and then sat up, controlling an instant's dizziness by holding her head between her hands. There was something going on . . . something more than the usual crowd of sightseers. An accident . . . ? That thought, and the instantaneous stampeding of imagination through which most mothers suffer agonies of needless torment, brought her to her feet. In that moment, Sim was maimed, crippled, dead. She offered him frantically, in an anguish of remorse, to Lorna, to anyone, if only he might still be alive and unharmed. She stood up and put on her hat with shaking hands. She went out, her high heels clicking on the stone floor, and stopped dead on the steps of the church, her hand outstretched for support to the wall beside her, her face paling and shrinking with incredulous horror. For in that first startled second she looked straight over the heads of the crowd at the young man throwing the beer bottle. From her vantage point on the top of the steps she could see him quite clearly, a young Hercules, his face dark and disfigured by hatred, and yet, to some corner of her brain which half-sought and half-repelled recognition, familiar. Who was he? Who? The question faded from her mind, for she was staring unbelievingly at Manning-Everett in his Rolls, sagging against the shoulder of his ghost-white chauffeur, his bald head obscenely scarlet.

And the young man had vanished. The crowd had swallowed him. Far across it, near the corner, she could see a movement, a progressive movement such as one might see in the tops of long grasses where a hunted animal fled, and she watched it, conscious of an odd, incomprehensible anxiety. Yes! For a second she saw him again, knew him by his size and the white sling across his breast, glanced about her with a fear which she did not think of explaining to herself to see if he were being pursued. She did not see him again, but she thought of all the upper windows along the street, crowded with spectators, and realised that it was incredible, impossible that no eyes had followed him but her own.

She looked down with a feeling of unreality on the small group of wedding guests still clustered about the steps. Lady Burton, she noticed, was vociferously refusing to get into her car until the crowd was dispersed, protesting with more than a note of hysteria that where there was one lunatic or assassin or Bolshevik or whatever he was, there might be half a dozen more. Several girls, farther back, who were not yet aware of the bottle-throwing incident, and were trying to disguise a youthful excitement beneath a fashionable pose of insouciance and ennui, were telling each other in clear, far-carrying voices that the proletariat was really going quite life-in-the-raw, don't you think? And that it was all, my dear, too, *too* bloody and thrill-making. She saw little Diane Barry, with a really amusing histrionic gesture, wave the next car forward and cry: "Bring forth my tumbril! I must to the Guillotine!" She looked away over their heads again at the now surging crowd.

For the young man's sudden action had broken it up. Nine-tenths of it wanted to see fun, not murder, and the sight of blood had a sobering effect. Lady Hegarty noticed for the first time the rough division of the crowd into two crowds, one mainly composed of men and the other mainly of women, and it crossed her mind confusedly that here one saw demonstrated the fundamental difference of outlook between the sexes. You would never, she thought, persuade the mass of womankind that a political demonstration was more important than a wedding! You would never win them from their unconscious, unorganised, universal allegiance to the first principles of life, of which this ceremony, silly as it had been made to appear, shallow and meaningless as it might seem even to its chief participants, was the symbol. This was what women wanted. They said: "This is bedrock. Your evolutions and your revolutions, your constructions and your destructions, your order and your chaos, your inspirations and your imbecilities, are all founded on this. God help you if someone didn't put it first!"

Lady Hegarty found herself thinking that strange things might grow out of that unassailable conviction. Perhaps men had not fully realised yet the uncanny adaptability of women? Within her own lifetime, what had they not gained in power and in scope for their intelligence. Just how long would they put up with this bungling, this mutilating of the life which they produced? How long, holding the trump card, would they refrain from playing it? Were they not, perhaps, in the form of a world-wide falling birth-rate, playing it already? "War? We will bring no more children into such a world. Hunger? Fear? Unemployment? We will not populate a world for that." Violence, such as this which she had just seen, growing inevitably out of a not inevitable misery—had not some woman borne that desperate-looking young man in agony as she had borne Sim—for this . . . ?

That involuntary connecting of him with her son stirred her memory, brought recognition which was a flash of torment. Jack Saunders. . . ! Sim's playmate and "twin." She had not seen him for some years now, but she felt a strange pain, as if the danger and the despair of a man whose mother's birth-pangs had coincided with her

269

own gave him some claim upon her which was only less than Sim's. Her memory, with anguish and with shame, brought her fragments of a conversation from some lost world of opportunity: *"He only had a pocket-knife . . ."* *"I'd give him some of mine . . ."* *"We have heaps. . . ."* *"Why?" "Why?" "Why?"*

She turned away wearily, and went back to the room she had left, and sat down on the couch with her hands clasped in her lap, staring at the floor. She was so tired and so disheartened that she felt no further interest in the crowd. No further interest in the wedding. No further interest in anything—in life itself. She thought dejectedly: "We begin all right. But somewhere, fairly early in life, we go wrong. Babies, little children—a limitless wealth of unspoiled human material. Energy, candour, joy—and then the process of distortion begins, and the foundation is laid for scenes like this. . . ." She thought with humiliation: "It's our fault. The mothers. We bear them and nurse them and then we allow them to pass out of our hands into a world not fit for them. We give them physical life and spiritual death. We prepare their clothes, their cribs, their nurseries with love and anxious thought—but we don't prepare their world for them. . . ."

Her idly clasped hands clenched suddenly in anger and bitterness.

Mothercraft! Study your charts, learn your rules, follow your routines. Feed them and bath them and weigh them. Spend all your love and intelligence on the building of their bodies in health and beauty. Perhaps some day they will be blown into small and bloody pieces by shell, or perhaps they will be gassed and their skins will peel off, or perhaps they will drown, choking, imprisoned in a submarine, or perhaps they will fall, blazing, from the sky. Or perhaps, if they are very lucky, the beautiful foundation of health which you laid for them will crack under the strain of under-nourishment, unemployment, anxiety, fear. . . .

And if they are really unlucky, they will be like Sim,

270

my son Sim, strong and healthy and handsome and rich and carefree in a tormented world. . . .

She did not even know that she had risen, but the sound of her high heels on the stone floor brought her back to herself. The crowd north of the church had almost dispersed, although it was still thick at the southern end of the street. She was tired, but the remnant of her bitterness lent her an implacable determination. She would not go to the wedding breakfast. She would not wait for the car. She wanted to be by herself for a time, and not to have to talk. She was old; she had wasted and worse than wasted her life, but in the few years which remained she would do something—something. . . .

She went down the steps and turned towards the harbour. A salt breath from it blew up the street, keen, strong, invigorating. She set off slowly with her rather ponderous gait towards the Quay, her heart full of some nebulous but passionate resolve.

PART IV
THE FERRY

"Among the conveniences which were now (1793) enjoyed in the colony, must be mentioned the introduction of passage boats, which, for the benefit of settlers and others, were allowed to go between Sydney and Parramatta . . . from each passenger one shilling was required for his passage; luggage was paid for at the rate of one shilling per cwt; and the entire boat could be hired by one person for six shillings. This was a great accommodation to the description of people whom it was calculated to serve. . . ."

From "An Account of the English Colony in N.S.W.," by David Collins, Judge-Advocate and Secretary of the Colony, 1798.

Lo i s reached the wharf with nearly twenty minutes
to spare. She bought a paper, and found a corner seat where she could put her feet up and
lean her head against the wall, and then she took her hat
off and lit a cigarette. The show, she decided crossly,
had been foul—a sheer waste of time. After the Professor
had left her and gone off to change his book she had
been captured by a lanky young woman in a brightly
patterned smock who had backed her into a corner and
talked a great deal, very fast and very earnestly. Lois
had suspected from the first that it was rubbish, but
she was often uncertain of the hair-thin line which divides
eccentric brilliance from eccentric nonsense, so she had
been, at first, polite, attentive and non-committal. The
young woman had said many times: "Don't you agree?"
and "Am I right?" and "What do you think?" but as she
had never waited for answers Lois had come at last, thank-
fully, to the conclusion that she did not really want them.
She had talked very fluently and most bewilderingly for
a quarter of an hour while Lois had stood uncomfortably
against the wall, growing hotter and hotter, and glancing
now and then at the doorway of another room where
tea was being served. Great names were fluttering from
the untiring tongue like autumn leaves in a high wind,
and Lois, who had now decided that it was rubbish after
all, had become more and more bored. She had said at
last with quiet desperation:

"Will you excuse me? I have a ferry to catch. . . ."

"You must? Well, it has been such a treat to hear
your views, Mrs. Marshall. . . ."

"Denning."

"Mrs. Denning. Of course. But do tell me before
you go . . . if it isn't an impertinent question . . . your
strange and beautiful philosophy, which shows so clearly
in your pictures . . . did you work that out *consciously,*

or was it . . ." she had fluttered her hands coyly
". . . must I use that old, *old*-fashioned word 'inspiration'? I believe I must! Was it inspiration?"

Lois had stared at her helplessly. She was still quite humbly willing to believe that this alarming person knew a great deal more about Art with a capital letter than she did herself, but she was convinced that her own art was her own business, and she scowled a little as she answered:

"I . . . don't think I have a philosophy, really." It was on the tip of her tongue to say "I'll ask my husband," but she realised in time that its truth and sincerity do not always prevent a remark from sounding ridiculous, so she added doubtfully: ". . . and I haven't ever had an inspiration that I know of. I don't really know anything about . . . about . . ."

She stopped. She had meant to say "artistic technicalities," but she knew this was wrong. She did know a great deal about technique, and inspiration, whatever it might be, was certainly not that. The word Oliver would have promptly supplied in place of "technicalities" was "patter," but the young woman had waited only for a pause to capture the conversation again.

"But, of *course*, you do! Such brilliance as yours isn't *accidental*! But here . . ." she had swept a hand, incredibly disdainful, round the room ". . . in this *small* community, so *far* from the influences which worked together to create, for instance, Van Gogh, Picasso . . . so *far* . . ."

Lois interrupted crossly:

"That's silly. There are influences everywhere."

The young woman had pounced.

"Ah! That is just it, that is *exactly* it! You have put your finger on the heart of the trouble, Mrs. Marshall. . . ."

"Denning."

"I beg your pardon? Oh, yes, of course! But among ourselves, in our little fraternity of art, you are still Lois Marshall. . . ."

"I sign my pictures Lois Marshall, but my name is Denning."

"Of course. Now you were just speaking of the influences."

"I wasn't. It was you."

The young woman had begun to shake a bony finger at her, as if to prepare her for the weightiness of her next pronouncement, but Lois, watching it, could only think fretfully that if people must have crimson claws instead of finger-nails they might at least be clean, so she only heard the end of the sentence:

". . . and it is that influence which is ruining art. . . . I speak widely to include all the arts . . . in this country! One cannot . . . one *cannot* . . . escape the influence of one's environment!"

Lois had asked, with a flicker of interest:

"Why should one?"

"Why . . . ? But, my dear Mrs. Marshall, an environment that stifles . . ."

Lois said, hiding a yawn:

"Well, Van Gogh had an environment, too, I suppose. He seemed to survive it."

"Ah, but what a *different* environment! Just imagine, Mrs. Marshall, if you and I had . . ."

Lois, her boredom momentarily lightened by a gleam of malice, did some vivid and enjoyable imagining, so that again the beginning of a sentence was lost to her, and she returned to hear:

". . . environment is *everything* to an artist. Atmosphere. The sense of unity, of oneness, an environment sympathetic to one's art, without hostility. . . ."

Lois said dryly:

"It seems to me that you provide the hostility. I'm quite certain the environment doesn't. It wouldn't be bothered. I don't find it hostile."

"You don't? Ah, but you are not *quite* of this world, Mrs. Marshall. It . . . passes you by a little. One sees that in your charming, *charming* pictures. But for some of us who want to express *reality* . . . the soul is starved

277

for its food in a community which has no understanding of one's work, no appreciation of one's struggle, no culture. . . ."

Lois asked in bewilderment:

"But . . . why? If it's reality you want . . . well, I mean it's all round you, isn't it, wherever you are? You aren't implying that our environment's an illusion, are you?"

The young woman had laughed with hollow despair.

"Indeed *no!* Quite the contrary! To most of us it is a most terrible fact! We strive and strive against it. . . ."

"But *why*. . . ?"

"Because it is lacking in all those graces and traditions which belong to culture. Because it is . . . inimical to art."

Lois, who used up all her patience on her work, had said wearily but distinctly:

"Oh, bosh!"

The young woman had baulked, offended; then, clutching at some impression that to be offended was bourgeois, un-Bohemian and inartistic, she had mustered an unconvincing laugh, and asked:

"Can you account, then, for the *small* amount of first-class artistic work we have produced? Can you tell me why, as a nation, we are artistically negligible? Can you explain why this country is culturally a desert? . . ."

Lois, her natural politeness totally exhausted, had suggested:

"Could it be, do you think, because there are too many people like you in it?"

She had walked slowly down the room, then, wishing that she were taller, but already conscious that her annoyance was merging into an anticipatory enjoyment of the moment when, describing the incident to Oliver, and embroidering, perhaps, just a trifle here and there, they would laugh at it together, and his accurate and ordered brain would form into words for her the amorphous feeling she had been so childishly unable to express.

She reflected now, opening her paper so that she

would not have to talk to any neighbour or acquaintance who happened along, that she never felt humiliated by her intellectual dependence upon Oliver as she had with her first husband, Kit. Kit had had a habit of sweeping aside kindly but firmly her own disordered and half-formed ideas, as an adult might sweep aside rubbish in a littered room and lift a child to a clear space saying: "Now, stand there, dear!" He had told her that she might take it from him that this was so, and that was so; and because she knew that he was clever and she was not, and because at the time she had been too young to separate in her own mind cleverness and wisdom, she had taken it. But Oliver actually seemed to enjoy poking about among her jumbled thoughts, and sometimes, to her astonishment, he brought to light cloudy fragments of ideas which looked surprisingly well when his tongue had decked and polished them with the words she could never have discovered, and set them out in order for inspection.

She knew that he would be able to clarify her own instinctive belief, her conviction which, clarified or not, would still remain unassailable, that to the true artist one environment was as good as another, and that a great deal of nonsense was talked about "culture" and "tradition." For what was environment to any artist, but the negative pole to his own positive, and what was his work, but the crackling spark which leapt to life between them? Was that right? Or would Oliver tell her that her metaphor was wrong, or her syllogism faulty, or that she had an unconnected middle, or something like that? She thought again of the young woman with the claw-like finger-nails, and was ashamed of her rudeness, which now seemed merely cheap, feeling a pang of compassion. For how dreadful it must be to know oneself out of tune. How disastrous to the leaping spark if one of the poles was not functioning properly, and how natural that the one pole should insist that it was the other one at fault. Lois realised that she was getting into deep water with her metaphor again, so she abandoned it, and reflected that it was no wonder that the young woman was so thin and haggard and voluble and distraught. No wonder that she painted so very badly. Would she paint better, perhaps, if she were transplanted to the environment she craved? No; her quarrel was not really with her environment, but with her own spiritual limitations, and these would pursue her. Lois sighed, feeling guilty that she herself should be so rich in contentment, so firmly and serenely at home in her environment, and torn by no spiritual conflicts save those intermittent frenzies and despairs which go with the spade-work and technique of artistic composition.

Over the top of her paper she caught a glimpse of Professor Channon walking down from the turnstiles, and heard behind her the churning of water, the clanging of back-thrust railings, the rattle of gangways which told that the boat was in. She glanced at her watch and yawned, and in the midst of her yawn noticed Mrs. Trugg ushering the three children through the turnstile. That made her think of the pie which, after so much earnest consultation, was to provide their evening meal, and of her own domestic shortcomings, and she resolved that when she went on the boat she would sit somewhere near the children and keep an eye on them in case their father did not turn up after all. She read, idly and inattentively, a couple of paragraphs in her paper, and was mildly surprised, glancing up again, to see Arthur Sellman, who usually drove his car to and from the city every day, walking down towards the boat with a folded newspaper in his hand. Her eye was caught and held by the sudden appearance, on the paved floor at her feet, of a patch of wavering light, delicate circles of it always moving, always changing, reflected from the water somehow by the glass windows above her, or perhaps from some window or mirror on the ferry. She did not look about for an explanation of its mysterious appearance. She was not interested in it as an example of complicated reflection and refraction, but as something which made a familiar little impact upon her consciousness, rousing in her, painfully, a desire to express it in her own particular way. It was, she thought, her paper fallen to her knees, incredibly delicate and beautiful, and the patterns which it made in its incessant movement were wayward, fortuitous, but unfailingly harmonious. With her head against the back of the wall she watched it in a trance of attention, its circles expanding and melting, flowing and contracting in endless, hypnotising beauty. A shaft from the declining sun lay in a bar of warmth and light across her folded newspaper, her clasped hands, and the steadily ticking watch upon her wrist.

*   *   *   *   *

Mrs. Trugg, having shepherded the three children through the turnstile, leaned over it to call parting admonitions.

"Mind you go straight on to the boat now, and sit where you can watch out for your dad. D'you hear me, Denis? And look after Brenda. You take her other hand, Jonathan, there's a good boy."

"She won't let me, 'cause she can't hold Burrendong if she does."

"Oh, well, never mind. Good-bye, love, don't you move away from the boys, will you? Go on, now; you've got 'eaps and 'eaps of time—the boat don't leave for another ten minutes."

They waved good-bye to her. When her stout and waddling figure was lost to view on the footpath, Denis remembered that he had not said: "Thank you for taking us," and he sighed, readjusting the grip of his hot hand in Brenda's, and thinking that Jonathan was clever the way he always managed to be on the side where she was carrying Burrendong. It wasn't that he minded holding her hand really, but he could see Bobby Younger over there on the seat, and he was so big and went to such an important school that he might think it was a sissy thing to do.

Jonathan remarked:

"There's Chloe's mother over there."

"Where? I can't see her."

"She's reading the paper and holding it up in front of her, that's why. And there's Bobby Younger. . . ."

"I saw him long ago. Don't talk so loud, Jonathan."

"Why not?"

"It's rude."

"Gee, Denis, he's got his bat with him. I bet he's a good batter, don't you?"

"You don't say batter. You say batsman. Come on."

When they reached the sloping ramp which led down from street to boat level, Brenda's body knew faintly that prickling moment of fear which assailed it when it encountered the unexpected, and she said with gentle reproach:

"You didn't tell me we were at the slope; mummy always tells me when there's slopes or steps coming."

Denis, remorseful, glanced at her anxiously, but Jonathan declared:

"You ought to know by now. You've walked about here often enough. Gee, Denis, see the propeller down under the water. It looks big, doesn't it?"

"I bet the propellers of the Manly boats must be beauts."

Brenda asked:

"What's the propeller?"

They looked at her in a momentary silence of astonishment and mental readjustment. Denis explained laboriously:

"Well, it's a kind of a sort of—well, wheel. There's one at each end, and they look dark in a sort of—of a—well, the water all round them looks pale green, and they go round and round."

"All the time?"

Jonathan said impatiently:

"No, of course not! What would they go round for when the boat's at the wharf? Hey, Denis, it's like a fish's tail, isn't it? Like some of those ones at the Zoo?"

Alone in the quietness of her brain Brenda moved through strange arrays of thought which only she could understand. Among its intently and laboriously conceived ideas she felt her way as one familiar with it feels his way unerringly in a dark and crowded room. A wheel—that was form, easy form, and her fingers had taught her long ago to know wheels. But Denis had said dark. Darkness was night, when you went to bed, but it was not night now. Perhaps he meant shadowed, which was a little bit like night; when she went out of the sun into the shade she knew, not only from the fading of warmth upon her skin.

And green. She sighed. Green was one of the things which would not live in her mind at all. Those things were called colours. Not all her examination of its furnishings would yield her even a fleeting notion of green. A long time ago she had thought that she knew it, and she had picked up some leaves from the ground one chilly evening and held them out to a little girl called Pat, who was playing with her, and said proudly: "Look at my green leaves!" But Pat had laughed and said they were not green, but yellow; and for a long time that night she had sat feeling and feeling them, the faintly hairy surface, the prickly edge, the little ridgy veins—but still they had felt green.

Now she knew that green was one of the things she couldn't feel. This frock she was wearing was yellow, but it felt just the same as the ones mother said were pink and green and white and blue. And it felt quite different from the thick one she wore when it was cold which was green, too. So it was no good trying to understand about green water.

And fish's tails. She knew those all right, because she had been on the beach at the Bay when the nets were pulled in and all the children ran about catching the small scattered fish in their hands. But they were not like wheels at all. Perhaps there had been some at the Zoo with tails like wheels? She had not been able to touch them there, and she had not liked the cold, shadow-place very much, with its endless steps and its endless little glass windows; the cries and the delighted exclamations of Mrs. Trugg and the boys had been confusing. She had

283

felt cross, and she had very nearly been naughty and screamed and cried. Because it was no use Mrs. Trugg saying: "Bless your pore little 'eart!" and telling her over and over again that they were "like jewels, my pet. As bright as rubies and emeralds." Mother had jewels. They were hard and they had sharp edges and they didn't move. Fish couldn't be like that.

Denis said:

"We're at the gangway, Brenda. There's a little tiny step up."

That was easy. Her hand, holding Burrendong, went out to touch the iron railing, and she walked confidently across on to the boat. Jonathan was saying: "Upstairs in front, Denis, you can see better there." But Denis was lingering; she could feel his pull on her hand. Suddenly Jonathan joined them. She felt the boys kneel on a seat and she kneeled, too, with her arms on a kind of railing, and a hot breath of air, queerly smelling, heavy, oily, came up into her face. Denis was saying:

"See those handles? They're like the ones in a railway signalman's box, only smaller. What do you think those round, flat things are for, Jonathan?"

"What, those sort of iron things on the floor?"

"They aren't iron, they're steel."

"Bet you they're polished iron. Look at all the clocks."

"Those aren't clocks, they're—well—they're sort of—well, they aren't clocks, anyhow, because they haven't got figures like clocks, and they've only got one hand, and they have all those copper tubes leading to them. See those things down there? When the boat's moving you can see them go up and down."

"I've seen them. Millions of times."

"Ar, you're mad! You couldn't have. . . ."

Brenda twisted round and sat down on the seat holding Burrendong and singing to him in case he was tired after his long and exciting afternoon:

> *"There was once a baby 'roo,*
> > *Baby 'roo,*
> *In a valley where the mallee and the grasses always grew;*
> *He would hop and skip and jump,*
> > *Baby 'roo,*
> *Such a happy little chappie, such a pretty fellow, too;*
> > *And when he . . ."*

Denis grabbed her hand again.

"Come on; we're going upstairs."

She counted the steps hurriedly. A little tiny one first. One, two, three, four, five . . . Burrendong was slipping from under her arm . . . six, seven, eight, not many more now, Burrendong, nine, ten, eleven, twelve . . . there! She hitched him more firmly under her arm and trotted along the passageway between the jostling boys. Now they were outside, for she could feel the freshening of the wind on her face, and she sat down again on a seat which was so pleasantly warm to her behind that she lifted and spread her yellow skirts to enjoy it better. Denis called:

"Look, Jonathan, why don't they have a No. 6 wharf, do you think?"

"Gee, isn't there a six?" Jonathan began to count loudly: "There's one and two and three on that side, and four and five and—gee, there isn't a six! But there's two sevens! 7A and 7B. Gee, Denis, there must be a six somewhere. Hi, look, Denis! Look over there where it says 'Cars Without Drivers.' What would be the good of a car without a driver?"

"I dunno. I say, Jonathan, I haven't seen dad come on board yet."

"Well, he might have missed it. Gee, Denis, there's that fat lady I threw the sand on this morning. Look, there's Bobby Younger coming on board. Do you think he might come up here? Hi, Denis, come round here and look at this. . . ."

In a few minutes they were back again and Jonathan said:

"I say, Brenda, there's your father coming down the

wharf. He hardly ever comes on the boat, does he? Do you want to go down and sit with him?"

Brenda said indifferently:

"No, what for?"

Denis and Jonathan looked at her and then at each other. It was an odd but undeniable fact that Brenda did not seem to like her father. They considered this eccentricity for a moment, soberly, and then, deciding that, like all her other small eccentricities, it had something to do with her blindness, they dismissed it from their minds. Denis said:

"I expect he'll stay down in the smoking cabin. I say, Jonathan, I wonder why dad doesn't come?"

"Look, they're pulling the gangways on. He's going to miss it. I don't care, though. We're heaps big enough to go home by ourselves. Gee, look at that lady with only one shoe! Look, over there with the man. That's the man we saw go down the cliff at the Gap one day. Why do you think she's only got one shoe? Look, her hat's all torn, too. Gee, do you think she's been in an accident, or something. . . ?"

"Look, here's the Captain coming into his sort of cabin-thing. I'd like to see in there some day, wouldn't you, Jonathan? Do you s'pose the wheel's hard to turn?"

"Bet you I could turn it. Easily. Hurrah! She's off!"

Yes, she was off. Brenda knew that by the little shivering that ran through the whole ferry and then settled down to a rhythmic throb. Jonathan squealed excitedly:

"Look, Denis, quick, quick! There's Mr. Smith and Mrs. Smith and their baby! They'll have to jump! Gee, do you think she can? Look, he's taking the baby from her. Look, they're going to! Gee, she's not a bad jumper for a lady, is she? Come on, let's get to the very front, we can see better there, and I'm going to pretend to be steering. . . ."

But Denis was staring open-mouthed up the wharf. Ian was running down it, his eyes searching the boat for them, so Denis waved and called: "Dad! Dad! Here we are! Yes, all right, Dad. O.K., Dad!" They waved frantically to his diminishing figure, and when they had seen him turn to walk away up the wharf again, Denis, tugging at Brenda, said:

"Come on!" But she pulled her hand away and did not move. Sometimes, just occasionally, she got tired of Denis and Jonathan. Everything they said began with "Look!" and they were always going somewhere else because they could see better, and those were parts of their life which did not mean anything to her except that she was somehow different. To her this spot where she was sitting was just as good as the spot a few yards away where they were now arguing and exclaiming, and she felt happier alone, hugging Burrendong, humming her song to him, listening, feeling; in her own world which she could inhabit without the perpetual strain of trying to understand, she felt a sense of rest and relaxation. Her song went on contentedly in a crooning monotone, and she swung her legs so that her heels kicked right up against the seat underneath her.

> *"And when he was tired of play,*
> *Baby 'roo,*
> *Niddy-noddy, sleepy-body, do you know what he would do?"*

There was a perpetual noise which was the water—a silky, swishing noise, and another, fainter and mixed up with it which was the noise of froth. One day she had touched some on the water, and she had asked mother what it was. Mother had been surprised at first to know that froth had a sound, but when she listened carefully she said she could hear it too.

> *"Jump into his mother's pocket,*
> *Baby 'roo,*
> *Curl up warm there, safe from . . ."*

The sound and the feel of the engines went together. There was one throb that sounded a little louder than the others, and when it came the seat gave a tiny bounce. That was a Manly ferry hooting quite near—their hoot sounded

different from the others. And there was another noise—
what was that? Distant, clear, faintly exciting—a sort of
music . . . ?

"Denis, what's that noise? Is it a sort of a trumpet?
Where is it coming from?"

Denis was not sure and said so. Jonathan was not
sure either, but he declared with confidence and authority:

"It's a sailor. On that warship over at Garden Island.
Blowing on a sailor's hornpipe. They have to when the
sun goes down."

"Is the sun going down now?"

"Yes, it'll be nearly down when we get home. Hi,
Denis, look. There's a mail boat going out. Can you
see her name? N-E-P-T. I can't see the rest. Do you
think she'll catch us up? Gee, she's big, isn't she?"

Brenda pulled her hat off and held it by its elastic.
She liked the feel of the fresh wind which blew strongly
up from the sea, lifting her hair from her hot neck and
forehead, fluttering her skirt about her bare knees. She
liked the sun and the movement of the boat, and the feeling of being borne forward through an invisible but
familiar world. She liked the feel of Burrendong, plump
and furry, in her arms. She hoped the boys would not
talk to her for a little while.

* * * * *

Professor Channon stood up as the ferry came in to
the wharf, gathering together the scraps of paper on which
he had been making notes, and placing them for safety
in the book he had just got from the Public Library. He
went down and waited while the deck-hands threw their
ropes and adjusted their gangways, but when he was
aboard he stood for a moment, hesitating. He liked best
to sit upstairs, but it was always breezy there, and he
wanted to go on making notes from his book, so he turned
into the smoking compartment below and settled himself comfortably in a corner. He adjusted his spectacles
and began to read, but his mind, strangely unruly, pulled
away again and again from the printed words as a dog on

a lead pulls away exploringly from the path he is being forced to tread. It was an increasingly familiar symptom, this lack of concentration, and he put his book down at last, considering it, facing it as another obstacle to be overcome, another delay in his race against time. It was, he supposed, a result of his illness, or perhaps, more accurately if less simply, a result of his knowledge of the inevitable outcome of his illness. His mind, struggling to maintain detachment and serenity, was yet fearfully aware of being held captive in a doomed prison; it rebelled fruitlessly, bruising the wings of its own achievement on the unyielding wall of his mortality. Conscious of what it had still to do it yet impeded its own progress with these waves of physical fear. Bent sternly to a certain goal it shied away, turned, rebelled, set off upon long, aimless quests as if in a panic hope that even at this late hour it might come upon some revelation, some shining proof of the ultimate human victory in which so far it could only achieve a sometimes wavering faith. How far and how much should one discipline it? And how early? The "inattention" of little children in school, for instance. What precious, delicately expanding filaments of awakening consciousness does one destroy to force into their reluctant minds the harsh reality of twice two are four? At what stage does mental discipline become coercion and repression? Were these involuntary excursions of his own thoughts inspirational, to be followed, or merely a senile "wandering," to be controlled?

The released mind, he thought, taking off his spectacles and settling himself wearily in his corner, had a strange habit of following easily to their logical conclusion tempting by-paths of thought which became darkened and confused by conscious reasoning. It was a kind of mental sleep-walking, when the thoughts, unhampered by a directing consciousness, led safely and confidently through places where reason might boggle, and custom drag upon them. Only with the awakening, the return to awareness of oneself, came the urge for action. Was this another of the rhythms of man's being, another example

19

of the balance, the poise and counterpoise of his construction, by which an equilibrium is maintained for his actions, functions and emotions? Conscious action was, perhaps, the logical result of unconscious meditation, just as the ugly and painful physical function of birth is the logical result of an instinctive and ecstatic emotion. Just as grief and joy, like madness and genius, are parts of a circle and no one can say where the one ends and the other begins. Yes, he thought, there are rhythms which govern us, from the crudest physical functions to the sublimest flights of the psyche! An austere, unvarying pendulum swing—lust and satiety, activity and rest, eating and excreting, exhilaration and depression. And the balance exists, inexorably, far beyond the functions of the body into the functions of the soul where each man is his own accuser and his own judge. That, surely, should be enough to convince mankind that his search for salvation must begin—and end—within. For justice is seldom done by one man to another, but always, inevitably, through the cosmic rhythm of his being, by any man to himself. From that rhythm, as from the rhythm of night and day, there is no escape, and no appeal. That is the ultimate law which never fails or alters. As you sow you shall reap, and in your own being you carry your own destruction or salvation.

What more, he wondered, could be needed to provide for man his universal religion than this simple recognition of his own infallibility? The infallibility of a being who, by desiring something to worship, has revealed that something in himself and cannot escape from it. Memory stirred an echo in his brain and he began searching for half-remembered words. Milton, was it? Something about man sinning against Heaven—"the high supremacie of Heaven" that was it—"affecting Godhead."

It seemed, the Professor reflected, a strange perversity. A strange refusal to see that by his own first awed recognition of divinity within himself he made the first step toward worship. And that, fearing the inexplicable power which governed him, he made the second false and fatal step of conceiving it as apart from himself, so that instead of standing erect in confidence he began to bow down in humiliation, to cry: *"Mea culpa!"* and "I am a miserable sinner!" and other ridiculous things. From there, like a man led astray by an incorrect compass bearing, his spiritual progress had diverged farther and farther from its straight and simple path, leading him on fruitless quests for a peace which he had driven out of his own heart. Leading him to starve and scourge and otherwise torment the body which Christ clearly described as "the temple of God." Leading him at last to an entirely vicious and harmful mistrust of and contempt for himself.

The Professor's involuntary sigh turned into a yawn. He put on his spectacles again and returned reluctantly, but with determination, to his book, but he had read no more than a line or two when, glancing up, he saw with surprise his son-in-law enter the compartment. Arthur noticed him, hesitated, paused. They exchanged greetings with the wary reserve of incompatibles. Arthur added vaguely:

"Been a dreadful day."

"Very."

"Might get a southerly later."

He stood staring out of the window over the old man's head, but his gaze was absent. The Professor, astonished by this unnecessary prolonging of their conversation by one whose only desire, as a rule, was to avoid him, replied: "Let's hope so," and began to read again. But seeing from the corner of his eye Arthur's crisply creased trousers and well-polished shoes still immovable beside him, he glanced up curiously, and found himself thinking: "He doesn't look well."

Arthur's face was sallow. His blue eyes, which had grown slightly protuberant lately, were heavy, the flesh about them darkened and puffy. His collar was . . .

The Professor's roving and observant eyes fastened in some astonishment on Arthur's collar. It was awry—he seemed to have lost a stud—and that was strange enough. But it was also dirty. Not just dubious. Not, by any

291

stretch of imagination, just showing the effects of a hot and humid day in the city. It had marks on it, as if dirty hands had been dragging at it. While he still stared, Arthur sat down heavily beside him on the seat and said:

"Did you—see that crowd?"

"Crowd?"

"Mob of unemployed. Started demonstrating outside Parliament House. Disgraceful affair."

Professor Channon, still eyeing the collar, said:

"I did notice that there seemed to be a lot of people coming from the top of that street when I went to change my book. I thought it was a wedding or something."

"So it was—part of it. George Hegarty's wedding. The two crowds got mixed up and out of hand. Some hooligan threw something at Manning-Everett and cut his head open. They took him to hospital. That sort of thing's the thin end of the wedge for out and out Communism. It's . . ." He turned on the old man a face suddenly dark with anger and accusation, his lips parted for a flood of words. But the eyes which he met reminded him of Winifred's, and they were watching him with an impersonal curiosity so that his words died unspoken, and thinking moodily: "Oh, what's the use?" he slumped back in the seat, his hands in his pockets and his legs spread across the narrow passageway between the seats. The Professor asked:

"You were there?"

He was a little surprised by Arthur's swift, oblique glance and his hurried denial.

"I? Oh, no, no—I just happened. to—I was going up to get my car and I ran into the edge of it. . . ."

His father-in-law said suddenly, sharply:

"Winifred? Was she at this wedding?"

"No—good Lord, no. She wasn't going. She said so this morning. No, she wasn't there. She . . ."

The uneasy, staccato sentences ended on that word. The Professor, puzzled but relieved, asked:

"And the Manning-Everett episode? Did the police make an arrest?"

Arthur scowled.

"If you ask me the police were pretty casual about the whole thing." He added with angry haste: "I don't know if they got anybody. I tell you I wasn't there. How should I know? The fat chap with the beard . . ."

The Professor prompted him silkily:

"The chap with the beard?"

"Someone said the ringleader was a chap with a beard. If he's not in gaol by now he ought to be."

He opened his paper with an irritable crackle. He regretted already the impulse which had made him sit down beside his father-in-law when he could easily, with a casual greeting, have passed on. The truth was he had been a bit shaken by that affair. When a man is not in the best of health, and beset with domestic worries into the bargain. . . . Although he was clear of it all now, he had still been conscious of an obscure nervousness, a sense of solitude which he had never known before. The threat of danger which had been in the air, the shattering awareness of a seemingly impregnable security as being something essentially precarious, had awakened in him some herd instinct for companionship, and his lingering beside the old man had been like the gesture of a child who puts out its hand to find its mother's in the dark. An uneasy memory of his own panic, and an unwillingness to appear in an unfavourable light, had combined with his natural secretiveness in prompting him to lies which, far from the spirit of the truth, were near enough to its letter to deceive himself. He did not even consider whether they had deceived the Professor. Anything which was hidden had always seemed to him to be, to all intents and purposes, non-existent. His egoism, like Lorna's, relied upon a genius for detachment. At the moment the old man had no reality outside Arthur's need of him; having fulfilled that need, having spoken in a familiar voice, having demonstrated by his mere presence the continuation of a familiar world, he had no longer any useful function in Arthur's life, and was discarded. Slowly, but surely, the rents in his self-esteem were being mended. Already his hour of sloth in the hotel wore the guise of legitimate weariness after a hard morning's toil, and the emotional stress inflicted by a perversely wayward wife. Already he had persuaded himself, quite finally, that Winifred had not been at the wedding. Already his moment of terror at the sight of Manning-Everett's bloody head had become transmuted from fear for himself into a horrified indignation on behalf of his friend. Already his ignoble flight was the disdainful and philosophic withdrawal of an orderly citizen refusing to be embroiled in a violation of the peace. Life was restored to normal. Here was his father-in-law beside him, casual and irritating as ever. Here, drifting in by ones and twos, were other dwellers of his neighbourhood, settling down with their evening papers, lighting cigarettes, nursing their hats on their knees, relaxing after the day's work. Here was the familiar salt smell of the harbour which came in through his bedroom window every morning; here was the uninterrupted routine by which his safe world progressed and prospered—unchanged. Another world, unwillingly glimpsed, faded as a nightmare fades with daylight. A moment when he had been forced to realise that his life was like a city which feels for the first time the ominous, subterranean tremors of an earthquake, had passed, and he felt the crust of custom and convention stable beneath his feet again. He nodded genially to a passing acquaintance, gestured greeting to another across the compartment, and settled down to read his paper.

The Professor, with his eyes on the open book, was not thinking of the printed words they saw, but from them, using them as a diver uses a springboard, as the taking-off point and the impetus of his own reflections. He was thinking that his own anxious and urgent desire to finish his book before death claimed him represented a paradox which was an essential of the creed he now embraced. What any human being as an individual might achieve was negligible; and yet, that it should be achieved was of tremendous, of colossal importance. For what mattered was that one should use oneself and the power which was in one to its utmost limit. That spending of oneself was the important, the imperative duty. He thought of the man beside him whose whole life was dedicated to an anxious hoarding of himself. To preserve his comfort, to guard his possessions, to ensure his future, to cherish his illusions—for these things he lived. It was obvious, and interesting, that though, so far, he had quite brilliantly accomplished these aims, he should be so manifestly unhappy. Again the Professor found words waiting in his memory to link with and expand his own thoughts towards completion: *"Man's Unhappiness, as I construe, comes of his Greatness; it is because there is an Infinite in him, which with all his cunning he cannot quite bury under the Finite."* Those words, *"with all his cunning,"* the Professor thought sadly, brought vividly to one's imagination the perversity of man, endlessly trying to tear apart his own inviolable entity, and in his resulting agony staring wildly into a void in search of some other and more merciful judge than the one he is afraid to recognise within himself. His mind is dizzied with the lunatic fancies of his maddening need, and his body tormented by a thousand grim, self-made tabus, but in his pain and through his madness and in spite of all his wilfulness, the law, the godhead in himself, works on serenely, and he faces at the end no far and disembodied deity, but the being, such as it may be, whom he has spent his life in fashioning.

There came a noise of clanging gangways and of churning water; the ferry shivered, throbbed, and began to move. The Professor, glancing over his shoulder, saw his young neighbours, the Smiths, running down the wharf with their baby, and he glanced a little anxiously at the widening strip of water. But it did not daunt them, and he chuckled with enjoyment and appreciation of the girl's spirited jump, her skirts flying above shapely knees, her cheeks flushed with exertion. Passing the door of the cabin they saw him and waved, and he thought as he responded how pretty she looked, and how happy, taking the baby back from her husband's arms, exchanging with him, over its head, a glance still bright with the shared and mischievous enjoyment of their leap. Arthur, who had risen, too, to watch, remained standing. For suddenly there came tearing down the wharf to stop breathless opposite his window, that fellow Harnet. Well, he missed it. The strip of water, Arthur observed with satisfaction, was too wide for even an Olympic champion now. Ian was scanning the upper deck, and suddenly he waved and shouted: "I'll meet you at the wharf, Denis. I'm going home by taxi." And then he saw Arthur. For a second or two they stared at each other through the closed window-pane, and then Ian, expressionless, turned away and walked back towards the turnstiles, and so out of sight.

Arthur, frowning and slightly red in the face, fumbled for his cigarettes as he sat down again.

* * * * *

Lady Hegarty went very slowly up the stairs to the top deck, holding on to the railing and pausing midway to regain her breath. She had stopped being surprised at herself now; although she had hailed a passing taxi when she had accomplished less than half the distance from the church to the Quay, she felt tired, and was conscious only of relief that for the next three-quarters of an hour she had nothing to do but sit still and watch the harbour. She sat at the top of the stairs fanning herself with an evening paper which she had bought, but was too idle to read, and watching, through her window, the other passengers coming aboard. She supposed that she had done an inexcusable thing. George would be rather angry and a good deal upset. Mrs. Stewart would be offended. Sim would be anxious, unless Lorna contrived that he should not miss her. Veronica, who despised her, anyhow, would put another black mark against her name. But really it would not matter at all. A few discreet questions would be asked, and discreetly answered. "But dear Lady Hegarty —where is she? I don't see her here." "She was not very well—such a pity—we are all so very disappointed. The heat, you know. . . ."

She smiled with a touch of grimness and then leaned forward in surprise staring down at the wharf. Arthur Sellman, of all people, coming aboard! Arthur, who never travelled in trams or buses or ferries, and seldom even in trains! She did not remember seeing him at the wedding, or Winifred either, for that matter, but there had been such a crowd, and her memory of it was a confusion of heat and heavy perfume, and the colours of the stained-glass windows blurring before her eyes.

Her surprise at seeing him was instantly over-whelmed, however, by another—a half-shocked amazement. For there, just limping on to the gangway with only one shoe, holding a bedraggled hat by its brim, and followed by a man to whom Lady Hegarty spared hardly a glance, was Maud! She realised that, for all her attempt to treat this naive child as a human being, she had not fully suc-ceeded in grasping the fact of a life which she lived away from the house where she worked, of clothes which she wore when her uniform was temporarily discarded, of experiences she might have apart from the carrying of morning tea-trays.

They disappeared from her view to cross the gang-way and she caught another glimpse of them as they came up the stairs on the opposite side of the ferry. A little per-turbed, a little anxious, she watched, as well as she could, for intervening heads of other passengers as they went for-ward and sat down with their backs to her almost opposite the steps which led into the master's little raised cabin. She remembered now that Maud had proposed to see the wedding, and realised that she had almost certainly been caught in the melée about the church. Relieved as she felt to have the girl's disordered appearance accounted for, she found herself still wondering a little uneasily about the man. Maud, after all, was very young, a mere child, and from the country. Was this her bus-driver, perhaps? She was surprised to find how concerned she felt for the girl's safety and well-being, and still more surprised that without reasonable excuse she had some sense of an important factor unknown, and that her feeling of uneasiness persisted. She had been too occupied with her startled scrutiny of Maud's dishevelled state to spare a thought for her companion, whose bent head had made his face invisible to her. Nevertheless, some chord of memory had been struck; enough to make her study what she could see of him—the back of his bare head and neck, the slope of his shoulders—with a puzzled and almost subconscious effort at recognition. She thought with compunction:

"Poor child—I hope she wasn't hurt, or very frightened. . . . I'll get her to give me her arm up the steps from the boat, and then I can get a good look at her young man. . . ."

She leaned back in her seat wearily, glancing at her wrist watch. It was just ten-to-five, and the deck-hands were already pulling the gangways on board. She stood up to open her window, and watched with bated breath the last-moment leap of the young Smiths. Then she sat down again, feeling gratefully the fresh wind on her face, abandoning herself with a relief which was the measure of the day's previous strain to this little voyage which meant, for a time, compulsory inertia, compulsory isolation, compulsory peace.

The Smiths were coming up the stairs in front of her. The girl paused, smiling, the baby in her arms.

"How do you do, Lady Hegarty. . . ."

"How do you do. You made my heart stand still just now when you jumped on board. With the baby, too!"

"Oh, I won the broad jump three years running at school! And we simply have to get home by six or it puts all baby's feeds out. She's still on four-hourly."

Lady Hegarty smiled, pushing one grey-gloved finger into the baby's curling palm.

"You young mothers are so conscientious nowadays. It's wonderful of you. But—how about this? Is this allowed?" She lifted a dangling dummy by its pink ribbon. The young parents exchanged an abashed and apologetic glance, and Mrs. Smith protested hastily:

"Oh, *no!* The clinic sister would simply never forgive me! But we've just been to see Dick's mother, and —well, you know how it is—I let her pin it on. But, of course, I wouldn't *dream* of using it. I'll burn it the very *minute* we get home. Well, we're going up the other end where Dick can smoke. Good-bye, Lady Hegarty."

She watched them go, smiling faintly, and then turned to her window and a scene familiar to her since childhood. The tall Norfolk pines still stood in the garden of Admiralty House, and the little steps which had intrigued her as a child still led down to its wharf and the deep water, golden-green over the yellow rocks. Lawns and trees sloped to the harbour edge on Kirribilli Point, but there were more flats and fewer houses than when she was a girl. Gulls perched on the lights and buoys; in those far-off days she had found the same joy in watching them which she felt to-day, admiring the curve and movement of their wings alighting, the silver gleam of the sun on them as they wheeled and sank, the peevish forward thrust of their beaks as they stood balancing.

The bays swung into the land down the long northern shore, Neutral Bay, Shell Cove, Mosman, Sirius Cove, Clifton Gardens; the red roofs of the houses and the mingled greens of gardens and bushland came down to meet the grey of the rocks at the water's edge, and the still sunlight of late afternoon, so deep that it was amber rather than golden, lay over the hilltops. Her tired eyes saw it all without awareness, but it brought tranquillity; she put her hand up to the window and spread its fingers to feel the cool air rushing between them.

Maud, she noticed presently, had risen and gone across to a window to look at something. The young man turned partly round on the seat and Lady Hegarty found herself looking at the arm which thus came into view. Was it an artificial one? . . . The hand was buried in the coat pocket, but there was an odd . . . She saw his profile, and her heart thudded. So he had got away! She

299

thought anxiously, incredulously: "Maud? Could Maud have been mixed up in that . . . ?" Yes, she knew now what the hard ridge beneath his sleeve meant, and she wondered with a pang of compassion what his injury was, and how much it had hurt him to dispose of his sling.

Then Maud saw her. She came instantly, with her usual naive impulsiveness, and stood before her employer on her shod foot, curling the other round its ankle to hide a hole in the toe of her stocking. She said:

"Why, fancy you being here, Madam! Gee, wasn't it awful at the wedding? It was a real shame, I reckon. Did you—I mean weren't you . . . ? I thought you'd be at the reception, Madam. . . ."

"I wasn't very well, Maud, so I didn't wait. Did you have any trouble in the crowd, child? Where's your shoe?"

"It came off, Madam—they were a bit big, really— my sister gave them to me. I was real frightened, and me and my girl-friend got separated, so—he—that chap . . ."

She half-turned, indicating her companion, and Lady Hegarty looked past her into the young man's eyes. The expression in them startled her, but only for a moment. She thought: "Of course! I represent danger to him, everything that's against him. And punishment. . . ."

She said to Maud:

"Yes, I know him. He used to go swimming with Mr. Sim when they were little boys. Is he a friend of yours?"

"Oh, no, Madam—I just happened to meet him and he helped me down to the boat. He was caught in that crowd, too. He got his arm hurt. He's—he seems real nice, I think. . . ."

Lady Hegarty said:

"I see."

He was not looking at her now. She could see only his back, bent forward, his head lowered, as if he were thinking. What would be his thoughts? Wondering if she had seen him throw that bottle? Telling himself: "She can identify me?" She thought: "I told Maud I knew him. And I do—I have known him, in a way, nearly all his life." She was surprised to find how complete her knowledge of him felt though she had not spoken to him for years. Their scattered meetings during his childhood, boyhood, young manhood, made a sequence of pictures clearer than she had ever realised, a chain of knowledge building up a conception of him which she could not feel to be faulty. She tried conscientiously, mistrusting her instinct, to put her thoughts into words: "What he did was wrong, and mad, and violent; but he isn't an anti-social person—he's only unlucky—and astray. . . ." With a faint shock she confronted a question of her own individual responsibility. What was behind a mad action like that but hatred? And what was behind hatred but accumulations of injustice? Words returned to her like an echo: *"There's that young fellow Saunders outside again, Madam, asking for a bit of work. Shall I tell him to wash Mr. Sim's car?"* And from farther back still Sim's urgent and bewildered cry: *"He only had a pocket-knife . . . Why . . . ? Why . . . ?"*

It was that memory which brought her recollection and inspiration. She thought with a strange feeling of excitement: "It was this very day sixteen years ago!" She did not know why that coincidence seemed so important, or why she found in it a hint of poetic justice, but she felt gratefully that it was somehow fitting that upon this day of all others she should be reoffered at least a fragment of the opportunity she had somehow failed to seize so many years ago. She said almost eagerly:

"This is his birthday, Maud. I remember because it's the same as Mr. Sim's. Go and wish him many happy returns of the day from me."

She watched the girl return and give the message. She saw the young man listen, think, hesitate, and then turn. His smile, she thought sadly, was not the frank and ragamuffin grin of his childhood, but it was a smile, and he lifted the hand of his uninjured arm to her in an awkward salute.

*   *   *   *   *

301

Bobby Younger selected a bull's-eye from a sticky paper bag and put it in his mouth. He had a book which Goat Mason had passed him in History that morning, in exchange for a pulley and half a nulla-nulla, but although he held it open on his knee he felt too idle and too much at peace with the world to read. This particular spot, downstairs at the very stern, was his own, sacred. The only person he ever welcomed there was Mr. Harnet, the father of those two little kids he often saw down in the Cove. From him he had learned a number of interesting things. He could tell the names of all the lights, for instance, and what colours they were at night, and whether they were fixed or flashing. And he had explained the difference between dioptric and catoptric, and about the eastern channel leading lights, which stood one on the foreshore and one high on the hill, quite near your home. When you asked him, for instance, what the green winking light was which you could see from your bed on the verandah, he could tell you at once that it was the eastern Channel Buoy off the Sow and Pigs rocks, sixteen feet high, five miles visible, Sixth Dioptric Acetylene Gas, and that it shone for one-third of a second and was eclipsed for two-thirds. He knew that the light off Bradley's Head and the one on the tower of Fort Denison had bells which sounded continuously during fogs, and that the red neon tube diamond in the centre of the bridge was a hundred and eighty-five feet above the water. He could tell you what the ships entering the port had to pay for pilotage—except whalers—and the total distance round the foreshores, and how many square miles of water there were, and, in fact, anything else that you asked him, so that on this daily voyage he was a companion to be cultivated and not repelled. Not many people intruded. Bobby had, indeed, some trouble with lovers seeking solitude; only this afternoon when he arrived there had been a couple spooning, but he had found from long experience that such people, by the mere fact of their bemusement, were easily dealt with. He never embarked upon his homeward journey without a bag of "chews" to sustain him, and one of these, well-licked and generously smeared along the seat behind the lady's back, was almost invariably enough to send her, with exclamations of dismay, from his domain. The bull's-eye which now so comfortably distended his cheek had secured his present solitude, and he put his feet up on the stern railing and reclined at ease, his fingers absently caressing the smooth surface of his new bat, which lay across his knees, and his eyes, half-closed against the glare of the declining sun, glazed with a contented inertia. Funny the city looked, receding into that golden light. As if it were not real. Even the bridge looked insubstantial, and Fort Denison a dark speck, shapeless in the dazzling water. That liner, the *Neptune,* was overhauling them fast. He eyed her critically, feeling himself an authority on liners since his visit, last year, to New Zealand. Two gulls wheeling and swooping near the ferry claimed his attention. One had a fish and the other was bent upon piracy. There, he'd dropped it, the poor mutt! Gosh, but they could dive! He had it again, and he was soaring away ahead of them, out of sight, while the other, discomfited, came down to bob cork-like on the foamy waves of their widely spreading wake.

*   *   *   *   *

The Professor was writing on his scraps of paper in his neat, small handwriting:

> ". . . *so that it is useless to contend that humanity has not yet found a method, an ethic, by which to live at peace. That ethic was given to it two thousand years ago, and whether one believes it to have been expounded by the Son of God or by a Galilean carpenter . . ."*

As he wrote he could feel the pain stirring. Keeping one hand over his pages so that the draught from the door would not carry them away, he straightened his back and pressed the other against his side, thinking that he might as well submit to his operation and get it over as quickly as possible. Increasing pain, Denning had said.

303

Well, if it increased much more he would get no work done at all. Already it was clogging his brain, so that thought came heavily and reluctantly; already it thrust itself up through his difficult concentration, so that a sentence which had been clear in his mind faded and was gone before he had got it on to paper. He began to write again, slowly, one segment of his consciousness fastened apprehensively on the pain. So long as he kept quite still, so long as he breathed quite carefully. . . .

The writing was small and clear and firm. It crept steadily down the page, and Arthur, curious, glanced at it sideways now and then from behind his paper.

" . . . for as long as the founder of that creed remains the Son of God, so long will His teaching and His example remain an abstraction, a far light, something beyond the achievement of unaided mortals. But in the moment when He becomes, for all men, human like themselves, begotten by man, born of woman, lit and driven and sustained by no power which they also may not claim, His teaching will become practical and intimate and real, a not impossible standard of human behaviour and of human thought, a demonstration to man that godhead is innate within himself. For Supernatural greatness may evoke awe, but natural greatness will provoke emulation, and by . . ."

He stopped. He had one of those startling and swiftly fading moments of mental lucidity when one sees truth as so extraordinarily simple that the civilised brain cannot deal with it. He recognised wearily that when a truth becomes a platitude its essence is gone, for the brain, like the rest of the body, sets up its immunities. Only in such rare moments as this one can truth return to flash and fade like a lighthouse beam across the sky. Mankind has only one wealth, the earth and its fulness; only one power, the power of his creative spirit. That was his thought, but with the passing of his moment he could find no revelation in it. It had been said too often; man had been inoculated by so many repetitions of it that it had no power, now, to set ardour raging like a fever in his blood, and he felt its resplendency tarnish as his brain began to work on it, felt it disintegrating, fading, tried to hold it, lost it, and suddenly, with a movement of despair, tore his pages across and across. . . .

*　　*　　*　　*　　*

When Jack subsided on the seat with a grunt of relief, Maud, beside him, nursing her unshod foot childishly on her knee, had said: "Well, I didn't think we'd catch it, did you?"

He made no reply. When she looked at him his face was clouded and preoccupied, his narrowed eyes were staring at the floor; she thought that his wrist must be hurting him a good deal. Secure in his obvious unconsciousness of her, she studied him out of the corner of her eye, admiring his size and the rough-hewn handsomeness of his dark face, already turning in her mind the phrases she would use in describing to her girl-friend this romantic encounter. When the boat began to move she was hardly aware of it, though her hot and weary body welcomed the cool gush of air which blew in through the open doors. She was wondering where he lived, and what he did, and when she would see him again.

He sat with his shoulders bowed wearily, his injured hand still buried in the coat pocket from which he dared not take it. It was hurting him wickedly, a burning, throbbing pain which ran from finger-tips to elbow, and with the slackening of the physical effort necessary for escape, fatigue and dejection had settled upon him. The cops were sure to get him. There must have been hundreds of eye-witnesses, dozens who had watched his retreat. He realised, now that he had time to think about it, all the circumstances which were against him. If it had been any other wedding but that one! Why had he not realised that at the time? He had mowed lawns, washed cars, repaired launches, clipped hedges and sold fish at the homes of a dozen families which had been represented there this afternoon. Sim had been well away before it

305

happened, but it was too much to hope that no one else had recognised him. Here on the ferry, travelling down the long, familiar waterway, he was safe for the moment but when he thought of the jetty at the Bay he knew a sick tremor of fear, imagined that the police would be waiting for him; and moving restlessly in his seat he made again that involuntary and incoherent sound of torment and despair.

Maud asked with swift concern:

"Gee, that wrist of yours must be fierce! Do you think it might be sprained? Rubbing it might be good. My brother . . ."

He said hastily to deflect her attention:

"It's nothin'—gives me a twinge now and then. Look at that liner be'ind us. 'Ow'd y' like to be on board 'er Goin' to China or Japan or somewhere?"

She said wistfully: "I always did want to go to Japan. I seen a picture once where all the cherry blossoms were out along a sort of lake with bridges. It didn't hardly look as if it could be real. . . ."

She jumped up and went to the window to stare back at the big ship which was following them down the harbour, and he watched her standing there with her arms along the back of the seat, and her hair whipped round her cheeks by the breeze. A dull emotion of pain and frustration stirred in him. He thought: "Me to think of marryin'! That's funny, that is! And after to-day—after that. . . ! If that bloke dies, and they get me, it's—murder. . . .

"Where the hell's she goin'? . . ."

He turned to watch her. The slow insidious fear which his own last thought had awakened in his brain was galvanised into a shock of terror. For there was Sim's mother—Sim's mother who should be at her son's wedding, sitting near the steps and looking straight at him.

His heart pounded wildly for flight or action. But here on this little ferry in mid-harbour neither flight nor action was possible. He turned his back, his whole body cold with sweat, and the energy which could find no physical release set his brain churning and grinding in an agony of thought.

What was she doing here? What the hell was she doing here? Why hadn't she gone off with the rest of the wedding party to eat and drink and dance and talk about the dirty criminal who had thrown a bottle at their friend, Mr. Manning-Everett? She must have seen him. She knew him like she knew her own son. She must have followed him, and when she got home she'd ring the police and . . .

His brain plunged wildly among plans of escape. Here he was helpless. No good trying to hide down at the Bay, even if they didn't get him at once. That little spit of land could be combed . . . unless . . . there were places he knew of along the cliffs, but how would a man exist there, and how would he get there with one hand useless? He might take a launch and risk getting away up the coast. . . . That one of Sellman's, it was the fastest on the harbour, and he knew it from doing repairs to it. . . . Robbery . . . what's robbery beside murder? . . . What's she telling the kid down there? What are they gassing about?

He wanted to look round, but some obscure instinct kept him motionless, feeling, as Winifred had felt earlier in the day in a different crisis, an irrational sense of safety in the mere absence of action. And then Maud was beside him again. He glanced up at her wretchedly, suspicion, defiance and appeal warring in his eyes. She was saying happily:

"She says it's your birthday. She said to wish you many happy returns. . . ."

For a moment he could not think. Out of a strange blankness he felt relief emerge in tiny filaments, wavering uncertainly, fearfully ready to retreat. He said: "Eh? What's that?"

She repeated it. Suddenly he knew that it was, quite finally, reprieve. From her, at all events, he had nothing to fear. She had not seen him. She did not know. Hope surged back into him. His birthday—he'd forgotten that. Was there luck in it? She had wished him . . .

He turned in his seat and looked back at her. She was a decent old dame. Her face was kindly, and she was smiling at him. His answering smile and his gesture held a hint of boyish elation and bravado.

Maud was saying:

"You never told me you knew her."

"I don't know 'er much. I just used to see 'er on the beach with Sim when we was kids. And I done a few jobs at the 'ouse from time to time. . . ."

"I s'pose that's why you went to the wedding. Funny, I was thinking you didn't look the sort that went much on weddings."

He glanced at her, pleased with her plausible explanation of his presence, gloomily aware that he would not have been quick enough to think of it for himself if she had asked him earlier, point-blank, why he was there. He muttered:

"Well . . . I just thought I'd go along . . . I 'adn't anythin' better to do. . . ."

She asked:

"Did you get a good view? Were you right up in front? Me and my girl-friend . . ." He interrupted her sharply:

"I never got near the front. I 'ardly saw a thing. See, that ship's catchin' us up. What's 'er name? Can y' read it from 'ere?"

She looked over her shoulder and he watched the lovely line of her strained throat and lifted chin with a sombre, hungry admiration. Her lips were moving as she spelled out the name, and her face was bright with a childish triumph as she turned to him again.

"*Neptune*—that's it. I can't see the last two letters, but that's what it'd be. Can you read it? I got pretty good eyesight. Up in Gundagai . . ."

Suddenly, clumsily, he tried to joke with her.

"Gundagai, eh?

" *'The dog sat on the tucker-box
Nine miles from Gundagai'*."

She interrupted with pretended petulance:

"Oh, give it a rest! We get that tired of the dog on
the tucker-box up there. . . . And, anyhow, it isn't nine
miles, it's seven, 'cos me brother measured it on his
speedometer; he's got a delivery van."

Jack asked slowly:

"Pretty good country, ain't it? I often thought I'd
like to get outback a bit—y' get tired of the city. . . ."

She did not speak for a moment. In that brief interlude of silence she sat with her hands clasped in her lap,
and an absent look in her eyes which made her seem
strangely sad. She said at last with a sigh:

"It's not so bad. When I was there, well, I was just
mad to get to the city. But now I'm here I get that home-
sick I don't know how to get along sometimes. Where I
lived we weren't even on the railway, so it was that
slow. . . . But it was real pretty. You ever been up that
way?"

He shook his head. She went on eagerly, a new ani-
mation flushing her cheeks:

"We used to drive from Gundagai in a sulky when I
was little. Now my brother has the van it's quicker. All
along the road it's real pretty—you know, just paddocks
and trees, nothing special, but being so hilly makes it
sort of . . ." She paused, at a loss for the word she wanted,
and finding, instead, another thought, she flickered a
moment's coquetry at him. "There's a bit of poetry about
that, too, seeing you're so strong on poetry. My father
used to say it to us when we was kids, driving home. I
can't remember all of it—something about:

" *'The mountain road goes up and down
From Gundagai to Tumut town.'*

Gee, so it does, too! I've got an auntie in Tumut. Her

309

husband got killed coming down from Talbingo one night on his horse. . . ."

He asked:

"Did y' do much ridin'?" She laughed:

"I was ridin' before I walked, pretty well! We used to ride ten miles to school every day. What's wrong? Smut on me nose, or something?"

For she could no longer pretend to disregard his steady, disconcerting stare. Her eyes were brilliant and her colour high with excitement as she met it, but excitement deepened suddenly to something which was half-ecstasy and half-fear. He was looking at her, one corner of her brain recorded, as if she were something in a shop window which he greatly coveted but could not afford. He asked slowly:

"Ain't y' goin' back there?"

"Oh—I s'pose I might—some day. . . ."

He relapsed into silence and abstraction again, but now she did not watch him, being busy with thoughts of a home and a life which, with absence, distance, had acquired a secret glow, an appeal half-sad and half-romantic, so that when he did speak again she looked at him vaguely and reluctantly, answering her own thoughts as much as his question.

"What's the chances of gettin' work up there? I'd like farmin'. What d'y' grow there? Wheat?"

"We had some wheat, but it was mostly dairyin' we did. Yes, I reckon I'll go back. I dunno if you'd get a job, things've been pretty bad. . . . I 'aven't got used to it here yet—wakin' up in the morning and seein' the water out me window instead of the paddocks. And the people aren't—well, so friendly-like as they are up home."

Her voice trailed out into a silence which neither of them noticed. She was faintly surprised herself by the poignant ache of homesickness which her own words had stirred in her, and she looked ahead down the glittering water with blind eyes, seeing far-reaching paddocks going up to meet the hills, and long tree shadows barring the pale sunlight of early morning; and even, with a tranced objectiveness, herself, bare-footed, running down through the frosty grass with her milk pail swinging in her hand. The picture she saw was memory, clear and fine-edged, but Jack's, confused and uncertain, was imagination. There were ploughs in his picture, and sweating horses, and wire straining between fence-posts, and trees falling. It was a picture in which he saw himself as always violently in action, and in which Maud, when she did for a moment appear, seemed merely, like the earth itself, something for him to spend his strength upon. He looked vaguely through the open window at the tree-clothed slopes of Bradley's Head and the white tower of its light upon the point, and a resolve began to shape itself in his brain. He asked:

"'Ow far is it? To Gundagai, I mean."

"It's—oh, about three hundred miles, I reckon."

He nodded, thinking again. He'd get up the country. He'd walk it, humping his swag and making what he could along the road. S'posing you did twenty miles a day? Well, he thought with a grim humour, at least you were getting some exercise! And somewhere—somewhere in this vast country there must be . . .

Through the dark web of their preoccupations and through the bright actuality of their physical world there came tearing one of those incredible moments of tragedy and horror which rob life of reality. At one moment there were quiet and thoughts, and the noise of water and the throb of engines. And the next a siren scream so shatteringly close, so madly urgent, that the heart stood still under the shock of it; and then only shrieking and shouting and chaos, the bright harbour no longer a picture for you to gaze at, but a menace, a terror, death waiting.

* * * * *

The Professor's hands were arrested in mid-movement by the shattering blast of the *Neptune's* siren. Holding aloft the torn fragments of his pages, he sat motionless in a second which seemed like an eternity, conscious of sharply lifted heads, startled faces, a poised

311

moment of uncertainty and apprehension. Then there was a crash. The whole ferry heeled over, and the Professor found himself and Arthur, and half a dozen other men who had been sitting on the same seat, lying on their backs against the closed windows; and through such windows as were open, and through the door, green water was rushing in upon them.

When the Professor struggled to his feet it was already round his knees, and he was aware of Arthur shouting and struggling just beside him. He gasped out: "Dive for it!" and prepared to launch himself against the rising wall of water which poured through the open doorway. It was their only chance, he knew, and a slender one. The alternative was to die here, trapped in the filling cabin, and he braced his body, aware even in this moment of its weariness and of its inadequacy to meet such an emergency as this. He found it difficult, gripped about the thighs now by the swirling water, to keep his balance, and suddenly he felt Arthur clutch him by the shoulder, dragging him backward. For a second, as he turned, startled, he stared into a face quite insane with fear. He clutched for support at the top of the door, now leaning diagonally above him, and suddenly Arthur's feet drove violently against his stomach, using his body to provide the necessary impetus for a frantic upward dive through the narrow aperture.

Professor Channon fell backward. His consciousness was nothing but a flame of pain, red-hot, consuming. But some instinct forced him, as he felt water close over his head, to struggle upward. What had been the opposite wall of the cabin was now its roof, and winning to the surface again he saw its windows not far above his head, and lifted one hand weakly to clutch at some support. It grasped one of the little brass rings by which the windows were raised and lowered, and he held on, keeping his head above the rapidly rising water. It would be only moments. He found himself thinking that quite clearly. It would be quick. For himself it would be quicker, better, than the death he had been awaiting. Farther along the cabin he saw other men trying to break the glass, but he had no strength left for that, and already water was splashing over the windows outside, so he doubted whether escape lay that way. It occurred to him, too, that it was perhaps strange and foolish that he should cling thus to his few remaining moments of life, the end being so inevitable; and then he knew with a sense of comfort that it was not foolish after all, but right. To spend yourself to the utmost, to use yourself to the last second, to fight death with life till there was no more life left to fight with. . . .

The physical agony of that one moment had passed now into a steady, numbing pain, but another agony remained, an agony of sorrow and of doubt. For Arthur's action had been his own last contact with the humanity, to which, finally, after a lifetime of searching and disillusionment, of hope and despair and renewed effort, he had finally pinned his faith. He thought of Arthur without resentment, wondering whether he had escaped or whether some wreckage had trapped him and foiled his attempt; and he thought, too, with the haziness of flickering consciousness, that it was strange and rather sad that Arthur should have fought so desperately for so warped and trivial a life, abandoned all pity, all generosity, all shame, denied those truths by which man finds himself, for a few more years of unprofitable existence, for what shall it profit a man . . .

He knew with weary resignation that his mind was wandering again from the laboriousness of thought to the easiness of quotation. But there came to him, slowly this time like the steadily expanding light of a sunrise, that sense of revelation which he had already found—and lost —so many times. The water was round his mouth and ears now, lapping against his cheeks and over his closed eyes. But he was possessed by a faith which his clouding brain would have no time to tarnish, a truth which to his dying cells and the slowing rhythm of his life, was Truth at last, complete, unassailable, serene. For what shall it profit a man if he gain the whole world, and lose his own soul . . . ?

It remained. His wilful and destroying intellect was numbed, impotent to harm it. The last glimmer of his consciousness, sinking away in slow whirlpools of sound and darkness, was the gladness and contentment of discovery.

*　　*　　*　　*　　*

Arthur struggled up through the roaring water. Quite incapable of coherent thought, he was yet vividly conscious of outrage. This was too much! His resentment was formless, and without direction, but its very intensity was his strength. He resisted the elements which were thus assailing his physical safety with the same ferocious panic with which he had resisted less tangible perils earlier in the day, astonished to incredulity that he, Arthur Sellman, should be vulnerable to such brutal assaults upon the security of his mind and body.

His head broke the surface of the water, the sun dazzled in his eyes. It occurred to him that not once in a year did he travel by ferry, and his sense of injury swelled, fastening with hatred on the crowd, the malcontents, the riff-raff who had driven him to it to-day, and was not shadowed, not even touched by any suspicion that no power on earth but his own cowardice had brought him here. He thought: "My God, it was close! Got to act quickly in a crisis, got to keep your head. In another second or two. . . ." That was as near as he ever came to a consciousness of what he had done. He was alive. Down there in the water-filled cabin, old Channon's body might be floating, but he, Arthur Sellman, was alive. To be alive, was to be sentient, to be kicking your arms and legs, to be thinking again and again with awed self-congratulation: "My God, it was close! I might have been caught, too! I might have been there, but I escaped, escaped, escaped. . . ." The word ran on through his mind like a refrain while he battled with the water. He was not a bad swimmer, but he was out of condition, and he had eaten too much lunch, and his clothes weighed

314

him down. He looked about, tried to hail a launch, swallowed a mouthful of water, and felt a cold chill of fear. For there was a suction which seemed like a weight pulling sideways on his legs, and it took all his strength to fight it. All and more. Twice his head went under, twice it came up again, and once he had a glimpse of people hauling a woman out of the water on to a launch, and shouted to them chokingly, and saw that they did not hear. He became very tired, and the word "escape" went on beating insanely in his mind as if the very rhythm of his pounding blood had caught it, and would not let it go. He felt his open hand slap down weakly, helplessly on the surface of the water, he heard a kind of report, had a strange feeling that the water was hot. Something hit him sharply on the forehead, and the word "escape" leapt out of his mind, and stood before his eyes, vast, illuminated, and then shot away into darkness with an explosion and a hissing like a rocket. His last gleam of consciousness was of an overwhelming, an intolerable solitude.

*   *   *   *   *

Bobby sat up suddenly, his eyes widening, the rhythmic, sucking movement of his jaws suspended. He had opened his book and read a page or two when something had made him look up. His eyes bulged with astonishment. He stared at the *Neptune* incredulously. It was . . . it was . . . jolly close, wasn't it? It was making straight for them. He thought uneasily. "I guess I'll move away . . . I . . ."

The siren of the big ship shrilled out horribly, and almost immediately came the impact. Bobby's only conscious thought was of his bull's-eye. "Gosh, this'll choke me!" He spat it out as he was hurled forward and the water closed over his head. He went down and down and down, struggling. He was aware of noise, tremendous noise, but whether it was from above or from within his own roaring ears he could not tell. He thought fiercely: "I mustn't open my mouth!" All the same it opened and he swallowed helplessly, still fighting, and conscious now

315

that he was rising. Suddenly the sun was glaring in his eyes again, and dark, tremendous shapes loomed about him. He trod water, choking, feeling sick, and grabbed instinctively at something floating past him. It was a broken bit of one of the ferry seats, and he clung to it, gasping, thought and sight returning, and looked about him. The *Neptune,* inconceivably vast, towered away above him towards the sky, its railing lined with shouting and gesticulating people. As he watched a man dived from it, and Bobby became aware for the first time that the water was dotted with the heads of struggling people as well as with bits of broken wood and *débris* from the shattered ferry. He noticed, too, with a queer sense of astonishment that familiar objects such as bags and hats and folded newspapers looked unbelievably strange when you saw them floating in the water. They gave to the whole confusing scene an added touch of grotesque impossibility, and when he saw his own bat bobbing past him he stared at it incredulously, hardly able to believe that anything so ordinary as a bat, anything belonging so intimately to his normal school-day world, could be sharing with him this impossible experience in which the infallible arrangements of infallible adults were suddenly overturned. He left his support for a moment to retrieve it. He was not frightened any more. He was as much at home in the water as on dry land, and already he could see boats making for them—launches, rowing boats, a Manly ferry.

A little gleam of enjoyment actually began to creep into the whole affair. Gee, this was a score! He'd have things to tell at school to-morrow! He'd nearly caught the earlier boat, too! Gee, what luck! Suddenly he wondered where the ferry was, and turned to look. His enjoyment faded, and a prickle of horror touched him like an electric shock. She was right on her side, what he could see of her, and she was black with madly moving humanity; he realised that the air was loud with the noise of people, grown-up men and women, screaming, yelling, panic-stricken. With a horrified check in his breathing he remembered that there were people who could not swim. He seemed to be a little apart from the others; he supposed that he must have been one of the first to be flung clear of the ferry. But there was a woman about twenty yards from him, and she was floundering and throwing up her arms in a helpless sort of way, so he began to swim towards her on his back, dragging his bit of wood with him as he dragged his canoe sometimes in the Cove. But it was heavier than the canoe, and he made slow progress. When he thought that he had gone far enough he trod water and looked about for her, but she was gone. He began to feel sick again, and a little frightened. Then he saw another woman, an elderly woman, whose grey-gloved hand beating the air seemed to him even at that moment incongruous, and he yelled out to her: "Hang on, I'm coming!" and began to swim hard, pushing his bit of wood this time so that he should not lose sight of her. When he reached her and saw her hands clutch at the support he felt with some astonishment that he must just hang on himself for a while before he did any more rescuing. He hung on, eyeing her across the bit of wood rather anxiously. She looked funny. He hoped she was not going to faint or anything. And he thought he knew her, though he could not be sure. He said, spluttering, as a wave splashed over his face: "Are you O.K.? Here, rest your elbow on it and kick a bit with your legs." The faint contortion of her face was hardly a smile, but it made him recognise her. Gee, how different women looked with their hair down and all round their faces, and their powder washed off! She looked about a hundred years old, and her mouth was all sunken like a witch's. She must have had false teeth and spat them out like he had his bull's-eye, so they wouldn't choke her! But she was Sim's mother, the mother of his hero, Sim Hegarty, who flew a plane, and owned a car that could do eighty, and swam races with him down in the Cove with a long, effortless crawl-stroke that he tried ardently to imitate. He was filled with a sudden earnest sense of responsibility, but with it there came ignominiously an ominous feeling which made him tighten his own grip of their support, while a cold rim of perspiration formed on his wet forehead, and saliva gathered in his mouth. He gulped, staring across at her with growing alarm. She looked very queer indeed, and he said urgently, with more than a trace of impending tears in his voice:

"Do you feel crook? Hang on, there's a launch coming this way. Here, give us your hand across . . ."

But he could not take it and he could not speak any more. A dreadful nausea surged up in him; there was a suffusion behind his eyes, a deathly sickness in the pit of his stomach, a horrible taste of mingled salt water and bull's-eye in his mouth, and he didn't care a bit whether he drowned or not. He thought with weak misery: "I'm going to be sick!" His hands tightened instinctively and convulsively on his support, his head spun dizzyingly, his eyes closed.

When he opened them again there was a slowly clearing darkness before them. He was weak and empty and resentfully conscious of a desire to cry. And then he saw a grey-gloved hand slipping away out of sight on the other side of their support, and he grabbed at it instinctively, but it was out of his reach, it was gone. Bobby, unaware that he was sobbing hysterically with some emotion which was composed equally of fear, sickness and rage that his rescue should have been thus foiled, began to dive. But it was no good. Somehow he couldn't do it. He had no strength left, and all he could manage was to get himself under, face downward, floundering, kicking, and then roll over helplessly with his face to the sky, hearing dimly a sound of gasping sobs which he could not quite account for. And then, more by accident than design, his shoulder touched his support again, and he put his arms over it and hung there, his panic fading out into a dim misery through which he noticed, without caring, that his bat was still safe, lying where he had placed it on the support between two jutting bits of wood. When, a few

minutes later, he was lifted on to a launch, he remembered
it. Someone asked:

"Feel all right, sonny?"

He answered hazily with chattering teeth:

"Gee, I'm O.K., thanks. But get my bat, will you?"

*　　　*　　　*　　　*　　　*

At the first sound of the *Neptune's* siren Jack had
leapt to his feet. So strongly if only subconsciously was
he afraid of the consequences of what he had done, that
in the first split second of tumult he imagined it as being
directed against himself, and he swung instinctively
into a position of defiance, his body crouched and his
sound fist clenched for battle. Maud's terrified scream cut
through his mental confusion like a knife, and he found
himself gripping her by the arm and staggering drunkenly
on the tilting floor. The steel-plated bow of the liner,
biting into the wooden superstructure of the ferry, was
turning her over and pushing her along through the
churning water. She turned slowly until her keel-plates
showed above it, and all the time her terrified passengers
fought upward from the slowly submerging side, clinging
desperately to seats, posts, railings, clutching at each
other, trampling on each other in their frantic efforts to
keep out of reach of the rising water. The *Neptune,* still
carried forward by her own impetus, bit deeper and
deeper, cutting through the ferry amidships as if she
were no stronger than a matchbox, until at last she was
completely severed, and the two halves floated away to
north and south of the liner. Jack, steadying himself on
the reeling side of their sinking half of wreckage, yelled
to Maud:

" 'Ere, 'ang on to me! Christ, no, not on to that
arm! 'Ang on to me belt!"

One arm! Here, at last, was a use for his strength,
and he had only one useful arm! He cursed, fighting
through the confusion of maddened people and splintering wreckage. All his enormous physical energy welled
up in him, rushing to meet this moment which demanded

319

action; but at every turn and with every movement his injured arm mocked the surging willingness of his muscles, and he felt a sweat of pain pouring down his face. He stood for a second, staring desperately about him, Maud clinging to him, white-faced but (he had a second of approval to spare for it) dumb. They were on top now, but the whole section was sinking rapidly. Below them people trapped in the broken and fallen woodwork were struggling to free themselves, and he saw three men and two women go under, and the water close, bubbling, over their heads. Their own temporary refuge would be, in a moment or two, a refuge no longer, and he realised with a shock of fear that when it went down it would suck them with it.

In such a crisis time is no longer the steadily moving vehicle of human consciousness, advancing unhurriedly in minutes as regular and unvarying as the tramp of soldiers on parade. A second expands, becomes monstrous, a minute stretches achingly into eternity, burdened with the intensity of ten years of normal life. Shock, closing the beleaguered brain, flicks hours away unlived, uncomprehended, or senses expand, widening their focus like the lens of a camera, recording avidly, and thought accelerates with the mad accuracy of a racing movie-film. There lay in front of Jack, during the few minutes while he stood lurching on the side of the shattered and sinking ferry, a scene which his brain accepted reluctantly, because there went out from it to resist the inflowing evidence of his eyes some vague but tormenting memory which told him he had seen it all before. Like an echo of the actual clamour which his ears were recording, this memory brought him thinly, as from far away, the cries of doomed men and women being sucked down into a gulf of waters. It was the stern of the *Neptune* which was visible to him now, and while he watched a girl's body being snatched towards it by the suction of the whirling propellers, saw her distorted face and wide-open mouth for a moment before she vanished, the memory was still there, and he found himself struggling with a dark, familiar fear in some uncharted region between past and present. There was a woman standing erect on a drifting piece of wreckage. She was alone and she stood quite still with her hands hanging by her sides, screaming. But that, too, belonged to memory as well as to sharply functioning eyes and ears, for he had heard those screams in some other experience which had no time or place, but which brought with it a fear in the midst of which at last he had been drawn down into a dark green, glassy silence, and consciousness had ceased. . . .

He said hoarsely to Maud:

"Can y' swim?"

She lifted a face from which even fear had been blasted by shock, and answered: "No."

He put his good arm round her, measuring the distance to the water with his eye. It was important beyond everything else that she should be saved, for she was his luck, his mascot, his promise, his awakener of hope. With her advent, dim and confused, but still alluring, new possibilities in life had drifted through his mind. They were too amorphous and too precarious to be called plans, but they were something which lay gladly and gratefully in a mind long burdened with hopelessness, and they had their origin, their obscure and mysterious origin, in her. He said roughly:

"We're goin' to jump. We'll be drawn under if we don't. Come on now, and don't struggle when we get in the water."

He jumped, dragging her with him. The impact of the water on his injured hand sent pain flooding through him, but worse than the pain was the knowledge that with only one arm his strength was halved. The weight of her, clutching him round the neck, held him down; he fought upward with bursting lungs. They broke the surface of the water and he flung his hair back from his eyes, his breath sobbing in his throat. Roughly, with a desperate effort, he freed himself of her strangling clutch. He had no breath for words, and in her panic she would not have heeded them, so he tried to get behind her;

321

but all her consciousness was governed now by the fear of the non-swimmer in deep water, all her instinct bade her cling to anything within reach, and she clung so determinedly that twice they went under and twice by superhuman efforts he won to the surface again. The second time he grabbed at a bit of floating driftwood. It was not large, but it would support her alone, so he freed himself, and dragged her arms over it. He was so exhausted now, and so stupid with pain, that he could do no more than turn over on his back and float, and he had a dim, delirious notion that all his being was flowing into his bandaged arm so that it was becoming vast, inflated like a balloon, and sailing away rapidly over the water, faster and faster, dragging the rest of his body behind it.

Suddenly, quite close to him, he heard a voice. It was not a loud voice or a despairing one, or even a very fatigued one. It spoke with a kind of detached fierce concentration, as if the breath which fashioned the words were, irrevocably, the last breath, and must be made to serve. It said, not imploringly, but imperatively: *"Take my baby, take her quickly, I can't . . ."*

He strove not only to turn his body but to steady his flickering consciousness, realising with the bewildered opening of his eyes that they had been shut. But there was no one near him. Grunting with pain he trod water, looked about. A dummy on a pink ribbon bobbed against his cheek.

He turned again, a hazy anxiety sharpening into fear, to look for Maud. She was all right. They had floated apart, but he could see a couple of men in the water supporting her, and one of them hailing an approaching launch. He searched his tired body for a reserve of that once limitless energy, goaded it into action, began to swim clumsily toward them.

But he had drifted near to the section of the ferry upon which they had been standing, and now it went under, and the water foamed together over it as over a submerged shoal. There was a dull, muffled explosion as the boilers burst, and a cloud of steam and a shower of flying timber went up into the air. Jack felt a fierce suction, stronger than the undertows he was used to battling with on ocean beaches, and a rush of warmth as the water nearby boiled like a cauldron. Suddenly he saw a man quite close to him—the back of his head, his hands flailing the surface of the water clumsily as if he were utterly exhausted. And as Jack watched he saw one of the many bits of wreckage flung up by the explosion hit him squarely on the temple, and distinctly heard, with shocked amazement, a small crack of breaking bone. The man's arms flung above his head for a second in a reflex jerk of agony; the next moment Jack had him by the shoulder. He did not consider his action at all. His strength in such a nightmare as this was not only the strength of great muscles, but the stolid strength of a brain to which at all times coherent thought comes tardily, and to which, when action is demanded, it quite simply does not come at all. Instinct and muscle functioned; reason lay dormant. Thought came, but only in disconnected snatches. Fighting with one arm for two lives, he did not question the action at all, but merely recorded in his own mind that it was as well the bloke had fainted and could not struggle.

His legs moved mechanically, his good hand gripped, his other moved weakly and almost uselessly. That, for the moment, was all that life held, and it seemed natural to him that there should be no more. It did not occur to him to free himself, by unclasping his hand, of the burden which he supported. His creed was not unlike the Professor's though he had never consciously formed it, and had never learned that it might apply to moral as well as physical strength. But to abandon the man while there was still an ounce of unused energy in his body would have been to him a denial and a betrayal of himself. His awareness narrowed, contracted to a tiny circle enclosing his endurance and his task, and matching the one against the other. Even when, at last, he heard a familiar voice hailing him by name, he did not immediately relax his grip or cease the rhythmic kicking of his legs.

When he had been dragged on board a launch, and seen the other man, limp and sodden, dragged up beside him, he noticed without surprise that it was Ted Billings, from the Bay, who had called out to him, and that it was upon the fish-smelling seats of Ted's launch that he and the man he had saved were stretched. For the present he did not want to move or to think. His labouring breath was still coming in gasps, and the weakness of exhausted effort flooded his whole body with lassitude. The pain of his hand went up his arm to the shoulder now, in long, stabbing shafts, and there was a faint taste of blood in his mouth.

Ted's seventeen-year-old son, Maurice, was leaning over the side of the launch. Jack could see his head and shoulders moving as he straightened up to throw a hat, a walking-stick and a small fibre suitcase on to its floor, but he was irritably conscious that not only his thought but his sight was blurred and distorted, and he put his right hand up clumsily to his eyes as if he could rub away the film of exhaustion which was dimming them. Ted, working at the arms of the prone figure on the opposite seat, remarked:

"This bloke looks bad. Must 'a' swallowed a lot o' water or somethin'. . . ."

Curiously enough, while sight was dimmed and diminished, sound seemed incredibly magnified. Ted's voice was like thunder in Jack's reluctant ears, and he moved uneasily, struggling with a dim memory of a blow on the head, someone being hit on the head with something. . . .

But his brain was not equal to any disciplined effort just now, and it slid away and was lost in a fog of amorphous impressions, shot with momentary gleams of fear. For all the time there was a knowledge at the back of his mind which was trying to thrust itself forward. The life to which he had clung so desperately was still precarious, the world to which he had won back with agony and endurance was still inimical, and the problems which had been temporarily annihilated by crisis were still there confronting him. That knowledge, unexpressed, inchoate, was like an intermittent glare of light illuminating the confusion of pain, sleep and physical exhaustion in which his brain toiled helplessly and, goaded by it into a blind unreasoning desire for action and escape, he stumbled to his feet, and stood for a moment, lurching, staring down at the other man, motionless and senseless on the seat. The face he saw was nothing but a white, spinning circle at first; and then, as a fast-revolving wheel slows and its spokes become visible, the spinning circle became a face, and its features strangely, and as it seemed to him, amusingly, recognisable. He heard his own laugh, and felt Ted and Maurice grab him and lower him on to the seat again, and knew that he was still laughing. It occurred to him that he should try to tell them this extremely funny joke—that he, Jack Saunders, had rescued Arthur Sellman from death—and then he became worried because he could not think why it was so funny after all. His arm, now, was his whole body. There was nothing of him at all but his arm and his lurching consciousness. He was not sure whether it was pain which was inhibiting thought, or thought which was creating pain, but he could still hear with abnormal clarity, and he heard Ted say thunderingly to Maurice:

" 'Ere, make for the Bay as fast as she'll go, son! 'E's in a fever or somethin'. And this other cove's bad, too. . . ."

Jack's whole being shrank and shuddered away from the noise of the started engine. It was incredible, unendurable; it was like hammer blows, and beneath its assault his remaining consciousness was extinguished, and a darkness which was partly sleep and partly swoon closed over him.

*　　*　　*　　*　　*

At the bow of the ferry the wild and piercing suddenness of the siren had brought Brenda to her feet, trembling all over. She heard one of her worlds, the world of sound, go mad about her, distorted and ugly with unfamiliar noises, shouts and screams, the splintering of glass, the sickening crack of breaking wood. Simultaneously her touch-world failed her; the floor betrayed her with a sudden lurch, and she felt herself falling backward and cried out in terror: "Denis! Denis!"

His hot hand clutched hers, but he did not speak. From the first second neither he nor Jonathan had uttered a sound, simply staring, petrified. At her call he had acted automatically, and now he looked along the heeling ferry and saw, with horrified and unbelieving eyes, people fighting each other, hitting each other, scrambling over each other like swarming ants to keep out of reach of the water which somehow seemed to be coming up at them. His heart pounding madly he began to scramble, too, dragging Brenda with him, and followed by Jonathan. They had to climb through the railing which usually stood vertically, surrounding the deck, and now hung horizontally over the churning water, and there they stood for a moment or two, breathless, sobbing with fright, on what was normally the side of the ferry.

Denis became aware of Brenda's clutch upon his hand; he saw Jonathan's face looking puckered and unfamiliar, and suddenly, like a revelation, the thought flashed through his mind: "I'm the eldest!"

That had never seemed to matter before; Jonathan never waited for anyone to lead. But now. . . . The image of his father rushed up before his eyes and past them as a car or train rushes up to and past a moving-picture camera. That was no good. Father wasn't here. Brenda was calling wildly: "Mummy! Mummy!" but that was no good either. The world was not that world any more where you were cared for and protected. It was full of terrible and incomprehensible sights and noises, confusion and panic, and the evil reek of fear. . . . The ferry gave another violent lurch, and they were thrown forward on to their hands and knees, and suddenly the water came much nearer to them, and Denis looked at it. His mind fastened on to it in a very ecstasy of relief. Why, it was only the water! Harbour water, green and deep and clear, the good, familiar water which was their playground! Not it, but the pandemonium about them, frightened him. He shouted to the others as they scrambled to their feet again:

"Look, Jonathan, it isn't any higher than the Pulpit! Come on, Brenda, we're going to jump like we do in the Cove. Get hold of her hand, Jonathan. . . ."

Jonathan got her hand. Denis found that now, at last, he was on the same side as Burrendong, but he could not make her loosen her grip of the toy bear. She only held it tighter, and said: "No! No! No!" so he grabbed her wrist and said loudly: "Ready? *One . . . two . . . three. . . ."*

They jumped. The water closed over their heads. That was nothing, it happened a dozen times a day. But this was different, and suddenly Denis knew why. Clothes made it different. And shoes. You didn't shoot to the top like a cork, buoyant; you had to struggle and fight your way up, your heart choking you as if it were something huge and heavy in your chest, your eyes bursting, a tiny, frightened spark of knowledge in you that you had lost Brenda's hand, and this was not a game after all. . . .

And then you were up. Your held breath went out of you with a sob, and a new terror clutched you when you couldn't see Jonathan. Or Brenda. Then you saw Jonathan, his face visible for a moment quite close to you, and then vanishing under the water again. He wasn't swimming or floating, he was struggling, and twice while Denis fought heavily through the few yards which separated him his face bobbed into view and then there was only the top of his head—as if something were pulling him down.

The water was full of people, and the air was still full of noise, but Denis did not hear it now. He could see that there were several launches making for them, and a couple of ferries, but he only wanted to get to Jonathan, and at last he did. His feet kicked at something soft under the water, and Jonathan gasped: "Brenda—she's holding—on to me. . . ." Denis submerged himself clumsily and wrenched at Brenda's clinging hands, and the second time he got them free and she came up to the surface, and he saw the little printed animals on her frock with a sense of astonished recognition. But she looked queer with her wide-open, unseeing eyes and her face a funny grey colour. And when he let go she just rolled over in the water and began to sink. Denis was tired. He did not know that, but he knew the water was somehow inimical again, and he shouted desperately:

"Here, Brenda, swim, can't you?"

But she did not seem to hear him, so he said to Jonathan: "Come on, get her other arm and float on your back."

Jonathan, treading water, protested aggrievedly:

"I feel heavy. I feel—like sinking. . . ."

Denis became really angry. He yelled:

"Ar, don't be mad! Come on—swim!"

Jonathan, spitting out a mouthful of salt water, asked:

"Where to?"

But Denis had no more breath for words. He jerked his head in the direction of an approaching launch and turned over on his back, grasping Brenda's shoulder and kicking with his legs.

The sky looked peaceful and very far away. There was a long, filmy drift of white cloud across it like a veil. He had a silly but not unpleasant feeling that he was going up towards it, sea and all, and that he must try to keep awake till he got there. He wanted to stop kicking and go to sleep comfortably, but he knew that he must not, although he had forgotten why, so he went on kicking, though not very hard, because his legs felt weak. Some water splashed over his face and that reminded him of the seals at the Zoo; the seals at the Zoo, he thought, were shiny and black, all except one which was yellow and had little pictures of animals all over it, and it made a strange noise, different from the others, louder, terrifying, a siren scream, and it leapt out of the water at you, vast, menacing, so big that you couldn't possibly save yourself from it, it was so big, too big, and you were the eldest, but it was too big, there was nothing you could do but kick and kick, never stop kicking, never stop. . . .

PART V
THE SUNSET

"As, upon a summer's eve, one stands upon the well-known heights overhanging Mr. Wentworth's villa of Vaucluse . . . one beholds, as one looks seaward, the heaving swell of the huge billows of the Pacific outside the Heads; then, turning the eye towards Sydney, it rests upon the tranquil waters of the harbour within. . . .

"Beyond, the spires of the city rise. . . ."

From "Reminiscences of Thirty Years' Residence in N.S.W. and Victoria," by R. Therry, Esq., 1863.

OLIVER came through the dingy little shop on to the footpath, and said: "Whew!" and then, under his breath, "Blast!" as he almost fell over the child who, till an hour ago, had been the youngest of the shop-keeper's family. She was sitting on the asphalt, sucking stolidly at a long and villainously coloured stick of some-thing which, Oliver thought irritably, would do her no good; and he turned away from his car, which stood waiting at the kerb, and crossed the road to the steps which Ian and his sons had climbed that morning.

Childbirth, he reflected, was an ugly and painful business at the best of times. A healthy young woman, well cared for in an up-to-date hospital, was bad enough. A middle-aged one, already exhausted by five confine-ments in too rapid succession, struggling through her labour in an ill-kept room on a hot November after-noon, was the very devil. He went across to the railing above the Gap with the word turning in his mind, and looked out to sea, feeling in his pockets for his pipe and tobacco.

He lit his pipe and rested his arms along the top railing of the fence. The breeze came sharply up into his face, cool against his hot scalp through his close-cropped hair, blowing against his eyelashes so that his eyes watered, whipping the hem of his belted dust coat about his legs. The surface of the ocean was slightly ruffled, pitted—a shivering, goose-flesh look, he thought, glancing up at the sky for signs of rain. But there were none. Its blue had softened now—a forget-me-not blue rather than the intense, midday blue of cornflowers, and the only clouds were high and white and filmy, drawn out across it like driven smoke. Already the shadow of the high cliffs stretched across the water beyond the lazy swell which broke in surf against them, and from this height the depths looked glassy and malign, heaving a little, gathering, lifting, receding with a movement that was hypnotic and disturbing.

A voice behind him said:

"Hullo, Doctor. Don't you know that solitary people loitering here are always suspected of contemplating suicide?"

He found Lesley Channon beside him, and, wondering where she had acquired a really ripe-looking bruise upon the cheek, he answered:

"Doctors hardly ever commit suicide. It's an ingrained habit of saving a life at any price, even if it happens to be your own, and you don't want it. How about young women who write stories?"

She laughed:

"They don't, either, because they deal in melodrama so much in fiction that they acquire a horror of it in real life. So we have both come to look at the view."

"Perhaps." Glancing at the bruise again he added: "And to regain our composure."

She looked at him quickly, seemed about to speak, checked herself, and asked lightly:

"What has been upsetting you?"

"Just introducing another unwanted infant into the world. I should be hardened by now. And you?"

"Me?" Her laugh, he thought, was a little forced. "Oh, I've had a most crowded twenty-four hours! It ended with being involved in a street brawl and—getting engaged."

She was looking down at the rocks below, her chin on her folded arms, and he realised that for all the airiness of her tone she was, indeed, struggling for composure. He suggested:

"Let's take the brawl first. I hope you gave something in return for the bruise on your cheek?"

She said soberly:

"I kicked. It was all rather—alarming. It was a mob of unemployed demonstrating outside Parliament House. Have you ever heard a lot of people together being— really angry?"

"Yes. What happened?"

"Nothing much at first. Then some man threw a beer bottle at one of the cars leaving the church after George Hegarty's wedding."

Oliver said thoughtfully:

"Ah, yes. George Hegarty's wedding. A great deal of pomp and circumstance, I take it?" She said impatiently:

"The usual circus. But you can see how it was all a bit . . ."

"Provocative?"

"Yes. And the bottle cut Gerald Manning-Everett's head open. Then things got rough for a while."

"They would. Was he badly hurt?"

"I think so." She added fiercely: "I hope so."

He looked at her curiously.

"Why?"

"I don't like his papers."

"Nor I. But it's possible that he isn't personally responsible for the policy of his papers, you know. It's a company."

She insisted with the relentlessness of youth:

"Then he ought to be. A newspaper isn't just a—a living, it's too important, and too powerful. If you own a newspaper it's your *business* to be responsible for its influence."

He pointed out:

"It's also possible that he sincerely thinks its influence is good, and its policy right."

She said forlornly:

"If black were black and white were white how easy life would be! What a pity there isn't a song-writer here —he could have that first line for nothing. It's all these greys that get one mixed up."

He agreed.

"It's certainly difficult. If, for instance, one could be definitely pro-Manning-Everett, or pro-bottle-thrower, and not afflicted by a sneaking sympathy for both of them. How about the bottle-thrower, by the way?"

"I don't know. I didn't see him. I heard someone say he was a very big, dark young man with his left arm in a sling. I think he got away. But Roger and I were busy getting out and rushing for a tram."

Oliver said: "Oh," and knocked his pipe out on the fence, feeling a little disturbed. There were plenty of big, dark young men, plenty of men with left arms in slings, innumerable men in a mood to throw bottles at Mr. Manning-Everett. But he found his memory returning with surprising accuracy to a patient who, only that morning, in his surgery, had answered to all those three descriptions. He had felt at the time, he remembered, that there was an obscure hostility in the man, a resentment banked and dangerously smouldering, and that he himself had been oppressed and saddened by some sense of spiritual distortion. He frowned. More than once a polite message from the local police had requested him to notify them if a man suffering from this wound or that disability should seek treatment of him. It was not a rôle he liked, and he was thankful that so far he had never been faced with the necessity for playing it, and he found himself wondering now if they might trace their quarry to this neighbourhood and seek information from the local doctors upon recent left arm injuries put up in splints. . . .

He moved his shoulders impatiently as if he could shake from his body as he was shaking from his mind a problem which had not yet emerged from imagination into reality, and looked down at Lesley thoughtfully. A lively curiosity about her engagement, which he had temporarily suppressed because he suspected that it, and not the bruise, was the chief cause of her distress, made him ask now:

"And may I hear about the engagement? Is it . . . ?"

He stopped. He realised that he had no idea at all whether it would be Roger or Sim. Sim, indeed, seemed the more likely, for her father, in speaking of his own illness, had told him that quite lately she had been entirely unaware of Roger as a suitor at all. She was looking up at him intently.

"Who do you think it is, Doctor?"

He shook his head. She insisted:

"Who do you think it should be? I really want to hear what you . . ."

He protested:

"Good Lord, Lesley, how can anyone know who it should be but yourself? You do know, don't you?"

She nodded.

"Yes, I know. But it still seems so queer that . . ."

"Roger Blair."

"Yes. It *is* queer, isn't it? Everyone thought it would be Sim. I thought so myself. And then suddenly it isn't, and I know it never could have been. . . ."

Her face, turned upward to him for a moment, held some misery and some mute appeal which stirred him to a painful compassion. Groping, guessing, he said:

"There are . . . emotional moments and states that one never quite escapes, or forgets. Their importance. . ."

He hesitated, unsure of his ground, but she asked urgently, her chin on her folded arms again:

"What *is* their importance? That's exactly what I want to know."

His mind travelled back into his own past years, finding an answer for her and for himself.

"I think simply the importance of any sensuous experience. Music you know well and can hear in your mind. The picture of that harbour behind you that you can see without turning round. Things that . . . what shall I say? . . . enrich your life. Any emotion that's strong enough to form a lasting memory is liable to hurt—at first."

She glanced at him out of the corner of her eye with a flicker of her father's humour.

"So long as it doesn't go on hurting! But I suppose in the end it's like those creased letters you keep in the bureau, all tied up with faded blue ribbon, and cry over every Christmas Eve."

337

He answered imperturbably:

"The difference is that one day when you go to have your annual weep you discover that your cherished memory isn't recognisable any more. It and the rest of your life have got all mixed up—to their mutual advantage. It's really," he added seriously, "very well arranged."

She straightened up with a sigh and glanced over her shoulder.

"I hope you're right. After all, it's your business to be right in such matters, isn't it?"

"I'm not," he reminded her, "a practising psychologist."

"Just a conversationalist. I've heard father say you have a wholesome respect for words."

"That—from him—and to me—is a great compliment."

"Why—to you?"

"I belong to the profession which calls an ear-nose-and-throat man an oto-rhino-laryngologist, and talks about a lacto-fructo-vegetarian regimen. One can easily become debased. What are you looking for?"

"Roger. I sent him home to change his trousers."

"Didn't they match his coat?"

"I don't think they ever do. But they had only one button at the back and that got torn off when we were escaping from the brawl. When we jumped for the tram I thought the worst was happening. Not that Roger cared. He just yelled with laughter and told the tram-guard all about it, and he yelled, too." She glanced over her shoulder again, and added: "There he is now. We're going for a walk along the cliff-edge up near the light-house. He's wearing shorts. You know . . ." Oliver, interested and a good deal amused, noticed a sudden softening of her eyes. "I shouldn't be surprised if he only *has* one pair of trousers."

She was so intent upon Roger now that Oliver could study her face at his ease. Youth, he reflected, no matter how serious, no matter how priggish, no matter how "hard-boiled," preserved some air of vulnerability which made it touching. Some combination of ardour and

338

hesitancy, some eager sincerity which made possible this temporary obliteration of the twinkling light of humour by the strong light of compassion and awakening love. Suppressing, therefore, his unruly desire to laugh, he said hastily:

"Very probable, I should think. Well, now that he's coming I expect he'll supply all the conversation you need. Good-bye."

Although her eyes met his then he knew that the brilliance of her smile was not for him. She said:

"I'm glad you happened to be here. You might as well be conventional, and wish me happiness before you go."

He answered over his shoulder as he went down the steps:

"You've got it, haven't you?" She nodded.

He saw Roger join her as he turned his car in the narrow street, and watched them set off arm-in-arm up the steep hill-path towards the lighthouse.

*   *   *   *   *

The taxi, driving out from behind a labouring bus, rushed round it and up to the crest of the last long hill. Winifred's hand, imprisoned in Ian's, lay between them on the seat; the pressure of their fingers had been, since leaving the Quay, their only communication. For there was nothing to say. No hope lay in words, but a little comfort in the mere fact of each other's presence, and they felt that the more keenly in silence. There had been a happiness in their hour which trembled on the edge of torture, and they were both weary now, feeling the burden of their humanity which shrank from such exquisite pain, telling themselves with self-reproach that they could not bear any more such meetings as the one they had just stolen, or such partings as that which faced them now. What, Ian found himself thinking, had they gained from it? A brief illusion of joy. And he wondered with the bitterness and scepticism of nervous exhaustion whether all joy was illusion, all ecstasy a dream from which one awakened. The hour they had spent together seemed only a dream already. It had no substance, no strength, it lacked the solid backbone which the everyday experience, the commonplace routine of life, lends to those moments of happiness which are securely welded into it. There, he thought, was the strength—and the weakness—of marriage. For the mortal mind, consistent only in its perversity, longed for freedom when it had security, longed for security when it had freedom, struggled peevishly to combine them, demanding the best of both worlds. That hour of theirs, snatched from its context and dedicated to an impossible, an already repudiated joy, had been filled with the poignancy, the febrile intensity of a delirium, and now, in the violence of inevitable reaction, he found his very memory shrinking from it. It had been too brilliant. Senses, over-alert and tuned by frustration to a pitch of painful awareness, had absorbed what they could get too greedily, seeking compensation for what they could not get and so ardently desired. Sunlight was more than sunlight, and colour more than colour. The blue of the sky, the glimpsed green of curving breakers, the glimpsed gold of a long beach, seemed to have been recorded otherwise than by sight alone; the noise of surf and crying gulls not only heard but felt, as if all the senses, in an orgy of desperate functioning, had overlapped into each other's provinces, making of one's being nothing but an unreasoning organism vibrating with a torment of receptiveness. That, he thought, restlessly, might be the particular hell of madness or of genius, and out of it anything might grow from depravity to inspiration, from great music to brutal murder. For himself and for Winifred, normal mortals craving normal life, the tension was too high, and the reaction too violent. For them it was necessary that the water should be H_2O as well as intoxicatingly blue, and the breeze, not only cool and sea-smelling, but from the south-east. He remembered Kim, who used the multiplication table as an anchor to hold him from the drifting, perilous world of illusion, and he thought sadly that such an hour could have had nothing real or lastingly beautiful unless it were possible to descend from it to some sober level of every-day existence in which there would be cares and quarrels, children, bills, and anxieties, and long, passionless nights filled with the quiet contentment of a shared life.

But here they sat, together and immeasurably apart, tense with the awareness of suffering ahead, and strung to a pitch of dangerous endurance. He glanced at her averted face. She was leaning back against the seat, her mouth drawn with weariness, looking absently down at the harbour. There was a smoky, copper glow over the city, and the water looked as flat and polished as brass. The light tower off Shark Island stood out against it in black silhouette; it had a grotesque resemblance, he thought, to a giant human figure standing knee deep in the water, and holding a bucket in its hand. He could see in the distance the little ferry which they had missed coming towards them down the bright path of sunlit water. He said, breaking their long silence with an effort:

"There she is."

Winifred was watching her, too.

"Yes; I should have thought she would have been nearer home."

"She must have called at Garden Island."

"We'll be in plenty of time."

He gripped her hand tighter and told her what he had not mentioned before.

"Darling, Arthur was on the boat. Would you rather I didn't come down with you to meet it?" She turned to him in surprise.

"Arthur? On the boat? Are you sure?"

He nodded.

"I just caught a glimpse of him downstairs in the smoking cabin. He saw me."

"And me?"

"No."

He watched her brows contract and her lips twist into an expression of such bitterness that he persisted quickly:

"Don't—don't, Winifred. What is it, dear?"

341

"It was just myself. Caring whether he saw me or not. Why should I?"

He said quickly, trying to comfort her:

"I know. One is forced into situations. . . ." She gave his hand a little squeeze and smiled wryly.

"That's generous of you, Ian. Nobody forced me into this afternoon's situation. I rushed into it myself. Against our arrangements. I'm not . . . *What is it, Ian . . . ?*"

For he was staring past her over her head and the colour had dropped from his face. His fear communicated itself to her, and, because to her fear could mean only danger to Brenda, her head turned wildly, instantaneously, to the spot where, only a few moments ago, she had watched the ferry which was bringing her daughter home. There came from between her lips one of those ugly and involuntary gasps with which people, badly winded by a blow or a fall, struggle for breath. For the ferry was no longer coming towards them, and in the middle of the shining waterway things were happening which her brain for a second refused to grasp. She was stupidly conscious that Ian's grip on her hand seemed to be breaking her fingers, and then that something was trickling down her temple, and then that her whole body was wet with perspiration. She heard herself speak to the taxi-driver, clearing her throat after the first words, because her voice was so hoarse as to be unintelligible, and she thought: "What a good thing I can still think clearly!"

"Drive fast! Drive as fast as you can! Faster! Why don't you . . . ?"

But after all that was not what she should say. He was looking back at her over his shoulder with an expression of startled enquiry, and she heard Ian say:

"There's been an accident to that ferry. Look! Our children are on it. . . ."

There was no need to say more than that. The taxi leapt forward to plunge down the long curving road, its tyres screaming at every bend. Winifred spoke only once.

"We can take the launch."

He nodded. She did not know when he had released her right hand, but it lay now, tightly clasped with her left, in her lap. She strained her eyes over the harbour, but what she could see had no detail, no coherence; it was all wrapped in that golden light as in a web of unreality. They did not see the road as they swooped down it, but when it brought them so low that only glimpses of the harbour were visible their eyes met for a moment. Silently, with an obscure and terrible hostility, they looked, and looked away. "Because of you," their eyes said to each other, "I am here and not there where I should be." Their hearts, lately open and eager for unattainable union, contracted jealously over a lonely agony of parenthood, seeing only Denis, serious and loving, Jonathan, ardent and lovable; Brenda doubly alone, doubly helpless in an always bewildering and now terrifying and menacing world. Denis and Jonathan in their fragmentary bathing suits, their brown and wetly shining bodies turning and tumbling in the deep water of the Cove. . . . *"They swim well—they both swim really well. . . ."* An incoherent prayer, protest, assertion, something to cling to, to say over and over, treading down into obscurity the other thought which insists: "If they get the chance." Brenda, the plump curves of babyhood just fading from her sturdy limbs, Brenda, fearless in the water, swimming out to the raft with her hand on the boys' shoulders. *"But she won't have their shoulders now. They're only children. She'll be alone—calling to me. For the first time in her life she'll call me and I won't be there. . . ."*

The taxi stopped with an abruptness which flung them forward against the front seat. Winifred's own gate was there before her eyes. She saw with confusion rather than with surprise that Martin was just backing the long, blue car into the garage; his unexpected presence roused no thought of Lorna in her mind, but etched there, with a sharpness of detail which made her flinch, a picture of his back and Brenda's only a few hours ago, her short

343

legs, rosy-tan between her socks and her brief yellow skirt, trotting beside his polished black leggings, her hand in his, her head tilted not to see but to hear him. . . .

And yet through this picture a thought did thrust its way. "He understands the launch better than I do." She called, already out of the car and running for the gate: "Martin! Come here, quickly!"

Something in her face and voice startled him. He was at the gate holding it open for her before she reached it; as she ran down the path she heard his voice and Ian's in a hurried exchange of words behind her. Her legs felt so weak that she was vaguely surprised at the way she was racing down the steps; she was crying, too, but that did not matter. Nothing mattered so long as every second was taking her nearer to Brenda. She remembered the key of the boatshed, but she did not remember going in to the house for it. That was strange, but again it did not matter, for here it was in her hand, and they were running down the remaining steps, down and down to the water's edge, and Ian and Martin were unlocking the door. For a few minutes she had to wait, doing nothing. The torment of that was almost unendurable; without physical activity thoughts welled up and rode in upon her, bearing her down with them like breakers: *I thought that was pain, I thought that was misery! Let her be alive and unhurt and I'll never see him again, never think of him again. . . . Let her be alive, and not hurt, and not too frightened. . . ."*

Ian, working almost automatically with Martin, had abandoned himself to an unreasoning conviction. He was making them swim. They were in the water, and somehow, by some strength in himself, he was keeping them afloat. Not his lips, not even his thoughts, but some inner concentration of energy was commanding them fiercely: *"Swim, Denis! Swim, Jonathan! Go on, swim, swim . . . !"* He held that picture of them in his mind, the picture of them swimming manfully; held it obstinately, tenaciously, because behind it, dim and evil, there was another picture of them going down and down slowly

344

in the green, deep water, fifty feet down to the harbour bed, turning slowly, and sinking as they turned, resting at last among wreckage and dark seaweed. . . .

Martin was talking. He was saying: "There!" and "Come on, now, together!" and "Well, you've got the fastest launch on the harbour for it . . ." and "They'll have been picked up, Madam, don't you worry. A wetting and a bit of a fright—that's all . . ." and "Now she's set . . . !" Neither Ian nor Winifred answered him, but they were conscious of a dim relief at the mere sound of his voice, at the mere knowledge that not all the world, but only their own part of it, was twisted like metal in a furnace to some unrecognisable distortion; that not everybody, but only they themselves, lay under this numbing spell of shock, frozen beyond speech, almost beyond thought. It seemed to offer them, if not a promise, at least a hope, and when they found themselves in the launch at last and heard the spluttering throb of the engine as Martin started it, their eyes met for the first time since that look in the car, and they were the eyes of sleepers slowly awakening.

*   *   *   *   *

Somewhere Winifred had discarded her hat, and the wind whipped her hair back from her forehead. The salt taste upon her lips might have been from the spray which wetted her face or from the tears which had dried stiffly on her cheeks. Ian, now that Martin needed no further help, was beside her; into the agony of their first fear was seeping a compassion for each other which turned them from hostility towards tenderness. She said his name once or twice, but had no other words. They were still both struggling with the incredulity which makes one's personal disaster almost easier to bear than to believe, and with that absurd amazement with which one sees, from the midst of one's own cataclysm, the sun still shining, the trees still growing, the world of other people continuing, untouched.

In a garden on the foreshore there was a woman

watering her lawn with a hose; Winifred, staring at her as they passed, found her mind groping stupidly for some conception of how it would feel to be so quietly occupied. There had been days, she remembered with hazy wonder, when she, too, after the fierce heat of some midsummer day, had stood idly with a hose in her hand, enjoying the fading sunlight and the noise of splashing water, and the smell of wet earth; watching the small, thirsty birds, tits, and bul-buls, and honey-eaters fluttering down from their leafy retreats into the spray, and up again, flirting their wings, on to some half-hidden branch. She even wondered if that woman, too, so peaceful and so unaware, might be waiting for the ferry to come round the Bottle and Glass headland, to wave to some home-coming husband, son or daughter, who, perhaps, would not come home, and she felt her own terror enlarge and choke her as if she were bearing, too, the poised terror of many other people still unconscious of bereavement.

When they shot out to round the Point the dazzle of the westering sun along the water blinded their forward-straining eyes so that they could tell only that its golden surface was broken by innumerable black objects, formless in the glare, ringed with strange shifting haloes of light. As they drew nearer these became boats and wreckage; a Manly ferry and two others, rowing boats, innumerable launches, the lowered boats of the now anchored *Neptune,* were all gathered about the spot where the accident had occurred; but of the little ferry there remained only a portion of its top deck still floating. On one of its seats, quite still, with folded hands and blank eyes, a woman was sitting with a bunch of flowers and a soaked brown paper parcel on her lap, talking inaudibly to herself. There were no longer any people in the water. The launches and small boats were hunting now among the *débris* for such articles of possible identification as they could retrieve. Martin, slowing down and manœuvring among the wreckage, called to a man on a nearby ferry:

"Hi, Digger, seen anything of a little girl and two little boys?"

The tightening of Ian's hand over Winifred's was, like the stiffening of her fingers in his, only a reflex, a physical manifestation of supreme spiritual tension. As an impression rather than a formulated thought, they were aware of it, conscious that upon the answer to that question much would depend, and that the freedom they had both so ardently and rebelliously desired might be too dearly bought. The man was shaking his head.

"No, we just got here." He looked at them, and added awkwardly: "Sorry."

They went on. Two men on the deck of another ferry were practising artificial respiration upon a prostrate figure. Martin called his question again, and one of them looked up to answer.

"No; survivors are mostly being taken up to the Quay. Might be there."

Martin turned to Ian, and nodded westward into the golden light.

"Follow those launches, eh?" Ian, his arm round Winifred and his heart like a stone in his chest, answered: "Better cruise about here for a minute or two—they might be on one of these boats. . . . *What is it . . . ?*"

For Winifred had moved so violently, drawn her breath into so dreadful a sob of fear, that he felt the sweat break out on his forehead. She was pointing at a small straw hat floating past, and her eyes stared at it, dark-ringed from a pinched and grey-white face. Ian said hoarsely:

"Is it hers? Is it?"

She nodded, still staring. Martin said noisily:

"Lord, that don't mean anything! Look, there's half a dozen hats floating around. Everybody must have lost a hat. A hat's nothing. Come on, let's chase those launches up to the Quay—that's where they'll be. They got a bit of a start, but we'll soon catch 'em!"

The engine throbbed again, the wind woke and the spray flew in their faces, but Ian and Winifred, side by

347

side, were quite still. They overtook one launch, and Martin, nearing it, shouted his question:

"Got a little girl and two little boys aboard?"

"No."

They only had breath for the bare word, for there was a young man shouting and struggling, and it was all they could do to hold him. Ian recognised him as his neighbour, young Smith. His voice was hoarse and ragged with exhaustion. "Let me go! My wife's drowning! Look! Look, she's got the baby to hold. . . . Let me go, blast you! Let me go . . . !"

The wind and the sound of their engine carried his voice away; Martin was passing another launch, calling again:

"Any children aboard?"

The shouted answer was clearly "No," but something followed which they could not hear. Martin slowed down and drew alongside. A man shouted to them through curved hands:

"You looking for children?"

"Yes—two little boys and a little girl."

He ducked his head and held out his hand to someone in the launch, and then straightened again, holding something aloft. Winifred for the first time felt her pain rip her self-control from her like a garment, leaving naked panic, and she fought Ian's restraining hands, feeling herself swinging down into some chasm of insane indulgence where she could scream and scream her misery away, unhindered and alone. Ian, leaving her, called:

"Yes . . . it's ours. Did you see . . . ?"

"I reckon the kid must have been picked up. Eh? No, but there was dozens taken on to the launches. Could they swim? Eh? Oh, *well!* They'll be O.K. Here, I'll chuck this thing—it was just about sinking when I got it. . . ."

Burrendong's sodden body sailed through the air and fell heavily at Winifred's feet. She was quiet again now, shaking as she remembered having shaken during a bad attack of flu, with heat and cold chasing each other over her aching body, and her teeth chattering. She was holding her head between her hands, her elbows resting on her knees, and she looked down at the lump of wet, grey fur, distorted by the blurring of her eyes, and thought with a dangerous lurch of her brain towards hysteria: "That would be funny! That would be very funny indeed. . . ."

Now they were going fast again. It was a good thing, she thought wearily, that Arthur had the kind of snobbery which demanded the best and the latest of everything. His cars must go faster, his launch must go faster than the cars and the launches of other people. He . . .

The shock of rudely startled memory steadied her wandering thought. She looked up slowly, wonderingly, at Ian's averted face. Arthur! Then, because her mind, already overloaded with emotion, stripped thought to its uttermost simplicity, she realised that she had forgotten him because he was not important. In this life which held only one question, one fear, one dimly enduring hope, he was not at all important. She forgot him again, and, stooping, picked up Burrendong.

They were nearing another launch now. She rose, wondering that in the unnatural calm which had followed her nervous collapse, her heart should be pounding so heavily; she listened, her face expressionless, to Martin's hail:

"Any children aboard?"

"Got a boy. . . ."

Ian moved violently. But it was Bobby Younger's face which was thrust forward for his inspection, and he turned away, hardly knowing whether his fear that it should be only one of his sons had been less than his heartsickness that it should be neither. But Bobby was shouting something, and Martin, straining his ears to listen, slowed down again to bring them within earshot. Bobby yelled:

"They're all right, Mr. Harnet. They got picked up."

"What? What did you say?"

"They got picked up. The kids. I saw them. They're on one of the launches ahead."

Ian's wild throb of exultation was steadied by Winifred's hand on his arm. She asked with dull quietness: "Brenda, too?" Ian called:

"Brenda? Mrs. Sellman's little girl . . . ?"

"Gee, yes, she was with them. They all got picked up together."

Their moment of almost stunned gladness was broken by Martin's yell. They stood looking at him with stiff, uncertain smiles, still half-mistrustful of this sudden resplendency over a life so lately darkened by despair. But on the other launch, led by Bobby, who was himself again, they joined in Martin's cheers, and suddenly Ian found himself cheering, too, and wringing Martin's left hand while the launch bucked and shied beneath his right.

Winifred sat down weakly in the stern. She felt no desire either to cry or to cheer. Her fear was transmuted now, not into elation like Ian's, but into a hungry longing. For him the knowledge that they were alive was all-sufficient; his physical bond with them was so slight, and played so small a part in his love for them, that they could be, to him, an almost purely intellectual joy. But for her there was the old, inescapable torment of the flesh which makes maternity at once so invincible and so dangerous. The savage possessiveness of a creature who will give her life not only in defence of her young, but slowly, unspectacularly, by inches, to serve their daily well-being, may become, insidiously, a possessiveness which demands their life of them; and now, in a turmoil of released emotion, she sat silently, hungering for a moment when she could feel the life she had borne still warm and breathing in her arms, hugging those arms, still achingly empty, across her breast, crying in her heart that only here, in this prisoning circle, could the child find true shelter; only here could she be really safe at last.

*   *   *   *   *

Ian, coming quietly to sit beside her and looking at her face, so mask-still now, so intently inward-looking, wondered whether there had yet returned to her, as it

350

had been uneasily returning to him, a knowledge which, for a time, fear had utterly obliterated. He spoke her name, tentatively, as one might speak to a sleep-walker:

"Winifred . . . ?"

She looked up. Her smile and her eyes were her own again, he thought, with a stab of love for her. Her own, but dimmed with fatigue, and absent, as if some part of her had not yet won back to normal life.

He asked slowly:

"Had you . . . ?"

But his thought seemed to leap the gap between his mind and hers. She said: "Arthur?" and they looked at each other for a moment searchingly. He found himself remembering Oliver's words: "No thought is impossible to live with." And he wondered if ordinary people like himself, people of no particular intellectual adventurousness, people lacking that flame of rebellious individualism which he had felt sometimes in Winifred, needed such an ordeal as this to release their thoughts from the bondage of convention to the rather alarming freedom of naked logic. For he hoped with all his heart and soul that Arthur was dead. He even felt slightly exhilarated to realise that there was no uneasy division within himself, no holding back, no nervous recoil from a desire too crudely and robustly savage. He felt no vindictiveness, no bitterness; he saw Arthur with a cold lucidity, not as a man between himself and Winifred, but as an obstruction in the path of some fitting and logical progress. With certainty and composure, he saw him as an obstacle to a marriage, and not as a partner in one which he himself was invading, for a marriage meant, if it meant anything, a uniting, and between Arthur and Winifred there had been no unity. She met his eyes calmly; when she spoke her voice was low and roughened like the voice of one recovering from a long and exhausting illness, but her words were as dispassionate as his thoughts had been.

"It's strange that we should both have forgotten him." She shook her head. "I can't think about him now. Not yet. Not till we have the children."

He nodded. They looked ahead in an idle, almost sleepy relaxation. The shadowed green of the Gardens and the skyline of the still distant city were veiled by a kind of misty bloom like the bloom of a ripe plum; the long ribbon of water, receding westward out of sight, was too dazzling to look at, and the peak of Martin's cap was jammed shieldingly over his eyes. They were overtaking two more launches, and far ahead it was just possible to see a third already mooring at the Man-o'-War Steps to unload its freight of dazed, soaked, unsteadily walking people to the care of waiting ambulances. But their own was hardly up to Garden Island before, overhauling the one ahead of them, Jonathan's voice shrilled out in sudden welcome:

"Dad! Hi, Dad, we were wrecked! We swum! We all jumped in the water, and we swum. . . !"

Ian, his throat tight, waved and shouted heartily:

"Good man! Are you all right? Where's Denis? And Brenda?"

"They're here. They were sick with salt water. I wasn't, not . . ."

Denis' face, pale, pushed into view. His smile wavered and his eyes were anxious, but he protested:

"It was the cream puffs, you sap! Hi, Dad, are we coming on that launch with you?"

Martin, parleying with the owner of the other launch, had drawn close alongside. Ian warned:

"Wait, Jonathan. Wait till we're ready. Where's Brenda?"

"A man's nursing her. Here she is."

Wrapped in a tweed coat, her fair hair darkened by the water and her pale face paler still by contrast, she was handed across into her mother's arms. The clutch, feverishly tight, of the small arms around her neck was to Winifred pain and joy so closely merged as to be indistinguishable, but there was now, at last, the blessed alleviation of service, of activity, of ministration, of crooning comfort and reassuring words.

"Darling, you're going home now. Lift your arms,

352

and I'll take off this wet frock. See, here's Martin's coat to put round you—aren't you grand with all these buttons? We'll give this one back to the kind man who nursed you. There, now Denis and Jonathan are aboard, and we can go home. When we get there . . ."

Words, quiet and ordinary. Bully your voice, keep it light and cheerful. Guard your tongue, no questions yet, no hint of your own terror. The tightness of this clutch about your neck means fear; this silence, this hurried breathing, this sharply throbbing little heart all mean fear.

"Was it nice at the Zoo, darling? Did you ride on the elephant? What did you say? Yes, it's our own launch —no, no, sweetheart, of course it won't sink. Are you quite warm? Oh, darling, don't, don't . . . what is it?"

For suddenly there was a shuddering through the child's body, and words, incoherent at first, ending in a wail:

"He got drowned . . . he got drowned. . . !"

Winifred sickened, thinking suddenly of Arthur. Why had this not occurred to her before? What had happened in those dreadful moments when the ferry was first struck? Had he known that his daughter was on board . . . tried to reach her? Spoken to her?

She asked as steadily as she could:

"Who did, darling?"

Brenda sobbed:

"Burrendong."

Winifred cried quickly, eagerly:

"No, no, darling, he didn't! We found him. He's wet, like you, but he's quite safe, and we'll dry him by a radiator while you're having your bath, and then he'll be ready to go to bed with you. And to-morrow . . ."

But already the heartbeats were less violent, the sobbing quieter, the clutching arms slackened. Winifred, holding her jealously in the shelter of Martin's coat, knew she would soon be asleep. She looked up, met Ian's eyes, and smiled contentedly. Jonathan, too, wrapped in his father's coat, was growing heavy-eyed, but he was sitting

353

up with determination, staring ahead to gloat upon the scene of their great adventure. Denis, on his father's knee, was still, but very wide awake. The fingers of one hand were playing idly with the buttons on Ian's waistcoat, but his eyes were absent, and now and then Winifred saw his lids flutter and a tremor pass over his face like wind over water. For he was seeing all the time what he had seen in those hazy moments, when hands were lifting him from the water—a straw hat with a striped hatband, slowly turning over, filling, sinking with an awful and relentless symbolism, so that he had cried out wildly, the shy and speechless hero-worship of the small boy for the big boy—torn from him for the first time in words; and voices, kindly and well-meaning, had assured him. "Bobby? Is that your little brother? He's all right, sonny, he's here, he's quite safe. . . ."

But Bobby was not here. He had watched Bobby's hat turning over, sinking; beyond the strange horror of that sight his mind would not take him. Bobby's hat with the striped hatband was the symbol of Bobby's magnificence, and the water had taken it. Denis' eyes could see only that—Bobby's hat, turning over, filling, sinking. . . .

Jonathan shouted excitedly:

"Hi, Denis, look! We're coming to it! Look, the *Neptune's* still there. Gee, she must be strong, it didn't hurt her a bit! Look, Denis . . . Denis, why don't you look . . . ?"

Denis moved impatiently:

"Ar, shut up! I don't want to look!"

Suddenly he began to cry. He sobbed heavily and quietly, his head against his father's waistcoat. Ian, after one question had brought no answer, asked no more, but held him closer, patting his back, exchanging anxious glances with Winifred.

Jonathan, sobered, moved up towards Martin. Brenda was asleep, and Denis, incomprehensibly, crying; the parents, he reasonably allowed, had their hands full. So he talked to Martin in loud whispers as they passed the scene of the accident again, finding each piece of floating *débris* choicer and more exciting than the last, wondering eagerly how many people had been drowned, and why did they sink, Martin? And would sharks get them? And when they had all jumped into the water he, Jonathan, had not sunk, although Brenda was holding on to his legs, so that was pretty good, wasn't it, Martin? And had *you* ever been in a shipwreck, Martin? No? Well, some day there might be another one . . . and couldn't we go just a bit slower past here, Martin, because didn't people float up to the top again sometimes?

But now they were past it all, and ahead was the little cove where they swam, and on the water-front their own home with the big rock in the garden, and Brenda's house beside it with its flag-staff and its green lawns and its curving white steps. Jonathan began to feel sleepy again. He asked, a yawn breaking the question in half:

"Gee, Martin, if you hadn't come . . . would we have gone in an amberlance?"

"Well, I s'pose you might. Why?"

"Only . . . well, it was a bit of a pity you came just *then*, because . . . I haven't ever been in an amberlance. Have you . . . ever been in an amberlance, Martin?"

But he did not hear the answer. Ian, holding the still wide-awake Denis, watched him slide down to the floor at Martin's feet, yawn vastly once or twice, and then fall headlong into sleep, his cheek uncomfortably pillowed against a polished legging.

*　　*　　*　　*　　*

The noisy chugging of Ted Billings' ancient launch diminished, and, as if it alone had been holding him fast in unconsciousness, Jack came up out of the darkness again, imagining that he was climbing the cliff at the Gap as he had climbed it that morning, in a fog of pain and mental turmoil. But when, clutching at the side of the launch, he lifted his heavy head and opened his eyes, it was the Bay he saw, its mirror-still water, its cluster of old, brown houses about the shore, its grassy hillside, dotted with huge rocks and the scattered buildings of the barracks. He glanced round dazedly, not troubling to collect thoughts which instinctively he feared, content to find in the familiarity of the scene an emotion which was less reassurance than apathy. He was too exhausted by pain, hunger, mental stress and physical effort to examine the future, but the Bay, serene under the pollen-gold evening sunlight, fostered an illusion that it could hold nothing very different from the past. They swung in to the land almost under the bows of the *Captain Cook;* from where he lay Jack looked up at the figure-head with its lifted hand shading its eyes, and the spy-glass tucked beneath its arm, and he saw the gulls, disturbed, rising from the buoy and the mooring rope as they passed. He lay in a kind of waking trance, watching the pale blue sky where filmy wisps of cloud hung motionless, watching the gulls sweep across his line of vision, changing from white to grey, from grey to gold, as they turned in the tranquil sunlight. When Ted bent over him with encouraging words he stared hazily as if at someone from an unfamiliar world. He did not want to answer the words, or to return to the world from which they came, but he could not stop the slow awakening of memory and thought, and their relentless quickening once they had awakened. The interval of unconsciousness had sufficiently renewed his vitality to place him once more at the mercy of his fear. He shut his eyes and kept them shut, but he could not help knowing from the silencing of the engine and from the slowing movement of the launch that they were almost in, and that in a few moments at most he must begin to contend with his life again. He could not help remembering that on the opposite seat Arthur Sellman was lying, and he knew now, though he did not find it funny any longer, what had so amused him in that first moment of recognition. A chap had more money than he knew what to do with, but it didn't help him when he was drowning; neither his wealth nor his influence had kept him afloat, but the one sound arm of a man who had nothing on earth but great physical strength and a sullen, indomitable obstinacy. And who now must bend his already overtaxed energy to the task of escaping from a law which would never threaten Arthur Sellman. For he knew again now, thinking quite clearly behind his still closed eyes, that if Manning-Everett died of his injuries, or was already dead, he, Jack Saunders, would be . . .

But his thoughts leapt into angry protest. That was wrong, that was false, he was no murderer! He conceived murder as something brutal and premeditated, and felt a flare of indignant repudiation. But when you are desperate and bitter, he thought, and always rather hungry, when the days are endless with idleness and your strength burns in you like a fire, when you are in pain and people keep on jolting your arm, and you can feel mounting passion and excitement all about you, when your brain is still echoing with illuminating words, and your heart bursting with the knowledge of injustice, when you are looking at a car which would buy you the farm of your desire, and bunches of flowers whose cost would feed you for a week, and an endless stream of people who have never known that a sixpence is a precious thing, and a pound note riches. . . .

He heard a groan and opened his eyes wearily. A couple of men were lifting the limp figure from the seat opposite, and a swinging arm hung down. Jack studied it without moving. He noticed smooth, well-kept nails, a square gold watch on a wide strap, gold sleeve-links; and then he shut his eyes again indifferently, for he was not really interested in Arthur Sellman, and his thoughts were already returning with restless urgency to his own problem. As soon as he got ashore he must get Ruby to dry his clothes, for he had no others, and he must remember to keep his bandaged hand out of sight as much as possible, and he must clear out . . . somewhere . . . somehow. . . .

Ted was back again now.

He asked:

"Can y' walk, Jack?"

For another second or two he kept his eyes closed; he

357

supposed he could walk, but he did not want to try. Not only physical weariness but the utter hopelessness of the life confronting him filled him with a childish, rebellious desire to arrest time, to extend this passive interlude. But Ted's arm was under his shoulder, lifting him, so he sat up, shrugging it away rather peevishly, and said:

"I can manage. I ain't hurt . . . only got a sort of giddy feelin'."

His head was spinning, and there was a singing in his ears, but after he had sat for a moment with his hand pressed over his eyes, he felt better, and got awkwardly to his feet. His wet clothes clung uncomfortably to his body, but he felt hot rather than cold, and he found when he began to walk that he was glad enough of the support of Ted's arm. Another man stepped forward from the curious crowd surrounding them, and helped to lift him ashore, and then Ted asked:

"Cripes, what y' done to y' hand, Jack? I seen the bandage when we hauled y' aboard, and then I forgot it. Y' bleedin' like a pig!"

Jack looked down stupidly at his crimson dripping fingers, wondering if this was the reason for his faintness. He muttered:

"It ain't nothin'. I cut 'em about on the rocks this mornin'. . . ." Ted said cheerfully:

"Well, Maurice is ringin' the doctor for the other cove, so 'e can 'ave a look at you, too. We . . ."

Jack interrupted:

"What doctor?"

"Denning . . . 'e's the nearest."

"What y' done with Sellman?"

"Who?"

"Sellman. Didn't y' know . . . ?"

"Was that Sellman? Hell, if I'd known that I'd 'a landed 'im at 'is own place on the way round. 'E's bad, Jack."

"What y' done with 'im?"

Ted released his arm to push open the sagging gate of Jack's cottage. The crowd had followed them, and Jack

358

stood unsteadily looking at them, his eyes blurring again with a fiercely mounting irritation. Ted answered, shepherding him up the path:

"We brought 'im in 'ere. I didn't like the looks of 'im. 'E's lyin' on the bed in the front room."

Again Jack heard that short laugh from himself, born of an amusement he did not attempt to analyse. The thought of that bed had crossed his mind several times during this difficult journey from the launch to the cottage; he had planned to crawl beneath its two tattered blankets while Ruby dried his clothes, but it looked as if he'd have to do with the camp stretcher young Bruce used to sleep on in the other room.

Ruby was at the door. He could see that she was in one of her tempers. Scarcely glancing at him, she stormed at Ted:

"What's the idea, dumpin' this chap on us? What d' y' think we are, a boardin'-'ouse, or an 'ospital or what? Where the . . ."

Jack shouted at her in the fury of taut nerves and hotly stabbing pain:

"Shut up! It ain't your 'ouse, any'ow. . . ."

Holding on to the door he looked down the path at the crowd still gathered, staring, outside the gate, and the ungovernable exasperation of fear rushed up in him again. They were looking at him, blast them, noticing his bandaged hand; they knew he had been on the ten-to-five ferry. This doctor who was coming had tended his injury, had told him to put his arm in a sling. In the morning, even if he wasn't nabbed before then, the papers would be full of the business . . . his description . . . there might be a reward offered. . . .

Panic gripped him; he felt the wild, mistrustful desire of the hunted for solitude. To be alone, alone! There was no one to trust but himself, nothing to save him but his strength which, for the first time in his life, seemed to be failing him. He said harshly to Ted:

"I'm O.K. now. Y' better go and see to y' boat. . . ."

But Ted protested heartily:

"Not on y' life! I'll wait till the doctor gets 'ere. That 'and of yours . . ."

"It's nothin' I tell y'! For Christ's sake get them gapin' idiots away from 'ere! . . ."

Ted looked at him dubiously. Jack's temper was known and respected in the Bay. Only for his blood-stained bandages and his soaked clothes he looked much as usual, his body slouched against the door, his eyes looking upward with a subdued smouldering from beneath his heavy brows. Ted answered uncertainly:

"Well . . . all right. The doctor should be 'ere in a few minutes. So long, Jack, I'll see y' later. . . ."

He went off down the path. By the time he reached the gate the door had closed.

Jack stood in the passage, his head bent over the injured arm which he was nursing now across his chest. With the door shut it was almost dark, and he peered at Ruby, not even toying with the idea of telling her his trouble, but dimly resentful because such an idea was so obviously unthinkable. She said sourly:

"Well, now I suppose y' want me to get the stove alight and dry y' clothes. But don't get the idea that I'm doin' any waitin' on that. . . ."

He shouldered her aside. He could hear heavy breathing from the front room where Arthur Sellman lay, and he went in and stood for a moment looking down at the figure on the bed. Not much of the waning daylight came through the one small window, shadowed outside by a sloping verandah roof, but it was enough to show him that his rescue had probably been in vain. He bent stiffly and tried to take off Arthur's wet coat, but with one hand it was impossible, so he called roughly for Ruby. She came, and under his angry eyes and the suppressed menace of his voice, she helped him unwillingly to take off the wet clothes and cover the unconscious man with the two thin blankets. When it was done Jack felt so exhausted that he stumbled over to the chair beneath the window, and sat there breathing heavily and cradling his left arm across his chest. Ruby, fighting her own particular demons of resentment, came grudgingly across to him and laid an ungentle hand on his shoulder.

"C'mon, give me y' coat. . . ."

He flung her hand off and said low and fiercely, with hatred:

"Get out!"

When she had gone he bent giddily and tried to take off his wet boots and socks. The soaked laces were tight and unyielding, and he fumbled at them clumsily with his one hand. There was a knot which defied him; he struggled with it, cursing, rage blinding his eyes again, until, overwhelmed by this final humiliation of helplessness, he flung his arm out along the window-sill and dropped his head on it, and only Arthur's laboured breathing disturbed the silence of the darkening room.

*   *   *   *   *

Oliver glanced at his watch as he drove home from the Gap. It was just after half past five. In a few minutes, he thought, he would go down to the wharf and meet Lois. She would be hot and tired, and perhaps the pictures would have made her cross, and she would snap at him, or perhaps they would have amused her, and she would describe them with that rather comically remorseful malice of hers. But in any case she would be there, and they would walk up the long concrete pier with the water lapping under it, and up the longer flight of concrete steps, and along the street to their own gate with his brass plate on it and his unlighted red lamp over it. Going down the path through the garden she would put her hand in his, and when they got indoors she would turn and lift her face for his kiss. It was, he reflected amusedly, a very simple programme to fill one with such a pleasant glow of anticipation; but if one learned anything from years of unhappiness it was to value contentment, and to seek it where it habitually dwelt—in just such unsophisticated joys as these.

He stopped the car outside his own garage, and left it there for the routine visit he must do later in the even-

ing, and then, as there was no sign yet of the ferry rounding the point, he opened the gate and went down the
path and through the waiting-room into his surgery. He
could hear Chloe practising at the other end of the house;
her scales ran up and down, a silvery ladder of sound. He
hung his dust coat behind the door and opened the shuttered French windows on the shadowed garden. His book
on the desk caught his eye, and he leaned over it, resting
his palms on the polished surface, and read a sentence
or two:

> *"What is of worth is the world of men; redemption is
> not deliverance from the flesh, but transformation. Faith is
> allied with hope, not with hopelessness. . . ."*

Footsteps made him look up. The grocer's boy, a
loaded box on his shoulder, went by to the back door.
Oliver, intent on his book again, was vaguely conscious
of his ring, and of the cessation of Chloe's scales.

> *"But optimism apparently can only have two grounds
> —the unaided powers of man, or supernatural interven-
> tion. . . ."*

A small sound behind him made him look up sharply.
Chloe was standing in the doorway, holding on to it, her
face a white mask, her mouth slightly open. He went to
her and she put out both hands towards him in a groping
gesture as if she were blind. He said gently, taking them:

"What's the trouble? You mustn't . . ."

But she pulled violently against his hands, and words
came from her lips distorted by terror into the thick,
blurred sound of drunkenness or paralysis:

"Mother—on the ten-to-five boat—it's sunk, Oliver,
it's sunk, *it's sunk . . . !"*

The awful blankness of intense shock descended on
his brain. For a second which seemed to stretch interminably out of the present into some dark, malignant future,
he stood struggling for the sense and understanding which
had forsaken him. He caught Chloe roughly by the
shoulders.

"What are you talking about . . . who said . . . ?"

"An accident . . . there's been an accident. The grocer told me . . . he s-saw from up on top of the hill. . . ."

He broke away from her. His whole body felt stiff as if the power of movement had left him. What is prayer? What is prayer but a longing so great, so deep, so agonising that all the spirit is dominated by it, all the body is unheeded, forgotten, all life suspended waiting for a reply? What is it but desire, silent or articulate, for that beauty whatever it may be, which for any man makes life a dearer thing than death? Not consciously, kneeling, a true prayer is born, but only out of agony and need, not in words not even in thought, but in some violent travail of the spirit which sends force rocketing through space, and power like lightning across the sky.

What are those material things which in the moments of one's blind sanity seem so real, so indisputable? Chairs, tables, walls, the bodies of other people? There comes some gust of monstrous reality and the little three-dimensional world which harbours them sways like the backcloth of a stage setting; wrenched clear of it all, seeing it from a vast distance, it becomes grotesque, impossible, a fantasy dreamed and half-forgotten, an absurdity, remote, unimportant, receding from sight and knowledge. . . .

The wind and turmoil of this dreadful region deadened his thought and paralysed his understanding. He felt something come close to him and was not sure if it were peril or revelation. Something seemed to be waiting either to destroy him or to reveal itself, he was not sure which, but he was conscious that he must struggle against it, he must return. . . .

Return to a voice speaking some words which once, in another life, he would have understood. Return. To turn back, to do something with his awkward, clumsy body, to command it in some way, to use it as a vehicle, to . . .

"Oliver, answer it, quickly. . . . It might be . . ."

His brain returned to its normal functioning. He felt the very instant of its return—as clear and definite as

363

the click of some piece of a dismantled machine returning neatly to its appointed socket. He was standing in
his consulting-room, Chloe opposite, and the telephone
was ringing on his desk. He was strangely weak, drained
by an effort which even now he felt might have been to
evade a revelation rather than to master an emotion
which had bordered on insanity. He stood over the desk,
leaning heavily on one hand, and put out the other to
lift the receiver. Fear ran through his body, doubling it
up as if with pain. Hurt . . . ? Missing . . . ? Dead . . . ?
He put the receiver to his ear and spoke into the mouth-
piece.

"Yes?"

"Oliver? Oliver, it's Lois speaking. . . ."

His knees gave way suddenly. He groped for the
chair and sat down, his eyes shut, his free hand stretched
out behind him in an instinctive summons to Chloe. She
came, saying: "Mother? Is it mother . . . ?" and, with her
head close to the receiver, heard the small, far-off voice
say: "Is Chloe there?"

"Yes, I'm here. Where are you, Mother?"

"Darling, were you worried? I'm all right—I wasn't
on the boat. I only heard about it a few minutes ago, and
I rushed to ring you up. Where's Oliver, isn't he there?"

He opened his eyes. Already normality had so far
returned that he was interested to observe its return, and
he answered:

"I'm here. A bit winded with relief. Where are you,
darling?"

"I'm at the Quay. Oliver, listen . . ."

"Why weren't you on the boat? Did you miss it?"

There was a slight pause. Then her voice came to
them both, for Chloe's head was close to Oliver's, a small,
rather abashed voice, confessing unwillingly:

"Well . . . I was *there* in time. . . . But I went to sleep
on the wharf. . . . Oliver. . . ."

Oliver began to laugh. Laughter shook and possessed
him till his sides ached and his breath failed, and Chloe,
taking the receiver from him, said indignantly: "Never

mind, Mother, he won't be able to tease you about it again."

Lois said:

"Tell him I'll get a taxi home. But I want to speak to him."

Chloe repeated obediently:

"She says she'll come home by taxi."

"No, *no!*" He stopped short, astonished by the vehemence of his reaction. Disconcerted, but indulgently, by his sudden terror and mistrust of taxis, trams, trains, boats, streets, all the malignant forces which might yet wreck their life—their precious life still so miraculously intact! He went on:

"Stay exactly where you are. Don't move. Go to sleep again if you like. I'm coming in to fetch you."

But she said urgently, a break in her voice which startled him to attention:

"No, no. Listen, Oliver. Those children were on the boat. . . ."

His elation flickered, checked like a flame under a dash of water. He said: "Yes, yes, of course. . . ." And he remembered, as he knew she, too, was remembering, a prostrate weeping figure on the raft; imagined, as she was imagining. new horror added to an already overburdened life. He asked with sudden hope:

"What about Harnet? Wasn't he on it?"

"No—he was here—with her. They missed it. It was the sound of his running down the wharf that woke me up. And . . . Oliver . . ."

"Yes?"

"Professor Channon was on it, too."

Oliver, shaken, said: "Good God!" and heard her voice add something else, without at first taking in her words. For he was filled with a strange conflict. His medical consciousness, seeing the old man as a patient, told him that if he had found death it was merely by a shorter and an easier road than that to which he himself had pointed earlier in the day; but another self, remembering only a friend, was chilled and saddened by the thought of wisdom and tolerance perhaps already lost to a foolish and intolerant world. He asked with an effort:

"What did you say, darling? I didn't get it."

"I said Mr. Sellman was on it, too. I don't know if she knew. So I don't think you had better come in for me, Oliver. In case . . . I mean, if she . . ."

"Did she see you?"

"Yes. She said they were going home in a taxi, and she offered me a lift, but of course I said no. Oliver, do go and see if . . . I'm so anxious. I feel . . . responsible. I arranged it all with Mrs. Trugg. If those children . . ."

He could hear that she was crying. He said quickly:

"No, no, you mustn't feel that. I'll go over there now and see if there's anything I can do. Darling, what will you . . . ?"

"I'll get a taxi, Oliver. I won't be long."

"All right." An urge, born of shock and panic, to add: "Tell the man to drive slowly," almost overcame him. He shut his lips on it grimly. Once you let yourself become afraid of life, he thought, you're done! She must come home through the ordinary, everyday perils of thronging traffic; she must take the everyday risks of faulty mechanism, faulty functioning of some human brain, a moment's failure in co-ordination, a blow-out, a drunken driver. . . . And he must wait, and attend to his job, trusting life to give its best, ready to defy it if it should give its worst. But he was conscious of fear like a small, hard core in his heart, for under so dark a shadow of tragedy its worst seemed strangely close, strangely and dreadfully possible. He repeated:

"All right. I'll go and look for Mrs. Sellman now. Good-bye."

He put the receiver down and glanced at Chloe. Her small face seemed more pointed than ever, and her habitual pallor had the tinge of sickness. He said:

"Get some tea ready for your mother, like a good kid."

She looked up at him so strangely that he added:

"What's the matter?"

366

"I hadn't ever seen . . . " she stumbled.

"What?"

"A grown-up man . . . frightened before."

He admitted, looking at her thoughtfully:

"Yes, I was frightened all right. I suppose that's part of what you pay for being happy—to be scared almost out of your life sometimes. Would you say it was worth it?"

She cried ardently:

"Rather! Oh, *rather!* Wouldn't you?"

He nodded, and went out through the open French windows into the garden. But he was not more than a few paces from the house when he heard the telephone ring again. His bondage to it was now so much an accepted part of his life that his return and his lifting of the receiver and his questioning "Hello?" were performed automatically, and only when an answering voice began to speak did he detach his mind from his own preoccupations.

"Is that Dr. Denning?"

"Yes."

"Look here, we've just recovered a body from the ferry wreck; we were out fishing near there when it happened. It was an elderly chap, and we got his name from his bank pass-book and other papers in his pockets. Channon. H. J. Channon. Did you know him?"

"Yes. I knew him."

"He had one of your prescription forms in his pocket with your address and 'phone number on it, so we could see he was a neighbour of yours. Can you hear?"

"Yes."

"I thought it might be better if I rang you rather than his own home. Shock for them, and all that. . . ."

"Yes. . . . Thanks."

"Will you let them know, then? The body's been taken to the Morgue."

"Yes. I will. Good-bye."

He put the receiver down carefully. He found himself looking fixedly at the chair in which the old man had sat that morning. It was difficult to understand all at once that he was dead. There were a few rare people, he thought, in whom vitality was so strong and clear a flame that some of it seemed to remain even after death, as the warmth may linger in a room where a fire has been extinguished. Here his voice lingered, and his smile, and words were reborn in fragmentary echoes. *". . . it's a strange thing that as you grow older you mind the thought of dying less and less. . . ."* That is true. Every doctor sees that tranquil acceptance. But when there is work to be done. . . . *"I need at least six months." "You keep me alive long enough, doctor, and . . ."*

Oliver swung round abruptly. He forced his thoughts away from the regrets which crowded darkly upon them. He remembered, with a more painful anxiety than ever, Winifred, who had lost her father and perhaps her child as well, and urged by the strange, but comforting illusion that one may serve the dead by caring for the living whom they have loved, he ran up the garden again, and out on to the street. The Sellmans' big blue car was standing half out of its garage, one door swinging open. That, Oliver thought, banging it, suggested haste, and he opened their gate and walked quickly down the smooth-trimmed, terraced garden, a superficial thought flickering across the troubled depths of his mind that unlimited money often seemed to have a fatal effect upon gardens. It became too easy to meddle, too tempting to tidy and "improve," until the lovely waywardness of growing things was curbed, and a beauty to which one should humbly minister became a beauty which one presumed to discipline.

The front door stood wide open. He rang the bell without result. Then he walked round to the front of the house, and there, crowded against the railings just above the landing stage, were the cook and two maids and the gardener, all straining their eyes under shading hands, and pointing at a black, swift-moving speck advancing across the bay.

He went quickly down and stood beside them. He noticed that the two girls had been crying, and that the cook was still sniffing unashamedly, and he thought: "If it could be husbanded and directed, this sympathy, this compassion, this decency which is in almost every human being!" And, remembering the sullen-eyed young man with the broken fingers, whose sullenness, if his guess were correct, had exploded into enmity and violence, he realised that there was, essentially, no such thing as hatred of man for man, but merely hatred of man for his own blunders, for those errors in judgment, those failures in imagination, whereby the graciousness of life was denied to half of humanity. In this moment, he knew, no sense of injustice or of inequality marred the generous anxiety of the four people beside him, and if to the anxiety there was added a streak of excitement and anticipation which struck him as a little ghoulish, it was only another difference in outlook which environment and circumstance had forced upon them. It was a primitive outlook, more robust, perhaps, than his own; it admitted frankly an unsophisticated joy in crises—and what crisis save birth was as exciting as death? He realised with a faint shock that he was thinking, theorising, deliberately allowing his mind to wander in order to delay the question which he now abruptly asked:

"Where's Mrs. Sellman? Has there . . . have you had any news of the children? Or . . ."

He stopped. One of the maids answered:

"No, Doctor, and we've been that upset! The poor little love, and her blind and all! Mrs. Sellman came rushing in . . ."

"She came home?"

"Oh, yes, Doctor, she came rushing in to get the key of the boatshed. I spoke to her, but she didn't seem to hear me. And then she and Mr. Harnet and Martin went off in the launch, and we've been waiting ever since, because what she'd *do* if anything was to happen to . . ."

Oliver asked the gardener:

"Is that their launch coming back now?"

"It's 'ard to say, Doctor, against the sun, like. But from the pace it's makin' I should . . . look! They're wavin'! That there's Martin, that is, wavin' 'is cap! The kids must be all right! Cripes, Cookie, what're y' howlin' for *now?*"

But Oliver was not watching the launch any longer. Chloe was beside him, breathless.

"Oliver, someone just rang up from the Bay to ask you to go at once. They've brought in two men from the ferry, and one of them is very bad. This is the address. I'm going straight back because mother might be home any minute. . . ."

He stood looking at the slip of paper she had thrust into his hand. Jack Saunders' house. That was the name of the young fellow whose broken fingers he had treated, and of whom he had thought instantly when Lesley told him of the bottle-throwing incident. So he *had* been in town! He glanced up again at the approaching launch. He thought as it came alongside the landing stage that Winifred, sitting motionless with the dark bundle which was Brenda in her arms, was probably a person more at peace with herself than she had been that morning. He called to her:

"Are they all right, Mrs. Sellman?"

She looked up at him. It was strange, he thought, how shock laid its mark upon a face; no mark you could separate or analyse, but a dim stamp of unfamiliarity, as though minute and seldom used muscles had set tensely, drawing the features closer, contracting the brows, pinching the nostrils and the corners of the mouth. And yet in this face the eyes were no longer the restlessly wandering, seeking eyes he had noticed earlier in the day. They were still and deep with a contentment which reaction had made almost sluggish. He looked at them uneasily, conscious that it might be for him to drive peace from them again, wondering if, wrapped in that armour of reprieved maternity, she were beyond the reach of even such pain as he might inflict. She answered:

"I think they only need hot baths and bed, Doctor. But will you make sure?"

He replied, noticing that she would not let Martin take the child from her arms as she stepped ashore:

"I'll look in a little later. I've just had a message to go round to the Bay to see someone who is badly hurt. You'll be at home, Harnet? I want to have a word with you when I get back."

Ian, with Denis still wide awake in his arms, nodded, and Oliver, turning away, ran up through the garden again and got into his car. He looked up the hill as he started it for an approaching taxi which might be returning Lois to him, but there was none, and he drove back the way he had come only a short while before, and parked his car near the tramway terminus. At the pier a man stepped out from a group to accost him.

"That's the 'ouse, Doctor. I brought 'em in my launch. Mr. Sellman looked pretty bad to me."

Oliver said sharply:

"Sellman?"

"Yes—Mr. Sellman from the Cove. When we picked 'im up 'e was all out to it, and Jack was 'oldin' 'im up. 'E 'asn't come round yet, and 'e's breathin' funny, too."

"I see. That's the house, is it? With the broken fence?"

"That's it, Doctor."

Sellman. Well, Oliver thought grimly, pushing the gate open, life might be tragic or it might be comic, but it was unfailingly surprising. Not in such a place as this would he ever have imagined visiting Arthur Sellman; and as there was no immediate answer to his knock he stepped into the dim hallway and listened. The sound of laboured breathing guided him. Only the evening light through the unblinded window made the room he entered visible to him. Arthur was a dark shape upon a disordered bed, and silhouetted against the window there was another, with bowed shoulders and a white blur of lifted face, whose eyes, mistrustful, he could feel upon him from the moment he entered. A sound in the doorway made him turn; he saw a young woman standing there, and said to her:

"I want some light here. A lamp or something."

She brought half a candle thrust into the neck of a bottle and lighted it. Oliver put his bag down on the floor and beckoned her nearer, bending over the bed. A voice came surprisingly from the figure at the window:

"'E got a crack on the 'ead from a bit of flyin' timber."

Oliver answered without looking up:

"I see. Yes. You came to my surgery this morning, didn't you?"

There was a sound which might have meant anything. Oliver took it for assent, and asked:

"How's the hand? Did you hurt it much?"

"A bit." There was a pause. "I 'ad to get rid of the sling when the crash came."

His faint tone of triumph, Oliver thought, betrayed him. He had spoken as a man might speak voicing an inspiration, and he was too pleased with his explanation to realise that no explanation had been necessary. Oliver, pushing up Arthur's eyelids, said: "Of course," and continued, almost mechanically, his methodical examination. Arthur was darkly flushed, and his breathing was stertorous. His pulse was slow and bounding, and the pupil of one eye was normal and that of the other enlarged. Oliver, in spite of a preoccupation which was as much concerned with Jack as with Arthur, was still capable of recognising in himself a new, and, therefore, an interesting reaction. Never before in all his medical experience had he bent thus over a patient hoping to find him dying. There had been times when his reason told him that death was often more merciful than life; but the instinct which had led him to his trade was an instinct for life, and death had always been, emotionally, an enemy to be resisted with every weapon at his command. Now he knew his attitude reversed. His reason told him that the life in this prone figure must be cherished and tended, and with all his skill and knowledge he would so tend and cherish it. But his instinct, still strongly and indomitably for life, found only barrenness and frustration

372

in something which must be, at best, merely a continued existence. The grief of bereavement, he reflected, is often full of an unreasoning bitterness and resentment. It is often guilty of hatred for the living merely because they live when another, dearer, and perhaps worthier, is dead. This feeling stretched, at the back of his consciousness, a thin, taut line of illogical anger, and he acknowledged and condemned it as he worked. For Arthur was alive; but far more strongly in Oliver's mind was the thought of a death which had come before its time, a life not precariously hovering like this one beneath his hand, but irrevocably gone. He said abruptly, speaking impartially to the woman standing behind him, or to the still figure at the window:

"I must get him to a hospital at once. Is there a 'phone nearer than the post-office?"

The woman answered "No," and Oliver, crossing to Jack, said sharply, irritated by some half-veiled truculence in her tone: "Bring that candle here."

Its light showed him not only a hand which was much as he had expected to see it, but a face whose exhausted pallor, whose misery and despair startled him. He took the candle from the woman and said to her: "Go and boil some water—a good deal of it. I'll hold this." When she had gone he turned again to Jack.

"I must go and ring up for an ambulance and arrange with a hospital for Mr. Sellman. But I'll come back at once and fix your hand. Keep it up like this."

He went out of the house without waiting for a reply, and walked rapidly across the park to the post-office. When he had secured a bed for Arthur at a nearby hospital, and summoned an ambulance, he spent a few minutes looking up numbers and jotting them down on a scrap of paper. He began to work through them methodically, and at the third he was rewarded.

"Dr. Denning speaking. Have you got a Mr. Manning-Everett in there with a head injury? . . . How is he? . . . Will you find out, please? . . . Yes. Yes, I see. Thanks."

He rang off and held the door of the small, stifling booth open with his foot while he searched for yet another number. This time it was Ian's voice which answered him. He explained rapidly:

"I've got Sellman down here at the Bay; I'm having him moved to hospital. An operation may be necessary. He's very badly injured, I should think almost certainly fatally." He went on quickly so that no comment from Ian was necessary or possible: "I thought you might tell Mrs. Sellman."

"I will, at once. Should she . . . go to him? She's with Brenda now."

"I think it would be foolish. He's quite unconscious. How is Brenda?"

"Only frightened, I think."

"And your youngsters?"

"Jonathan's fine. Sleeping soundly. I'm a bit bothered about Denis. He seems nervy. You might look in later if you have time."

"Yes. And . . ." now that the moment had come he found it even harder than he had expected ". . . did you . . . does Mrs. Sellman know about her father?"

"Her father? Good God, Doctor, was he on that boat, too?"

Oliver, who had let the door swing shut, kicked it open again, wondering irritably what it was which made the characteristically foul smell of telephone booths; he could feel perspiration trickling between his shoulder-blades. He said:

"Yes. I had a ring from some people who . . . found him. He was dead. I'd like to speak to her myself later, Harnet—there's something I can tell her that might help her a bit. I'll look in to-night. Good-bye."

He came out into the fresh air and stood for a moment breathing it in gulps. Then he walked back across the park to Jack's house, and as he entered he heard a voice say roughly from the kitchen:

"I'm goin'! So hold y' row! I'm in a bloody jam, I tell y'. I got to get away!"

Oliver went into the front room. The candle, dripping grease, was still standing on a chair by the bed, and he lifted it, looking down at Arthur's dark-flushed face. It was just possible, he thought, that a trephine might be successful, but there was, for the moment, no more that he could do, so he picked up his bag and went down the hall and into the kitchen. A couple of inches of candle was standing upright in its own congealed grease, and the draught from the open doorway was making the flame smoke and sway so that shadows leapt grotesquely up and down the walls. Jack was sitting on an up-ended packing case at the table. His injured arm lay along its edge, his other was curved over it as if in some futile effort at protection, or alleviation of the pain which was making a white mask of his face. The woman was standing opposite, and although Oliver had heard no words from her, and though she spoke none now, the callousness of the shrewish woman was clear to him, not in her face, for she had turned her back on him, but in Jack's. His torment was not only physical. Now, less than ever, had the life for which he had battled a place for him; now more than ever it was endlessly inimical. Even from this woman, of whom, unknowing and hardly capable of imagining love, he had sought some illusion of comfort, he was meeting nothing but hostility and bitterness. He did not move, but under the leaping, twisted shadows he seemed to move. Oliver, in whom visual imagination was strong, saw him as grotesquely contorted and flung about by life, abased and maltreated and stripped of human dignity, and, in a violent reaction of anger against so intolerable a sight, he said sharply to the woman:

"Go along to the chemist and get this made up. Wait for it."

He scribbled on a page from his notebook, tore it out and handed it to her. She went with no protest beyond a contemptuous grunt, and he took her place at the table, looking across it into Jack's watchful and mistrustful eyes. He asked, opening his bag on the table:

"Now, let me have that hand. Where's the water? Are you going far?"

The injured hand twitched violently between his own. It was not a movement of pain, and Oliver knew it, but he said woodenly: "Sorry. It's sure to hurt a bit." Jack muttered vaguely:

"Far . . . ?"

Oliver, rummaging in his bag for bandages, replied casually:

"I thought I heard you say something about going away as I came in." He worked silently for a few minutes and then added: "Bad luck to be in a ferry smash the day you break your fingers." Jack said nothing; Oliver went on conversationally:

"They tell me there was a disturbance in town this afternoon. Manning-Everett, the Southern Newspapers man, was slightly injured, I believe."

Jack cleared his throat, moving restlessly. Oliver was aware, for the first time, of a quick upward glance, doubtful, searching.

"Slightly . . . ?"

"Well, a scalp wound. They bleed like the devil, but they're soon mended. I heard from a friend of mine who's an honorary at the hospital they took him to." He stopped, listening. "That must be the ambulance. Hold this firm till I get back. I'll just see they get him off all right."

Jack sat quite still. He could hear voices, the sounds of several people coming and going. He was grappling with a thought whose strangeness made it difficult to for mulate. This afternoon he had done two things. He had tried to kill a man, and he had tried to save a man. But he was glad the man he had tried to kill was still alive, and quite indifferent to the fate of the man he had tried to save. That in itself was enough to baffle him, but behind it he was conscious of something stranger still. For his relief at the news which Oliver had given him was not only relief for himself. There had come to him some shadowy conception of a power which had not only the

376

poor but the rich at its mercy. He did not know what it was, nor how it functioned, but he saw, dimly, that it was possible that not only himself, but Manning-Everett, too, might be caught in the toils of some system which neither of them had created. He had a moment of detachment when he saw quite clearly that it might take far greater courage, far greater vision to abandon than to win. He liked Manning-Everett no better than he had liked him before, but he found that he could see him now as being not so much served as mastered by his wealth, and as Oliver came in again he said, still half-lost in his thoughts:

"I reckon money can get hold of a man . . . like drink. . . ."

Oliver, glancing at him curiously as he went on bandaging the hand, replied:

"I suppose so. It means power, of a sort."

Jack did not speak again; when his hand, neatly bandaged into a new and smaller splint, lay before him on the table, he still sat motionless, his eyelids sagging with fatigue. Oliver said:

"I'll have to go. How about getting some sleep now. You weren't thinking of going away to-night, were you?"

Jack's shoulders moved slightly in an abortive shrug.

"It don't matter much . . . now. I'll take a chance. . . ."

Immediately he was afraid of his own unwary words, and his sharp upward glance was so full of suspicion that Oliver turned away abruptly and stood at the open door looking out at the rank grass and the broken palings, and the folded purplish flowers of the morning glory. He said without turning:

"I have some clothes, if they'd be any use to you. We're about the same height. There's a dust coat with loose sleeves. . . . I'd keep that splint on if I were you. Where were you thinking of going?"

Jack mumbled unwillingly:

"I . . . thought I'd . . . I 'ad a chance of a job . . . up the country."

"I see. Well, will you come for the clothes in the morning?"

This time the pause was longer. Oliver thrust his hands in his pockets and prayed for patience. It was like training an animal, he thought, remembering a rock wallaby whose confidence he had won years ago with slow, infrequent words, and careful movements, and endless waiting. In his own time this shackled and mistrustful brain would find its own way. In his own time, because suspicion was something grafted on to him, and not inherent, he would recognise and accept an aid offered as instinctively as his own had been offered not an hour ago to the unconscious man in the water. Oliver turned round.

"Well, think it over. That prescription I sent up to the chemist will ease the pain and get you a night's sleep. Take a dose when it comes. And get out of those wet clothes. Good-night."

He left the house again and walked quickly back to his car. Lois would be home by now. With the healthy egoism of the man who knows when to be selfish, he thrust Jack from his mind, thrust Ian and Winifred and Arthur Sellman from his mind, smothered even the dull sense of loss with which the Professor's death oppressed him, and opened all his being to his own joy.

*　　*　　*　　*　　*

Winifred closed the front door when Lois had gone and walked slowly back to Brenda's room. She was grateful that the news of Arthur's death should have come to her through that matter-of-fact, almost childishly direct little person. It had been so easy, with her, to be honest; it might have been so easy with someone else to be hypo critical.

"Someone just rang up Oliver to say that your husband died in an ambulance on the way there. Oliver's not home yet, so I thought I had better come and tell you."

She did not say she was sorry, she did not offer condolences. Her eyes were so honest that it had been possible to meet them honestly. It had been possible to acknowledge first the naturalness of her own awareness of deliverance, and then allow, without hypocrisy, the tears which were now streaming down her cheeks. It was possible for her to weep for Arthur Sellman, who had lived according to his lights; quite impossible for her to weep for a husband whose existence had stultified her own and Brenda's. The grief which was shaking her now was not a personal grief for someone loved and lost, but an impersonal grief for that tragic element of bitterness in their marriage which had been neither his fault nor hers.

Outside Brenda's room she paused to dry her eyes. It was strange, she thought, that she should have wept for Arthur and not for her father. Some people so serenely dominated their lives that death, when it came, even suddenly like this, seemed less an extinction than a last voluntary step which it dictated. Ian, holding her in his arms, had told her. It might be, she thought wearily, that in the comfort of that embrace, and in the knowledge of their children's safety, she had felt a rightness which the old man would have been the first to applaud. She looked down into the garden through the hall window, and saw Roger and Lesley there, and drew an added comfort from the knowledge that this, too, was what he would have wished.

The curtains in Brenda's room were drawn, and she tiptoed in, peering down through the dim light at the child's sleeping face. But there was a fluttering of the eyelids, a faint twitching of the brows, an occasional uneasy movement of the small hand upon the coverlet which told of troubled dreams, and Winifred sat down beside the cot and took the curled fingers in her own.

She could feel deep within her, unreleased as yet, but confidently waiting, a core of profound and lasting happiness; but over it her thoughts wandered with the restlessness of a mind not yet entirely relaxed after the feverish activity of crisis. She wondered where Lorna was, and if she knew yet of her brother's death. She wondered rather sadly about Sim, seeing him as she had seen him that morning on the beach, helpless and hypnotised by Lorna's beguiling beauty. She came back with a start to Brenda's voice, slurred with sleep, her eyes brilliant slits under her heavy lids.

"Say me . . . stories, Mummy."

Winifred began, speaking softly and almost mechanically:

> *"There was once a baby 'roo . . ."*

The eyes widened, the hand twitched convulsively under her fingers.

"No, no! No, Mummy, no . . . !"

"All right, darling, don't cry. Not that one." She smoothed the hair away from the child's forehead, wondering anxiously what obscure legacies of fear and nervous torment might remain to her from the day's experience, and began in a low monotone:

> *"Little Jika-Jika, all the darkies like her*
> *In her dainty Sunday dress and pinny;*
> *Give her wattle blossom, and a joey possum. . . ."*

"Mummy."

"Yes, darling?"

"Where's daddy?"

Winifred answered slowly:

"He isn't home. Are you warm enough, Brenda?"

"Did he get drowned, Mummy?"

Winifred's heart checked. For there was no apprehension in the question, no grief such as that which had shaken the child's voice when she had feared for Burrendong. And she wondered again what had happened on the boat, and whether Brenda had some last memory and knowledge of her father which his wife would never share. She said:

"What makes you ask that, darling?"

"Denis and Jonathan saw him come on the boat. If he isn't home yet I expect he got drowned. Go on with the story, Mummy."

Winifred went on. Her mouth felt dry, and there

was a faint, sick horror in her heart. Her mind cried out in a torment of pity that he had not surely been such a monster. . . . But then she realised that to Brenda he had not been a monster at all. He had been merely unimportant. A voice which spoke to her rarely, a presence to which she said obediently: "Good-morning, Daddy," and "Good-night, Daddy." Someone who had not touched her affections while he lived, and who would leave no gap in them now that he was dead. Someone, obviously, logically inevitably, far, far less important than Burrendong. . . . She went on stroking, reciting with the absent-minded fluency of habit:

> "*And she lives outside Benalla with her father Doutta-Galla,*
> *Who eats snakes for breakfast till he's pale.*
> *He kills them with a waddy and devours the head and body*
> *And little Jika-Jika eats the tail.*"

She leaned forward, peering at the heavy lids, and they lifted momentarily.

"Go on, Mummy."

Winifred's heart gave a sudden leap. The happiness in it would no longer be denied; she could not subdue it, could not resist her desire to spread it out and turn and examine it, to fly it like a banner before her eyes, to shape it into plans and hopes and all the vital stuff of life so long denied to her. There was a faint, unsteady throb in her voice as she began again:

> "*The man from Menindie was counting sheep,*
> *He counted so many he fell asleep . . .*"

Brenda breathed deeply and regularly. Her lashes lay still on her cheeks. But Winifred's hand went on stroking, and her voice went on low murmuring, for now her thoughts had leapt forward to seek the future, and all of the past that she cared about lay beneath her hand.

*　　*　　*　　*　　*

Lois, looking at it sadly, said:
"So it got burnt after all!"
Chloe shut the oven door resignedly.

381

"Well, darling, you wouldn't expect me to think about pies while you were drowning, would you?"

"But I wasn't drowning."

"But you might have been. Anyhow, Oliver won't mind. He won't notice, even. And it *is* eatable." Lois confessed:

"I was really thinking of Mrs. Trugg. I'm afraid she'll be rather disgusted with us. Is that Oliver coming in . . . ?"

With her tea-cup still in one hand, and a thick slice of bread and butter in the other, she went quickly up the hall. Oliver was just coming through the French windows of the surgery when she reached its door, so she could not see his face clearly, but she thought that he looked tired and worried. He held her closely for a long time, silent, and she shut her eyes and threw her bread and butter on the floor so that she should have one arm free to put about his neck. He said at last, without moving:

"So you went to sleep?"

She explained:

"It was some light moving about on the ground. I was watching it, to . . . to . . . well, I wanted to watch it, and it made me sleepy. And it was dreadfully hot, and I hadn't had any tea because a woman in a smock would talk about art, and . . ."

He asked:

"Are you apologising for going to sleep?"

"Well . . . in a way, I suppose. It is a silly habit. I always feel apologetic about it." His arm tightened.

"Never again."

"No. But I've got something else to apologise for. The pie got burnt."

"Pie?"

"Your dinner, darling."

"Oh. Well, anyhow, I can't eat anything now—I must go and do another visit. Did you know about the Professor? His body was recovered. And Sellman's alive."

"No."

He loosed his arms and held her away from him,

peering at her face in the dusk. She explained, picking up her bread and butter and placing it carefully in her saucer:

"They rang up from the hospital you sent him to. He died in the ambulance. I went over at once and told her. She knew about her father. I don't think she properly realises anything yet except that Brenda's safe. Must you go out again at once?"

"Yes. Come with me. It's just up to the top of the hill."

"All right. I'll tell Chloe."

When she came back he was looking at two X-ray photographs on his desk. He thrust them into the waste-paper basket and said: "Come along. If we're quick I won't need headlights."

As they drove up the long, curving road the red after-glow of sunset was working to its climax. She sat close to him with one hand on his knee, but she was thinking of the light. There must be bushfires somewhere, she decided, for the red-gold brilliance had a smoky solidity, so that you almost expected when you moved your hand to feel a faint resistance.

At the top of the hill Oliver turned down along the tram line towards the lighthouse. The breeze had fresh-ened, and it was cooler here on the high land between harbour and sea. He stopped the car and got out.

"I won't be long."

But on the other side of the road he paused, looking down now, just after sunset, as he had looked just before sunrise, at the harbour. Then it had been grey and silver between its dark headlands, but now in this fierce light it was molten, burning with a polished brilliance which hurt the eyes. For a moment Oliver played with the idea that it was not the sun which wrought that change, but the turbulent human life which had passed over it and round it in this day. This morning it had looked prime-val and aloof; in the night hours while its invaders slept it had returned to an ancient memory, and dawn had found it still touched with the grandeur of past solitude.

Since then the conflict which had begun a century and a half ago had painted it with the colours of flame and blood. But in the end, he found himself thinking, the land will win, the land must always win. One generation resisted it, crying aloud of exile. Others, following, denied it with always dwindling strength, but the land is eternal and it can wait. It takes them and torments them with fire and flood and drought; it pours wealth about their feet. It shows them strange, gaunt places to chill the heart, and it spreads beauty lavishly before their dazzled eyes. It kills them in the bush and in the desert, and even here on this water which has looked all day so blue and bright and kindly, it has revealed again, suddenly, the hidden menace of its strength. Its rule is aloof and dispassionate—not an enmity, but a discipline with which to mould and drive its people, hurt them, gladden them, terrify or exhilarate them, kill or save them so that they must become, whether they wish it or not, shaped to some pattern which will make them one with it at last.

Oliver looked up at the sky. It was ridged with flame which faded as he watched. The long waterway beneath lost itself in a western haze of paling gold, the bridge spanned it like a rainbow, the city skyline sank into a lavender-coloured mist. He turned with a sigh which was the released breath of contentment rather than regret, and looked down at the shadowed sea. A little sailing boat with all her canvas out was racing for the Heads, making for the harbour like a bird homing.

THE END.